MW01133623

Grey Areas
The Saga
(Books 1-4)

BRAD CARL

ISBN-13: 978-1522946366
ISBN-10: 1522946365

Cover art adaptation by Matt Downing Photography
Copy Editing by Free Range Editorial

G13 8-14-18

The following is a work of fiction. Any resemblance to actual businesses or persons, living or dead, is purely coincidental.

I'd like to use this page to extend a massive thank you to both Brandon Nichols and Matt Downing for their help. They use their brains and abilities to make me look good and I am forever grateful.

I

"Do you believe in life on other planets?" Bruce Townsend asked.

Henry Fields stared across the counter. He wanted to pull the stray white hair sticking out from Townsend's nose. But he also wanted this job.

"Do you?" Henry asked back.

Townsend smirked. "Answering a question with a question. Classic deflection. I like that. When can you start?"

Henry wasn't surprised. The sign in the window of the Corner Store read "Help Needed" not "Help Wanted," implying desperation. He'd only noticed it because the speed limit slowed him down to thirty miles an hour as he drove past the store on Highway 57. It was as if Gable, Iowa, had chosen him.

"Whenever you want me to," Henry replied, looking around the small store.

"How about tomorrow morning? Be here a few minutes before six. Since you've never worked in a convenience store or gas station, there are gonna be a few things I need to show you. Where do you live?"

"Nowhere yet. You got any suggestions?"

"Well, welcome to Gable, first of all. You'll find some

great food at Stubby's Diner right across the street there," Townsend said, pointing. "If you're a single fella you can get some porno mags right over here," he continued, strolling to the magazine section of his store. "Or when you need groceries to cook an anniversary dinner for your better half, you might wanna head twenty miles south to Adler. It's the main hub around here, a much larger town. Or you can always get your grub here but, as you can imagine, our selection for that kind of shit is limited."

It was obvious to Henry that Townsend was trying to learn more about him. Bruce Townsend was a man in his mid-fifties, bald head, medium height, pot belly, and two days' growth of white beard showing.

"I'm on my own. Just a thirty-year-old bachelor. So, do you have some thoughts on where I might live?"

"Oh yeah, sorry. Sometimes I get sidetracked. You could live in Adler, but you're gonna spend less in gas and rent living in Gable. Plus, we don't have the crime that Adler has. Tom Chumansky has a little farmhouse just west of here. He built himself a big mansion behind it. Owns a couple of electronics superstores in Adler. I heard he's trying to rent out the farmhouse. It's a decent place."

"Sounds good to me," Henry said. He had driven through the small city of Adler less than an hour ago and estimated its population at around a hundred thousand. It seemed like a good spot, but saving money right now was Henry's best move. As Townsend began writing down directions to Chumansky's house, he remembered something else.

"One more thing," he said. "The employee you're replacing was also my accounting person. Now, I don't expect you to take that part over, but would you mind getting paid by personal check? I'll get the other paperwork and stuff handled later."

Henry decided this might be a good opportunity to push the envelope.

"How about you pay me in cash?" Henry suggested. "Banks annoy the shit out of me." May as well drop a curse word back at Townsend and let him know it doesn't offend me, Henry thought to himself.

"I know what you mean," Townsend responded. "They're always finding reasons to charge you extra—returned check fees, overdraft charges, minimum balances, the whole nine yards. Fine, then. Cash it is."

Henry walked over to Townsend and collected the directions to the farmhouse.

"Thank you for the opportunity, Mr. Townsend. I won't let you down," Henry said, holding out his hand.

"I know you won't, kid," Townsend replied, shaking Henry's outstretched hand. "And why don't you just call me Bruce."

"Will do," Henry said. He walked to the door and pulled his car keys out. A thought crossed his mind as he exited. He turned and added, "You can call me Hank...if you want to."

"See you bright and early tomorrow morning, Hank."

Henry walked to his dark blue Honda Civic and got in. He sighed as he turned the ignition. A new beginning. A chance to start again. Gable seemed quiet. And small. "Population 879" read the green sign that had welcomed him to town.

Following Bruce's instructions, it took less than ten minutes to arrive at the farmhouse. Henry turned in to a long gravel driveway and drove a quarter mile before he saw a small white house on his right. Sitting behind it another quarter mile or so down the drive was a large brown house.

Looks like this is the place, Henry thought as he looked around. There were trees, bushes, weeds, and grass on three sides of the small house. A faded red barn sat at the edge of a wooded area about a hundred feet in front of the house. Around the corner of the barn, Henry spotted a man driving a riding lawn mower through the yard. He was smoking a cigar and doing his best to cut the grass around two German shepherds that were frolicking in his path. The man noticed Henry, who by now had come to a complete stop. He turned off the mower as Henry exited his car and began walking towards him.

"Would you happen to be Mr. Chumansky?" Henry inquired.

"That's me," the man responded, pulling himself off the seat. He wasn't a large man, maybe five foot six, thin, with sandy blonde hair, squinty eyes, and a squeaky voice. "What can I do for you?"

"My name is Henry Fields. Bruce Townsend at the Corner Store told me I should check with you about renting a house."

"Oh yeah?" Chumansky said with a deadpan expression as he continued to approach Henry. Chumansky looked to be in his late thirties and was a good half foot shorter than Henry. But that didn't stop the smaller man from getting as close to Henry as he could. They were almost toe to toe when Henry answered him.

"Is that a problem?" Henry asked, once again answering a question with a question. It was a confrontational inquiry, but he said it in the least threatening manner possible. Henry wasn't looking for a fight; he was looking for a place to live. Chumansky immediately slumped down and took a step backwards.

"Naw, I was just messing around," Chumansky said. Henry had seen guys like this before. Taller men often referred to it as "short man syndrome." Pint-sized guys with an attitude, at least until someone stood up to them or knocked them out.

"Tom Chumansky. Nice to meet you, Henry." Chumansky stuck out his hand. Henry returned the gesture. He could feel the calluses on the man's palm.

This guy might be in the electronics business, Henry thought, but he has spent some time working with his hands, too, more than likely on the farm.

"This is the house right here," Chumansky confirmed as he began walking in that direction. The dogs followed, occasionally jumping on Henry. He wasn't much of a dog lover, but that didn't stop Henry from making an attempt. The problem was, every time he pet one it only encouraged them both to jump on him even more.

"My wife and I just moved out of it a couple of months ago," Chumansky continued. "We finally got the idiot contractors squared away and finished with the new one. You might've seen it when you were coming down the drive."

"Yes, it looked nice back there. Kind of imposing with the woodsy backdrop." Henry dropped the compliment like a butt-kissing used car salesman.

"Thanks. You know, whatever makes the wife happy. And she's happy. For now, anyway. Cost me a fortune, but what the hell. You only live once, right? Can't take the money with you when you clock out, so..."

Chumansky opened the front door of the rental house, and the two men entered the living room. The dogs remained outside.

"We left the old furniture here and put all new stuff in the new house. That's the lazy man's way of moving. The only things you won't have here are a TV and a phone. I can get the electricity and water turned on with a phone call."

Henry was happy to see the furnishings, especially the bed. Otherwise he'd either be sleeping on the floor or driving to Adler to buy an air mattress that evening.

"The sheets on the bed are clean, as are the towels. They're yours to use. There's even a washer and dryer downstairs, so you don't have to haul your clothes to the laundromat. A couple of empty rooms down there, too. Otherwise not much else. Well, maybe a mouse or two. This was a farm, you know." Tom Chumansky was quite the talker.

"Don't do any farming anymore?" Henry asked. He

didn't really care, but thought he should pretend like he did.

"When my old man died I phased most of it out and invested in the electronics business. I've got two stores in Adler called Mecca Warehouse. Gadgets, iPods, TVs, headphones, DVD players, CDs...hard to believe we sell any CDs these days, but we do."

"How much you want?" Henry asked, cutting to the chase. He was getting hungry.

"For CDs or for this place?" Chumansky chuckled.

"This place," Henry replied. "I'm more of a radio guy, myself. I prefer a variety."

"I can understand that. But just so you know, you can get outstanding variety on an iPod," Chumansky said.

This guy doesn't miss an opportunity, Henry thought. He was almost scared to find out how much rent Chumansky wanted.

"Two-fifty, including utilities," Chumansky offered, before Henry could ask again. "I won't even charge you a deposit."

"That's a fair price," Henry said. Actually, it's an excellent price, he thought to himself. "You've got yourself a tenant, Mr. Chumansky."

"Mr. Chumansky was my father. Everyone around here calls me Chum," he declared. "Well, everyone except for the darling creature who shares my bed, of course." he added.

"Makes sense...Chum," Henry responded with a smile while reaching into his front pocket. He pulled out a wad of bills and counted out some twenties. "Here's my first month's rent," he said.

"We're already five days into the month," Chum said. "Let's just call it a prorated two hundred."

"Fair enough," Henry replied, handing him ten twenty dollar bills.

"A cash man. I like that. I think we're gonna be buddies," Chum proclaimed.

***

There was one speed limit sign on the county highway leading from Henry's new home back to Gable, and he was pretty sure it read fifty-five, but he couldn't be certain. Nonetheless, he found himself hitting seventy-five during some stretches, and he didn't really care. Henry was so hungry he was beginning to feel sick. He couldn't remember the last time he had eaten.

The only parking available for Stubby's Diner was on the street. Henry thought about parking at the Corner Store but didn't want to push his luck before even working an hour for Bruce. He parallel parked on the street and entered Stubby's through the creaky screen door.

It was clear to Henry that Stubby's Diner had been around for a while. The wooden floor was worn. The tables, chairs, and booths looked as though they had been around since the early seventies. The place smelled like burgers and fries. Henry could tell by their uniforms that many of the clientele were first-shifters from the dairy plant in Adler. The rest were older folks having an early dinner.

Henry sat down at a table for two near the middle of the restaurant. The older, portly hostess brought him a glass of water and a menu, and let him know that his server would be with him shortly.

It had only been a couple of hours, but Henry was already growing rather fond of Gable. It seemed quiet, cozy, and unsuspecting. He felt confident he was going to like it here.

"Well, you're new," his waitress proclaimed as she interrupted Henry's thoughts and stood next to him. Her light brown hair was pulled back in a ponytail, and her hazel eyes sparkled in the dim light of the mid-afternoon as she smiled.

"Yes," Henry said. "I'm new...I guess." He looked up and returned the smile. She was attractive despite the fact she had been working in a grease pit for God knows how many hours.

"What brings you through town? Business? Family?" she asked, wiping up a wet spot on his table.

"Actually, I just moved here," Henry answered. "Moved into Tom Chumansky's farmhouse just a while ago," he said, pointing with his thumb over his right shoulder.

"Oh, really? Interesting," she said. "Chum, eh? Quite a character, isn't he?"

"That's a fair way of putting it. My name's Henry Fields," he responded, holding his hand out.

"Claire Mathison," she said, shaking his hand delicately. "What are you drinking?"

"Coke would be good. And how are the fish sticks?" He was so hungry he couldn't wait a second longer to get his order in.

Claire inhaled deeply through her nose. "You smell all the grease in here? Fried foods are our specialty. The fish sticks are huge and fried in their own vat so our French fries and onion rings don't taste like Chicken of the Sea."

"Fish sticks it is then," Henry agreed. Claire grinned and walked away through the kitchen door.

Henry leaned back in his chair and took a drink of water. He ran his hand through his brown hair and gazed around the restaurant. The middle-aged barmaid was chatting it up with two older men sitting at the bar. She wasn't wearing a wedding ring, but these days that didn't mean much. It was just far less likely for a married woman to be ringless than it was for a man.

Two men were sitting in the corner booth, yakking over their beer and nachos. Occasional bellows of laughter would erupt and rapidly die down. Henry guessed they were talking about their boss, but for all he knew they could be talking about him. He was a stranger in this town, and Claire had proved it by immediately picking him out of the afternoon crowd. Maybe this place wasn't such a good idea after all,

Henry thought.

Before he had time to contemplate further, Claire was placing a huge glass of Coke on his table. She stood next to him for an extra beat as he thanked her.

"So, how'd you end up in the middle-of-nowhere-Iowa?" she asked, handing him a straw.

Henry wasn't in the mood to construct a backstory at the moment, so he elected to keep things short.

"It's a long story," he said with a sigh. "I'm from out there." Henry pointed towards the door. Claire smiled again. "Being here just kind of happened, I guess," he explained.

"Gable doesn't just happen to people," she said. "Not usually, anyway. I was born and raised here. Went to high school right out there down Highway 57. For some reason, I'm still here. It's like the Mafia. If you're born in it, it's almost impossible to leave."

"Maybe you just haven't found the right reason to leave yet," Henry suggested while picking up his Coke glass.

"Maybe," Claire replied. "Fish sticks are coming in about three minutes," she said, changing the subject and heading to the kitchen.

Henry's meal arrived shortly after and he inhaled it as fast as his mouth would allow him to chew and swallow. Claire was polite but not as chatty while he ate. Traffic was picking up in Stubby's as the evening hours approached. He paid for his twelve dollar tab by laying a twenty on top of the check. As he moved towards the door, Claire called out to him.

"Hey, Henry!" He stopped and turned as she walked up to him. "What was your reason for leaving where you came from?"

This girl is relentless, he thought.

"Fate, I guess," he said with a shrug.

"Wow," Claire said with a wry smile. "You're relentless, Henry."

Henry grinned and shook his head as he opened the

door. He was going to like this girl, which was good since she obviously wasn't going anywhere.

"Thanks for stopping by, Mystery Man. Come back and see us soon!"

***

Henry lay down on his new bed and put his hands behind his head. His two duffel bags and backpack were still on the floor next to him where he had dropped them earlier after returning from his meal. It was now nine-thirty in the evening. The house was dark. The entire area was quiet except for the occasional bark from a German shepherd or two. The dogs seemed to be guarding the area and protecting the land from owls, deer, and passing cars.

As Henry drifted off to sleep he chuckled to himself. He wondered what the Vegas odds would have been a month ago that he would end up living on a farm in Iowa, by himself. This wasn't what he'd had in mind when he was growing up. His parents had always led him to believe he could do anything he wanted in life. He'd spent hours daydreaming about being a fireman, a detective, a doctor. Almost every day it was a new career, a new life. Sometimes his daydreams were influenced by a TV show or a movie, like the two-week period he became a Jedi after seeing *Star Wars* for the first time.

It was nobody's fault he was here now. Henry had stopped playing the blame game a long time ago. Like the saying goes, "Life is twenty percent what happens to you and eighty percent how you react to it." He was reacting to life every day now.

"There's only one thing you can control in this world, son," his father had told him when he graduated from high school. "You. You have total control over your emotions, your words, your actions. You can't stop someone from wronging you, but you have complete control over how you react, or whether you even react at all."

His father was the glue that held the family together.

He always had advice for his two sons but never forced anything on them. Sports, camping, hunting, fishing, Boy Scouts; he was close to both of them. And he treated their mother with the respect a woman deserved and needed, helping to keep her sane while raising two boys. There was little doubt she would've preferred a daughter in the mix. She never said a word about it to her sons, but their father more than likely knew. It was as if he always knew exactly what everyone in the house was thinking and feeling at any given moment.

Henry dozed off for the night thinking about how much he missed his father and how he wished he could speak to him now.

II

Henry pulled up to the Corner Store at five forty-five the next morning. He wasn't surprised Bruce had yet to arrive. Henry had left plenty early knowing that being late on his first day would not have made a good impression. Five minutes later, Bruce pulled in with his Ford Explorer.

"Here's your copy of the key to this joint," he told Henry as he handed him a key ring with one key on it. "We didn't talk much about a schedule, but it's just you and me splitting this thing up until I get a part-timer to help out."

"Not a problem," Henry replied.

"It means no days off, you know?" Bruce said with a cringe.

"I don't mind. I can use the money."

Henry's boss exhaled. "Whew, I didn't think about it until I went home last night. Thought you might be pissed. The weekends will be some good overtime for you."

Bruce showed Henry how to use the cash register, credit card machine, and gas pumps. By the time Henry felt comfortable, it was six fifteen and customers were already filing in. Some came for gas, but most were there for a morning cup of coffee or a bag of prepackaged donuts. Bruce explained that the Corner Store was more of a mini-grocery store than a convenience store. They didn't carry any ready-made, warm food like hot dogs, taquitos, or nachos. If customers wanted something like that they could go across the street to Stubby's. They also opened at six and provided sit-down breakfasts as well as to-go style foods like breakfast burritos.

"It's a small town thing," Bruce said, summing up his explanation. "Stubby's was in Gable long before this gas station added a food section."

"Stubby still around?" Henry inquired.

"His wife is, but Stubby died about six or seven years ago."

"I assume 'Stubby' wasn't his real name," Henry surmised. He handed a male customer his change for a bottle of water and a small cup of coffee. The customer stopped and turned to Bruce when he overheard Henry.

"I always wondered, what was Stubby's real name?" the customer asked with a smile.

"Rodney was his birth name, and how he got the nickname is kind of inspiring," Bruce began. "Everyone knew him as 'Rodney' or 'Rod' up until when he was about twenty years old and he had an accident. He was a farmer's son, and one day he got his hand caught in a clogged corn picker. Lost the four fingers on his right hand at the first joint."

"This part of the story I've heard," the customer said to Henry while walking towards the door. "It's a good one, though, so keep listening. I'll see you tomorrow!" The man waved and jogged to his car.

"So anyway, Stubby—Rodney—didn't let the missing fingers hold him back much. He had such a sense of humor about it he began referring to his hand as 'old stubby.' That's kind of what the hand looked like with those half-sized fingers: a stub."

"So, the name just stuck?"

"Pretty much," Bruce said. "He told me what happened was one time, someone misunderstood him. They thought he was referring to himself instead of his hand. Which is funny because Stubby always weighed about one sixty soaking wet."

"Not a big guy, eh?" Henry asked.

"Not short, but not fat either. It just goes to show how most people never gave it a second thought. Many of them weren't around here forty years ago when the accident happened. They didn't even realize Stubby had a handicap because he never let it affect him. Once the nickname stuck, I think he stopped referring to his hand at all. It just became a part of him. Which is ironic since he also lost a part of him."

"Good point," Henry said. "Good story, too."

"One hundred percent authentic," Bruce replied. He grabbed his keys and changed the subject, lowering his voice even though no one else was in the store.

"A couple more things before I take off for a while," Bruce began. He moved to the back corner behind the register and reached under the counter. "The silent alarm is set and turned off back here. You might've noticed when we came in, there was no noise. I came back here and turned it off while we were opening. The code is 1221. Don't forget to turn it off when you open this place. Otherwise you'll have an army of trigger-happy, small town law enforcement pointing their guns at you in no time flat. You've got sixty seconds before that silent alarm is triggered."

"Got it," Henry replied with a soft chuckle.

"And speaking of guns," Bruce continued, "I've got this here, too, though I've never had to use it."

He reached under the counter beneath the cash register and pulled out a SIG Pro semi-automatic pistol. He turned to Henry.

"You ever used one of these before, Hank?"

"Probably not one like this," Henry replied, taking the gun from Bruce.

"Just pull the trigger...and don't miss," Bruce instructed, taking the gun and placing it back in its hiding spot.

"I can handle that," Henry said, though he couldn't imagine getting held up in a town this small. Bruce headed to the door.

"I'll be back a bit later to let you grab some lunch while I watch the register," he said. "If you have any questions just call my cell. The number is right behind you on the board."

"Got it," Henry said.

The day flew by more quickly than Henry had expected. Idle chatter with customers kept his mind busy. When the store emptied out, he wandered over to the radio on the shelf behind the counter. He went up and down the dial and finally settled on a classic rock station that was playing a Journey song.

Around ten o'clock a uniformed police officer walked into the store. Henry nodded to him as he entered but wasn't certain the officer had returned the greeting, which seemed strange.

Maybe he didn't see me, Henry thought. The police officer shuffled around the store for a minute or so. Henry tried not to stare, but he couldn't help notice the officer looking his way several times.

What is he doing? Henry wondered. Worse yet, what had Henry done to warrant this attention? He'd been in town for less than twenty-four hours. Had he done something wrong? Was there a problem with his license plate, maybe?

Finally, the officer headed over to the beverage counter and poured a cup of coffee. He emptied two sugars in the cup and secured the lid. On his way to the register he grabbed a fruit pie off a stand. Whatever Henry had done, he was about to find out.

The officer placed his coffee and pie on the counter and began to reach for his wallet. There was a moment, only a split second, where Henry thought he might be reaching for his gun.

"You're new?" the officer asked. His name tag was shining so bright Henry had to squint to read it: JACKSON.

"Yes, I am," Henry responded, reaching for the fruit pie to scan it. "Henry Fields," he said, extending his right hand across the counter. Jackson returned the gesture with a quick shake. Henry also noticed "Sergeant" engraved on his badge.

"John Jackson, Gable Police," he responded. It sounded to Henry like Jackson had spent a lot of time practicing the inflection of that phrase. "When I first walked in I thought you were somebody else," Jackson continued.

Henry's heart sunk to the tips of his toes.

"But then I remembered that guy was six nine. I played basketball against him in high school."

Henry recovered, realizing he had been on high alert for no reason. It was a ridiculous notion anyway, he thought.

Henry chuckled out loud at the thought of playing basketball in high school. Or being six foot nine. Sergeant John Jackson was around forty years old, average height, with a burly build. He had a full head of hair and big, piercing brown eyes. As the policeman left the store with a quick, "see you tomorrow," Henry tried to imagine Jackson playing basketball. The only thing he could come up with was the image of Jackson getting his shot blocked by a giant doppelgänger of Henry.

Around eleven o'clock Bruce returned to give Henry a lunch break. After a quick question and answer session about some job specifics, Henry walked across the street to Stubby's for a meal. As he approached, he saw Claire standing outside the restaurant, smoking a cigarette and drinking a Coke.

"What's up, Mystery Man?" she called out to him.

"First day of work," he pointed with his thumb over his shoulder.

"Pumping some gas, printing some lottery tickets," Claire joked, taking a drag of her smoke.

"No gas pumping. I can't even remember the days of

full-service stations," Henry shot back.

"That one used to be full-service," she pointed with her cigarette.

"I figured as much." At that moment Henry's stomach gave him a friendly reminder in the form of a growl. "I'm gonna head in for some food," he said. "I didn't have breakfast."

"Grab a menu and I'll be right in to take care of you," Claire said with a smile.

Henry walked through the door and sat down at the same table as the day before, all the while wondering if Claire had just hit on him.

***

Claire chatted with Henry for a moment each time she brought something to his table. Eventually the subject of Chum came up again. Henry told Claire about meeting his new landlord for the first time and moving in to his farmhouse.

"Chum's quite a character, isn't he?" Claire asked while refilling Henry's water. "Almost too much to deal with, at times."

"He definitely has moxie," Henry agreed. "Seems manageable, though."

"Just wait until you meet his main sales guy, Eddie. Now that guy is a real piece of work," Claire explained.

"Lots of personality around here for such a small town," Henry observed. They exchanged smiles as she left for another table.

He didn't mind making a new female friend, or any friend for that matter. The stimulation was good for him. Henry just wasn't sure he wanted things to go any further with Claire than they already had. She seemed genuinely interested in him, but he also knew this was the result of a pretty girl living in a small town her entire life. She was too close to the people in Gable, knew them all too well. A new guy moving to town was something fresh in her mundane life of waiting tables and hearing the same jokes over and over again. Claire now had something to look forward to and explore. Henry knew he was making himself even more appealing to her with his elusiveness. But the alternative was to get Claire to talk more about herself, and he was aware this would have the same effect. It was human nature.

He watched her as she dealt with others in the diner. It didn't matter who she was talking with, she always seemed sincere. There were no crossed arms, no steps backward. She was always leaning into conversations and attentive to her surroundings. No one waited long for a refill or extra napkins. She kept things moving. He figured some of this was the process of working for tips, but there was little doubt waiting tables for a living was not for everyone. Henry had never done it and was certain he never could. Working the register at a gas station was about the best he could do when it came to customer service. It wasn't that he didn't like people. In fact, the problem was he knew and understood people too well. No, Henry liked people. He found them intriguing. That is until they let him down or crossed him. He found it hard to forgive and forget. Fool me once, shame on you because I'm done, he thought to himself.

As he finished his club sandwich and side salad, Claire dropped the check on his table.

"Here you go," she said. "And there's no need to leave me a tip today."

Henry glanced up at her with a confused look. Before he had a chance to reply, Claire spoke again.

"The eight dollars you left for me yesterday will cover today's service, too," she explained.

"I didn't have any change," Henry countered with a wry grin.

"I did," Claire said, shaking her head and folding her arms across her chest.

"Your prompt service and conversation were worth

extra money to me," he said with a shrug. He knew she was angling at something, but he wasn't sure what it was.

"I appreciate you saying that," she said. "It's not every day someone drops a seventy percent tip on my table. But I prefer keeping things legit. Working here is an honest living and anything more than twenty-five percent feels like a bribe."

Interesting, Henry thought. He considered continuing to make light of things but could tell Claire was dead serious.

"Fair enough," he said. There was only one thing he could think of that anyone would bribe her for, and that just wasn't something Henry would ever do. But he also knew Claire couldn't be sure of this. Especially when he wasn't willing to tell her much about himself.

As Claire walked back to the kitchen to get another customer his lunch, Henry pulled his wallet from his pocket. He had made some change earlier at the Corner Store and would be able to pay for his lunch in the exact amount of the check. Henry liked Claire, but even before her dignity speech he'd had no intention of leaving her eight dollar tips for the rest of whatever. He couldn't afford it. Especially not on minimum wage. He set the money on the table and walked out the door without saying goodbye.

***

Henry finished his first day of work at three in the afternoon when Bruce came back to take over. Instead of spending the money to eat out yet another time, Henry elected to buy some food at the Corner Store to take home for meals. It had been a long first day, and enjoying some relaxing time around his new home might do him some good.

He said goodbye to Bruce and grabbed his shopping bag. It was full of microwave burritos, cereal, bread, cheese, eggs, peanut butter, and milk. When he got back to the house he put the groceries away, took a quick shower, and put some fresh clothes on before exploring the place. Henry hadn't had much time to check out the rest of the house the day before.

As Chum had told him, just about everything he needed was already here. A refrigerator, a microwave, even a bed in the second bedroom, not that he was expecting company anytime soon. The closet space was minimal but that didn't matter much to Henry.

He walked down the narrow staircase in the kitchen to the basement. The old steps creaked so much that Henry expected to crash through them with every move he made. When he reached the bottom he noticed a clothes washer and dryer on the left. To the right were two more rooms. He walked into the first one and immediately saw that it was deserted. It had a closet that was also empty. Not that Henry expected to find buried treasure or anything. He was just curious and preferred to be aware of his surroundings.

After discovering the other room was vacant as well, he returned to the kitchen and made himself a peanut butter sandwich. He sat down on the couch, put his glass of milk on the carpeted floor and ate with his plate in his lap. He stared at the empty entertainment center that most likely once housed a television set. From what he had seen, there was no radio in the house, either.

I'm going to need to find a hobby, Henry thought to himself. He soon fell asleep on the couch, still sitting up, with the plate in his lap.

III

Over the next few days Henry settled in to Gable, his job, and his new home. One morning he woke up to discover he did, indeed, have a roommate. The plate he had left on the kitchen counter overnight no longer had bread crusts on it. Discovering this sent a chill down Henry's spine. It wasn't that mice frightened him. After all, they were always so fun to watch in cartoons: Mickey, Speedy, Jerry. But there was something creepy about real ones. The way they lived in houses and did as they pleased. And they were never seen by the human eye until after they grabbed that fatal final piece of cheese—Snap!

But Henry had another idea. Something that he hoped would wind up being far more entertaining. One afternoon following work he made a quick trip to the pet store at the northern end of Adler. For a nominal fee Henry adopted a black cat; he named him "Wilson" after Tom Hanks' volleyball friend in the movie *Castaway*. Now he had a real roommate and not a squatter.

Henry hadn't seen Claire since she told him not to tip her so much, but he hadn't been back to Stubby's either. Instead, he had been bringing his lunch to work or buying it at the store. If Bruce came to relieve him he would either sit outside and eat or take a walk up and down Main Street. One day Bruce wasn't able to make it in to give Henry a break, so he just ate behind the counter while continuing to take care of the register. Bruce made it up to him by letting Henry take off an hour early and still paying him for that hour.

When Friday of his first week in Gable rolled around it was time for Henry to work his first night shift. He and Bruce had worked out the schedule: Bruce would work six to three during the day on Friday. Henry would come in from three until eleven and close the store. Then he would return on Saturday morning to work from eight to three. Bruce would then cover the next two shifts so Henry could have some time off over the weekend. Henry would return to work at three until close on Sunday and go back to the day shifts for the week starting Monday morning. Bruce was a married man and had grandchildren to spend time with, but Henry wasn't sure what he'd do with his time off. Working this job hadn't even seemed like work, so far. It was a laid-back gig. People were, in general, nice to him. Or at least they were reserved and quiet, which was fine with Henry.

His first afternoon working at the Corner Store was like the mornings had been. But there were fewer people buying coffee and more buying beer this time of day. It was Friday, after all. Around seven o'clock, an elderly man had a difficult time getting the gas pump to work. Henry locked the door to the store, something Bruce had taught him on his first day, and jogged out to help him. The man was grateful and even came inside after pumping his gas to tell Henry what life was like when he was Henry's age.

The next several hours were uneventful. The sun began to go down and Gable became rather quiet. Henry assumed it was because many people went to Adler for dinner and entertainment. He had also heard about another town north of Gable on Highway 57, called Merchant. It was bigger than Gable, but not nearly as large as Adler.

At eight fifteen, Henry was passing the time listening to the radio when he heard a loud crash outside. He sprinted to the door and opened it, attempting to look up and down the highway. He couldn't see much of anything that way due to the location of the Corner Store building. It seemed no one else had heard the noise, which surprised Henry. If anybody else *had* heard, they didn't find it urgent enough to investigate. But Henry did.

He reached into his pocket, grabbed his keys, and locked the door to the store. He jogged to the edge of the property and scanned north then south, up and down the highway. When he looked south he noticed something white sticking out of the ditch on the west side. Henry's instinct kicked in and he began a brisk jog down the shoulder of the highway, toward the white object. Had there been a car accident? He couldn't see far enough to tell for certain. The sun had gone down just enough that details from a distance were impossible to see. Henry kept jogging for what seemed like an eternity.

I should've driven my car, he thought to himself.

Finally, Henry reached the scene of what appeared to be a one-car accident. He saw a white sedan planted upside down and nose-first in the ditch. There were other cars pulled over on both sides of the highway, and a few of the drivers were beginning to get out.

"Did you see anything?" Henry called out to them. "Is the driver still in the car?" No one answered but he could tell they were speaking among themselves up on the highway. He stumbled down into the ditch towards the overturned car. There was no fire that he could see, only smoke mixed with clouds of dust and dirt floating through the air from the impact. Henry approached the driver's side door and knelt down. He looked through the empty upside down frame, where there'd once been a window.

"Hello!" Henry yelled into the car. "Anybody in there?" No one answered; the car was empty. The driver and any passengers must have been thrown from the vehicle. Henry stood up and spun around. He began searching for signs of life...or death.

"Anybody out here?" he yelled. "Hello!" Henry could

feel his heart racing. His breaths were short and quick. He tried to take a couple of deep ones to prepare himself for what he might see next. The grass was long enough that any person thrown from the car would be hidden. Henry kept moving and yelling in an attempt to find the driver or a passenger. A couple of other men from the cars that had pulled over on the shoulder began coming down to help.

Approximately sixty feet from the car Henry finally spotted something red amidst the tall ditch weeds. He ran over to the area, about ten feet from a barbed-wire fence. The red he had noticed was a man's shirt. The man wearing the shirt was lying on his back, attempting to sit up. As Henry reached him, he called out to the other two men who were searching the area.

"Over here!" he shouted, waving his arms and beginning to help the man in the red shirt sit up. "Was anybody else in the car?" Henry asked. The man seemed more in a daze than in pain.

"No," the man replied. He looked Henry in the eyes as he was finally able to sit straight up. "My arm..."

It was at that exact moment Henry realized the man's left arm was missing. His shoulder was a mass of blood and wreckage. The arm was nowhere in sight. Henry tried to think of a reassuring statement but came up with nothing.

Just then the other men ran up behind Henry and the victim.

"Holy shit!" the heavyset one exclaimed, out of breath from the ninety-foot jog. He stared at the man's bloody socket.

"Is there anyone else?" the second man asked.

"No, just him," Henry answered.

"I've got some towels in my truck. I'll go get them!" The chubby guy hustled back up to the shoulder.

"We've got to get him out of here," the other man said. "I'll go call 911. My phone's in the car."

Something told Henry neither of the men wanted to

stick around and look at the victim's injury. He tried not think about it or look at it as he spoke to him.

"What's your name?"

"Alan...Alan Walker," the man answered.

"Do you think you can walk if I help you, Alan?" Henry asked. He wasn't sure if moving him was a good idea. At this point he was working on adrenaline and instinct, not experience. After all, this kind of thing didn't happen to a convenience store clerk every day.

"I think...yes," Alan responded. His black hair was matted down with a combination of blood, sweat, and dirt. He had a deep cut on his forehead that was still bleeding. His eyes were as big as saucers as he continued to stare at Henry for answers.

It surprised Henry that Alan hadn't passed out yet. He must have lost large amounts of blood when his arm was severed. As Henry helped Alan stand, he saw a pool of blood where Alan had been lying. He reached around Alan's waist and let the injured man balance his weight against him. Fifteen seconds felt like fifteen minutes to Henry as they crept to the highway. When they passed the wreckage of the car, Alan turned and looked at it. The look on his face made Henry wonder if the man even understood what had happened. As they reached the edge of the highway, Alan began to lose his balance.

"I can't..." he said as he fell from Henry's grip and to his knees.

He's going to pass out soon, Henry thought.

"An ambulance is on the way," the chubby man said as he hustled to Henry and handed him some towels, as if he were a paramedic. Henry took the towels and looked down at Alan, who was balancing on his knees, swaying from side to side. He was beginning to shake.

"I don't think there's enough time," said Henry. "The ambulance has to be a good twenty minutes away."

"I can drive him there," a female voice piped up. "I was heading to Adler, anyway."

"I'll ride with you," Henry said, completely forgetting he was supposed to be working. "What color is your car?" he asked her.

"Silver," the woman replied. She looked to be in her mid-fifties. "It's a Murano."

The man who called the ambulance had also made his way over. Henry turned to him and asked, "Can you call 911 again? Ask them to tell the ambulance to be on the lookout for a silver Murano heading south, flashing its brights."

The man nodded, pulled his phone from his pocket, and walked back to the shoulder to make the call. Alan was lying down on the ground again, this time on his side—the side that still had an arm. He was conscious, but his breathing was labored and he was beginning to shut his eyes for brief periods. Henry enlisted two more men who had pulled their cars over to carry Alan to the backseat of the woman's car. He gave them two towels and kept one for himself.

"I'll be right back," he told them. "Just give me sixty seconds." Henry ran down the ditch in the direction of the overturned car. He tried looking inside through the glassless, passenger-side window but couldn't see much of anything. Nightfall was continuing to creep down on the countryside.

Wrong side, anyway, Henry thought to himself. He darted to the driver's side, where he had first looked for victims. He reached inside and felt along the roof that was now on the ground. He reached up to the floor. Nothing. As Henry pulled his arm out of the car, it brushed against the seatbelt. He could immediately tell it wasn't just an empty harness. He looked up and saw Alan's arm in a bloody, tangled mess of nylon mesh.

Henry didn't have time to think about how nauseating and surreal this was going to be. He reached up and began untangling the arm. The skin was cool. As he worked at twisting it out of the seatbelt, Henry could feel the flesh and bone protruding from the severed limb, but at least it didn't take long to free it. Henry wrapped the arm in the towel and sprinted back up to the highway. The lady in the silver Murano had pulled up to the shoulder and was waiting for Henry.

"Could you pop the hatch, please?" he called out to her. Henry figured it might not be a good idea to make Alan ride shotgun with his arm. He placed it in the back, still swaddled in the towel, and closed the hatch door. He scurried into the backseat and squeezed in next to where Alan was stretched out.

"Let's go!" Henry exclaimed. The woman pulled onto the highway and began to pick up speed. Alan had passed out. There were two towels near his wound. It looked to Henry as though Alan had been trying to apply pressure to it. Henry pressed his own hand hard against the bloody towels.

"What's your name?" the woman asked.

"My name's Henry. His name is Alan," he answered.

"I'm Rose," she offered. "You do this often?" She caught Henry off guard with her sense of humor, but he managed a soft chuckle when he replied.

"I can't say that I do," he said. "First time, actually."

"Me, too," Rose said. "So I assume your plan is to shorten the ambulance's drive time and get Alan to some EMTs faster?"

"It might not be standard operating procedure in an emergency situation, but it made sense to me at the time," Henry explained.

"Makes perfect sense to me," Rose agreed. "How's he doing back there?"

"I'm no doctor, but I'd say he needs professional medical attention soon."

"Then it's a good thing we're doing this," Rose replied. A few seconds of silence passed, then she spoke again. "Did you put what I think you put back there, in the towel?"

Henry looked down at Alan. He was still passed out.

"Yeah," he answered. "I figured if there was any hope..."

"You did the right thing," Rose told him. "A good thing."

Up ahead and off in the distance, a vehicle was approaching. Rose and Henry noticed it through the twilight at the same time.

"There's the ambulance!" Henry exclaimed.

"Flashing my brights!" Rose reported.

Within seconds, the ambulance and the Murano met nose to nose on the right shoulder of Highway 57. Henry jumped out immediately and stood by the door. He hadn't let up the pressure on Alan's wound until now.

"He's in the backseat here!" he shouted to the paramedics. One of them came over immediately and stood face to face with Henry. He was an African-American of average height and build, and he was all business.

"What do we have here?" he asked.

"He was in a car accident about seven or eight miles north of here. Looks like he was thrown from the vehicle. When I found him his arm was missing. I think it got caught in the seatbelt. The accident happened roughly thirty minutes ago. His name is Alan Walker."

Henry stepped aside and let the paramedic look in on the injured man.

"I've been trying to keep pressure on it," Henry explained. He's been passed out for maybe ten to twelve minutes."

The paramedic pulled his head out from the vehicle and waved to the other two paramedics, who were bringing the gurney. He turned to Henry again.

"Only ten minutes or so?"

"Give or take, I'd say. Is that bad?" Henry had no idea. All this stuff he had been doing was guesswork. He had never broken a bone, never had surgery, and never spent any time in a hospital other than to visit someone.

"No, I wouldn't say so. But it's not necessarily good either. Just a bit unusual," the EMT explained. He pulled Henry aside a few more feet as the other paramedics began to move Alan out from the backseat and onto the stretcher.

"Hey, uh...you wouldn't happen to have recovered the severed limb, would you?" he asked.

Henry had almost forgotten.

"Yes, yes I did." he replied, moving to the back of the vehicle. The hatch was still unlocked and Henry raised the door. Not requiring a cue, the paramedic immediately leaned in and pulled back the bloody towel to confirm it was, indeed, a human arm.

"We'll take this with us," he explained, folding the towel back around Alan's arm and picking it up.

"Of course," Henry said. The paramedic took the towel-wrapped appendage to the back of the ambulance, where the other two EMTs had just transferred Alan. Henry stood by the driver's side door of the Murano and waited to see if they needed anything else. Rose rolled down the window.

"Looks like it's out of our control now," she said.

"I guess so," Henry sighed. "I hope he's okay."

"You did your part," Rose assured him. Just then the African-American paramedic jumped into the driver's seat of the ambulance. As he did, he gave Henry a quick wave of the hand as if to say "thanks." Henry waved back.

"Did you want to follow them to the hospital and find out how things turn out?" Rose asked Henry as the ambulance U-turned onto the highway and sped away with the lights flashing and siren blaring.

All of a sudden, Henry remembered what he had been doing less than forty-five minutes earlier.

"I can't," he said. "I need to get back to work. Can I talk you into driving back to Gable?"

Henry was grateful when Rose didn't hesitate to

accommodate him. On the way he explained everything to her. He told her how he had been working at the store when he heard the accident and instinctively ran up the highway to investigate.

Rose was a saleswoman who lived in Adler and had been on her way home from a business dinner in Merchant. When she noticed several cars pulled over on the highway she only slowed down to be safe, at first. But when she discovered what had happened, she elected to pull over and see if she could help.

When they drove past the accident scene again, there were two Gable Police cars on the shoulder, lights flashing. Henry thought one of the policeman might be Sergeant Jackson, though he couldn't tell for sure in the darkness.

When they pulled up to the Corner Store, all looked the same to Henry as when he had left it a little more than an hour ago. He turned to Rose and thanked her for helping and for bringing him back.

"Don't mention it," she said. "You would've done the same for me or anyone else."

Henry wasn't quite sure how Rose knew this, but he felt certain she was right.

"By the way," he remembered, "you're gonna have some blood on the seat back there." Henry looked down at his shirt; it had several spots on it, too.

"That's not a problem either," Rose replied. "It's a company car, and I'm due for a detail cleaning from top to bottom. Company dime!"

Henry thanked her again and got out of the car. He unlocked the door to the Corner Store as she drove away. There was no telling how many customers he had missed while he had been gone, if any. He would have to come clean with Bruce, but it could wait until tomorrow afternoon. Henry only hoped it wouldn't cost him his job. Bruce seemed like a reasonable guy, but you never can be too certain about people. This much Henry knew from experience. A lot of experience.

He saw three customers before closing. Only two came inside the store, both to buy beer. It was dumb luck neither of them noticed the bloodstains on his shirt because Henry didn't have the energy to explain himself. When Rose dropped him off he realized just how worn out he was from the experience he had just had. His body wasn't tired, but he was feeling emotionally drained. Henry had turned off every other thought or feeling he had in his mind to concentrate on the situation at hand. Now that the ordeal was over and he had time to process what had happened, it was overwhelming.

At eleven o'clock sharp Henry set the store alarm, locked the door, and fell into his car. The drive to his house was relaxing. So relaxing, in fact, that he had to struggle to stay awake. When he walked through the front door of the house, Wilson immediately greeted him with four meows. Henry replied with a couple meows of his own and filled his cat's food bowl. Then he poured some cornflakes in a cereal bowl for himself and took it with him to his bedroom while he changed clothes. He peeled off the bloody shirt and threw it in a corner. Henry knew he would more than likely end up throwing it away, but he didn't want to think about it at the moment.

After putting on a pair of shorts and finishing his cereal, he crawled into bed. On cue, Wilson jumped on the comforter and curled up behind Henry's knees. They were both happy to be in bed. All was quiet.

And then there was a knock at the door. Henry had already dozed off and wasn't sure if he was having a dream. He waited and listened. Another knock. It was real.

Henry rolled out of bed; Wilson followed behind. There was another knock before he got to the door.

"I'm coming," he growled. He thought for a minute how if he still lived in a city he wouldn't even be answering it.

When Henry opened the door he was surprised to see Claire, standing on the top step, holding a bottle of white wine and two glasses.

"Howdy stranger," she said.

IV

"I kind of feel like I owe you an apology," Claire explained. She batted her eyelashes just a bit and flashed Henry a smile. "Can I come in?" she asked.

"Well, I guess," he said. "I had a long day, but..."

Claire walked into the living room, not giving him a chance to finish his sentence. She stood behind Henry while he closed the door.

"The place looks good," she commented. "Similar to how Chum had it. Want some wine?" She walked to the kitchen bar and set the bottle and glasses down. Then she reached into the back pocket of her jeans.

"I even brought a corkscrew."

"I'm not much of a drinker," Henry confessed as he followed her to the kitchen.

"More for me then, I guess," Claire replied, wrestling the cork from the bottle. Henry watched as she poured a large glass. She then took the second glass and poured a small amount, handing it to Henry.

"Just in case," she said with a smile and took the large glass for herself, strolling back to the living room. She pounced on the couch and took a drink as Henry sat down next to her.

"Forgive me for slowing things down here,

but...you've been in here before?" Henry asked. Claire nodded.

"Several times," she said. "Chum throws a party every few months and invites the entire town. I mean, not everyone shows up, but it's always a good time. Lots of booze and food. Usually roasts a pig. It's pretty freaky to pull the meat for your sandwich from something that's staring at the guests."

"That does sound...different," Henry said. He'd never been a fan of eating anything that still had eyes. Claire laughed at his response.

"Of course, if you drink enough first you'll be so hungry you won't care where your food is coming from," she added, taking another swallow of her wine. Henry placed his glass on the coffee table in front of them.

"You say you owe me an apology?" he asked. Claire took another quick sip and set her glass on the coffee table next to Henry's.

"The other day when I got on your case about the big tip you left me," she began, "that wasn't fair."

Henry shrugged.

"You hadn't done anything to deserve that kind of attitude from me," Claire continued. "I gave you good service and you tipped me what you felt it was worth. There's nothing wrong with that. I just have...issues."

"It's no big deal," Henry said. "We all have little things that set us off."

Claire's eyes lingered on Henry's during a few seconds of uncomfortable silence. She rubbed her left wrist with her right hand.

"I haven't seen you in a few days," she said in a softer tone. "I thought maybe I'd scared you off."

Henry wondered if it was customary for her to stop by a customer's house with a bottle of wine to apologize for her peculiar behavior. He decided against posing the question out loud.

"No, no," Henry replied. "I've just been getting settled

into a routine and stuff. Nothing personal."

Claire reached for her glass of wine.

"You not been eating any meals this week then or what?" she asked him with a wink.

Henry playfully threw his hands in the air.

"Hey, I can't afford to eat out every day," he said. "Besides, walking across the street goes both ways, you know? We have donuts, wine, and cigarettes. You should stop by sometime."

You can even tip me, Henry thought to himself, but elected not to say it.

"Hi, kitty-kitty! How are you?" Claire blurted as Wilson walked into the room, helping to change the subject.

"That's Wilson," Henry explained to her. "He's new in town, too."

"He's cute," she said. "Come here, Wilson." Claire made some kiss noises and the cat jumped on her lap.

"I guess he knows his name," Henry said.

"Or he knows a good thing when he sees it," Claire countered. She began petting Wilson on the head and scratching his ears. It wasn't long before he was purring. "You don't seem like a cat-guy," she continued.

"He earns his keep by scaring the mice. Living on a farm doesn't come without a price," Henry explained as he stood up and stretched.

"You're a poet and didn't know it," Claire said, laughing.

Henry thought about it for a moment before he realized what she was referring to.

"I guess you're right," he said and chuckled. "Sorry. I'm a little slow right now. I had a long day."

"You need to talk about it?"

"I need to sleep."

"Is that a hint?"

"Just a fact, ma'am."

The laughter the two continued to share proved they were becoming increasingly comfortable with each other. Henry sat down next to Claire again and began telling her about the evening's events. As he did, Claire listened intently. By the time he had finished the story her mouth was gaping, wide open.

"So you have no idea what happened to him?" she asked.

"I don't," Henry said.

"You might've saved his life!" Claire exclaimed.

"Well, there were other people there," he said.

"Yes, but you said yourself they weren't being terribly energetic," she replied.

Henry shrugged and yawned. He looked at the clock. It was twelve thirty. He needed to get some sleep, but he knew Claire had other ideas.

"You had to touch—carry—his detached arm...pulled it out from the car? That's so...weird," she said.

"I try not to make it a habit," Henry replied. By now Claire had finished her glass of wine and had almost consumed another. Henry was also certain she'd had a glass before she knocked on his door. Some liquid courage, so to speak. There was another short, uncomfortable silence before Henry finally spoke again. "I don't mean to seem rude, but I really need to get some sleep." Claire's eyes widened.

"I came here for a reason," she explained as she slid closer to Henry. Wilson didn't appreciate the juggling. He ended his extended stay by jumping from Claire's lap to the floor and returning to the bedroom. Henry knew what Claire meant, but elected to force it out of her.

"I thought we established that already," he replied.

"We did, but there's more," Claire began. "I need to tell you..." She looked down at the floor. "...that I am attracted to you." She finished the sentence by looking back up and into

Henry's eyes.

Henry smiled.

"I'm flattered," he said.

"But..." Claire said. Henry held his smile.

"There's no 'but,'" he insisted.

"You didn't say it back," she said.

"You're not a patient person, are you?" Henry said without thinking first.

"Who is?" Claire responded, leaning in and pressing her lips against Henry's. They held the kiss for a few seconds before Henry pulled back.

"Was it that bad?" she said with a strained look on her face.

Henry grabbed one of her hands and held it while placing his other hand just above her knee. He leaned back in. Not so much that she would expect another kiss, just enough that she would know he was serious.

"Claire," he began, "I am attracted to you, too. I'm just not the kind of guy who takes advantage of situations." Claire raised an eyebrow at him. Henry went on to explain himself. "Rushing into intimacy is never a good idea," he said. "It complicates things."

She smiled and leaned a bit closer to him.

"I agree," she said, "that's why I'm perfectly fine with just making out." Claire placed her mouth back on his and this time slipped her tongue between his lips. Henry reciprocated, but only for a few seconds before pulling away.

"Ok, ok," he said, "that's good, that's good."

Claire gave him another perplexed look, as if to ask for another explanation. Henry obliged.

"I can already tell you I enjoy kissing you. But Claire, I don't think right now, at this moment, is a good idea."

She leaned back and let out a heavy sigh.

"Rejected," she said.

"How can you call this a rejection?" Henry asked. He had spent enough time around women to know the routine. But understanding them was a completely different story. This was getting ridiculous, and he was tired. Drained.

"Claire," he said, moving closer to her. "Would you be willing to just lie here with me tonight?" Henry put his arm around her and pulled her closer. Claire placed her head on his shoulder.

"Maybe," she answered.

"Let's just slow things down," he told her. "There's no hurry." Henry kissed the top of her head. Her hair smelled like strawberries. He lingered for an extra second. They lay down next to each other on the couch, Claire on the outside, Henry behind her with his arm around her waist.

"I still don't know anything about you," she whispered.

"I don't know much about you either," Henry reminded her. "But since you've put yourself out there the way you have tonight, I'm willing to offer you something in return." He paused for a moment. "A while back I had a pretty good job," he began. "It paid well, provided good benefits, and had lots of flexibility. Life was pretty good. But something happened that changed my mind about all of it. Now I live my life day-to-day, paycheck-to-paycheck, more or less."

"That sucks," Claire whispered. She pressed herself back against Henry.

He gripped her tighter, his face in her light brown hair, until they both fell asleep. Henry's sleep was restless as he dreamed a cloudy haze of car accidents, missing body parts, and girls with raging hormones. At three thirty in the morning, he woke up. His body was stiff and sore from being in the same position for several hours. He eased himself over and out of Claire's grasp, leaving her to sleep comfortably on her own. He took the afghan and draped it over her before retiring to his bedroom.

***

At seven fifteen, Henry woke up to some mid-morning nuzzling from Wilson. When he looked at the clock, he bolted out of bed and beelined for the shower. As he left the bedroom he could see the couch was no longer occupied and the wine glasses were still on the coffee table. The half empty wine bottle remained on the kitchen bar. Henry wasn't surprised Claire had taken off. In fact, he was kind of glad. It would've been awkward pushing her out the door so he could go to work. But he did feel as though they had accomplished a slight breakthrough last night. For what it was worth, he was still uncertain.

After taking a ninety-second shower, Henry dressed, filled Wilson's food bowl, and grabbed a banana before heading out the door. The sun was already bright in the sky when he pulled his car away from the farmhouse. There was little doubt that working all these hours was tiring. But he'd finally get twenty-four hours to himself this afternoon to do whatever it is he might want to do.

As he drove to town, Henry found himself thinking more about Claire. It was clear to him there was more behind Claire's "don't tip me so much" rant. But pushing the envelope on such a thing last night could've been disastrous. She was certainly an aggressive young woman. But Henry also knew there was an underlying sensitivity about her. Or maybe that was just because she was a waitress and pretended to care too much—for tips. He wasn't quite sure yet, but the irony was not lost on him.

Henry also wondered how poor Alan Walker was doing. It was crazy enough to untangle and carry a guy's severed arm around a crash site. But Henry couldn't imagine what it must've been like to be driving down the road without a care in the world and out of nowhere have an arm ripped from your body while being thrown from your car. He remembered reading once about a man who was mountain climbing alone. Somehow he ended up with his hand and forearm stuck under a rock. In order to free himself and survive, the man had to cut his own hand off. It was mind-blowing and nauseating to think about. Henry wouldn't wish something like that on his worst enemy.

At seven fifty-five, Henry turned off Main Street and into the north side of the Corner Store lot. This area had become his personal parking spot. It kept his vehicle out of the customers' way and gave him easy access to head home when his shift ended.

After getting out of his car, Henry began the short walk to the front of the store. When he turned the corner he was surprised to see Bruce's Explorer parked near the front door. On the other side of it was a Channel 6 TV news van. Henry looked inside the store before entering and saw Bruce talking to a female reporter and a cameraman. His boss spotted him through the glass and waved him in.

V

"Get in here, Hank!" Bruce exclaimed with a grin. "We've been waiting for you. It sounds like you had quite a night last night."

Henry walked through the door and let it close behind him. The newswoman was holding a microphone and smiling at him while the cameraman pointed the big camera in his direction.

"I guess I did," he agreed.

"You probably don't know Balinda Simmons," Bruce explained. "She's with Channel 6 in Adler. And this is Craig with the camera. They heard about your heroics last night and wanted to talk to you about what happened."

Henry raised his eyebrows. "Heroics?" he said.

"Yes," Balinda Simmons piped up. "You saved a man's life!"

Henry had never been a big fan of the news media. Most everything they reported seemed one-sided or at the very least slanted in a direction, probably to meet an agenda. Henry looked at Bruce and spoke, lowering his voice, "Can I speak to you for a minute, boss?"

"Of course," he replied. After asking Balinda and Craig to wait outside, Bruce turned back to Henry. "What's up?" he asked.

"I really don't want to be on TV," Henry explained.

"What do you mean? This is great! You did an awesome thing last night—at least from what I understand. You should be proud of yourself!"

This was going to be more difficult than Henry thought.

"You realize I locked the store up during business hours to do this, right?"

"That's the beauty of it all," Bruce explained. "Saving a guy's life was far more important to the Corner Store than making a few bucks!"

For years Henry had operated under the assumption that the only things people cared about were themselves and how they could benefit, personally, from a particular situation. Bruce seemed no different than the rest of them.

"It's just that I'm extremely camera shy," Henry explained, trying to sound as desperate as possible. "I passed out during a televised spelling bee in sixth grade."

Bruce's arms were crossed and he was stroking his chin, trying to figure out how to cash in on this opportunity for his business. Henry really couldn't blame him. Owning a business had to be a constant battle of sleepless nights and bottled friends. Something like this could be good exposure for the Corner Store. It wouldn't make Bruce a millionaire, but it could bring a spike in sales for a few days. While the story was still fresh, people might travel an extra twenty minutes out of their way to get some gas for the chance to meet a real-life hero.

"All right," Bruce said, "let's see what we can do about this. Stay here for a minute." He walked outside and over to the Channel 6 van. Henry could see him speaking to Balinda Simmons and her camera guy. As he watched their pow-wow, a customer strolled through the door for a cup of coffee and some donuts. Henry quickly went behind the register and handled the transaction. It was, after all, his shift.

As the customer walked out, Bruce and the news duo walked back in. Craig still had his camera.

"I'm hoping we have a compromise worked out here, Hank," Bruce said. He went on to explain that the news team would still like to interview Henry but would be willing to do so off camera, recording only his audio.

"We'd really love to hear what happened in your words," Balinda explained with a hopeful look on her face. She was about five six with her heels on, blonde and attractive, with rosy-red lips. Henry succumbed.

"I guess I can do that," he obliged.

"Excellent!" Balinda clapped her hands together in excitement.

"Is he ok?" Henry asked her. For a brief moment, she looked puzzled.

"Oh, uh...yes, yes," Balinda said. "He was in surgery all night. They reattached his arm. So far everything looks to have been successful."

"That's great to hear," he replied. At the time of the accident, Henry wasn't sure there was any possibility of Alan's arm being reattached, but going back to get it seemed like the right thing to do. It wasn't like Alan was in any condition to remember it.

Balinda and Craig quickly set up their equipment and turned to Henry for the interview. She stood next to Henry while Craig adjusted audio levels.

"I'm here with Henry Fields who is an attendant at the Corner Store in Gable. Henry was first on the scene of a one-car accident on Highway 57 around eight fifteen yesterday evening. Henry, can you tell us how things happened from your perspective?"

Balinda Simmons thrust the microphone in Henry's face and he went on to tell his story. Bruce stood behind the counter and listened. When Henry was finished, the reporter spoke again.

"Henry Fields, a true hero right here in small town Iowa. I'm Balinda Simmons reporting in Gable for Channel 6, Adler."

"Clear," Craig reported.

"Great. Thank you so much, Henry," Balinda said, holding her hand out. "You did a superb job for a man who doesn't like being on camera. Most people enjoy this kind of recognition."

Henry returned the handshake.

"Well, thanks," he replied. "I'm just not that interested in being a 'hero.' This was all quite a shock to me so early in the morning."

"Well, you can thank Rose McNeely for the exposure," Balinda explained. "After she dropped you off here last night she went to the hospital to follow up on Alan, the victim's, condition. She couldn't stop singing your praises to the doctors and nurses, and word got back to us."

Henry wasn't surprised. Rose had seemed like a very nice lady. He could've done without the attention, though. Was it really this difficult to stay off the grid, even in Iowa?

"She was very helpful last night," Henry said, heading over to the cash register to take over his shift. Balinda and Craig thanked Henry and Bruce one more time before leaving the store.

After finishing a transaction with a customer, Henry turned to his boss. "I'm really sorry about locking the store down last night," he told him. "I just reacted on instinct. I mean, it wasn't busy at all. But that's no excuse..."

Bruce responded by patting Henry on the back. "I already told you, it's not a problem," he assured him. "You did a good thing last night. It was all for a good cause. You're a good Samaritan and you should be proud. I'm proud of you, Hank! So proud, in fact, that I'm going to pay you for your first week of work today when I come in at three. Sound good?"

"Sounds great, thanks!" Henry said. Bruce really was

starting to seem like a pretty good guy and boss, but it was still too early to tell for certain. Henry was always looking for signs.

Bruce left Henry to his shift a few minutes later, giving him an opportunity to sit down and reflect. It didn't feel like he had slowed down much at all since hearing the car accident twelve hours ago. Rushing up the highway to help, thinking fast on his feet, riding with Rose towards the ambulance and then back to the store, finishing his shift, and so on. Sure, he made it to bed. Twice. But the quality of sleep was nowhere near up to par.

Henry was emotionally exhausted more than anything. He hadn't been in town a full week yet and he had already helped a car accident victim, been interviewed on TV, bought a cat, and almost had sex. Certainly not under the radar, by any definition. He hadn't meant to get so involved. Responding to the car accident was by complete chance as was the unfortunate arrival of Balinda Simmons. It was simply in Henry's nature to help. Most people spend so much time worrying about themselves they rarely pay attention when an opportunity presents itself to help others. On the surface, Henry played the game with other people the way he should by being polite, complimentary, helpful, and interested in their lives. The problem was Henry could see through most people's crap. It drove him nuts to have to be phony himself to deal with a phony world. But the alternative was speaking his mind and becoming completely transparent. And that just wouldn't fly in most situations.

When Henry was in middle school, his father was fired from his job as the operations manager of a trucking business. The company had hired some consultants to come in and tell them what they were doing wrong and how they could do things better. Henry's father was caught in the cross-fire of the changes. It wasn't that they wanted to fire him, but his father was so openly opposed to many of the changes that were being mandated, his employer felt it was best to part ways with him after ten years of service. Three years later the company went out of business. Henry had just turned sixteen and was looking for his first job at the time, so the subject of his father's dismissal was a good dinner topic one evening.

"Does it make you feel better knowing they went under after you tried to tell them they were wrong about so many things?" Henry asked his father.

"It makes me feel better because they did me a favor," his dad explained. "If they had kept me around, I would now be known as the guy who helped sink it."

"But that wouldn't have been true," Henry replied.

"No, probably not. But how would anybody else know that? It's like being on a bad football team. Is it the coaching that stinks? The players? The ownership?"

"You had a lot of the answers. You could've helped them," Henry said.

"I could've if they were willing to listen. But they weren't."

The pained look on Henry's face told his father to explain more.

"Son, the one regret I have—the one lesson I learned from this experience is—you can talk and plead all you want, but if you're talking and pleading with someone who has already made up their mind, you're wasting your time and energy. Always assess a situation before opening your heart and mind to anyone. You simply have to know what they will do with what you provide them, or if they even care."

"In other words, lie?" Henry suggested.

"Be in control," his father clarified. "I should've shut up and looked for another job. Instead, I let my emotions get the best of me and had the door shown to me."

The situation with Claire was one that probably could've been easily avoided had Henry not tipped her eight dollars. This gave her a reason to roll out the drama and let him know up front she had more baggage than JFK International. This wasn't intentional. She was only trying to get Henry to notice her. It was like a boy pulling a girl's hair on a playground because he likes her. Henry was thinking things might be better if she had simply pulled his hair.

When she didn't see him for several days, Claire worried she had run him off with her outburst. Naturally, she overcompensated for this concern by getting drunk and throwing herself at him. Henry liked Claire despite what he already knew about her. He was only human. And he was attracted to her, of course. But getting wrapped up in an intimate relationship was at the bottom of his to-do list right now.

Around nine o'clock, Sergeant Jackson strolled into the Corner Store for his morning cup of joe. The door had yet to close behind him when he began speaking.

"Rumor has it our little town has a new hero," he belted in Henry's direction.

"I don't know if I'd call it that, but you know how the media is," Henry replied.

"At least they're not calling you a 'super hero,'" Jackson said, walking to the coffee machine. "I've always found capes to be kind of femmy."

"There really aren't a lot of them that don't wear a cape, are there?" Henry mused.

"You almost sound like you believe in superheroes," Jackson said, laughing.

"No, no. Not anymore," Henry admitted. "I used to know a lot of adults who probably did, but I'm not one of them."

"I know what you mean," Jackson said. "I've worked a comic convention before. Strange folks, most of them." He finished pouring his coffee, added his sugars, and grabbed a fruit pie while heading to the register. "Sounds like you were involved in quite an ordeal last night," he said.

"Let's put it this way," Henry replied, "I'm hoping it doesn't happen again tonight."

"You and me both," Jackson commented while

handing a five dollar bill over the counter. "I was lucky enough to be off duty and at home in Adler during that one."

"I could've used your help," Henry said.

"Sounds like you did okay."

"Flying blind," Henry admitted. "Everything I did was either instinct or something I saw on an episode of *ER*."

"Pretty gruesome, wasn't it?" Jackson asked with frown. "I remember the first bloody call I got sent to," he recalled. "Suicide attempt. Gunshot to the chin."

"Attempt?" Henry clarified.

"Yup. He lived. Three-fourths of his face was gone. It was just a giant, bloody crater. His tongue was hanging halfway down his chest. Shortly after we arrived and the paramedics began working on him, the guy started digging into what used to be his face to try and clear an airway and help himself breathe."

"Wow," Henry said, handing Jackson his change. "That tops last night by a mile."

"What's sad is I've seen worse, but I won't bore you with the details now," Sergeant Jackson said as he opened the front door. "I've got to get back to business."

Suddenly, Henry felt a jolt in his memory.

"Wonder Woman!" he blurted out.

Jackson stopped, the door still open. "What's that?" the police officer asked.

"Wonder Woman doesn't wear a cape," Henry said with conviction. Jackson considered this for a moment before replying.

"I tell you capes are femmy, and the first superhero you come up with that doesn't wear one is a woman?" He chuckled.

"I'd look weird in that outfit of hers, wouldn't I?" Henry said with a chuckle of his own.

"See you later, superhero," Jackson said as he walked

out the door with a smile.

Henry was glad to see Jackson had a sense of humor. In the past, he hadn't received any warm and fuzzies from police officers. His first experience with one set the tone for years to come.

One snowy winter night, eleven-year-old Henry was lying in bed. He had just fallen asleep when someone came to the front door. The sound of the doorbell woke Henry, but he didn't think much of it and began going back to sleep. That is, until his mother opened his bedroom door and told him there was a police officer outside who wanted to speak to him about a stolen motorbike.

The officer claimed he had followed a set of footprints in the snow from where the bike was stolen, and the tracks led directly to their front door. He had not stolen the motorbike, but when Henry told this to the policeman it was, of course, not good enough for him. He asked to see Henry's snow boots for comparison's sake.

Even though Henry was innocent, he was flooded with overwhelming emotion at the thought of having to prove it. This police officer came to his family's home believing that a thief had recently walked into it. Despite the principle of being innocent until proven guilty, Henry received a vibe from the officer that was the complete opposite. It felt more to him like the policeman was saying, "I've got you, you crooked little brat and I'm gonna prove it." Henry wondered what life would be like for his parents after he became the first sixth grader in the neighborhood to go to juvie.

Thankfully, the officer was honest enough after a ten-minute investigation to come back to the house and admit he was wrong. For starters, Henry wore a size nine. The original footprints the policeman was tracking were much smaller. Apparently, the prints Henry had made on his walk home from school had blended at some point with the footprints the officer followed from the scene of the crime.

Of course there was no apology, no thank you for

helping. Just a quick explanation and he was on his way. Even at the age of eleven, Henry thought it was strange the policeman didn't notice the change in print size while he was sleuthing through the neighborhood. Or maybe he didn't want to notice. Maybe he liked scaring the crap out of children. Or maybe he was just so hell-bent on catching the bad guy that he missed the obvious clues that would have pointed him in a different direction.

Henry never heard what happened, if the motorbike was ever found. There were plenty of candidates in the area, but whether or not the police officer matched up the tracks with the culprit was a mystery. Maybe he just successfully pinned it on some other innocent boy.

Suddenly, the store phone rang. It startled Henry so much he jumped slightly from his chair.

"Corner Store," he answered.

"Hey, Henry. You're just the guy I was looking for. This is your buddy and landlord, Tom Chumansky."

Strange. I wonder what he wants, Henry thought to himself.

"Hi, Chum," he replied. "What can I do for you?"

"Well, I'm having a little get-together tonight at my house and I wanted to invite the local hero to join us," Chum explained.

"News travels fast in a small town," Henry said.

"That it does," Chum agreed. "It's hard to keep a secret around here. So, look, all the food and booze is provided by me. All you have to do is bring yourself. Dress casual. I'm not into that stuffy, formal shit. We live in a field for God's sake, right? We usually just hang out, tell stories. Nothing too crazy. Seven o'clock. What do you say?"

"Aw man, Chum. I'm still pretty tired from last night," Henry explained. It wasn't a lie. "I just don't know. It might be a better idea for me to get a good night's sleep."

"I'm not taking no for an answer, Henry," Chum said.

"Besides, I know where you live. If you don't show up, I'll just bring the party to you. It wouldn't be the first time we've had one at that house."

Just then, the door to the Corner Store opened and Claire walked in. She smiled at Henry but said nothing, noticing he was on the phone. Her hair was pulled back in a ponytail, and she was wearing her work clothes. She walked to the register and stood in front of Henry, still smiling. He returned her smile as he spoke to Chum.

"Can I bring a guest?"

VI

When Henry's shift was over at three, Bruce came in to manage the store and pay his only employee for his first week of work. As promised during their initial meeting, he paid Henry in cash. It was a thick block of money.

"I didn't think you'd want it all in hundreds, so I gave you a little of everything," Bruce explained.

"No problem," Henry replied. "It all spends the same."

"That's true," Bruce agreed. He grabbed a plastic merchandise bag and handed it to Henry. "It doesn't matter how small the town is—you'll look suspicious carrying a big wad of cash around." Henry took the bag and placed his money in it. Bruce continued speaking, "Big plans tonight?"

"Chum invited me to his place for a party or...whatever you want to call it," Henry said. "I think I'm going to try and sneak a nap in and then go over there for a while."

Bruce smiled. "Ah, yes. Chum and his parties. You'll meet some interesting people, that's for sure," he said. "You never know what might happen when you hang out with him."

"I figured as much," Henry said. "I'll keep my guard up."

After saying goodbye, Henry drove home and did exactly what he told Bruce he would: he took a two-and-a-half-hour nap. At five thirty his alarm went off. He was still groggy and felt like he could've slept another eight hours. After jumping in the shower and putting on some fresh clothes, he felt better.

Claire arrived at the house a few minutes before seven o'clock. She was dressed in white capris, a navy blue button-down blouse, and white tennis shoes. Her hair was down and Henry could tell she had used a curling iron to style it.

"Is this a date?" Claire asked when Henry opened the door. He was wearing blue jeans and a dark red polo.

"And hello to you, Claire," he answered her with a smile. "I thought we agreed we were taking things slow."

"No. You said that," she corrected him. "Technically, I never agreed."

"You can call it whatever you want," he told her.

They agreed to walk the quarter mile to Chum's new house along the extended gravel road. On the way they discussed the day's events at their respective jobs, almost like a married couple would. Henry told Claire about Balinda Walker's visit to the Corner Store and how he had to work around being on TV.

"I thought everyone wanted to be on television," she said, laughing. "What's wrong with you?"

"I guess I get nervous," Henry explained. "You know, your heart starts to beat fast and your breathing becomes heavy. Almost like hyperventilating."

"You're weird." Claire laughed again. "But I like weird."

"Is this the part where we talk about our exes?" he inquired, trying to change the subject.

"No, God no!" she exclaimed. "I need a lot of alcohol in my blood to start that conversation!"

They both laughed some more as they walked up Chum's concrete driveway. Henry did enjoy Claire's company. When she wasn't falling all over him or complaining about an excessive tip, that is. As far as Henry was concerned, "taking it slow" was code in his book for "you're gonna be difficult to get rid of if we ever have sex." He was just trying to take control of the situation by keeping his distance.

They walked up the front steps and Henry rang the doorbell. The Chumansky dogs began barking immediately as the bell played a melody Henry didn't recognize.

"That's the Mecca Warehouse jingle," Claire said, shaking her head.

"His modesty is overwhelming," Henry joked. Behind the door, Chum could be heard rounding up his dogs. After about thirty seconds, the door opened.

"I knew you'd show up!" Chum exclaimed. "Greetings to both of you. Claire Mathison, great to see you. It's been a while. I apologize for taking so long to answer the door. I threw Millie and Hazel outside through the back door."

He ushered his guests through the front door and into his recently built home. The walls had a lacquered wood finish, giving it a homey, country feel. Chum led them to the left where a petite woman was sitting on a sofa with a glass of wine. She was wearing blue jeans, a purple V-neck blouse, and sandals. Her brown hair was long and hair sprayed into a style that looked like it was from the eighties.

Some fashions never die, Henry thought.

"Honey," Chum said, "this is Henry, the guy who is renting our house."

The woman stood up and walked over to them. She extended her hand towards Henry and introduced herself.

"Maddison Chumansky. So nice to meet you, Henry. I heard you on the news today but didn't get to see your happy face."

Her voice and delivery were far more restrained than her husband's. She was an attractive woman and, like Chum, looked to be in her late thirties.

"Well, my happy face is here now," Henry responded,

changing the subject and shaking her small hand. "I assume you know Claire?"

Henry enjoyed moments like this. He could observe Maddison's reaction to Claire to see if there was an issue he hadn't picked up on yet between Claire, Chum, and his wife.

"Yes. Hello, Claire," Maddison said with a smile. "It's so good to see you."

Claire returned the smile with a compliment.

No contempt or glaring issues here, Henry thought.

"The new house looks fantastic," Claire said. "It's so big!"

"Yes, it is," Maddison replied. "Would you like a tour?"

"That would be great," Claire replied enthusiastically. She looked at Henry as they began to follow Maddison.

"Hey, wait!" Chum called from behind them at the front door. "Henry, come here. You can take the tour later. I want you to meet someone."

Henry looked at Claire and Maddison and shrugged.

"We'll catch up with you in a few," Maddison said. "The house isn't *that* big." Both ladies snickered and went on their way. Henry turned and walked to the front door where Chum was still standing, half inside and half out.

"Check this out!" he bellowed as Henry rounded the corner to the doorway. "Fire it up!" Chum yelled out the door. Immediately the roaring engine of a large motorcycle exploded through the peaceful early evening. There was a man with a Fu Manchu mustache sitting on the bike, revving it up. He was dressed in blue jeans and a black Harley-Davidson T-shirt. Chum looked at Henry with a toothy grin and then back at the man on the motorcycle. He made a throat slashing motion and the man powered the bike down.

"Purring like a pussy cat!" Chum shouted to the man climbing off the motorcycle.

He began moving in the direction of the door, where

Henry stood with his landlord. "A Heritage Softail with thirty-three-inch Samson True Duals, eighteen-inch Ape Hangers, no baffles and lowered two inches with lots and lots of chrome," the man said. "I'm in love."

"Eddie, meet the new guy," Chum said. "This is Henry."

"Hey, man. Eddie Clark," the motorcycle man said with a handshake.

"Fast Eddie," Chum added. Eddie shrugged.

"Dare I ask what's fast about you, Eddie?" Henry asked. People love to talk about themselves, and he felt certain Eddie was no exception.

"Well, Henry, I like fast cars, fast bikes, and fast women, for starters," Fast Eddie Clark explained as the three men walked into the house.

"And he's a fast-talking salesman," Chum threw in. "Walk into my store, and if Eddie isn't already with someone, he'll find you and sell you. You'll be leaving with an entire new home entertainment system."

The men walked to the kitchen and Chum opened the refrigerator. He pulled out two bottles of Budweiser, handing one to Eddie.

"Henry?" Chum offered.

"I'm not much of a drinker," Henry said.

"Neither am I," Eddie said, looking at Chum with a grin and taking a swig.

"Here," Chum said, reaching back into the refrigerator and pulling out one more bottle, handing it to Henry. "Humor me by carrying this around and making it look like you're having a good time. You can nurse it."

The men walked back to the room where Maddison had been sitting earlier. Henry sipped his beer. It wasn't that he didn't like alcohol or the feeling that a few drinks could give him. In fact, he loved it. He just didn't want to lose his wits right now. Plus, he was still tired from a whirlwind twenty-four hours, and the alcohol would only magnify this.

As they stood and waited for the women to return, Henry listened to Chum and Fast Eddie discuss the day's events at Mecca Warehouse. Eddie bragged about up-selling an elderly couple on high-priced items and long-term replacement/repair plans. Chum gave details on new inventory that was to arrive the following week and the sales plan to sell older products fast to make room on the showroom floor.

"Being in business is a never ending battle, Henry," Chum explained. "What did you do before you made your way to Gable?"

"Yes, Henry," Claire chimed in as she returned to the room with Maddison. "What did you do?" She smiled and walked up next to him, touching his arm.

Here we go again, Henry thought.

"I was in sales," he explained. It was a lie, but at least it would fit into some of tonight's conversation.

"Oh yeah? Where at?" Chum inquired.

"It was a small company. Mostly phone sales selling credit card services," Henry explained, making things up as he went along. He wished he had created a backstory in his head at some point this past week.

"Wow, what a shitty thing to have to be selling," Eddie spouted. He took a swig of beer and, with a smirk, eyeballed everyone. Henry nodded, but Chum spoke up first.

"You've got sales experience, eh? How much is Bruce paying you?" he asked.

"I didn't say I was good at it," Henry explained. Everyone laughed.

"We'll talk later," Chum said as the doorbell rang. He answered it and let in a few more guests including some local Gable folks and a couple of the Chumanskys' friends from Adler.

Everyone continued to mingle and talk, sometimes all together and sometimes in small groups. Henry was introduced to several more guests as the "new guy" and "hero." He remained modest about yesterday evening's happenings. Claire continued to cling to him while consuming a homemade margarita blended by Chum. Every few minutes or so Henry would take a sip of his now warm Budweiser.

Not surprisingly, Fast Eddie lived up to his name. Henry observed him from a distance and saw how much Eddie liked to talk. Quite often it was impossible for anyone else to get a word in when trying to hold a conversation with him. At one point Eddie came over and asked Henry about his interview with Channel 6.

"That Balinda Simmons is a hot little number, isn't she?" Eddie asked Henry. "They made you out to be Superman on TV!"

"I didn't see it," Henry explained. "I don't have a television." As soon as he said this, he cringed on the inside.

"You don't have a TV?" Eddie exclaimed. "Chum! You hear that? New guy doesn't have a television!"

"Well, I really don't have the time to watch," Henry explained.

"He'd have to buy a satellite dish out here," Chum added.

"Bullshit!" Eddie blurted. "I've got friends in high and low places, my boy. You buy a TV from me and I'll get you free satellite service!"

Henry looked around as if the satellite police might jump out and arrest someone.

"Free satellite? How come I don't have that?" Chum shouted at his salesman as he walked across the room towards him. Eddie took a swallow from his fresh bottle of beer before responding.

"Because you've never bought a TV from me," he explained. Chum stopped dead in his tracks.

"Well," he said. "I guess I can't argue that."

Everyone who was listening to the conversation

laughed. Henry tried to imagine Fast Eddie dressed for work, but it was difficult to picture him in anything other than his Harley attire. He wondered how Chum got hooked up with him.

"So, Henry," Maddison spoke up, "how did you end up here in the middle of Nowhere, Iowa?"

Henry held his expression, not wanting to give away his frustration at once again being asked about his past. More than anything he was angry with himself because he hadn't prepared. For years he had operated under the notion that people didn't care about him, they only cared about themselves. Yet here he was, playing twenty questions with everyone. Henry knew he could make up anything reasonable and just go with it. But he'd have to keep track of it all and remain consistent. All the more reason to not impair his brain with alcohol.

"I just happened to drive through and noticed the Corner Store was looking for help," he explained.

"That's...different," a guest named Abby said. "You just...drove through?"

"I guess you could say I was looking for a fresh start," Henry said.

"Looking for a fresh start?!" Chum exclaimed. "Did you ditch a crazy wife or something?"

Maddison punched her husband in the arm and came to Henry's defense. "He's still a young guy," she said. "There's nothing wrong with starting over, so to speak."

"Yeah, I start over every day," Eddie added. "Drinking, that is."

Another eruption of laughter filled the room. The party continued through the evening. Drinks flowed and Maddison served finger foods. Henry was particularly fond of her homemade bruschetta. He was glad to have the food available considering it was eight o'clock before he realized he had neglected to eat dinner.

Claire surprised Henry by taking her time with the margaritas. After the previous night he was beginning to wonder if it was normal for her to get some booze in her blood and throw herself at a guy. Women like that were the perfect companion until the next morning when the guilt kicked in along with the hangover. Henry was glad to see Claire had some self-control.

Fast Eddie was a different story. He continued to drink as if Chum had the last bottles of beer on Earth in his refrigerator. The more he drank, the louder and rowdier he got. Chum was Eddie's boss, but the personal relationship between the two men seemed to be completely different. And Eddie was larger than Chum, as was most everyone. Henry imagined the uncomfortable silence that would take place if Eddie were to get drunk enough to wrestle Chum to the ground and give him an atomic wedgie. The idea of Chum getting his underwear pulled out of his pants and over his head cracked Henry up. There was just something about the guy that made you want something awkward to happen to him.

"They've been friends since they were kids," Claire told Henry as they watched Chum and Eddie. The two men were in a deep discussion about the new big-screen televisions that had arrived at Mecca Warehouse.

"I can see that," Henry said. Claire turned and faced him.

"Do you have any friends?" she asked.

"Besides you?" Henry asked with a wink.

"You know what I mean," Claire continued. "Why are you so slippery about your past?"

Henry thought about it for a moment.

"The past has passed. The present is present," he told her.

"And the future?" Claire raised her eyebrows as if she would finally get a profound response from the new guy.

"To be determined," Henry said.

"That's pretty cryptic," a disappointed Claire responded.

"You have to admit it made sense," Henry said, trying to lighten her mood back up.

"Did you get that out of a fortune cookie?"

"I think it was on an episode of *Matlock*."

"You sure are something, Henry Fields." She shook her head and looked at the others across the room.

"Chum's wife seems pretty normal," Henry observed.

"Maddison? Yes, I guess you're right," Claire said. "A lot different than her husband. They say opposites attract, so..."

"She's not from Gable, though?"

"No. She's from another small town around here somewhere."

"I wonder how they met, then," Henry asked.

"I don't know for sure, but I do know that growing up in a small town can be suffocating," she explained. "We were always crashing other small towns or inviting people to Gable. We just wanted to spark some entertainment with new and different personalities. The entire school had about two hundred students when I graduated."

"That's pretty small," Henry agreed. "My graduating class was bigger than your entire high school."

"Wow!" Claire exclaimed.

"What?"

"You kinda-sorta told me something personal," she said. Henry smiled.

"Oops."

The evening went on with nothing eventful happening. Chum and Eddie would roar with laughter or disagreement on occasion, but it never amounted to anything serious. No one else seemed concerned about their activities, including Claire. Every once in a while, someone would ask

Henry a question about his past. He would proceed by dodging an actual answer, but everyone remained cordial with him. Most didn't catch on or mind that he was changing the subject on them. Henry knew the easiest thing to do was ask them about themselves or their children. Of course, he didn't really care what they had to say in response. This was survival.

Henry could tell, however, that Claire was aware of what he was doing. If the two of them were going to continue seeing each other on any level, he was going to have to get his story straight soon.

By ten thirty the party had died down to just six people. Remaining in the house were Chum and Maddison, Henry and Claire, Eddie, and Chum's accountant Marty. Marty was a nerdy looking guy who reminded Henry of Montgomery Burns from the television show *The Simpsons*.

With so few people left, the party had gotten much quieter. Henry was beginning to think about calling it a night himself when Chum disappeared for a few minutes and returned with a shotgun. Eddie immediately saw the firearm and let out a wail full of excitement.

"Yes, baby! Let the games begin!" he shouted with a fist pump and darted out the front door.

Chum followed Eddie and slapped Henry on the arm as he passed.

"Come on, Henry!" he said. "The night is still young! Don't you just feel like shooting something, sometimes?"

Before Henry had a chance to answer, Chum disappeared through the front door. Henry turned to Maddison and Claire.

"What's this all about?" he asked the ladies, figuring one of them would have an idea.

"I think they're going shooting out front," Maddison explained. She spoke as though it wasn't unusual; just another day in the life of the Chumanskys. Even if she objected, Henry doubted she would ever say anything.

He looked at Claire and then back at Maddison. Marty, the accountant, was rubbing one of his temples.

"In the dark?" Henry asked.

At that moment, everyone in the house jumped as a gunshot exploded from the front lawn, interrupting the conversation.

VII

The group of six gathered just outside the front door of the Chumansky house. With the help of several floodlights, Eddie and Chum took turns shooting clay pigeons in the dark of the night. The sight of the clay discs floating through the late evening sky reminded Henry of a nighttime baseball game.

While Maddison spoke with Marty on the front steps, Henry and Claire sat in lounge chairs near the garage behind the shooting.

"The electronics business seems to have treated Chum well," Henry observed. "Nice, custom built house with brand new furniture, lots of land..."

"That's for sure," Claire said. "To me he lives the life of a billionaire."

"What keeps you here?" Henry inquired.

"I guess it's familiarity. Gable is all I've ever known. I've worked at Stubby's for sixteen years."

"Sixteen years?"

"Since I was nine," she said, pausing for a beat before continuing. "Stubby was my uncle," she explained. "He was my dad's big brother."

"I see," Henry said. He thought it was interesting she hadn't mentioned this before.

"I like it here, I guess. I still live at home for crying out loud," she continued.

"You get along with your parents?" Henry asked.

"My dad died three years ago," Claire said. "Heart attack."

"I'm sorry," Henry replied.

A shout interrupted their conversation.

"Hey, Henry! Get your ass over here and take a few shots!" Chum hollered.

Henry stood up and stretched his legs. "I'm not much of a sharpshooter."

"Good. Then you'll make us look better," Eddie said. He handed the gun to Henry who looked at it as if it were from another galaxy.

"I wasn't kidding. I'm not a gun-guy," he reiterated.

Chum stepped between his tenant and his sales guy and gave Henry a quick thirty-second tutorial. Eddie stood off to the side and loaded the manual clay pigeon thrower.

"Call 'pull' when you're ready," Chum told him. Henry took a couple of deep breaths and held the gun up, aiming into the dark sky.

"Pull!" Henry said with authority. Eddie flung the disc of clay as far as he could into the air above the field. For a moment Henry lost sight of it. When he found it again he did his best to line the barrel up and pulled the trigger. Simultaneously, he felt the kick of the gun drive into his shoulder and heard the crack of gunfire. The clay pigeon made a soft "thud" as it landed in the grassy field, unharmed.

"I told you I wasn't any good," Henry said, glancing first at Chum and then turning around and shrugging at Claire. She covered her mouth as if to hide her laughter.

"Those things cost me almost a quarter apiece, Henry," Chum joked. "You better not miss too many more!"

"I'd go out there and bring it back but I don't trust

Eddie not to cap me," Henry retorted.

"Don't worry, he'd miss you," Chum joked again.

Fast Eddie snorted.

"You're so sure of that, you wanna run out there yourself?" he asked his friend and boss while putting out a cigarette on the driveway cement with his boot.

"Tell you what," Chum said, taking the gun from Henry, "I'd hate for you to accidentally kill me. I've got a better idea. A safer one."

Maddison's attention moved to her husband.

"I'm listening," said Eddie, taking a swig from his beer bottle.

"I'll step out twenty-five yards or so, holding a pigeon in the thrower," Chum explained. "I'll extend my arm with the thrower, exposing the pigeon as your target."

"So, you're gonna hold my target," Eddie confirmed.

"It's a nineteen inch margin for error, give or take," Chum said.

"You're on, hotshot," Eddie said, handing Chum the thrower and grabbing the shotgun.

"Tom, what the hell do you think you're doing?" Maddison shouted as she walked down the front steps and headed for her husband. Chum ignored her.

"One thing, though," Chum added, "if I let you do it, you have to let me do it."

"As long as I get to go first," Eddie agreed. "That way when you shoot me I'll at least have the satisfaction of knowing I beat you."

"Deal!" Chum said. He bent over and grabbed a clay pigeon and put it in the thrower. By now Maddison had made her way over to him. Henry moved back to his chair next to Claire.

"Have you two jackasses lost your minds!?" she protested.

Chum threw up his arms. "What?" he said. "It's not like we're having Henry shoot—no offense, Henry. Ed and I are both good shots."

"Good shots who've been drinking for four hours," Maddison added sharply.

"Nineteen inches, Maddie!" Chum bellowed.

"Yeah, at worst I'm only a couple of millimeters drunk right now," Eddie chimed in. Chum laughed. Even Henry thought that was pretty funny.

"You guys are making jokes now but what's gonna happen when one of you ends up hurt or...worse?" Maddison pleaded.

"We already have an experienced hero here." Chum pointed at Henry.

Good Lord, Henry thought. When's this "hero" garbage going to end? May as well play along.

"I'm not doing mouth-to-mouth, just so you know," Henry said. Claire smacked him on the arm.

"You're egging them on?" she asked him.

"Those two don't need any help. I'm just the peanut gallery," Henry explained.

By now, Maddison had given up talking sense into either one of them. She walked behind the two men to where Henry and Claire sat. Marty had also wandered over. The four of them stood and watched Eddie and Chum prepare for their circus act.

Chum walked into the front yard and turned around at about twenty yards.

"Go back a little more," Eddie told him. "I need some more distance between me and the target."

Chum took five more steps back, stopped, and spoke. "I'm not going back anymore. Your trajectory might get all jacked up."

"Trajectory shmajectory," Eddie said. "Stick that

puppy out there. Let's do this!"

Chum held his right arm out to the side, the thrower in his hand. The clay pigeon sat in the holder, awaiting its fate.

"I can't watch," Maddison said, putting her hands over her face but peeking between her fingers.

Henry figured the chances of Chum being hit, at least with Eddie shooting, were slim. The drama was much ado about nothing. Nineteen inches left plenty of room to make a mistake. Eddie was, from what Henry had witnessed in the last hour, a good shot. Still, the idea of something going wrong was intensifying the atmosphere. Claire had grabbed on to Henry's forearm with a grip strong enough to stop the blood flow to his hand and fingers. Maddison continued to cover her eyes and peer between her fingers. Marty was cringing with his head turned sideways, watching with one squinty eye. Henry, on the other hand, was treating this demonstration like a NASCAR race. Chances of a crash were slim, but the possibility of one happening is the only reason anyone watches.

"Hold it steady," Fast Eddie ordered his boss. He raised the gun and began to aim. Chum continued to hold his arm out and did not seem to move an inch. He didn't even look nervous. Henry wasn't sure if that was because he was half in the bag or just a little bit crazy.

As fast as he raised it and aimed, Eddie fired the shotgun. The clay pigeon shattered instantly. Chum staggered a little from the momentum of the bullet's impact.

"Score," Eddie declared coolly, pulling the gun back down.

"My turn," Chum said as he strolled back to the group.

"You sound like a child," Maddison told him.

"I'm just a kid at heart, baby," Chum replied. He walked up to her, gave her a kiss on the cheek, and walked back over to Eddie.

Henry turned to Claire. "Is this normal small town weekend behavior?" he asked her. Before Claire could respond,

Maddison did. "It is in our house," she explained. "I've been trying to get him to settle down for years."

"It could be a lot worse," Claire said. "He could be out doing God knows what."

Maddison sighed. The two men walked through the yard to where Chum had held the thrower to see if they could figure out how perfect Eddie's aim had been.

"I suppose you're right," she agreed.

"I had a wife that was always out doing God knows what," Marty added, making eye contact with everyone. "It really could be worse, Maddie."

"If it makes you feel any better, I think this is all for show," Henry commented. "It would be different if they had an apple on their head or something, but holding that thing out like that is pretty safe. I mean, as long as I'm not the one doing the shooting."

The four of them let out quiet chuckles as the two shooters walked back.

"Take two," Chum announced.

"It's not possible to hit it better than I did," Eddie said. "You can only hope to match me." He grabbed a clay pigeon and put it in the thrower. "Don't shoot me."

"Get out there," Chum told him. "I wanna get this done so I can run inside and get me another beer."

Eddie walked out to the approximate area where Chum had been only a few minutes earlier. He held his right arm out and waited with his left hand on his hip. He showed no concern for his safety. Chum raised the shotgun and began to aim.

Off in the distance, a vehicle could be heard rumbling up the gravel driveway. Only the headlights were visible as they moved past Henry's house and beamed towards the small gathering of people. Chum lowered the gun. As it approached, it became clear the vehicle was a pickup truck. They could see shadowy figures in both the cab and the bed.

"Ho...ly...shit," Chum managed to utter as he stared and watched the pickup jump off the driveway's slab of concrete and come to a stop on his lawn. Three Hispanic men leaped to the yard from the back of the truck. Two more exited the cab. Of the five, two of the men who had jumped from the truck's bed were a lot bigger than the others.

"What the hell...?" Henry said under his breath. He looked at Claire. She raised her eyebrows and shook her head, telling him she had no idea what was going on, either.

"Buenas noches, muchachos y muchachas," the passenger from the pickup cab said as he approached Chum. He had a black mustache and appeared to be the leader of the group. The driver stood next to him as the other three men followed behind. "I hope you don't mind us joining your party, Tomás," the man continued in English.

"Tom, who are these men?" Maddison asked her husband as she walked up and stood next to him in front of the strangers. Henry continued to watch from a distance with Claire and Marty. He could sense these men had not been invited to the get-together.

The man with the mustache reached out to grab the shotgun from Chum's hands. Chum immediately tried to jerk the gun back, but the man held his grip. As this was going on, the other man pulled a handgun from the waistband of his jeans and pointed it between Maddison's eyes. The cold steel pressed against her skin.

"Tom..." Maddison sobbed as she immediately began to shake. Claire let out a gasp and grabbed Henry's arm.

"Ok, ok!" Chum blurted, responding to the gun in his wife's face. "Here." He handed the shotgun to the man with the mustache. "Let her go, Franco."

Franco put his hand in the air.

"Eso es suficiente, Rafael," he said. Rafael obeyed Franco and released Maddison from gunpoint. She ran back to where she had been standing before, between Henry and Marty.

Fast Eddie began to walk in from his spot where he had been holding the target, but Franco stopped him. "Hold on, Eduardo," he said. "It looks like you were having fun. Stay there. I'd like to have fun, too."

Eddie stopped cold in his tracks, not knowing for sure what to do. When he began moving forward again, Rafael held up his gun and aimed it at Eddie.

"All right!" Eddie shouted and took five steps back, still holding the clay pigeon thrower.

"What the hell is going on here?" Henry asked in a whisper, looking first at Maddison and then at Claire. The fear on both of their faces gave no answers and confirmed this was no joke.

"I saw you two playing a game when we drove up. Hold that target out," Franco told Eddie, who hesitated to obey. Franco looked at Chum. "You like playing games, don't you, Tomás?"

Chum remained silent as Franco raised the shotgun toward Eddie. Henry sat in his chair not having a clue what was going on, but recognizing that getting up was not a good idea. There were too many guns out there.

One of the other three men moved to Franco and pushed the shotgun down. Placing his hand on Franco's shoulder, he spoke to him under his breath in Spanish. Henry couldn't make out a word the man was saying but assumed by his facial expressions he was attempting to calm Franco down.

"Yo sé lo que estoy haciendo, Carlos," Franco told the man as he pushed him aside. "¡Fuera de mi camino!"

Carlos retreated to his previous position with the other men. As he did, Henry could see a concerned look on his face. It was obvious Franco would now continue to terrorize the group.

"Hold it out there, Eduardo," Franco instructed, once again aiming the gun at Eddie. "Where is my money?" he asked Chum without looking at him.

"I don't have it, but...I'll get it...soon," Chum said.

"Then where is my coke?" Franco asked.

"I told you two weeks ago I don't have it," Chum answered. "I ran into a situation—"

Gunfire interrupted Chum's voice as Franco pulled the trigger. In a split second, Fast Eddie Clark grabbed his right leg and fell to the grass, wailing in agonizing pain.

Claire, Maddison, and Marty gasped in unison. Henry continued to process what was going on while remaining on guard. He began running through scenarios in his head about what might happen next and what he could do to help ensure everyone's safety. It surprised him that Eddie was still alive. Henry thought for sure Franco would aim higher.

"I missed," Franco said and then looked at Chum. "Or did I?"

"Come on, man," Chum pleaded. "Have I ever done you wrong? I'm going to make this right. I just need more time."

"I know you're going to make it right," Franco agreed. "One way or another."

Claire continued to stare at the scene, as if she were watching a scary movie.

"I'd heard the rumors," she whispered, "but I never thought they were anything more than...rumors."

"That Chum was dealing?" Henry asked, turning to look at her. Claire nodded. They both looked over at Maddison, who was now in tears as Marty tried to comfort her.

"Do you think she knew?" Claire asked Henry.

"I doubt it. She sure seemed clueless," he answered.

"What's going to happen?"

"I don't know, but..." Henry's voice trailed off. He didn't have the answers and he didn't want to say something corny. He was doing his best to keep his cool and stay in control and up to this point he had done just that. All the more reason it was a good idea to drink half a beer the entire evening. Despite being tired from the night before, Henry still had his senses. He was on high alert. Somebody needed to be.

"Llevarlos dentro de la casa," Franco ordered his men. "And get Eduardo a band-aid."

Carlos and the two larger men came over to where Henry, the ladies, and Marty were. They pulled out guns of their own. Maddison began to scream.

"I think they're just taking us into the house," Henry told her. He hadn't taken a lot of Spanish in school, but he knew enough to recognize the word "casa." Maddison immediately stopped screaming. Everyone stood up and walked into the house with the armed men following behind.

Once inside, the three men directed them to the sitting area where the party had commenced earlier. Following behind was Rafael as he helped Eddie limp his way into the house. Franco strolled in a few seconds later as Eddie fell onto the couch.

"He needs a doctor!" Maddison exclaimed as Franco made his way into the room.

"He does," Franco agreed. "But that's not my concern right now." He pivoted in a circle, scoping out the Chumansky home. "Rafael! Carlos! ¡Ven conmigo! It's time to search the house." He began to walk out of the room with his two main men but turned around and looked at Chum. "Where's my shit?" Franco asked him.

Chum looked at him in desperation. "I honestly do not have it. Just give me a chance to figure things out."

"I already have," Franco said. He turned and walked out of the room.

Eddie continued to groan in pain every thirty seconds or so. Chum and Maddison sat next to him and attempted to comfort him.

Henry grabbed Chum by the arm. "You're a drug dealer? Seriously?" Henry said, jerking his arm in rhythm.

"Man..." Chum said. He looked at his wife and then back at Henry. "Where do you think I got the dough for the stores?"

"¡Silencio!"

One of the big men watching them was not pleased with their chatter. He moved closer to enforce his command to be quiet.

At this point, Henry wasn't sure what to do next. He didn't know if Chum was telling Franco the truth or if they'd find anything as they searched the house. The fact that they were all at gunpoint didn't give them much of a chance to do anything. All they could do now was wait.

The clock ticked. An occasional rumble could be heard throughout the house. Henry assumed they were turning furniture over and throwing things around as they looked for their drugs and money. He held Claire close to him, wondering if they would ever get the opportunity to take their relationship to another level.

After twenty minutes, the three men returned, empty-handed and unhappy.

"Tomás, you've left me no choice," Franco said. "There is nothing here."

"That's what I've been trying to tell you!" Chum replied. "I'll get it taken—"

"Enough!" Franco shouted. He turned to Rafael. "Matarlos a todos."

Carlos hurried over to Franco again. This time his voice was louder and more desperate. "¡Franco, no necesitamos matarlos! ¡Debemos darles la oportunidad de conseguir el dinero!" he pleaded.

Franco held his hand in front of Rafael, who obeyed by pulling his gun out and placing it in his boss's hand. Without another word, Franco held the gun in front of Carlos and shot him in the head. Maddison and Claire both let out screams of shock as the man crumpled to the wooden floor, lifeless.

"Do it," he said to Rafael, handing the gun back to him. He turned and walked out the front door.

This can't be good, Henry thought.

VIII

Rafael and the remaining two men walked over to Chum and his guests on the couch. Eddie was still groaning in pain, but conscious. Maddison was in a panic, sitting between Marty and her husband.

"What are they doing? Tom! What are they going to do?"

Chum looked at his wife, then at Rafael, who was scratching his temple with the barrel of his gun. Henry had a pretty good idea what was about to happen if Chum didn't give them what they wanted. Scenarios like this were not what Henry had in mind when he pulled into town last weekend.

So, this is how it's going to end for me, Henry thought.

Suddenly, as if a traffic light had turned green, Rafael pulled the gun down, aimed it at Marty's forehead, and pulled the trigger. It happened so fast, Marty didn't even have a chance to beg for his life. His head snapped back and his body followed, falling limp on the couch. His eyes stared at the ceiling.

"Oh my God!" Maddison screamed in tears. Claire buried her head in Henry's shoulder as she also began to weep.

"Tom! Do something! Give them what they want!" Maddison pleaded with her husband.

"Even if I had the money or the drugs to give them, it wouldn't matter now," Chum said. "It's no use. We're all dead."

Henry's mind was racing. There had to be a way out of this. He remembered hearing the story of United Flight 93 on 9/11 and how the passengers and crew had fought back. They rushed the terrorists, who were armed with box cutters, in an attempt to regain control of the plane. But the odds were not good for something like that happening tonight. Guns were a lot more accurate from a distance than box cutters. Plus, Franco was still outside somewhere.

Rafael wasted no time as he moved a foot to his left and stood in front of Maddison. This time he was patient. He looked her in the eyes, at the tears streaming down her mascara- streaked face. She sobbed and grabbed her husband's arm. This seemed to freeze Chum with fear. So much so that he made no effort to protect his wife.

"Please! Please..." Maddison's voice trailed off as she spoke. "Please don't...don't kill me..."

Rafael did not react.

"I'm pregnant," Maddison said as a slight smile made a brief appearance on her lips. At first, Henry wasn't sure if she was telling this to Chum or to Rafael. But the look on his landlord's face and his verbal response said it all.

"You're...you're pregnant?" Chum repeated back to her. She nodded. Rafael began to raise the gun.

"Hang on! Wait! Stop!" Chum yelled as he tried to put his hand in front of the gun. The killer pulled it down to his side. He was curious as to what Chum would say next. So was everybody else.

Chum let out a sigh strong enough to make his bangs float off his forehead. He looked up from the couch and spoke to Rafael. "I'll take you to the stuff. Just leave everyone else alone. Please?"

Henry couldn't help but let the tiniest of smirks form on his face when he heard Chum add "the magic word" at the end of his offer to Rafael. This guy just put a hole in your accountant's head. Using a pleasantry wasn't going to faze him.

Rafael smirked, too. He put the gun down by his side, turned, and walked out the front door. The other two men stood in front of them, watching and waiting for further instructions from their boss. Claire huddled close to Henry. Maddison did the same to Chum, but while doing so glanced at Marty's lifeless body on the couch. She let out a gasp and buried her face in her husband's shoulder. None of them spoke at this point, not knowing what the consequences might be. The only noise was an occasional groan from Eddie. He was turning pale, looking sick. Ninety seconds passed before Rafael re-entered the house with Franco.

"Tomás, I understand you've decided to give me what I came for," Franco said.

"Yeah," Chum answered without looking up.

"Finalmente," Franco said. "Where is it?"

Chum continued to stare into space through all four of the armed men in front of him. "We have to go to my farmhouse up the drive."

"We? I don't think so, amigo," Franco said as he moved to the front door. "I will go by myself. Where in the house?"

Chum let out a chuckle and a slight shrug. "Suit yourself," he said. "Basement. Under the clothes dryer."

Franco moved back into the room and stood in front of Chum.

"What is so funny?" Franco inquired.

"Nothing. I mean, you might be able to disarm it yourself for all I know," Chum explained vaguely.

"Disarm what?" Franco asked, angry now. He pulled his gun out and aimed it at Maddison. "Start talking or I'm going to pick up where Rafael left off."

"Ok, ok. It's booby trapped—rigged with an explosive," Chum said. "You're going to need my help."

Franco put the gun down and looked around the room. First at the people on the couch, then back at his men. He looked at Chum.

"Get up," Franco said. He looked at Henry and pointed at him with the gun. "You too," he said.

"Me?" Henry questioned as he stood up. He looked down at Claire, who now had a strained look on her face.

"You two are coming with Rafael and me," Franco explained. He turned to the other two men and spoke in Spanish while pointing in the direction of Maddison, Claire, and Eddie. "No los deje fuera de su vista. Si intentan algo, matar a todos ellos."

"No funny stuff," Franco said to them. "I told these guys to shoot you if you try anything."

Rafael and Franco moved to the door.

"Let's go," Franco commanded Chum and Henry. Claire touched Henry's fingers one last time before he walked completely from her grasp. He turned and looked at her calmly, mouthing the words, "It's okay." She gave Henry a faint smile as he turned and walked out the door.

***

Franco insisted on using the truck to get to the farmhouse. Rafael drove with Chum riding shotgun, while Franco sat in the bed and kept his eye and gun on Henry. The ride was bumpy and short. Henry wondered why, if Chum had the money or the drugs the entire time, he hadn't saved Eddie's leg and Marty's life by giving it up earlier. This entire situation was difficult to fathom. Henry kept thinking how he should've just gone to bed tonight. Or gone home from the party earlier. More than likely he still would have ended up finding himself in the middle of this mess right about now. Henry imagined what it would be like to have these guys wake him up in the middle of the night.

It's better this way, he thought. At least I know what's

going on.

The pickup came to a stop next to the side door of Henry's rental house. The four men got out of the truck. Chum walked up to the door and almost ran into it, discovering the hard way that it was locked. He turned to Henry.

"You locked it?"

"Yeah. Is that unusual?" Henry asked, reaching into his pocket for the key.

"It is in Iowa," Chum answered. He took the key, unlocked the door, and handed the key back to his tenant. Henry assumed he was the only one in the group who found it amusing that Chum was giving him grief for locking a door while escorted at gunpoint by homicidal drug dealers.

"You live here?" Franco asked Henry as the men walked through the door and into the kitchen.

"For a week," Henry replied as Wilson greeted him in the doorway by rubbing against his leg. Rafael led them down the stairs to the basement. When the four men had gathered, they all turned and faced the clothes washer and dryer.

"Where is it?" Franco asked.

"Gonna need some help moving the dryer," Chum explained.

"He can do it," Franco said, motioning to Henry. Chum walked over to the clothes dryer and Henry followed. They lifted and moved the appliance, revealing a small trapdoor about three feet square. "What about the explosives?" Franco asked.

"I don't know what happened. They're gone," Chum said. He knelt down in front of the door and examined it.

"What do you mean?" Franco asked, moving closer to the hidden door.

"I mean, somebody disarmed it and removed the C4. It's gone!" Chum exclaimed as he fumbled his way through the combination of the attached padlock. He pulled the lock open and grabbed the latch on the door, opening it to the left.

"What the fuck?" Chum blurted.

"It's empty!" Franco shouted. "What kind of bullshit are you trying to pull here?" He grabbed Chum by the back of his collar and yanked him to his feet.

"I'm not pulling anything!" Chum insisted. "There were five kilos in there and two hundred and fifty grand—it's all gone!"

Franco stared at him as he tried to decipher the truth by looking deep into Chum's eyes.

"Maybe Eddie took it," Franco suggested.

"He didn't know where it was at, and even if he did he wouldn't do that," Chum told him. "The stuff was just here last weekend when I..."

Chum turned and eyeballed Henry.

"What?" Henry asked. Chum's head turned sideways, still staring. Then it dawned on Henry what he was thinking.

"You think it was me? I've been working the entire week until now. Work and sleep, that's all I've done. I haven't even been in this basement until now!"

The last part wasn't true, but Henry didn't think explaining himself would help his case. It was safer to lie.

"It was here last Sunday before I started mowing the lawn. You showed up and rented the place and that was the last time I was in here until now. Who else would it be?" Chum accused.

"It seems you've got plenty of enemies. Why don't you tell us who else it would be," Henry said. He couldn't believe this was happening.

"If you two don't figure this out in thirty seconds, I'm going to shoot both of you right here. Someone knows something. Come on, damnit!" Franco was growing impatient.

"Shoot both of us?" Chum cried out. "He's the one who stole the shit!"

"No. I didn't." Henry said in a much calmer tone than

Chum had just used to accuse him.

"Figure it out," Franco commanded them.

Henry looked at Chum, then at Franco and Rafael.

"This is bullshit. I'm being set up," Henry told them. He needed to figure something out, fast. Chum didn't seem interested in anything but pointing the finger and saving himself.

What an asshole, Henry thought.

"You just need to tell the truth," Chum pleaded with a worried look on his face. "They're going to shoot both of us!"

Henry wanted to punch him. Instead, he came up with the only solution he could think of.

"All right. I'll take you to it," Henry told Franco. "We need to go to the Corner Store."

Chum looked relieved and surprised at the same time.

"This better not be another game," Franco threatened.

"It's not," Henry assured him. "Let's go."

The men climbed back inside the pickup truck the same way they had arrived. Henry wondered how Claire was doing back at the house and if he'd ever see her again. All he could do right now was remain calm and keep his racing heart under control. He knew there was no way out of this train wreck alive if he didn't continue to think straight.

Less than ten minutes later they arrived at the closed convenience store. Rafael parked the truck parallel to the front door. It was now one thirty in the morning. The entire area was quiet except for the occasional sound of highway noise.

Henry unlocked the front door to the store and began to enter before Franco stopped him.

"Rafael will go first," Franco told him. Henry stepped aside to let Rafael through and then entered himself.

"No alarm?" Franco asked.

"Do you hear anything?" Henry avoided answering the question.

"Unusual for a store," Franco observed. He looked around for signs of a trap.

"No money kept here. Just food and beer," Henry explained. He knew bringing them to the Corner Store was his only hope of making it out of this situation. But Henry would need some help from Chum to turn the tables.

"So where's my stuff?" Franco asked. "I'm getting tired of asking the question."

"I need to get the key for the walk-in cooler," Henry said as he began to walk behind the counter. Franco followed with his gun drawn in his left hand even though there was barely enough room for both men in such a tight area. Rafael and Chum moved to the back corner of the building, near the cooler. Henry grabbed the key ring off the nail behind the counter next to the telephone and radio. As he did this he knew the next five seconds would be his only hope.

"Ok," Henry said, and what he was hoping would happen, did. One brief moment with his guard down was all Henry needed from the armed man. Franco made a half-turn to exit the tight space. This exposed his back to Henry when he should've been keeping an eye on him by walking backwards. Henry considered trying to knock Franco out with a punch to the back of the head, but feared the effort would fail. Instead, he made one swift move to get the gun out of Franco's left hand as he was completing his turn. The firearm was, after all, a much greater threat than Franco. Although he wasn't the fist-fighting type, Henry liked his chances against his captor, one-on-one. He put his hands together and swung both arms with all the strength he had. He slammed Franco's left arm against the gunman's body, bashing the weapon from his grasp. Reacting a split second too late, Franco turned in time to take another double-armed swing from Henry to the face and side of the head. The force sent Franco's head into the counter as his face kissed the metal cash register and flattened him to the floor with a thump. He wasn't completely unconscious, but dazed enough to give Henry time to grab Franco's gun from the floor and Bruce's from under the counter.

The commotion sent Rafael into a panic, causing him to hesitate. This enabled Chum to lower his shoulder and tackle Rafael against the walk-in cooler door. But the struggle was going to be a tough one to win, even for a scrappy guy like Chum. Rafael was armed, which meant Chum would have to hold the gun off while defending himself from Rafael's other fisted hand.

Not expecting him to last long in the fight, Henry darted to the other side of the store to help Chum while Franco remained on the floor, nursing a headache. As he did this a shot rang out through the store, but the brawl continued. Henry assumed it was errant gunfire caused by the combat. He reached the tussle with both guns drawn on Rafael, who was still on the bottom.

"That's it! It's over! Drop the gun!" Henry shouted. Rafael's eyes bugged out of his head when he realized what was happening. The hand holding the gun immediately went limp. Chum pulled the gun away and stood up, holding it on his attacker.

"Don't pull that trigger," Henry told him.

"Why? He killed Marty and damn near killed my wife!" Chum protested, still catching his breath.

"Because I work here and I don't want to have to clean up the mess." It was a terrible answer, but Henry didn't have time for philosophical justifications. "There's some twine in the storage closet. Tie him up and get him in the cooler. I'll do the same with Franco. The cops are on their way."

Chum didn't question anything. Not even whether the drugs or money were actually in the cooler. Henry kept the gun tight on Rafael while he reached down and found the truck keys inside his jacket. He placed them in his front jeans pocket. Chum helped tie both men up and drag them inside the ten by ten refrigerator. Less than five minutes had passed since the four men first walked into the store. Henry was expecting the police to arrive at any moment.

"So, now we just wait for the cops?" Chum asked.

"Yeah," Henry said. "Grab me one of those Gatorades over there, will you?"

Chum turned and walked to a shelf near the corner of the cooler. He tucked the gun in the back of his jeans.

"What flavor? Grape, Blue, or—"

Chum was unable to finish his sentence. Henry had approached him in silence from behind and began administering a blood choke. Within seconds, Chum passed out and was lying on the cold floor near the other two criminals. The choke hold was the only tactic Henry remembered from a two-week self-defense course he took during an interim period in college. The unconsciousness would only last a few seconds, so Henry knew he needed to act fast. He took the gun from Chum's waistband, left the cooler, closed the door, and locked it, leaving the key in the lock.

As he ran out the front door of the store, Henry could hear Chum pounding on the cooler door from the inside. A piercing blare of sirens was coming from the highway. Henry got in the truck, turned the key, and stormed off heading west, back to the Chumansky property. He wasn't sure what was going through Chum's mind after they had tied up Franco and Rafael, but Henry had no interest in spending another minute trusting him. Not after he had tried to get Henry killed. At this point, he didn't care about anything other than getting back to the house and helping Claire to safety.

The night was black on the winding country roads of Gable. Henry kept the high beams on to compensate for the darkness. Taking the curves at top speed, he used both lanes and the shoulder to help keep the truck on the road and out of the ditch. Henry prayed there was nobody else out for a late night drive.

By the time he approached the driveway he had formulated most of his next plan. He didn't have any time to waste and, just like the ambush he orchestrated at the Corner Store, there was only one shot at getting it right. This time he would have no help. Not from another man, anyway, since Fast Eddie was currently "Slow Eddie" at best, and more than likely passed out from the pain.

As he turned off the highway onto the gravel drive, Henry saw Chum's dogs, Millie and Hazel, bouncing in his direction. They hadn't been seen or heard from since Chum let them out the back door when Henry and Claire arrived at the house. Henry assumed they had found something more interesting to do for the past several hours.

Better late than never, you two, he thought.

IX

When he reached his house, Henry parked the truck next to the side door, jumped out, and raced inside. First, he grabbed a broom and a mop from the kitchen pantry. Then he dug out two bricks from the landscaping around the concrete steps outside. Millie and Hazel weren't much help, as the happy-go-lucky dogs pounced on him the same way they had the day he met Chum. He placed all the items in the cab of the truck and drove towards Chum's large house, where Claire and the others were still held captive. Instead of using the gravel driveway Henry kept the vehicle on the grassy field, hoping to keep his arrival silent. When he was approximately forty yards from the house, he shifted the truck into park but kept it running. He hoped the gurgling of the engine was not audible from inside the large house. Even if it was, Henry figured the two goons wouldn't budge after witnessing their coworker getting gunned down for questioning Franco.

He took the broom and mop and used their long, straight handles to stabilize the steering wheel in a straight-ahead position. Henry had seen this done on TV shows, but he wasn't sure how realistic it was to expect it to work in real life. The truck was facing the right front side of the house away from Claire and the rest, assuming they were still in the same place he'd left them.

Henry had gone over several plans in his mind during

the speedy drive back to the farm. He'd considered parking the truck a hundred yards out and laying a brick on the horn. But Henry knew this wasn't foolproof. If it failed, the two creeps guarding the others would know something was wrong. God knows what they might do to wipe their trail clean. He thought about using the simple approach of walking in the front door with two guns drawn to see what they would do. Once again, though, Henry didn't feel good about the possibilities. Especially if bullets started flying. There were too many innocent, unarmed people in the house. He knew he needed to take these thugs by surprise, and the best way to do it was with some good old-fashioned misdirection.

Henry didn't like the idea of jumping out of a moving truck, so a brick and some large sticks would have to do the trick. But there was still one problem. He needed to figure out a way to shift the automatic transmission from neutral to drive while the accelerator remained floored. This would not be an easy task. While conducting a couple of tests, Henry discovered the gearshift was close enough to the steering wheel that he could make the move by sticking his arm in and pulling it out before the truck took off on its own.

After reassuring himself everything was ready, Henry proceeded with his ruse. He put the pickup in neutral and laid a brick on the accelerator. The vehicle revved up but went nowhere. The RPM needle bounced inside the gauge like a flopping fish out of water. With one swift move, Henry flipped the gear into drive and pulled his arm out. The truck immediately took off on a beeline for the front of Chum's house. Henry bolted behind it as fast as his legs would carry him.

***

The scene inside the Chumansky house remained the same as it had been more than an hour ago. Claire and Maddison sat next to each other on the sofa. Next to Maddison was Eddie, half lying down, half sitting up. His entire left pant leg was drenched in blood, and he was barely conscious. None of them had spoken a word since the other men had left.

The two Hispanic men in charge of watching them were hovering near the sofa, taking turns pacing in and out of the room. They spoke in Spanish to each other often, and it was clear to the prisoners that their patience was wearing thin. The longer Franco and Rafael were gone, the more intense their conversations became. At one point they raised their voices at each other, possibly in disagreement about how to proceed if their superiors did not return soon.

The last thing anyone in the house expected at that moment was a truck driving through the front door. Drywall, wood, and bricks went flying everywhere as a wall of the house caved in from the force of the pickup truck ramming through the doorway before settling in the foyer. The instantaneous demolition caught everyone off guard. They were too stunned to react. The sound was nowhere near as disturbing as the jaw-dropping experience of watching the destruction take place. Even Maddison could only look on in shock.

"¿Qué demonios pasó?" one of the men screamed.

"¡Es la camióneta de Rafael!" the other man responded.

The men turned their backs on the couch and began investigating the truck, guns drawn. Millie and Hazel began barking outside. Debris covered the windshield and driver's side window. One of the men began brushing it off to have a closer look inside.

From the back hallway, visible only to his friends on the couch, Henry appeared at the same moment the two goons turned to examine the truck. Maddison and Claire both noticed him but did not say a word. Instead, they indicated that it was safe for him to enter the room. Before doing so, Henry removed his shoes. He walked past the three on the couch and motioned for them to be quiet and stay put. He held a gun in each hand. The third one was tucked in the back of his jeans, out of sight.

Henry felt like John McClane in the movie *Die Hard* even though he knew he was far from it. People will do crazy things to survive. He already knew this from recent personal experience. He moved silently as the two men continued to ramble at each other in Spanish. Henry kept his approach angled in the shadows so that when either man changed his position or turned his head, he would remain out of their line of sight.

By the time the two men were finally able to look inside the truck cab and discover there was no one inside, Henry was right behind them. He placed a gun barrel against the back of each of their heads.

"Don't move," Henry commanded. Neither of them did. But one of them spoke.

"Shit," he said.

"Good, you know English. Drop your guns to the floor. Now." Henry was firm and hostile on the outside. On the inside he was nervous as hell that one of the guys would make a move. Killing someone was not something Henry wanted to add to his résumé tonight.

Both men let their guns fall to the floor. Henry kept his guns pressed against the two men's heads.

"Claire! Maddison! Come grab these guns!" he instructed without turning around. Both women darted from the couch and picked up the firearms.

"What happened?" Claire asked him.

"Where's Tom?" Maddison asked in a panic.

Henry kept his guns in position and didn't turn his head to look at either one of them.

"He's fine. I'll tell you everything. But first you need to get something for us to tie these two assholes up with."

Maddison found some four-inch duct tape and called for an ambulance at the same time. Henry marched the men against a wall and forced them to sit on the floor. Then the ladies helped him bind the men at the wrists and ankles. When they were finished, Henry put his shoes back on and gave a limited overview of the events that had taken place at the farmhouse and store.

"We ended up luring them to the Corner Store, where we were able to ambush them," he explained, skipping over all the other details. He didn't think getting into Chum's questionable behavior or the fact that Henry had locked him in the cooler with the other two would be a good idea right now. He also didn't have the time for it.

"So then where is my husband? I missed that part," Maddison asked sarcastically.

"Sorry," Henry responded. "He's at the Corner Store waiting for the cops."

As far as Henry was concerned, this was the absolute truth, if not the whole truth. He was thankful she didn't ask more questions.

"I need a drink," Maddison declared, and began heading for the kitchen.

"Before you do that," Henry said, "I need to run back to my house."

"Why? What for?" Claire asked. She stepped forward and placed her hand on Henry's chest.

"It's a long story," he said, avoiding an actual answer. "I'm going to leave you with these." Henry handed each woman a gun. He leaned in to them and whispered. "If either of them tries anything, just shoot him in the leg," he said.

"I don't know that I can shoot someone," Claire said with a worried look.

"If you had to, I bet you could," Henry assured her, still whispering. "But I don't think you'll need to worry about it." He smiled and grabbed her empty hand. "The police and ambulance should be here soon. You're going to be fine," Henry told her. He leaned forward and kissed her softly on the lips. Releasing her hand, he turned toward the front door before realizing his error.

"I guess that one's out of service," Henry joked as he moved to the back door. Claire covered her mouth to hide her smile. Maddison could only stare at the pickup parked in her front hallway.

***

Henry sprinted as fast as he could back to the little white farmhouse he had lived in for a mere week. Entering through the side door, he ran through the kitchen and headed straight for the bedroom. He tossed his duffel bags on the bed and began gathering his clothes and other belongings. Wilson was in dire need of attention and made it known to his owner. He jumped on the bed and purred incessantly, rubbing up against Henry every time he came near him. On occasion, Henry would stop packing and pet his cat for a moment, or stroke his ears.

It only took Henry a few minutes to finish. Next, he took the cover off the old-fashioned vent in the bedroom and reached inside, pulling out his small backpack. Henry unzipped it and glanced at the cash inside. It was filled to the top. He zipped it closed again and slung it over his right shoulder.

It was now after two in the morning and Henry expected the police to be driving up to the farm property at any moment. After making sure Wilson had plenty of food and water, he turned off all the lights in the house. He left the house key on the kitchen counter along with the remaining guns. He then made sure all the doors were locked from the inside before heading out the front door. He popped open the trunk of his Honda and tossed his two duffel bags in. The backpack accompanied Henry to the front seat. Just before he turned the key in the ignition he noticed the glare of headlights in his rearview mirror. Henry twisted around in his seat to witness four cars coming down the driveway.

"Shit," he whispered to himself.

It has to be the cops, he thought. They were smarter

than Henry would've guessed, not turning on their sirens or lights. He reached down with his left hand and used the lever to recline the seat. This put him below the line of sight from outside the car.

There would be no reason for the police to stop at the little white farmhouse. Everything on this part of the property was dark and silent. They should be heading to the Chumansky residence, where there were still, as far as anyone knew, people in danger. Henry could hear the spitting of the gravel beneath the cars as they drove by. It was happening within a hundred feet of where he was lying in his car, motionless.

Henry wondered where Chum was right now. Was he in one of the police cars? If he was, was he in handcuffs? What had he told the officers? Was Sergeant Jackson one of the cops who had just driven by?

Once the sound of the cars faded, Henry put his seat back upright. He couldn't see what was going on at the Chumansky house from inside his car, but he assumed the police were just now noticing the destruction he had caused with the pickup truck.

Henry turned the car on but left the headlights off. There was enough light along the gravel road that he could make it to the county highway without them. When Henry reached the intersection to the highway, he paused and released a sigh.

Without a second thought, he turned the steering wheel to the right and headed north. After a quarter of a mile, he turned the headlights on.

And just like that, Henry Fields disappeared into the early morning darkness.

X

"Give me a quick briefing before you write your report, Sergeant," said Chief Nathan Perkins of the Gable Police Department. It was Monday morning and the entire station smelled like coffee and donuts. It had been a long and busy twenty-four hours, and Sergeant John Jackson was ready for some sleep.

"Around one thirty Sunday morning the department received a call that the alarm had been tripped at the Corner Store," Jackson began. "When officers arrived, they found the door unlocked and the lights on. Locked inside the store's cooler were three men: Franco Salazar and Rafael Menendez, both tied up, and Tom Chumansky."

"Tom Chumansky?" Perkins verified.

"Yes, sir. He was frantic and difficult to calm down or understand," Jackson explained, "but officers were eventually able to decipher that Chumansky's wife was being held at gunpoint in their house."

"Jesus Christ." Perkins was in his late fifties and had been on the force for almost thirty-five years. He could've retired long ago, but heading up the police in a small town with almost no crime had its advantages.

"When officers arrived at the Chumansky house, they immediately noticed a white pickup truck had been driven into it," Jackson continued.

"Into the house?" Perkins exclaimed.

"Yes, sir. Inside the house there were two more men tied up: Rodrigo Ramírez and Miguel Sánchez. They were being guarded with handguns by Chumansky's wife, Maddison, and Claire Mathison."

"Wait a minute. I thought you said the wife was being held at gunpoint." Perkins said. He took a sip of his fresh coffee and leaned back in his chair.

"That's correct. Give me one minute and I'll get to that, Chief," Jackson said. He was reciting the entire report from memory and knew if he got off track he would forget important details. "Also inside the house and suffering from a gunshot wound to the leg was Eddie Clark," Jackson explained. "An ambulance was dispatched immediately to the house. Clark was taken to Adler Regional, where surgery was performed to remove the bullet. He's in stable condition now."

"Thank God," Perkins mumbled sarcastically. "What would the world do without Fast Eddie?"

Jackson continued with his report as though he hadn't heard his boss's comment.

"There were two deceased bodies in the house, as well. Carlos Lopez and Marty Greenberg. Gunshot wounds to the head."

"Holy hell." Perkins hadn't expected this. There had never been a double homicide in Gable. The crime rate had remained extremely low for decades. Adler was a much larger breeding ground for murderers, thieves, and dealers. "So what happened?" Perkins inquired.

"What we've pieced together so far is this was some sort of drug related ambush," Jackson said. "Salazar and Menendez allegedly pulled the trigger on the two victims. We're checking ballistics, residue, prints, and such. But I'm confident it will be confirmed. They're in custody right now. Ramírez and Sánchez are also in custody for their role."

"Great, we've got our own 'Little Mexico' right here in our cells," Perkins grunted. "Maybe we should charge the Adler P.D. rent."

Jackson continued without missing a beat. "We're convinced Chumansky was involved with these characters, but the Hispanic guys aren't talking. Chumansky's denying knowing anything, calling it 'mistaken identity.' Frankly, we've got nothing on him."

"So, what about the truck parked in the house?" Perkins asked him.

"Apparently there was another man involved, a Henry Fields. For the past several days he has been employed at the Corner Store and was a guest at the Chumansky house Saturday evening. Somehow, to thwart whatever Salazar and Menendez were trying to do, Fields lured the men to the Corner Store, where he and Chumansky were able to take them over. Now here's where it gets weird, Chief."

"Oh, now it's gonna get weird?" Perkins joked.

"Yes, sir," Jackson said. "Chumansky claims he helped this Fields character tie up Salazar and Menendez. Then Fields blindsided Chumansky with a choke hold and locked him in the cooler with the other two."

"So maybe Fields is the one tied to these drug assholes," Perkins suggested.

"You'd think so," Sergeant John Jackson agreed. "But then why did he go back to the Chumansky house, drive Salazar's truck through the front door, and apprehend the goons who were holding the others hostage?"

"Why don't we just ask him?" Perkins suggested.

"We would if we could find him. It seems he skipped town shortly after this all went down," Jackson reported.

"See? Looks pretty guilty, don't you think?" Chief Perkins enjoyed making observations from behind the desk, even when he knew Jackson was going to have more to say. Asking the obvious questions helped his team think ahead.

Jackson was his best officer, too. There wasn't a week that went by when Perkins didn't breathe a sigh of relief that Jackson had yet to turn in his resignation to leave for a bigger city. Working as a police sergeant in Gable was mainly traffic accidents and an occasional domestic dispute. Nathan Perkins knew this fell short of what most police officers had in mind when they were playing cops and robbers as kids.

"Yes, sir," Jackson agreed. "Running away definitely makes him look guilty. The problem is, according to Claire Mathison, that entire notion is ridiculous. She doesn't know why Fields took off, but she confirmed that Salazar was there specifically because of Chumansky and some money or cocaine he owed them."

"Really? What did the wife say?"

"Not much. But when he found out Fields had disappeared, Tom Chumansky began alluding to the idea that Fields was the one Salazar was after."

"Fishy. So if Chumansky is the real reason this all happened, why did Fields bolt?" Perkins wondered out loud.

"That's the million dollar question, sir," Jackson commented. "Fields was renting the old Chumansky farmhouse. We're searching it again today, but so far we haven't found much of anything other than a lonely cat."

"Got anything else?"

"Hodge is questioning Bruce Townsend, the Corner Store owner. But for now I'm going to get to work on the report and, if it's okay with you, grab some sleep when I'm finished."

"Sounds good, Jack. Have at it," Perkins said.

***

John Jackson sat at his desk writing the official report on the weekend's events. Being on the police force wasn't quite as exciting as it sounded; not in Gable, anyway. But it was a good job that was getting him plenty of experience. This case from the weekend was the most intriguing thing to take place in the area since Jackson joined the force eight years ago. Before then he had bounced around between the military and security jobs. While serving in the Army, he was deployed to Bosnia and worked protective service. It had been Jackson's favorite job: wearing civilian clothes and carrying a concealed firearm while guarding high ranking officials. His "Billy Bad Ass gig" was what he always called it.

Jackson was so deep in thought with his report that when his phone rang he didn't notice it until the second ring.

"Sergeant Jackson," he answered.

"Hi, Sergeant. This is Balinda Simmons from Channel 6 in Adler. I understand you're in charge of the investigation of the incident that took place over the weekend."

Jackson rolled his eyes.

"I am," he conceded. "But the info you've got is all I can tell you right now."

"No, no," Balinda said with a chuckle. She was used to getting brushed aside by the authorities. "I'm calling because I think I might be able to help you with something."

His ears perked up, but he was still skeptical.

"Sounds good to me. I'm listening," Jackson said.

"Well, you're looking for this man, Henry Fields. And you might already know this, but he helped out with the highway traffic accident that happened on Friday night."

"Yes, I met and spoke with Fields a couple of times last week, and I know what accident you're referring to," Jackson offered.

"Well, I did an interview with him the next morning because of the help he provided on the scene. The thing is, he was pretty adamant about not wanting to appear on camera," Balinda explained.

"That's kind of strange," Jackson stated. Now he was listening with every ounce of attention he could muster from his sleep-deprived body.

"Yes, I thought so, too," Balinda agreed. "The interview we ended up airing was audio only, with his blessing. But..."

She hesitated.

"...we still managed to capture some video of him."

Jackson snorted.

"In my defense," she explained, "it's not like we filmed him head-on without his knowledge. This is just some footage that happened to get recorded while we were setting things up."

"Despite the fact I've met him, we have no record of what he looks like so this is helpful," Jackson said. "But I should also mention he's not actually 'wanted' for any crime. We'd just like to talk to him and get his side of the story."

"I understand," Balinda said. "I just wanted to help out if I could. I've got some screenshots here I can email you if you'd like."

"That'd be great."

After giving her his email address, Jackson hung up the phone and went back to writing his report.

***

Jackson was putting the final touches on his police report when Officer Ryan Hodge walked into the station. It was almost ten thirty.

"Just in time," Jackson called out to him. "You got anything I should add to this?"

"Maybe," Hodge replied while walking to Jackson's desk. He sat down in the chair across from him before continuing. "Townsend said he believes the alarm was engaged because Fields intentionally didn't turn it off. Also, one of the guns we found at the farmhouse was Townsend's. He kept it at the store behind the counter, just in case."

"No surprise there," Jackson said.

"Yeah, but he did mention something that I thought was peculiar," Hodge said.

"What's that?" Jackson asked.

"I asked Townsend for Fields' employee paperwork. You know, his W-4 and I-9. He said he hadn't had Fields fill any out yet," Hodge explained.

"Not that unusual," Jackson replied. "He only worked there a week."

"Yeah, but then Townsend said Fields requested he be paid in cash," Hodge added. Jackson stroked his chin.

"Did we dust for any prints at the farmhouse?"

"No, because we didn't think we had a reason to," Hodge said.

"Let's go ahead and do it," Jackson ordered.

"You got it, Sarge." Officer Ryan Hodge turned and walked out the door.

Fields might not be wanted by the Gable Police Department for any crimes, but his behavior was sparking curiosity that warranted some extra effort. Jackson pulled up the criminal database and entered the name "Henry Fields." There were two matches. One of them was African-American and the other one was white but looked nothing like the Henry Fields Jackson had spoken to on multiple occasions. Jackson opened another window on his computer and checked for an email from Balinda Simmons. When he found it, he opened the attachment and stared at the video screen captures of Henry Fields, the superhero without a cape. Jackson thought it was interesting that Fields was involved in what could be described as two heroic incidents on consecutive nights. Was this guy trying to be a modern day superhero? Was the conversation Jackson had with Fields about superheroes more serious than he had thought? Of course, the other possibility was Fields had been a victim of circumstance, twice. After the drug-related incident on Saturday night, he might have been so spooked he simply skipped town. There's no law against doing that.

Jackson heard footsteps behind him. He could tell it was the chief by the sound of the walk. Two knee replacements and a lifetime of weight problems had made Nathan Perkins a perfect desk jockey.

"Guess who's coming to dinner?" Perkins asked. Jackson turned from his computer and leaned back in his chair, looking up at his boss.

"I give up," he replied.

"DEA," Perkins explained. "They're gonna take Tijuana back with them, too." He pointed with his thumb towards the jail cells.

"So we got ourselves some big players here, eh?" Jackson surmised.

"Something like that," Chief Perkins said. "They'd like our report and evidence...everything."

"St. Louis?" Jackson asked.

"Chicago. They'll be here for lunch," Perkins said as he began hobbling back to his office.

"I thought you said 'dinner'?" Jackson called back to him, realizing a nap was no longer in his future.

"It was a figure of speech, Jack," Chief Perkins grumbled.

"Cary Grant?" Jackson recognized the phrase "Guess Who's Coming to Dinner" as a movie title.

Perkins let out a gruff belt of laughter before responding.

"Spencer Tracy and Sidney Poitier."

"I was close," Jackson retorted.

"No, you weren't."

***

When noon came and there was still no sign of the DEA, Chief Perkins sent Hodge to Stubby's to bring some sandwiches back to the station. Jackson had switched from drinking coffee to Diet Coke an hour earlier and after rummaging through the kitchen cupboard found a Nutty Bar that he split with the chief.

At twelve forty-five, a dark blue sedan pulled up to the station. A tall woman with long brown hair climbed out of the car with a briefcase. As she entered the building, she placed her sunglasses on top of her head. Jackson and Perkins rose from their desks to greet her.

"Chief Perkins?" she stuck her hand out and looked at him and then at Jackson.

"Yes, ma'am. That's me," Perkins responded by taking her hand and shaking it. "And this is Sergeant Jackson."

"I'm Agent Delia DeMarco," she said.

Jackson shook DeMarco's hand and sized her up at about five feet ten inches tall. This was an easy guess for him since it also happened to be his height.

The three of them sat down at the conference table. Chief Perkins offered her a sandwich, but Agent DeMarco declined, saying she had eaten something an hour ago. She explained that her initial intent was to be in Gable an hour earlier, but she ran into some road construction on Interstate 80 that slowed her down.

After giving her a brief rundown of Saturday night's events, it was time to discuss the next steps.

"We've never had anything like this go down in our small town," Chief Perkins explained. "Where do we go from here?"

"Well, we have a wagon on the way to take Salazar, Menendez, Ramírez, and Sánchez off your hands," DeMarco explained. "It should be here tomorrow." She began thumbing through the report as she continued to speak. "After that there's not much more for you to do other than provide a support system in case we need anything else. I'll take the rest of the day to conduct my own interviews with the witnesses.

Looks like there's Claire Mathison, Bruce Townsend, Tom and Maddison Chumansky and...you say this Henry Fields is M.I.A.?"

"Yes, it seems that way," Jackson replied and then snapped his fingers. "But I just remembered something."

He trotted back to his desk and woke up his computer by shaking the mouse. Balinda Simmons's email was still opened on his monitor. He printed the two screenshots of Henry Fields and brought them back to the conference room.

"Up until a couple of hours ago we had no record of what he looked like. I received these photos from a local TV station. We still don't think Fields was involved with Salazar. But since he took off the way he did...you may as well have these for your file."

"Interesting," DeMarco said. "I appreciate it." She gathered all the paperwork into her briefcase and stood up. "Thanks again for your help, gentlemen," she said.

"Our pleasure," Chief Perkins said, handing her a couple of business cards. "Here are our cards, just in case."

After saying their goodbyes at the door, the two police officers walked back into the office.

"They didn't make them like that when I was in the academy," Perkins said. "She's a hot number."

"She could probably kick both of our asses at the same time," Jackson commented.

"Wouldn't that be fun?" Chief Perkins joked. He then paused and looked at his worn-out sergeant. "Go home and get some sleep, Jack. Thanks for staying."

***

At seven thirty that evening, Delia DeMarco rented a room at the Stone Creek Inn in Adler. It had been a long day, and she needed a good night's sleep before hitting the road and heading back to the Windy City. The Stone Creek Inn was a comfortable and quiet hotel with an adjoining restaurant. After grabbing some dinner, she went back to her room, took a quick shower, and got dressed for bed. She opened her briefcase and laid the report and paperwork in front of her on the desk.

She picked up the pictures of Henry Fields and studied them for a moment. Nothing about him jumped out at her. She knew all the major players, of course, but there were always ones out there she didn't know.

Agent DeMarco reached into her briefcase for her smartphone. Using its camera, she scanned a picture of Henry Fields and uploaded it to the FBI database. She included a message that read: "Request facial recognition."

DeMarco didn't know if it would come back with any type of match, but having the FBI take a look wouldn't hurt anything. Chances were good this guy was just a drifter. He more than likely had had enough excitement and near-death experiences to last a lifetime and decided to run away from it all.

She set her phone down and went to the bathroom to brush her teeth. When she returned a few minutes later, her phone was already flashing. Delia picked it up, glanced at the results, and did a quick double take. She had expected the results to come back negative. Squinting to make sure she was seeing everything accurately, it became clear to her there was a match. But something wasn't right about it. Reaching into her briefcase, Delia grabbed the business cards she had received from the Gable Police. She tried to reach Chief Perkins first, but it went to voicemail. Sergeant Jackson answered on the second ring.

"Sergeant, this is Delia DeMarco," she said.

"Yes ma'am," Jackson replied as politely as possible. It wasn't every day the DEA called his mobile phone. He was sitting in a recliner watching television.

"I'm sorry to bother you so late," Delia said, "but I just discovered something I thought you should know before I turned it over to the FBI."

In one motion, Jackson pulled the lever on his recliner and sat up.

"Wow. Ok. What's that?"

"The Henry Fields story piqued my curiosity, so I ran the pictures you gave me through facial recognition in the FBI database. It came back with an eighty-one percent match."

"What does that mean, exactly?" Jackson asked, wondering if it meant Fields had a police record. But that wouldn't explain why DeMarco was turning it over to the FBI.

"Henry Fields is not Henry Fields," Delia explained. "His name is Barrett Greyson. And he's wanted for questioning about his involvement in a murder."

"Really?" Jackson exclaimed. His wife shushed him to not wake up their children. "Are you sure?" Jackson added, more quietly this time.

"Eighty-one percent sure, Sergeant."

Book 2
Ghosts of Winter

XI

The fifty-three-foot semi-trailer truck pulled in to the snow-covered Marble Industries parking lot and made a wide U-turn, positioning itself perpendicular to the loading dock. From the lone window inside the building, Ernie Saunders watched the truck begin to back in. Winter had hit its stride in Caribou, Maine, just like it always did by December. Thanks to Mother Nature, ice melt was a necessity in this part of the country. It kept Marble Industries in business and food on the table at the Saunders house. Ernie once estimated he had loaded close to ten thousand trucks during his twenty years with the company. But this year things would be different. Corporate had finally come through with the help he had been requesting for five years. As far as Ernie was concerned, he had earned the right to slack off every once in a while and make someone else go outside and freeze his ass off. When the driver had finished backing up to the dock, he jogged through the flurries and entered the small shipping office where Ernie sat.

"Man-oh-man, it's cold here!" the driver bellowed as he shook snowflakes out of his hair.

Ernie perked up from his seat behind the desk and pushed his glasses up his nose. "Where you from?" he asked, reaching for a folder full of orders.

"I live in South Carolina but I've been in New England all week. The weather up here is ridiculous."

"Well, you can't get much closer to Canada than Caribou," Ernie explained. "This snow is just another day in paradise. Who you picking up for?"

The driver pulled a bill of lading from his pocket and read the company name out loud. "Grigsby International," he recited.

Ernie paused for a beat before responding. He took pride in knowing what was going on in the ice melt industry. "Hmmm," he said. "Must be a new distributor."

"Beats me," the driver responded. "I'm just the chauffeur."

Ernie grabbed the two-way radio on his desk and spoke into it. "Hey, Dan. Got a pickup here for Grigsby. It's a full load. I'll help you."

Dan Scotwood had only been working at the warehouse for about six weeks. Ernie'd spent an entire day teaching him how to drive the forklift. It would've made more sense to hire someone with experience, but that would have cost more. Ernie hoped to impress corporate with the money he saved by teaching Dan himself and paying him less.

Ernie told the truck driver where he could find the restroom and coffee. Then he grabbed his gloves and coat, pulling the hood over his head. In the warehouse, Ernie hopped on his forklift. As he turned the key he could hear the other forklift approaching from around the corner. The brakes squeaked as it came to a halt next to Ernie. The driver was bundled from head to toe: boots, snow pants, coat, gloves, hood, and even a scarf wrapped around his nose and mouth. Only his eyes were visible beneath the hood.

"We need to get those brakes looked at," Ernie said to him.

The man replied from under the scarf, but what he said was unintelligible beneath the noise of the forklift engines.

"I can't hear you with that thing in your face, Dan," Ernie said, this time in a louder voice.

The man pulled the scarf down to his chin, revealing several days' growth of a beard and mustache. He grinned at

Ernie. "I said, I'll make a phone call as soon as we get done with this, boss," Barrett Greyson replied.

***

Agent Chase Sheehan of the Federal Bureau of Investigation drove his rental car into the Morning Glory subdivision of Aurora, Colorado. If he'd had the time he would've preferred driving all the way from D.C. instead of flying into Denver and renting a car. He hated flying. Not because he was afraid, but because his ears never seemed to want to pop. Today's flight had been particularly painful. The pressure in his ears was so excruciating that Chase used the plane's restroom to throw up. Ironically, the heaving caused his ears to pop a bit, making the rest of the flight more manageable.

After landing his ears were still plugged. Every so often Chase would pinch his nostrils, close his mouth, and try to exhale through his nose to relieve the pressure that was causing some minor temporary deafness. These attempts did nothing for his hearing, but at least his ears no longer hurt now that he was on the ground. The entire ordeal was just a nuisance now. One that he would have to ignore for a while. Chase knew a good night's sleep would solve most of the problem and he'd be back to normal by tomorrow.

The car's GPS announced he had arrived at 17402 Rockland Drive. Chase brought the vehicle to a stop at the curb and put it in park. He sighed and gripped his nose, making one more effort to pop his ears. No dice. He exited the car and walked up the driveway to the front door. After ringing the doorbell, Chase stood still and waited, arms crossed behind his back. He wondered if anything would come of this visit.

The door opened and a middle-aged woman with short auburn hair greeted him.

"Agent Sheehan I presume?" the woman said.

"Yes, ma'am," Chase replied.

"I'm Ella Greyson," she said, holding out her hand. "We've been expecting you, Agent. Come in."

Chase shook her hand then pulled his credentials from his breast pocket. Mrs. Greyson gave them a quick glance and led him to the kitchen.

At the table sat an average-sized bald man in his late fifties. He was drinking coffee and reading the *Rocky Mountain News*. When he realized there was a guest in the room he jumped up from the table.

"I guess I didn't hear the doorbell," he said. "Trapped deep in what I was reading, apparently."

"Honey, this is Agent Chase Sheehan," Mrs. Greyson said.

"Hello, Agent. Nice to finally meet you," the man said. "I'm Frank Greyson."

After shaking hands with Mr. Greyson, Chase was invited to join him at the table.

"Thank you for meeting with me on such short notice," Chase told them as he sat down across from Mr. Greyson. Mrs. Greyson took the chair next to her husband.

"I should mention," Mr. Greyson said, "I'm not sure we have anything more to tell you than what we already have over the telephone."

"I can appreciate that," Chase said. "Sometimes getting together face-to-face can help bring something to the surface that might've otherwise been overlooked. It's standard procedure, really."

"Up until a couple of months ago we had assumed our son was dead," Mr. Greyson reminded him. "I don't think we have any new information, but we're willing to help out in any way we can."

"I'm glad to hear that," Chase said. "Because I'm also here to ask you for a favor."

"A favor from us?" Mr. Greyson asked.

"Yes. I need you to hold a press conference and ask

your son to come home," Chase explained.

Frank Greyson looked at his wife and then back at Chase.

"A press conference?" Mr. Greyson echoed.

"We just don't have much to go on," Chase said. "The only good lead we have is the make, model, and color of the car he was driving when he left Gable, Iowa."

"Would he see the press conference? Do you think it would work?" Mr. Greyson asked.

"It's possible," Chase answered. "It certainly wouldn't hurt."

Mrs. Greyson glared at Chase.

"You guys only want to find him because you think he's a murderer!"

Her husband reached over and stroked her arm to help calm her down, but his gaze remained on the FBI agent.

"I know Barrett didn't kill Otto Clevinger," Mr. Greyson said with such confidence Chase almost believed him.

"Again, I can appreciate your stance," Chase said, realizing immediately this was a poor choice of words.

"It's not a 'stance,' Agent Sheehan," Mr. Greyson explained. "It's a fact. And my wife is right. The FBI only wants Barrett so they can throw him in prison."

Chase sighed.

Another family in denial, he thought to himself. Maybe they'll snap out of it when the DNA test results come back. Or maybe they won't.

"Look, Mr. and Mrs. Greyson. I know it sounds trite, but I'm just trying to do my job."

The three of them were silent for a few moments before Chase continued.

"You both have repeatedly told me Barrett is innocent. But can either of you explain why, if he did nothing wrong, he ran away?"

"Honestly, Agent," Mr. Greyson said. "We don't even know that he ran away. He left his wallet, driver's license, and credit cards behind. Doesn't that seem more like an abduction to you?"

"You think someone took him?" Chase asked. "Who would do that?"

"I don't know. I'm just throwing theories out there. Isn't that what you're supposed to be doing?"

"I'm supposed to look at the facts," Chase explained. "And the facts are that your son disappeared from the Denver area shortly after he was questioned by local police regarding the murder of Otto Clevinger. A few weeks later we learned he had traveled to Gable, Iowa, of his own free will, using the alias Henry Fields and driving a car that he did not own when he was in Colorado. Surely you can understand where I'm coming from."

Ella Greyson spoke for the first time since her outburst. Her tone was much calmer now. "Agent Sheehan, do you have children?"

"Yes, ma'am," Chase replied. "I have an eight-year-old daughter."

"Can you fathom the idea of her committing murder? Do you have any idea how you would react to such a thing?"

Chase put his head down and thought about this for a moment as she continued.

"I'm sure you love your little girl just as much as we love Barrett. And I'm sure you can also admit that you would do anything to protect your child from harm, no matter the circumstances."

Chase raised his head and looked at the two parents as Ella Greyson went on.

"I think my son is scared, Agent Sheehan," she said. "Not because he committed a crime but because he doesn't know if he can prove he didn't."

Chase held his hands open in front of him. "Help me

get him back home. In return, I promise you I will do everything I can to help prove his innocence. If your son did not kill Otto Clevinger, I need his help to find out who did. Can you understand that?"

The Greysons looked at each other and paused for a moment before nodding in unison.

"We understand. We'll do the press conference," Mr. Greyson agreed. "Just tell us where and when."

***

The snow had started to fall in Gable around four o'clock the previous afternoon. Now, sixteen hours later, there was almost a foot of it covering the small town and surrounding areas. Making matters worse were the gusting winds blowing the snow across Highway 57, causing drifts and making travel impossible for anything other than a snowmobile or a yeti. And, of course, the temperature was unbearable thanks to the wind chill. This was a winter storm in Iowa.

Claire Mathison lay in bed and stared at the ceiling. She listened to the whipping wind and the pelting of snow against her bedroom window. Wilson was curled in a ball, his head between Claire's shoulder and cheek. He had adjusted well to his new home, though there were fewer mice to chase than at his previous house.

The events of a few months ago had confused Claire to the point where she now questioned her judgment more than ever. Henry was not really a "Henry," but a "Barrett," and quite possibly a murderer. On the surface she found this unfathomable, though any involvement in such a crime would explain his elusive behavior when talking about his past. But he certainly didn't seem like a criminal. After all, he had saved Claire's life. Maddison's, too. It took poor Maddison less than a week to file for divorce, despite being pregnant. Finding out her husband was deeply involved in selling drugs had caused her to reconsider the relationship. The police and DEA had no evidence to convict Chum. No money and no drugs meant no case, Sergeant Jackson had told Claire at Stubby's a few weeks after the incident.

But maybe Henry/Barrett was a deranged psychopath. The kind of guy capable of pulling the wool over a woman's eyes, wooing her, taking her money, and disappearing. Or killing someone and disappearing.

Claire didn't know what to believe. What she did know as fact was that Barrett Greyson's boss had been found dead—murdered—in his house a few weeks before Greyson arrived in Gable as "Henry Fields." She had no idea why an innocent man would run instead of staying to prove his innocence.

Despite the confusion and all the questioning from the police, FBI, DEA, and reporters, Claire still found herself drawn to this mystery man. She had a difficult time thinking of him as "Barrett." In her head she still referred to him as "Henry." *Dateline NBC* had traveled to Gable three weeks earlier to begin filming a television news magazine story about Barrett Greyson. Claire found herself habitually referring to Barrett as "Henry" on camera when telling her side of the story. She couldn't help herself. When she thought of him, the only thing that came to mind was the limited amount of time she had spent with a nice guy named Henry. A man who had saved no fewer than four lives while in town for only one week. No, something just wasn't adding up. The Barrett Greyson the FBI and the national media knew was not the same guy Claire knew as Henry Fields.

Sergeant John Jackson agreed. He and Claire had chatted at length about the entire incident and neither of them believed Henry/Barrett had any involvement with illegal activity in Gable. It was clear that Chum had been and more than likely still was involved with selling drugs and that his wife had apparently been oblivious to it for years. To this day Chum still claimed he did not know the men who crashed his party, shot Fast Eddie Clark, and murdered Marty Greenberg.

Fast Eddie was not the type to rat despite his new limp, courtesy of his boss. But the stories of Claire and

Maddison tracked so well that at one point the district attorney was ready to move forward. According to Jackson, the DEA pulled the plug before filing charges. They wanted more evidence to make it a slam dunk and figured Chum would hang himself sooner or later. If they were really lucky he'd even bring more criminals down with him.

Jackson had had many conversations with Barrett Greyson while he was in Gable as Henry. Like Claire, he had a difficult time believing the guy had killed his boss in Colorado. But Jackson also reminded Claire that his personal opinion didn't matter. The truth was, Greyson had fled his home after being questioned by police. Just last week, Jackson had made some phone calls to the Denver police department and learned that DNA had recently been recovered at the crime scene. They didn't know whose DNA it was yet, but, as Jackson pointed out, if Greyson was innocent the easy solution would be to provide a DNA sample and clear his name.

The DEA had asked Gable Police to keep an eye on Chum. The theory was that placing a federal agent in plain sight in such a small town would be too obvious and counterproductive. Instead, Adler PD tracked him when he was in the city and working at Mecca Warehouse. The Gable Police did the same when Chum was in their territory. Agent Delia DeMarco called to check in on occasion.

Chief Perkins assigned Jackson the task of watching Chum while he was in Gable, but there hadn't been much to report since the dust had cleared. Maddison still lived in the big, recently remodeled home in the country, but Chum had moved to Adler after getting the divorce papers. It was painfully obvious to everyone—the police, the DEA, his wife, the prosecutor and the entire population of Gable—that Tom Chumansky was a criminal. Yet, no one could do a thing about it.

As for Gable, there was now an aura of suspicion that seemed to hang over the small, previously trusting community. Everyone in town was on edge. For weeks, the only conversations that took place inside Stubby's were about the murders. No one would ask Claire about it while she was working, but it was clear to her by the expressions on her customers' faces that they were thinking about it when she refilled their water or brought them the check.

Life had not exactly returned to normal for Claire. She'd been suffering from severe insomnia. When she finally was lucky enough to fall asleep, she'd often wake up shortly thereafter courtesy of a nightmare. Claire eventually made a trip to her doctor in Adler, who prescribed some sleeping pills and also referred her to a psychologist.

What once was Claire's daily routine of three cigarettes had turned into a full-blown, pack-a-day habit. She had done her best to curb the alcohol intake, allowing herself one glass of wine at night before taking the sleeping pill, convinced it would help her calm down just a little bit more. At the root of it all, Claire had found it impossible to clear her head of the gruesome snapshots that remained etched in her memory.

"People can't witness the things you did without it affecting them, unless they're sociopaths," her therapist, Dr. Sherrie Hammond, told Claire during their first session together. "You can't 'unsee' something. There's no erase button for the brain. That's why you feel so overwhelmed. You need to talk about what you saw and accept that it happened in your presence. Once you do, your mind will process the memory differently than it has been, in a much safer way."

Dr. Hammond didn't have the stereotypical couch in her office. She did have a recliner, though, and Claire took full advantage of it during her sessions with Hammond. Most of the time doctor and patient would have no eye contact during their conversations. This was because in the middle of their first meeting, Claire discovered Dr. Hammond had a nervous facial tic. Every few sentences while Claire was speaking, Hammond would unexpectedly get a wide-eyed look for a split second and then return to normal. Claire found her shrink's "surprise eyes" annoying and distracting. Although she didn't mention it to Dr. Hammond, she effectively solved the problem with the recliner. Claire would stare at the ceiling with the chair reclined as far back as it would go, pretending she was talking to herself instead of a professional. This worked well as far as she was concerned because Dr. Hammond never uttered the ridiculous phrase, "How does that make you feel?" during their talks. In fact, she didn't ask many questions at all. It was mostly phrases like, "Tell me about...," an occasional "Hmmm" or "Uh-huh," along with several recaps to show she was listening.

But there would be no therapy session today. No waiting tables and no tips, either. Stubby's was closed due to the winter storm. And there would be no cigarettes since Claire wasn't allowed to smoke in her mother's house. It was too cold and snowy to do much of anything today. The best she could hope for was a long nap or two and some soap operas in between. Today would be another day of remembering what had happened and wondering just why the hell she couldn't stop thinking about the man she knew as Henry Fields.

XII

"Just so we're clear, Agent Sheehan. I don't expect this to work," Frank Greyson said as he and his wife walked out the door to the front steps of their house. They had gathered in the living room and watched through the picture window as the four local television stations arrived with enough lights, cameras, and microphones to shoot a boy band video.

Chase wasn't fazed by Mr. Greyson's comment. "We have nothing to lose by trying," he said as they stepped out to the makeshift press conference. The weather in Colorado had been unusually mild for December, making it an easy choice to have the gathering outdoors rather than search for an indoor location. Wearing his navy FBI windbreaker, Chase squeezed between the Greysons and spoke to the media first.

"Thank you for coming today. My name is Agent Chase Sheehan of the Federal Bureau of Investigation. I am leading the investigation of the Otto Clevinger homicide as well as the disappearance of Barrett Greyson. As you may have heard, Barrett Greyson was recently sighted in Iowa. His identity was confirmed through fingerprints, but only after he disappeared again. Now that we know he is alive, his parents, here next to me, have agreed to hold this short press conference to read a statement."

Chase took a step back and held his hands out, signaling the husband and wife to step closer to the microphones held in front of them. Frank Greyson unfolded a piece of paper containing two paragraphs he had written while waiting for the media to arrive on his front lawn. He held his wife's hand while he read.

"Three months ago my wife and I were relieved to learn that our son, Barrett, was still alive. We are so grateful, in fact, that we called you here today to help us get the word out, to ask our son to come home."

Mr. Greyson paused for a moment. He then looked straight ahead and directly into the nearest camera before speaking again. As he did, the other TV station's cameramen frantically tried to squeeze into position for a better shot.

"Please come home, Barrett. We love you and miss you. We will get this situation sorted out and go on with our lives. We can't do this unless you come home. Your mother and I just want to help."

Mr. Greyson stopped speaking directly into the camera and addressed the entire congregation standing in his yard.

"Thank you," he said.

The instant Frank Greyson ended his statement, nine television and radio reporters spoke at the same time, asking the first question on their lists. The noise rendered individual questions indiscernible, but one correspondent was smart enough to wait until the others had finished before asking his question, loud and clear.

"Did your son murder Otto Clevinger?"

Chase quickly stepped forward again. "I didn't say the Greysons would be answering questions," he said. He leaned into Frank Greyson's ear and spoke softly. "You don't have to say another word. This isn't part of our agreement."

Mr. Greyson nodded his head at Chase and then looked at the reporter. "No. Barrett didn't kill Otto Clevinger," he answered.

"How can you be sure?" another reporter asked.

"He doesn't have it in him," Greyson responded.

Yet another reporter, a woman, piped up immediately. "Are you aware that the FBI is having DNA from the murder scene evaluated right now that could link your son to the crime?"

Mr. and Mrs. Greyson both turned and looked at Chase with question marks in their eyes.

"Okay, that's enough. Thank you for coming and...helping," Chase told the reporters and cameramen as he ushered the Greysons back inside their house.

Goddamn leaks, Chase thought. No one can keep a secret anymore.

When the front door closed, Mrs. Greyson spoke first. "DNA? Is that true?"

Chase looked at them both and sighed. He couldn't lie now. What would be the point? "Yes, but it's not as simple as she made it sound," he explained. "It's true that we did discover some DNA at the scene that wasn't Clevinger's."

"You didn't think it would be a good idea to tell us this?" she asked. "Why wouldn't you share this with us?"

Mr. Greyson didn't wait for Chase to answer. "Because if he had it would've risked us not doing the press conference," he informed his wife.

Chase folded his hands and looked down at his shoes.

"Why? Why would that make a difference?" Mrs. Greyson asked desperately, sure that her husband was onto something.

Chase looked up at the Greysons but still did not speak. He hated this crap.

"You don't want to tell her?" Mr. Greyson asked him.

The FBI agent finally responded. "You seem to have all the answers. Feel free," Chase said, placing his hands on his hips.

Mr. Greyson kept his gaze on Chase while he answered his wife's question. "He needs a sample of Barrett's DNA to compare to the DNA they found."

Mrs. Greyson's jaw dropped open. She glared at Chase but backed away from him at the same time. "You tricked us!"

she shrieked.

Chase could no longer contain his frustration. "If you're so sure of his innocence..." he muttered, letting them finish the sentence in their heads.

"Get out," Mrs. Greyson snarled, pointing a finger at Chase. She didn't say it loudly, but he knew he had worn out his welcome in the Greyson household, for now, anyway.

Chase drove his rental car down the street and out of sight. He parked a block and a half from the Greysons' home, where the media was continuing to pack up before heading to their respective studios for editing.

Chase had separated his emotions from his work a long time ago. Sure, the Greysons were pissed, but he was just doing his job. Screw them, he thought. They're so sure he's innocent, let him come home and prove it.

He plugged his earphones into his smartphone and opened an FBI surveillance application. As he continued to glance down Rockland Drive in the direction of the Greyson house, he listened intently to what was being said inside it.

"You're going to be late for your appointment, Frank."

"It's not like I'm in a hurry to get there."

"I know, honey. But..."

"I didn't mean it that way. We're going to do everything we can to make this nightmare go away. Come on, let's get going."

"I'm trying to figure out what we did to deserve two nightmares at one time in this family..."

Ella Greyson's voice trailed off as she and her husband exited their house through the garage. Chase could hear the garage door going up and the car engine turning over. He pulled the earphones out of his ears and unplugged them from his phone. He then slouched down as the Greysons' black SUV drove past him. After waiting an additional five seconds, he pulled out and followed the vehicle from a distance.

The surveillance bug Chase had dropped inside a

potted plant in the Greysons' living room was tiny, extremely powerful, and would never be found because it would disintegrate within twenty-four hours. That meant if he felt he needed to do more eavesdropping after tomorrow, Chase would have to be granted access to the Greyson home again. He would first try the easy way, but in a worst-case scenario there were always alternative methods.

He followed the Greysons for three miles until their vehicle slowed down and pulled into an industrial park. Upon witnessing this, Chase entered the parking lot from the back end and watched as the couple parked their car. From his position he was able to view Frank and Ella Greyson as they strolled across the narrow drive and through the revolving door of an all glass building. Once they were inside, Chase deemed it safe to drive by and have a closer look. As he did, he could read the sign on the front of the building: McCoy Cancer & Research Center.

***

"I'm so glad you're still in business," the heavyset man told Chum as he flipped through the settings on the remote control of the 54" television.

"Why wouldn't I be?" Chum asked him without breaking eye contact with the remote.

"Oh, I just meant with the bad publicity and all," the man clarified. "You know, drug dealers and...murder." He whispered the last word as if it were dirty.

Chum turned to the man and smiled. "Hey, shit happens, right? I mean, what could I do? Some guy comes to town, rents my old house, and turns out to be a dealer who owed money to some Mexican thugs. Lesson learned."

The man nodded.

"And I guess maybe I should put up a fence, too," Chum added before changing the subject. "I'll tell you what. I'm going to call over a real man to help you with this TV. He knows more about them than I do, anyway."

Chum scanned the store and flagged down his main man from the adjacent aisle. Eddie Clark rushed to his boss's side.

"You see that limp?" Chum asked the customer. "That's called loyalty, right there. The man took a bullet to the leg for all of us. Probably saved our lives. Have you met Fast Eddie Clark?"

After introducing the two men, Chum made his way to the back of the Mecca Warehouse store and entered his office. He sat down in the chair and began thumbing through some paperwork. Tom Chumansky had been out of sorts for the last few months. He wasn't sure which of the recent events were affecting him the most: a baby on the way, a divorce, a new home, and there was still that damned money.

From under a pile of papers the sound of the Spin Doctors song "Little Miss Can't Be Wrong" could be heard. Chum shuffled them around and found his singing mobile phone. The melody told him his ex-wife was calling.

"I didn't expect to hear from you so soon," he said when he answered. "Are you ready to get remarried?"

Maddison ignored the question. "Why don't you ever answer my text messages?" she asked him.

"What? I don't know. I just sat down and my phone was buried. I didn't know you had sent me one."

"Would you come outside to my car, please? I have something for you."

"You didn't just have the baby out there, did you?" Chum asked.

"Just get out here, peanut gallery."

Chum grabbed his winter coat from the back of his chair and hustled to the parking lot. It had been a struggle to accept the fact that Maddison no longer laughed at anything he said, no matter how hard he tried. His sense of humor was the thing that had won her over years ago. When he proposed he had done it by luring her to the store's television section. The same video was playing on all of the TVs. It showed Chum wearing only a barrel and talking about how he wasn't embarrassed to be himself around the love of his life, Maddison. On the video, he opened up a ring box before the screen went black. When Maddison turned around, Chum was standing behind her, wearing only the barrel and holding the open ring box. He asked her to marry him, she said "yes," and the customers in the store went wild with applause. Things were good for the couple for quite some time. Chum's laid-back attitude and Maddison's sensible thinking had been a strong combination. The key had been keeping his illegal activities off of Maddison's radar screen. When she found out, there was nothing Chum could say or do to change her mind.

When he reached his ex-wife's car, he joined her by sitting in the passenger seat. "What's up?" he asked. "Early Christmas gift, maybe?"

Maddison shook her head and sighed. "Tom, no offense. But shut up and just do some listening for a change, okay?"

Chum didn't respond. It was difficult for him to not make another cheesy joke like pretending to zip his lips. Instead, he gave his former wife his undivided attention.

"I did my part," Maddison began. "I played dumb and kept quiet about your illegal shenanigans, both to the cops and during the divorce. You got Marty killed, Tom. You may as well have pulled the trigger yourself. Eddie took a bullet for you and you could've stopped it from happening. You almost let them put a bullet in my head, too. It's obvious to me now that I never really knew you. But for the sake of our child having both a mother and a father, I'm giving you the chance to get your shit together. God knows I wouldn't have let you impregnate me if I'd known what you were doing. But now that I do know, I want it to end."

Chum swallowed hard and gave a slight nod of the head.

"I mean it," Maddison reiterated. "It has already cost you your marriage. Don't let it cost you fatherhood, too."

"I get it," Chum conceded.

"There's one more thing," Maddison added. Chum waited in silence for her to continue. "How much money do you have hidden and where is it?

Chum shook his head. "You never cease to amaze me, Maddy."

"I'm trying to help," she said.

"I don't understand how me telling you about this—"

Maddison didn't let him finish. "Maybe you should answer the questions first and then I'll explain."

Chum stared at her in rare silence.

"What? You don't trust me? That's hilarious, Tom."

"That's not it, babe," Chum said. "I realize I've made my own bed here. But you've got the house, you've got the child, and I'll be supporting both of you for the next two decades. I'm accepting it. Can't you just leave that ghost alone? Hasn't it caused enough anguish?"

"I probably should," Maddison agreed. She gazed into her ex-husband's eyes and leaned in his direction. "You still haven't answered me."

"Fine," Chum replied. "Two hundred seventy-three grand."

"Where is it?"

"Can you tell me why you want to know, first?"

"Has it moved since the night of the incident?"

"No."

"That's what I thought. Can't get to it, can you?"

"It's kind of hard when you're being escorted by Mayberry's finest everywhere you go." He pointed with his thumb over his shoulder when he said this.

"Yes, I noticed the police car when I pulled in," Maddison admitted.

"You'd have to be blind not to."

"I want to help you get the money, Tom. And then I want you to put half of it away for your child's education." Chum considered this as Maddison continued speaking. "I'd like to try and lead our child down a different road than us and hopefully provide him or her with a college education."

"And you want to pay for it with drug money? I can already afford to send the kid to school, Maddy."

Maddison scowled. "Which raises the question of why you felt the need to supplement your income by selling drugs in the first place! Now do you want to explain that to me or are you going to tell me where the money is so I can help you get it back?"

Chum sighed for what seemed like the millionth time in the past ten minutes. "It's in the woods behind the house. I have GPS coordinates. It's buried."

Maddison nodded and then smiled as he continued with more questions of his own.

"What about the other half of the money?" Chum asked her. "What are we doing with that?"

"My dearest ex-husband," she said, placing a hand on his cheek, "I'm not a total bitch. The other half is for you to keep."

Chum put his hand on top of hers. "I miss you, Maddison," he whispered to her.

She thought about asking him whether there was cocaine buried with the money but decided she didn't want to know.

***

Barrett Greyson entered the seedy lounge and took a seat at the bar. He had been instructed to sit there and wait patiently, that the man who could help him out would approach when the time was right. The bartender spotted Barrett immediately.

"What can I get for you, Boss?"

"Club soda," he replied.

"You got it," the bartender said. He was slightly shorter than Barrett, average build, with jet black hair slicked back and two full tattoo sleeves.

"What's going on tonight, Boss?"

Again with the boss thing? Barrett thought to himself. "Just hanging out after work," he explained. Why say too much?

"Cool. My name's Floyd," the bartender said, stretching his right hand and arm across the bar. Barrett hesitated for a split second before responding. One thing he had learned during his travels was that anonymity in a bar had become a thing of the past. Many bartenders were now introducing themselves to the patrons and, of course, expecting reciprocation.

"Cody," Barrett said as he shook Floyd's hand. It was the first name that popped into his head other than Henry or Barrett.

"Great to meet you, Cody. If you need anything else just flag me down," Floyd said and disappeared to the back.

Barrett wasn't sure how his connection was supposed to find him, but the toothless truck driver insisted things would be set up for his favorite forklift driver.

"I know this guy here in Caribou," the driver had said one day, very randomly. "He can get anything done for you, for a price."

Barrett was immediately intrigued by this notion. After all, he had a lengthy wish list with a major priority or two at the very top. "Anything?" he had asked the driver.

"I've never heard of him failing yet."

And just like that, here Barrett was, at the Main Street Bar and Grill, waiting patiently for the genie in a bottle to appear. He stirred and sipped his drink while intermittently surveying the establishment. There was a dartboard in one corner and a pinball machine in another. A jukebox sat near the front door. The only other customers in the joint were two couples sitting at a table and three men sitting together at the bar, jawing about something Barrett didn't care to pay attention to.

He continued to sit and wait with no idea exactly how long he was supposed to do so. Maybe the entire thing was a joke. Truck drivers were a strange breed. On occasion, one would make a pit stop at a casino, get drunk, and forget to deliver a load for several days. Others would tell the consignee they would be there in five hours but instead would end up neglecting the commitment once they made it to their girlfriend's bed. At any moment a truck driver's cell phone could mysteriously lose its signal for hours. Things didn't used to be this bad in the transportation industry before the government began regulating the number of hours of sleep a driver was required to have in a twenty-four-hour period. When the process became controlled, the need for drivers increased exponentially across the country and all kinds of derelicts came out of the woods to get a commercial driver's license. Barrett knew all of this long before he found work at Marble Industries thanks to his father's lengthy career in logistics operations.

After forty-five minutes of sitting at the bar, Barrett was beginning to wonder if he had been duped. It was only nine thirty on a Tuesday night and the entire place had emptied. As far as he could tell, Barrett was now alone with Floyd, the bartender.

"Another soda?" Floyd asked his only customer.

"Nah, three is my limit. I'll be up all night pissing as it is," Barrett explained.

Floyd didn't respond. Instead he moved his way around the bar and behind Barrett, walking to the door and locking it from the inside.

"Sorry. I didn't realize you were closing," Barrett said, reaching into his pocket for some cash. "I can head out."

Floyd strolled back to his place behind the bar and put his hands out in front of him, palms up, and spoke. "Why would you want to leave when you haven't gotten what you came here for?"

Barrett stopped all movement and stared hard into Floyd's eyes. The bartender smirked.

Holy crap, Barrett thought to himself. He's been the guy all along.

Floyd rested his elbows on the bar and leaned forward, stretching his legs out behind him.

"We're alone. What can I do for you?" he asked. Despite the fact no one was around, the volume of his voice had dropped significantly. As Barrett processed what was happening, he shook his head from side to side like a dog shaking off some unwanted touching.

"How did you know?" he asked.

Floyd backed off the bar and threw his arms into the air. "Man, it's what I do."

Barrett stared at the empty glass in front of him. After a moment of silence, he looked up at Floyd. "Canada," Barrett muttered. He assumed he didn't need to say more.

"Happens to be one of my specialties," Floyd said. "How much time can you give me?"

"How much are we talking?" Barrett asked.

"Depends on how much time you've got."

"I've got time."

"I don't ask people anything about their situation, so you're going to need to hear me out. Besides, I don't want to know your situation. Listen up to the options and then tell me what you want to do," Floyd said evenly. Barrett doubted Floyd was his real name, and he was pretty sure Floyd knew Cody wasn't Barrett's real name either. Not that Floyd wanted to know.

"It can be a tricky pain in the ass to set someone up to simply drive into Canada with the proper documentation if he's on the run and using an alias. Obviously most people are. Again, I'm not asking, so don't tell me. I'm not saying it can't be done, but there is a big risk. Plus, it's time consuming to tie up all the loose ends. And more expensive. What I do for most people instead is get them inside a cargo trailer."

"Aren't those checked by customs?" Barrett asked, already knowing the answer.

"Yes, well there's more to it than just walking inside a trailer and going for a ride," Floyd continued. "I don't go into details beforehand, but I can assure you this method has never failed."

"How much for getting on a trailer?" Barrett inquired, cringing as he waited for the answer.

"Four thousand. No refunds. If you chicken out, too bad," Floyd elaborated. He wasn't a tough-looking guy by any stretch of the imagination, but he spoke with plenty of confidence.

"How do I know you're not setting me up?"

"You don't. All I can do is look you in the eye and tell you it's real. If you think you have a better option, something you're more comfortable with, no skin off my back."

Barrett noticed Floyd hadn't called him "Boss" or "Cody" one time since he had locked the door. This guy was as serious as they come. There wasn't a lot of reason to doubt him. He wanted as little to do with Barrett as possible. It was a nice change of pace and just the way Barrett liked it.

"I'm going to need some time to think about this," Barrett declared. "Can I get back to you?"

"Of course. But when you come back you need to do things the same way you did tonight," Floyd said.

"Basically, wait...right?" Barrett assumed he understood, but the way the last hour had gone he couldn't be too sure.

"That'll do," Floyd confirmed.

"You really have this entire operation down pat, don't

you?" Barrett asked.

Floyd ignored the question and made his way around the bar. "I'll let you out," he said. His keys jingled as he pulled them from his pocket. Realizing the meeting had been adjourned, Barrett laid a few dollars on the bar next to his empty glass before moving to the door.

"Have a good night, Boss," Floyd said as he ushered Barrett out the door.

Barrett shook his head and let out a soft chuckle as the cold nor'easter wind punished his face. The door shut behind him, and Barrett headed toward his vehicle in the tiny parking lot. He hoped the thing would start. There had been mornings recently when Barrett thought he might need to take the bus to work. But so far the Taurus had been a champ in Caribou's winter weather. After leaving Gable, Barrett had sold off the Civic in Paducah, Kentucky. Then he took a Greyhound bus to Pittsburgh where he purchased the 2002 Ford Taurus and drove it all the way to Maine. He could have easily bought another car in Kentucky, but Barrett figured dumping one car and picking up another in the same place could come back to haunt him if he was being tracked. He was always trying to think at least one step ahead of the authorities, just in case.

Of course, Barrett wasn't certain he was even being pursued. When he left Colorado in the middle of the night approximately four months ago, he saw no signs of police surveillance. But that was the point. He was trying to stay ahead of them; he assumed the heat was coming. After driving for three weeks in what amounted to a giant half oval—Denver, Colorado Springs, Amarillo, Dallas, Fort Smith, Kansas City—Barrett grew tired of the road and on a whim picked Gable, Iowa, as his new home. The Civic he was driving when he arrived there had been purchased in Nowhere, Texas, after dumping the car he had fled Colorado in.

Every move Barrett had made since leaving his home was calculated, but that all went to hell in a handbasket in Gable. The small town had certainly made it difficult to stay under the radar: the car accident, the TV news, Chum's party and his side business, and Claire. Barrett didn't want to leave without saying goodbye to the one friend he had made in Iowa, but there had been no choice. He knew his fingerprints were all over the farmhouse and more than likely so was his DNA. If he had stayed it would only have been a matter of time before the authorities began asking questions "Henry Fields" couldn't answer. They'd dig deeper and eventually Barrett would find himself in a heap of trouble, maybe even arrested. Leaving that night was his best chance at avoiding such a fate.

And now the opportunity to get into Canada, presumably undetected, had presented itself. Maybe he could leave this entire nightmare behind. It wasn't ideal, but it was survival. The thought of spending even one day in prison did not appeal to Barrett. He'd rather never see his family again than take such a risk. At least that's what he kept telling himself during his long drives across the country.

As far as Barrett could tell, Floyd was the real deal. Four thousand dollars would put a dent in his savings, but it was still less than Barrett initially thought it would cost him to get across the border. When he left Colorado the only money he'd brought with him had been untraceable: a backpack full of cash he had been hiding and adding to since he was a teenager. He had been saving it for an emergency. This was undoubtedly an emergency.

Until now he had never had an interest in going to Canada. His father had traveled to Maligne Lake in Alberta once for a fishing trip with some friends when his oldest son was still quite young. The only thing five-year-old Barrett remembered was how scruffy his father's unshaven face looked when he returned ten days later.

Oh Canada, this will be interesting, Barrett thought to himself with the melody of the Canadian national anthem running through his head. He scratched his own unshaven chin as he drove through the cold winter evening to his apartment.

XIII

The day after the snowstorm, Claire was scheduled to be off from work, but her Aunt Carol asked her to bartend until three thirty. This worked out perfectly as it gave Claire a chance to make up some hours and tips and still make it to her appointment with Dr. Hammond at four thirty.

Bartending during the day at Stubby's primarily consisted of waiting on three tables and anyone who elected to sit at the bar. Beer could be sold at any time, so it was always fun for Claire to see how early the first beer of the day was served.

At three twenty-five she rushed home for a quick shower and drove to Adler for her session with Hammond. She arrived ten minutes early and after checking in sat down in the waiting room. Claire was always less than thrilled to be seen by patients who were leaving. The only saving grace was that Claire was able to see them, too. She wondered if it was normal to compare her own sanity to others' just by sizing them up for a few seconds.

Today a man in his early forties came out of the office. His brown hair was a mess and his eyes were red and moist. He wore a camouflage jacket and high-top sneakers, and he smelled like a combination of deodorant and incense. Today would be one of those days where Claire would feel superior to the opening act. No matter what happened during her session with Hammond, she would walk out of the building knowing she was at least in better shape than that guy.

Dr. Hammond held the door open for Claire. When it

closed behind them she spoke.

"How are we doing today?" she inquired.

"Okay, I guess," Claire replied although she hadn't really given it much thought. The two walked down the hallway to the psychologist's private office. Claire found her place in the recliner and immediately tilted it back all the way.

"Ready to go already?" Hammond asked.

"It's my dime, isn't it?" Claire answered. The copay was starting to suck her dry. Claire was beginning to wonder if she should get another job. There was also the option of ending the therapy. Claire wasn't even sure it was doing her any good.

"That it is," the psychologist agreed. She pulled out her laptop, notebook, and pen. "What's on your mind?"

Claire sighed. It usually took her a while to begin spilling her guts. "Same old shit, really," she began.

"How are you sleeping?"

"About the same. I don't have any trouble falling asleep, but if I wake up in the middle of the night I'm screwed," Claire said.

"What's keeping you awake?"

"Nightmares, visions of death."

"This is only your third session. It's going to get better," Dr. Hammond tried to reassure her.

"When?"

"When are you going to accept that it happened?" Hammond inquired.

"I'm trying, but it's a lot easier for you to say it than it is for me to actually do it," Claire remarked with another sigh. She stared at the ceiling.

"Claire, there is something we could try," Dr. Hammond offered. "Do you like to write?"

"I don't know. Probably not for fun."

"Well, this wouldn't be for fun," Hammond explained,

pulling a spiral-bound notebook from her desk and tossing it on Claire's lap. The sensation caused Claire to immediately sit up in the recliner. "This will be for therapy."

Claire thumbed through the empty notebook and glared across the room at her shrink. "What am I supposed to do, write some 'See Spot Run' books?"

"No. You're going to reprogram how your brain processes what you witnessed," Dr. Hammond explained.

"By writing about it?"

"Yes."

Claire paused before speaking again. "This is all a bunch of voodoo mumbo jumbo," she grumbled.

"No, it's not, Claire," Hammond said. "It's practically common sense. If you write about it every day you will force your mind to accept it as a part of you instead of trying to hide it in your subconscious. It's your subconscious that's rearing its ugly head in the middle of the night. You've got to force it out."

"While I'm awake?"

"Especially while you're awake."

Silence filled the room as neither woman spoke for thirty seconds.

"What do you have to lose by trying?" Dr. Hammond asked.

"Will you see what I write?"

"Only if you want me to."

"Yeah, probably not then," Claire said. "Okay. I guess I'll try it."

"Good idea," Hammond said.

"That's why you get paid the big money," Claire commented. Before her psychologist had a chance to reply, she spoke again. "Speaking of money, can we get back to my session of unloading before the timer goes off?"

***

When the session wrapped up, Dr. Hammond reminded Claire to write whenever she could and to read what she had written when she was finished. Out loud was the best method, but reading to herself would also work, if necessary.

Claire didn't give the writing therapy much thought as she drove to the nearest grocery store to pick up bread and milk at her mother's request. She pulled into the snow-covered parking lot, got out of her car, and carefully walked through the automatic doors. As always, it took her a few seconds to gather her bearings and remember which direction she should head first. After entering aisle four and searching for the best deal she could find on a loaf of bread, Claire headed to the dairy section and grabbed a gallon of milk. On her way back to the front of the store she picked out a lime green spiral-bound notebook from the discount section. She had turned down the one Hammond had thrown to her during their session because she didn't like the bright red color. The self-checkout lanes were not busy, so she could bag and pay for her items without waiting in line.

Ready to make the short trek back to Gable, Claire shuffled through the parking lot to her car. As she was getting in, she heard a car door shut loudly and glanced to the adjacent aisle in the direction of the sound. When she did, Claire noticed a pregnant woman dropping a mobile phone into her purse. For a moment it seemed surreal to Claire. She hadn't seen the woman for more than three months.

"Maddison!" she bellowed across the lot.

The woman turned her head and looked at Claire, who was already moving toward her. "Hey," Maddison said with a smile. "How are you?"

The two women shared a brief embrace before continuing to speak.

"You look fantastic!" Claire exclaimed. "How far along are you?" She took a step back to get a bird's-eye view of Maddison's baby bump.

"About five months," she replied. "Supposed to be due in April."

"Well, congratulations," Claire said, realizing she didn't know what to say next. Should she bring up Chum? Should she say anything else at all? Maddison seemed preoccupied. Maybe it would be best to say goodbye and move on. Before Claire could make a decision, Maddison spoke again.

"How are things for you?" she asked.

Claire brushed her hair out of her face before answering. "Oh, fine," she lied. "You know, one day at a time."

Maddison nodded. "Yes, I know that all too well," she admitted. She looked at the ground before speaking again. "You know Tom and I are divorced," she continued.

"Yes. Well, I had heard it was happening but didn't know if it was official yet," Claire explained. She wasn't sure if she was being asked a question or told a fact, so she thought it best to clarify.

"Last Friday," Maddison told her.

"That was fast," Claire observed. "Doesn't it usually take longer?"

Maddison smiled and patted her pregnant belly. "I have a bargaining chip," she said. The two shared a quick laugh.

"It's kind of cold out here," Claire said. "Probably not good for you or your baby. I'll let you get to your business."

"We should get together sometime," Maddison suggested.

The offer surprised Claire, but she recovered quickly. "Yeah, that would be great," she agreed, assuming it was just lip service. There was a slight pause as the two smiled nervously at each other.

"Well, I guess I'll see you around sometime," Claire said as she began to move in the direction of her car.

"Claire?"

"Yeah?"

"Can I get your number so we can get together?"

"Oh yes, of course," Claire replied as Maddison pulled her phone from her purse. The two ladies exchanged numbers and again embraced briefly before parting ways.

She's either really good at faking it or she actually wants to hang out, Claire thought to herself on the drive back to Gable. She couldn't imagine what it must be like to be recently divorced and pregnant with a first child. Maybe Maddison just needed a friend. They were both small town girls and probably had a lot in common. But they were also fifteen years apart in age and at different stages of their lives. After some consideration, Claire decided this didn't really matter. Heck, it might even turn out to be therapeutic to spend some time with someone else who witnessed the same violence she did.

***

Barrett drove the forklift up the aisle and turned left at row twenty seven. He found the product listed on the order form attached to his clipboard and loaded the pallet onto the forks. After reversing direction, he drove the forklift back up the aisle and to the outdoor section of the loading dock. He placed the pallet on the truck, jumped off the forklift, and asked the truck driver to sign the paperwork. After giving the driver his copy, Barrett stepped inside the shipping office to warm up. It wasn't the coldest day of the month, but it wasn't a warm one, either. The weather never seemed like this in Colorado. The winters in Maine were blustery, cold, and it probably wouldn't stop snowing until June. Barrett knew it wouldn't be any better in Canada.

He moved to the small space heater next to the shipping desk where Ernie was sitting, typing an email. Barrett removed his gloves and blew into his hands before holding the palms near the heater. When he finished his email, Ernie turned to Barrett.

"Danny boy, it completely slipped my mind earlier today but I've got a present for you," he announced. "Let's go out to my truck and put it in your car."

Going back outside was not at the top Barrett's to-do list at the moment, but it was the end of the day and he was, after all, receiving a gift. The two men walked down the dock ramp and over to the chain-link fence where their vehicles were parked. Ernie reached into the backseat of his extended cab pickup truck with both hands and pulled out a twenty-two-inch flat screen television.

"It's not very big, but hopefully it'll provide you with some entertainment," Ernie said with a toothy grin.

Barrett hadn't seen this coming. Ernie was always nice to him, but he certainly didn't give off the consistent warm and fuzzy vibes of friendship.

"Wow, I don't know what to say," Barrett said. "This wasn't necessary, but thank you very much. What can I do for you in return?" It was an awkward moment for Barrett, not just because he was on the run and using an alias, but also because it was in his nature to assume Ernie had ulterior motives.

"How about opening your car door?" Ernie suggested. "This thing ain't heavy, but it's cold out here."

Barrett was so consumed by the act of kindness he forgot he was standing outside in the bitter cold staring at his boss holding a TV. He opened his car's back door and let Ernie slide the set inside.

"You didn't go out and buy that for me, did you?" Barrett asked, although he was fairly certain he already knew the answer judging by the scratches on it.

"Ha!" Ernie responded. "Are you kidding? I don't like you that much." They both chuckled as they tracked back up the ramp and into the office. "My wife and I replaced our bedroom TV with a new thirty-two inch," Ernie continued. "An early Christmas present to each other. And then I remembered you had told me you didn't own a TV."

"Well, I can't thank you enough, Ernie," Barrett reiterated. He wondered if he'd be able to get any of the local channels to work without a satellite or a cable subscription. There was no sense in spending money on something like that, especially when he didn't plan on being in Caribou much longer. The only television Barrett had watched in the last several months was in the roadside motels he stayed in during his travels.

"There is one thing you can do for me in return," Ernie said as he removed his coat and hung it over his desk chair.

"What's that?" Barrett asked, hoping it wasn't something too ridiculous. It wasn't like he had asked for a TV.

"Don't screw me over," Ernie replied.

"How so?" Barrett inquired, raising an eyebrow.

"Let me put it to you this way, Dan," Ernie began. "Some people in this world don't take their jobs seriously. Sometimes they flake out and disappear. You don't seem like that type, so don't get me wrong. I just don't want to wake up one day and not have you be here for me. This is the busiest time of year and it's taken me a long time to get corporate to let me have some help. So...please don't flake out on me, okay?"

Barrett managed a meager smile before responding. "Sure. Of course."

***

Chase sat in the hotel lobby and dialed a number on his mobile phone. As he waited for an answer, he watched an elderly couple make their way to the front desk to check in.

"Hello?" Chase heard a female voice on the other end of the line.

"Good afternoon, Mrs. Greyson. This is Agent Sheehan," Chase announced. He continued speaking before she had a chance to yell at him. "I need to speak to your husband briefly, if I could please."

"Just a minute," she said dryly.

Still pissed, Chase thought to himself. He wasn't surprised. He wondered how angry she'd be if she knew about the bug that was now fertilizing one of her plants.

"This is Frank," a man's voice said through the phone.

"Mr. Greyson, this is Agent Sheehan. I'm sorry to bother you but I need to ask for your cooperation."

"Another favor, Agent?"

"Honestly, you'd be doing yourself a favor," Chase explained.

"And how would that be?" Greyson asked.

"I have in my hand right now a federal search warrant for Barrett's condo," Chase said, holding the paperwork in front of his face as if he were showing it to Mr. Greyson through the phone.

"A search warrant?" Frank Greyson said. "What for?"

Chase couldn't resist the temptation to poke a little fun at the absurdity of the question. "To...search..."

"You know what I mean, Sheehan." Greyson responded. He wasn't angry, but it was clear to Chase he shouldn't push his luck after that one. When people called him by his last name without saying "Agent" first, he knew it was time to put his game face on. Maybe it was his age or maybe it was the stress, but sometimes Chase had a difficult time taking his job too seriously. He was told during his time at the academy this type of attitude could get him in serious trouble, possibly killed, if he didn't keep his guard up at all times. Chase liked to think of it as "guarded fun." He was a good FBI agent and he knew it. So what if he got a little surly every once in a while?

"The police have already been in there once," Mr. Greyson continued. "They didn't find anything."

"This search warrant is a little different than that early investigation," Chase explained.

"I don't understand," Mr. Greyson said.

"Mr. Greyson, I'm not trying to be rude when I tell you...I'm not really at liberty to say any more than I already have," Chase explained.

"Then why are you calling me?"

"To offer you the chance to meet us there and open the door with a key," Chase said. "It's a lot easier and less of a hassle for you than having to clean up the splinters of a busted in front door," he added.

There was silence on the phone. Chase didn't fill it with any senseless talk. He waited patiently for Frank Greyson to resume speaking.

"What time?" Greyson inquired when he finally spoke again.

"We're ready now so you just tell me when you can be there," Chase answered.

"Give me an hour," Greyson abruptly replied and hung up the phone. Chase held his phone away from his face and looked at the screen to confirm he had just been hung up on. With a smug grin on his face, he dialed another number and instructed the Denver FBI office to send a standby team to Barrett Greyson's residence on Wright Street in the suburb of Lakewood. As he walked through the hotel parking lot to his vehicle, Chase wondered how Greyson would react when he found out the search warrant was for his son's DNA. The task itself should be a smooth one and prove much easier than waiting for Barrett Greyson to return to Colorado. Convincing Mr. and Mrs. Greyson to do the press conference was more about keeping an eye on them than it was to convince their son to come home. A man who was intelligent and disciplined enough to know how to not be tracked while on the run wasn't going to return to the scene just because his parents asked him to. It wasn't likely, anyway.

Not long after beginning his drive to the condo, Chase's phone rang.

"Sheehan," he answered through the Bluetooth speaker system in his rental car. He was shocked he had gotten it to work. Usually a rental car's Bluetooth system was a disaster, but this one had been working just fine for him. All except for the caller ID, that is.

"What's up?" a female voice responded.

"Heading to Barrett Greyson's place to hunt me down some saliva," Chase informed her.

"Sounds like fun. Anything new with the case other than that?" she asked.

"Not really. What about on your end?"

"My guy in Iowa, Jackson, has been keeping an eye on Chumansky. But nothing has been happening. Kind of weird."

"I don't think that's weird at all, Sis," Chase told her. "He's laying low."

"I wouldn't have pegged him as being that smart," she said.

"It's like Dad always said: 'Even a retarded squirrel gets a nut every once in a while,'" Chase reminded his older sister, Delia DeMarco.

"Yeah. The problem is everybody the DEA guns for is a 'retarded squirrel,'" Agent DeMarco replied. "Do you really think Barrett Greyson killed his boss Clevinger?"

"How much more does it need to be spelled out for you, Dee? The guy took off after being questioned once by local police. One time! How many innocent people do that? And then he disappeared in the middle of the night from Podunk, Iowa, after being involved with a drug deal gone bad!"

"He wasn't involved in that!" Delia exclaimed.

"How the hell do you know?"

"Because the only person who's trying to say he was is Chumansky. Do you believe him?"

The rivalry between the two had been going on for what seemed like forever: academics, sports, their careers. It seemed they rarely agreed. But when push came to shove they still had plenty of brotherly and sisterly love for each other. They just liked to compete.

Chase paused before responding. "No," he remarked, knowing she had a point. "You're right. I don't know what the hell's going on. All I can do is hope there's a DNA match with whatever we find here at the condo."

"I'll keep you posted," Delia told him. "We'll figure this out, Chase. We will."

She was always the one to level off the mood when the victory had been proclaimed, regardless of the winner.

"All right," Chase agreed. "I'll let you know what happens."

They hung up the phone as Chase found a parking spot outside of Barrett Greyson's condominium building. Delia and Chase Sheehan were twins—peas in a pod. Delia was born a minute earlier than her brother and had been riding that train since the two were old enough to understand what it meant. But when she went through her divorce, Chase was the person who supported her the most. Their parents had been mystified at the idea of her not trying harder to make the marriage work. They were also, to this day, unaware of Delia's ex-husband's violent nature. Chase would never forget the time Delia called him for assistance at home and he found her on the couch holding an ice pack to her left eye. Even now, years later, it took every ounce of willpower in his body for Chase not to hunt down Daniel DeMarco and crush his skull into dust.

He left his car and walked to the FBI van that was parked in two spaces. Out of the corner of his eye he noticed Frank Greyson strolling in his direction from across the lot.

"Forgive me if I don't shake your hand, Agent Sheehan," Greyson greeted him.

Chase wasted no time worrying about the snub. "You ready to do this?" he replied.

Greyson nodded and began to walk up the stairs to his

son's residence. Chase and four other FBI personnel followed.

XIV

Claire sat on her bed and looked down at the words handwritten inside her crisp, new, lime green notebook. She took a sip of White Zinfandel before following Dr. Hammond's instructions of reading her words out loud.

"Having Henry there helped calm me down. I didn't realize how serious it was until the one man put a gun to Maddison's head when we were outside. When they took us into the house and sat us on the sofa I had a horrible knot in my stomach. I felt like I couldn't breathe. I held on to Henry's hand very tight. The one guy who seemed to want to stop anything bad from happening was the first person to be shot by his boss. I've seen dead people before, even watched a few pass away. But seeing someone shot in the head and fall lifeless to the ground with their eyes open is like nothing I have ever seen before. It was horrifying. I immediately wondered if he had a family who would miss him. I didn't want to look at his dead body, but I couldn't stop. It was at this point that I realized my instinct was right. This was not going to end well. When Marty was shot and killed it happened so fast I had a delayed reaction. My God, I barely knew him. But I had been talking to him off and on all evening. Now he was dead, right there on the couch next to us. Now I knew for sure I would be dying that night. But when Chum caved after Maddison's pregnancy announcement, there was a glimmer of hope. I didn't want Henry to leave me but if that was what had to happen, well, I didn't really have a choice. When he came back and drove the truck through the front of the house I didn't know what was happening. I saw Henry come in from the back and when he captured the two men holding us I felt like I was in a movie. I didn't know why he left so quickly after, though. I was shocked and hurt when he ended up disappearing. Really hurt. I thought there was a connection between us. Apparently not."

Claire placed the notebook on her nightstand. She put her winter coat on and stepped outside to have a quick drag or two of a cigarette. For eight thirty in December it was almost tolerable outside. No sooner had Claire thought this, when a push of winter wind swept across her mother's back door, sending a chill down her spine. She quickly put the cigarette out and went back inside the house, closing the door behind her.

Walking to the kitchen, she noticed her mother sitting in the living room, watching a Lifetime movie. The program had more than likely been recorded the previous weekend. Instead of going back to her room, Claire joined her mother on the couch.

"Those things are gonna kill you," Trish Mathison told her daughter without moving her eyes from the television. Her daughter responded dryly. It was a comment she had heard a thousand times in the past three months.

"So I've heard..."

Her mother was a woman of few words. She always acted like she wasn't paying attention to her surroundings but would later catch you off guard with comments. It was as if she had been tucked away in your back pocket the entire time.

Claire stared at the screen with her mother. She knew they both looked like zombies in a bad late-night movie. But it didn't matter. Life had already handed Claire her own little slice of hell before the incident. Now there were added ghosts and demons that had joined the group. The idea she had buried deep inside her that Henry—Barrett—would sweep her away to a new beginning had been swallowed up by deceit and God knows what else. She had once again fallen for a man's bullshit. This time it was...a murderer?

I should probably be writing all this in my notebook, Claire thought as she began to doze off.

***

Barrett once again sat on a stool in the Main Street Bar and Grill and waited for Floyd to pick the right moment. Tonight's crowd was a busy one compared to his last visit. This wouldn't have bothered Barrett so much if he didn't have a bag containing four thousand dollars in the trunk of his car in the parking lot. It was unlikely anything would happen to it, but there had been a lot of things happening to him recently that weren't "likely." These days Barrett couldn't be too sure.

This time he had been wise enough to show up later than he had previously. The idea of waiting around all night to spend four grand didn't appeal to Barrett.

After Barrett had spent about an hour nursing a club soda and eyeing Floyd, the bar began to clear out, as if by magic. When the last patrons exited, Floyd locked the door and returned to the bar where Barrett was seated.

"You're obviously here again because you want something," Floyd said as he poured himself a glass of water.

"Yes," Barrett answered him. "I'd like Canada for four thousand, please." He almost made a Jeopardy joke with the request but thought better of it.

Floyd took a swallow of water and set the glass on the bar between them. He spun it a couple of times before continuing. "You're not in a hurry, right?"

"Not yet."

"Good. I just need a few days. You have the money with you?"

Floyd grabbed the soda fountain gun and refilled Barrett's glass.

"Yeah. It's in my car," Barrett said with a nod in the

direction of the parking lot.

"Well, that's good. But not necessary," Floyd told him. "I don't make an exchange here like this." Barrett gave him a puzzled look and leaned back slightly from the bar. Floyd immediately recognized the concern and continued speaking. "Look...Cody," he said, the sarcasm so slight that even Barrett almost missed it, "I'm not going to stand here and be a salesman. You either want what I got or you don't. If you do, you're gonna have to trust me. You got better options? Go trust someone else. I don't have time to wine and dine you."

The two stared at each other from across the bar. It was a standoff, but not the physical kind.

"I'm listening," Barrett said.

***

"How is it possible there's not one speck of DNA in that condo?"

Chase stood inside the Denver division laboratory and glared at the three technicians as if it were their fault the residence was spotless.

"I don't know what to tell you," Ta Nguyen, the lead lab tech, answered him. "I've never seen anything quite like it myself," he continued.

"Damnit," Chase mumbled under his breath.

"We can run some more tests on the samples we took and see what else we can find, but there won't be any clean DNA. That ship has sailed," Ta explained.

"Do it," Chase said. He turned around to head downstairs and outside for a breath of fresh air but caught himself first. "Please," he added, spinning around to once again face the technicians. "Thank you."

The men nodded in response and strolled back to their spots in the lab. Sometimes Chase let his emotions take over, causing him to forget his manners and the fact that he was not the only one who wanted justice. On his way downstairs he dialed his sister again to give her an update.

"I'm on my way back to Iowa," Delia told her brother before giving him the opportunity to tell her why he was calling.

"Sounds like a ball," Chase said. "What for?"

"Devling wants me to see if I can find something. Anything. He's worried Jackson is missing something with his surveillance."

"I guess that makes sense," Chase stated. Devling, Chase knew, was David Devling, the sixty-three-year-old Special Agent in Charge of the DEA in Chicago. It seemed he was never going to retire, making his sister doubt her future in the Windy City.

"I suppose so." Delia sighed and then changed the subject. "So what do you know?"

Chase quickly told her about the DNA sweep and how they had come up empty.

"I've heard of leaving a crime scene clean, but an entire condo that's DNA-free? That's pretty unusual...isn't it?" Delia felt the need to clarify. She was more used to dealing with cocaine and heroin whereas Chase was the DNA and blood guy.

"Yeah, it is. Especially if he didn't commit a crime," Chase replied and then paused for a moment before adding, "Wouldn't you agree, Sis?"

Delia immediately comprehended what he was implying. "All right, smart ass. I get what you're saying. You make a good point," she acknowledged with a snicker. Her twin brother's sense of humor could always bring a bright spot to even the darkest of situations.

The two said their goodbyes and, as always, agreed to stay in touch regarding their related cases.

Still frustrated but ready to refocus his energy, Chase fell into his rental car and pulled away from the FBI building. As he drove, he began to review the case in his head and realized there were a lot of details he had been brushing aside since arriving in Colorado. Chase had been focusing so much attention on Barrett Greyson he had been neglecting Frank Greyson's other son. Not to say he had anything to do with the crime, but it was possible he might be able to provide important information. Even more intriguing was the victim's son, Boyd Clevinger. Boyd was the heir to the throne of the family business. When his father was murdered, Boyd had been the benefactor in a multitude of ways. But he also had an alibi for the night of his father's death, making it far more difficult to pin the crime on him. He had motive, but that was about the extent of it according to the case file.

Chase figured it couldn't hurt to pay the guy a visit and see what else he might be able to piece together. There was a good chance he would learn absolutely nothing new. But there was also the slightest possibility he could solve the entire case by speaking with Boyd Clevinger, face to face. This was Chase's job. And he liked doing his job a lot.

***

Barrett sat down on his couch in the small one-bedroom apartment he had been renting in Caribou. He held the remote control out and turned on the television Ernie had given him. He didn't expect to get much to tune in without paying for some sort of service, but oddly enough Barrett soon discovered NBC was watchable through a slight haze of video snow.

After watching the end of a sitcom that wasn't very funny, he waited to see what would air next. It was eight o'clock on Friday night, making it difficult to say if anything worth watching would be on. Barrett recalled his father telling him as recently as this past spring that there was a time when the best shows aired on Friday, Saturday, and Sunday nights.

"In the mid to late seventies and early eighties everyone was home in front of their television sets at night watching all of the family shows," his father had said. "These days the programming has changed, there's more competition with cable TV and satellite, and frankly most of the shows stink."

Barrett was too young to remember any of that, but he always enjoyed hearing his dad's perspective on life then versus life now. He seemed to be full of so much wisdom. Barrett never thought of his old man as a know-it-all like his younger brother did. While it was true his father wasn't always right, he never failed to admit his mistakes. Barrett respected him immensely because of this; the world needed more people like Frank Greyson.

The advertisements ended and an all-new episode of *Dateline* began. Keith Morrison was reporting, which worked well for Barrett since Morrison happened to be his favorite. *Dateline* and other news magazine shows were somewhat of an addiction for Barrett. They disturbed him, but he couldn't stop watching them. And Keith Morrison had a way of making you want to listen to him tell a story.

Thanks for the TV, Ernie, Barrett thought. He was all-in tonight, ready to relax and enjoy a mindless activity for a change.

The show began harmlessly enough. Lester Holt introduced himself to the camera and mentioned a couple of things that would be coming up on the network over the weekend. As the anchor segued into the evening's story, Barrett could feel his jaw begin to drop toward the hardwood floor of his apartment.

"Tonight's story takes us to a small, unsuspecting town in Iowa...and leads us all the way to the Rocky Mountains of Colorado," Holt began. "Keith Morrison has the story."

"No way," Barrett said out loud to no one. The screen faded to a shot of a windmill, then a barn, a water tower, and finally a shot of an all too familiar convenience store.

"Our story begins in the small town of Gable, Iowa," Morrison announced.

"You've got to be kidding me," Barrett mumbled

under his breath. Not once since leaving his home in Colorado had he considered he might end up the subject of a *Dateline* investigation. This was not the kind of fame he had daydreamed of while growing up. The only saving grace was that it wasn't an episode of Chris Hansen creeping out of the woodwork and catching pedophiles red-handed.

Barrett watched and listened as Morrison gave background on the town. For a moment he thought there was an outside chance the story would be more about Chum and his drug buddies. But when the first face shown on the screen was Bruce Townsend, Barrett knew his initial instinct was correct.

"Henry was a nice guy," Bruce Townsend told Morrison on camera. Barrett could tell the video was shot inside the Corner Store, where just a few months earlier he had been employed as Henry Fields. "I needed a cashier. He came in one afternoon and I hired him on the spot. He did a good job for me."

"How did he ask to be paid?" Morrison inquired, already knowing the answer.

"In cash," Bruce answered him.

"You didn't find that...strange?" Morrison asked in a concerned tone.

"Not really. I'm a small operation in small town Iowa," Bruce replied. "It seemed like a harmless request at the time."

"But was Henry Fields harmless? Or was he someone...completely different?" Morrison said in a voiceover that included one of his signature pauses.

"Oh, for shit's sake," Barrett said, as if he were responding to Morrison. He got up from the couch and went to the refrigerator. Inside he found a bomber bottle of beer that had been given to him as an early holiday gift from the forklift maintenance guy at work. Barrett continued to listen to his own story being told on the television as he opened the bottle of Black Bear Brewery's Voodoo Bear Porter. Instead of going for a glass, he elected to return to the couch with just the bottle. He took a quick drink and sat down again. It had been quite a while since Barrett had consumed alcohol in any quantity. Now felt like the perfect time to break the dry spell.

He continued to watch as his one week in Gable, Iowa, was played back for him through the lens of an investigative reporter. When Claire was introduced, Barrett's heart sank. He had spent so much time trying to move on he had almost forgotten about the feelings he once had for her.

"Henry always treated me like a lady," Claire told Morrison. Barrett smiled when he saw the radiant expression on her face while speaking of him. He enjoyed watching her smile, which was probably why he had spent so much time trying to make her laugh during their short time together. "He was thoughtful and sensitive and had a way about him that made me feel secure," she continued.

"What did he tell you about his past?" Morrison asked her.

"Not much," Claire said. "I would ask him, but he would be elusive."

"Strange," Morrison said. He had this way of uttering one-word sentences that made it difficult to discern whether they were questions or statements. Claire seemed to recover nicely from Morrison's attempt to rattle her, though Barrett was aware it might just have been the editing.

"Yes," Claire continued. "But one day he finally told me something. He told me that he used to have a pretty good job, but that something had changed his mind about it and that now he lives his life day by day."

"That was the truth, too, Claire," Barrett told his TV as he brought the beer bottle to his lips for another swig. For the next twenty minutes the story of Gable unfolded right before his eyes on national television. The party, the drug dealers, the murders. Not surprising, Tom Chumansky and Fast Eddie Clark had declined to be interviewed by *Dateline*, but Claire and Maddison confirmed that Barrett had rescued them from the two Hispanic goons who had held them at gunpoint.

"He seemed to have nothing to do with any of it," Maddison Chumansky told Morrison. Barrett could tell she had been interviewed inside her house where most of the action had taken place.

"You divorced your husband for his involvement in the drug dealing," Morrison mentioned, coyly.

Maddison smiled back at him, as if unaffected. "We're separated, but it's in process," she explained. Barrett noted she hadn't actually confirmed she was divorcing him because of the drugs.

As the hour came to a close, Barrett prepared to kick back and reflect as the camera pulled back from the little farmhouse west of Gable. A Keith Morrison voiceover could be heard during the pan.

"But who was Henry Fields? And why had he left Gable so abruptly in the middle of the night?" Morrison asked the viewing audience. "Coming up during our second hour of *Dateline...*"

"Awww, shit. Of course there's more!"

Barrett had been so enthralled with the story and concerned with its accuracy that he never considered the show would run two hours and dig deeper into his past. He was also more than a little buzzed.

"Was Henry Fields a murderer?" a voiceover asked, previewing the forthcoming hour of the program. The last image Barrett saw before the commercials was a hazy picture of himself he had never seen. But it didn't take long to discover the origin of the photograph and all that had taken place in Colorado since leaving his home last summer.

"Thanks to fingerprints left in the farmhouse and the screen captures provided by local reporter Balinda Simmons, Henry Fields was identified as Barrett Greyson, a CPA at the Clevinger Group, an accounting firm in Denver, Colorado," Morrison explained when the show resumed. He went on to tell the viewers how Barrett had had a somewhat tumultuous relationship with both his boss Otto Clevinger and his boss's son, Boyd, who had recently joined the company.

"One evening this past summer," Morrison continued, "the Clevinger Group held a get-together for clients and prospects inside their building. Everyone from the company was in attendance including Barrett Greyson and, of course, Otto and Boyd Clevinger."

Barrett tipped the beer bottle back as far as it would go to be certain he had finished it before placing it on the floor in front of him.

"This is so freaking weird," he said, not taking his eyes off the TV. Barrett could feel his head begin to cloud from downing the beer so fast. He was glad he had done it, though. The alcohol was making this far more tolerable than it would've been otherwise. In fact, he wished he had another bottle.

Morrison and *Dateline* went on to get all of the facts correct. They mentioned how Otto Clevinger had car trouble that evening and Barrett had given him a ride home. The next morning Clevinger was found dead in his house.

"And so sixty-six-year-old Otto Clevinger, son of the son who began the family business almost seven decades earlier, was found the next morning on the floor of his living room, still dressed in his suit from the night before," Morrison told the viewers. "The cause of death...asphyxiation."

Morrison explained how the autopsy and police investigation determined quickly that Clevinger's death was a homicide but that there was no evidence to indicate how it had been done or who had done it. The last person to have seen him alive: Barrett Greyson.

During a commercial break, Barrett maneuvered himself until he was lying flat on the couch. His head was beginning to hurt. One would assume it was the alcohol, but Barrett thought it might be *Dateline*. The next segment of the report showed the police tape of Barrett being interviewed by detectives in Colorado about the murder of Otto Clevinger. If Barrett were an average viewer he would've found this clip boring as hell. But tonight he was no average viewer. He knew all too well those thirty seconds were condensed from three hours of questions. Questions that would change his life forever: Did you drive Otto Clevinger home on the night in question? You were mad at him, right? Did you kill Mr. Clevinger? Did you know you were the last person to see him alive?

No, it wasn't the seemingly uneventful police interview that pointed the finger at Barrett Greyson on tonight's episode of *Dateline*. It was when he disappeared into thin air the next day.

"Why would an innocent man who was questioned by police and then released, flee?" Morrison asked. "That was the perplexing question on detectives' minds."

The show continued to paint Barrett as having a motive: his anger, jealousy, and power struggle with Boyd Clevinger as the heir apparent to the Clevinger Group. Boyd, on the other hand, was presented as the poor soul who had lost his father too soon. A father whom he loved and respected dearly.

As if awakened from a dead sleep by a clap of thunder, Barrett bolted straight up and returned to a seated position.

"Holy crap, Keith!" he shouted in frustration at his TV. "You had everything nailed down pretty good until now! What the...?"

As soon as he screamed it Barrett realized he was really only mad at himself for the situation he had put himself in. Boyd playing the victim didn't surprise him one bit. It was something he had witnessed day after day at the office. But it was disgusting to see it on national television while his own name was being slaughtered by his longtime pretend friend, Keith.

The show began to wrap up with a recap of how Barrett had left Colorado and settled down a few weeks later in

Gable, Iowa. A video clip of his mother and father was also shown at what appeared to be a press conference.

"Please come home, Barrett," his father requested. "We love you and miss you. We will get this entire situation sorted out and go on with our lives. We can't do this unless you come home. Your mother and I just want to help."

Barrett stood up and walked closer to the television. His father looked tired. There were bags under his eyes Barrett couldn't remember seeing before. He had spent a lot of time missing his father over the past several months, but he hadn't really considered what impact his disappearance might've had on his parents.

"As the search for Barrett Greyson continues, his father wonders if he will ever see his son again," Morrison said, then paused. "Frank Greyson is currently fighting an uphill battle of his own against pancreatic cancer."

Barrett's legs instantly began to buckle when he heard Keith Morrison's words. He dropped to his knees on the hardwood floor in front of the television set instead of giving in to the faintness he was feeling.

Dad has cancer, he thought to himself. He tuned out the last fifteen seconds of the program as he processed the disturbing news he hadn't been prepared for.

Barrett knew pancreatic cancer was not known for a high survival rate. Hollywood actors Michael Landon and Patrick Swayze had both lost their lives to the disease and Barrett distinctly remembered the national media giving both men a death sentence before either had a chance to fight.

That's how bad pancreatic cancer is, he thought.

Still on the floor, Barrett began to twist the bare knuckles of his right hand into the floorboards. He didn't know what he was doing, or why he was doing it. He wanted to scream. He wanted to punch somebody. Barrett continued to push and turn his knuckles into the floor as if they were screws and his arm was the screwdriver. With tears in his eyes, he began to pound his fist into the wood. Barrett knew the noise might agitate his neighbors, but the pain felt so good, it was impossible to control himself. It wasn't until the blood from his knuckles began to spatter that he ended his torment.

XV

Chase walked into the lobby of the Clevinger Group and asked for Boyd Clevinger.

"Do you have an appointment?" the blonde female receptionist asked.

"No," Chase replied, as if he didn't care. He didn't.

"Can I tell him who's here?"

Chase began to reach for the credentials in his pocket. He stopped short, though, and instead pulled a business card from his wallet. Keep it simple, he thought.

The receptionist took his card and picked up the phone, pushing a couple of buttons on the keypad. Chase could hear the phone ring in an office that seemed so close it must've been around the corner. Then he heard a man's voice in the distance.

"Yes, Julia," it said.

"There's a Chase Sheehan with the FBI here to see you," the receptionist reported into the receiver.

"Who?" the voice down the hall said.

"Chase Sheehan," Julia repeated, this time more slowly and clearly annoyed.

"Is he a client?" This time the voice was louder.

Julia shook her head. "F as in Frank, B as in Boy, I as in...Idiot." She held the phone away from her and turned to Chase.

"It's regarding his father," Chase explained before the

receptionist had a chance to speak.

Julia instantly turned pale, as if she had forgotten the tragedy that had stricken the company several months earlier. She put the receiver back to her face.

"It's about your father," she told her boss, this time with a tad more sensitivity. There was a pause before a response was given, but this time Chase could not make it out.

"You can go on back," she said, pointing. "First door on the left."

Chase walked ten feet forward and ten feet to his left before entering an open office door. He saw a man in his mid to late thirties with blonde slicked back hair get up and walk in his direction from behind a large oak desk.

"Boyd Clevinger," he said, holding his hand out.

"Agent Chase Sheehan," Chase reciprocated.

"I understand you're here about my late father."

"Yes, yes I am," Chase said.

"How can I help you? Please, have a seat."

Clevinger walked behind his desk and sat in an oversized chair. Chase assumed that, up until a few months ago, the office had belonged to Boyd's father. Chase sat in a chair directly in front of the desk.

"I wish I could tell you I have good news, but at this point we are still a work in progress," Chase began. "I was wondering if you could go over the night's events from your perspective."

"All right, ummm, sure," Clevinger replied. "I've already done this a few times, but..."

"I understand, and I don't want to waste your time," Chase said, "But I really need to go over it again if you wouldn't mind."

"Sure, sure," Clevinger agreed. "Where should I begin?"

"Tell me how the night began for you."

"Well, my wife and I got ready for the open house, and our babysitter called because she needed a ride. I had to go pick her up because Fred wasn't ready yet. So after I picked her up and brought her to the house, we took off for the office."

"What about Fred?" Chase asked.

"She was with me. I said 'we,' didn't I?" Clevinger responded. He seemed genuinely perplexed and concerned he had misspoken.

"Fred is..." Chase began to put two and two together but before he could spit it out, Clevinger explained the misunderstanding.

"My wife's name is Fredrika. We call her 'Freddy' or 'Fred' for short."

"My apologies," Chase said as he chuckled to himself.

"No need. So we went to the party and everything went pretty well. I mean, we had hoped for a bigger turnout, but it was okay."

"Was there anything that stood out to you?"

"Not really. I mean, everyone pretty much did their thing."

"Why didn't you take your father home when he had a flat?"

Boyd Clevinger paused and stared at his desk full of paperwork. "I don't know," he answered in a mutter.

"What was that?"

"I don't know why I didn't take him home," Clevinger clarified. "You're the first person to ask me that question."

Chase saw an opening. "Did your father ask you to take him home?"

Boyd Clevinger continued to stare at inanimate objects on his desk. "Yes."

"What did you tell him when he asked you?"

"That he was a pain in the ass."

Chase was again not sure if he had misheard the

fortunate son. "I'm sorry. Could you repeat that?"

"I told him to figure it out himself, that I had a kid and wife to worry about. I called him a pain in the ass."

Clevinger explained this not with pride, but with remorse. That didn't change the fact that it felt extremely awkward to Chase.

"Were you having a bad night or something?"

"Not really. Like I said, the night went fine," Clevinger said. "I just...I was always annoyed by my father."

Chase raised his eyebrows.

"I'm not proud of it, Agent Sheehan. I pretty much treated my father like shit."

No kidding, Chase thought to himself. "I see," Chase said out loud.

"It doesn't make me a murderer...does it?"

"My understanding is you have an alibi?"

"As best I can, yes," Clevinger replied. "My father left at nine and I left with my wife at ten. I took the babysitter home at about ten twenty-five and I arrived back home for the rest of the night at ten forty-five. Obviously, you're welcome to verify all of that, though I'm sure it's already documented." There was a pause between the two thirty-somethings before Clevinger continued as he crossed his arms. "Why are we going over all of this again? I've been through it with the authorities already, multiple times."

"You're more than welcome to refuse to speak to me," Chase explained. "Which would kind of be like what Barrett Greyson did, though I'm not sure how that's working out for him right now. What are your thoughts on him?"

Boyd Clevinger paused again and uncrossed his arms. "I don't know where to begin. He and I had a love-hate relationship."

"Why's that?"

"I don't know. Maybe he resented me."

"Why?"

"Is this pertinent?" Boyd asked, aggravated.

"I'm trying to figure out why Barrett Greyson would murder your father."

"Honestly, Agent Sheehan, I think he resented me because he thought I didn't work for what I have but—"

"Do you think Barrett Greyson killed your father?" Chase decided to lay it out there before having to listen to the guy justify his position in the family business.

"I don't know what I believe anymore," Clevinger said with a shake of the head. "All I know is I didn't do it."

"It almost sounds like Greyson should've wanted to kill you," Chase suggested.

Clevinger's eyes bulged from his skull but quickly retreated. "I wish he would've," he said, though Chase wasn't buying it. "Barrett had a better relationship with my father than I did. I always figured he was the son Dad wished he had."

The phone on Clevinger's desk rang once, interrupting the awkward conversation.

"Yes, Julia," Clevinger greeted the receptionist.

"I'm sorry to disturb you, but your landscaping company in Arizona called and they wanted to know if you were okay with them working overtime to finish a couple of jobs," Julia reported from the speaker phone.

"Of course, why not?" Clevinger exclaimed. "We only pay those guys eight bucks an hour. Tell them to go for it!"

There was a slight pause before Julia spoke again.

"Boyd, could you pick up the phone please?" she requested. Clevinger picked up the receiver and listened. Chase was unable to make out what Julia was saying, but he listened with intrigue while standing up from his chair, preparing to leave.

"What?" Clevinger said. "Really? Wow." He paused as Julia spoke quietly from around the corner. "It's fine. Go ahead. Thank you." Boyd pushed his oversized chair backward and stood up. "Is that all you need, Agent Sheehan?" he asked as he walked around his desk.

"Yes, you've been extremely helpful," Chase told him. "Thank you very much for taking the time."

"I just want to help in any way I can," Clevinger said as the men shook hands. The two parted ways as the rookie CEO walked back to his desk, and Chase was left to see himself out. As he made his way to the front door he turned to Julia, the receptionist, and smiled. She noticed the gesture and for the first time during their brief encounters smiled back at Chase, revealing a small gap between her front teeth.

"Can I ask?" he said, holding his smile. The young blonde began to snicker.

"He didn't realize overtime meant paying them time and a half." Julia said this quietly so her boss would not overhear.

Chase shook his head as he pushed the door open, still turned toward the front desk. "It does?" he replied with a wink. Julia grinned again, watching through the glass doors as Chase walked to the parking lot.

***

Claire sat on her bed, legs crisscrossed and notebook open on her lap. She held a glass of wine as she began to read her latest journal entry out loud.

"Uncle Stubby would always leave money on my dresser. I would wake up the next morning and it would be there. When I was too young to know better, I thought it was a nice gesture. As I got older, I realized what was happening and I felt dirty. It was like years of ignorance had caught up with me. I ran to the bathroom and threw up when it all came together. I wasn't quite nine years old. When I confronted my uncle about what he had been doing to me for as long as I could remember, he just smiled at me."

Claire stopped reading as a tear fell onto the notebook. She wiped her eye with her empty hand before continuing to read.

"It wasn't really even a smile. It was more like a conceited sneer. The only thing he said to me was 'would you like a job?' It didn't make any sense to me at the time, but looking back now I realize he wanted to keep me around. He knew I was getting older and he would eventually lose me completely. In his own sick way he still wanted to have something to..."

Claire again stopped short for a brief moment before finishing the sentence.

"...something to pay me for."

Just then Claire's phone rang. After regaining her composure, she answered it even though she didn't recognize the number on the caller ID.

"Hello?"

"Hi, Claire. It's Maddison Chumansky."

"Oh, hi," Claire replied. She hadn't expected to hear from Maddison at all, let alone so soon after running into her.

"I was wondering if you'd like to come to my house tomorrow for some dinner," Maddison asked.

"Uhhhh," Claire said as she tried to recall her work schedule. "Sure. That would be nice. I'm off tomorrow night."

"Great, come on over at six thirty. The driveway is sufficiently plowed, so you should be able to make it in with no problem. But if you do have an issue just give me a call and I'll come out and push your car."

"Sounds good," Claire said before catching the joke. "Hey wait, you're pregnant. You're not going to be pushing any cars."

Maddison chuckled. "Nope. And you're not going to get stuck, either. See you tomorrow," she said and hung up.

***

It was six o'clock on Sunday night. Barrett packed his two duffel bags and backpack in silence. He hadn't turned on the television since watching the *Dateline* episode two nights ago. That Friday was also the same morning he had followed Floyd's instructions and paid him four thousand dollars to get into Canada, undetected. He was told to simply leave it at the front desk of the Hampton Inn in Presque Isle. The only caveat was that it had to be forty one hundred dollar bills in an appropriately sized bubble mailer envelope. Floyd had, in fact, gone as far as to tell Barrett specifically which one to use.

"A number one is what you want," Floyd told his client. "You use a zero and it will be too small. Anything larger than a one is too big and makes people wonder what's in it."

Barrett considered asking more questions, but decided against it. He didn't need any more lectures; he just wanted to get out of the country.

So after telling Ernie he would be late due to a dentist appointment, Barrett had made the twenty-minute drive to Presque Isle, south of Caribou, and marched through the front door of the Hampton Inn. As instructed, he left the package at the front desk for "Roger Gilmour" and drove back home. Later that evening the *Dateline* episode aired and Barrett fell asleep with a bag of ice on his knuckles.

Barrett assumed most people would find this entire process of getting into Canada a silly way of doing things. But he already knew all too well the complexities and attention to detail it took to be discreet. After all, he went to great lengths to remain under the radar the first several weeks of being on his own, and it was only when he let his guard down the slightest bit that he drew attention to himself. Even if he hadn't helped Alan Walker after his car accident, he still would've found himself in the middle of Chum's mess, and the authorities probably still would've figured out who he was thanks to the fingerprints in the farmhouse. Barrett hadn't given a thought to the prints until Keith Morrison mentioned them on *Dateline*. Short of wearing gloves for the rest of his life there probably wasn't much he could to do to prevent leaving fingerprints wherever he went. Besides, telling people he had a skin condition and had to wear gloves all the time would, ironically, draw attention to himself. He could burn his fingerprints off with acid and tell people he was burned badly as a child, but the entire notion of doing such a thing didn't appeal to him. He wasn't desperate. Not yet, anyway. No, the best way to move forward was to be more careful and prevent the need to disfigure himself to survive. Since arriving in Caribou he had done his best to avoid contact with too many people on a personal level, at least outside of work hours. His visits to Floyd and the trip to Presque Isle were rarities. The truck driver who had turned him on to Floyd in the first place presented little danger. From what Barrett's father had taught him about drivers, the guy had probably already forgotten about the encounter.

Despite the concerns he had for his own well-being and future, especially after watching his story unfold on television, Barrett couldn't stop thinking about his father's condition.

When he left town, Barrett believed deep down that he would see and talk to his father and mother again, somehow. Maybe he had lied to himself. The only way it would be possible would be if he was found, and maybe tried and convicted. Then he could see anyone that wanted to see him...when they visited him in prison.

Now the knowledge that his father had cancer, and a terminal cancer at that, was causing Barrett to lament. There were so many things he still wanted to talk to his dad about. Not just about this entire murder rap, but about life in general. The thought of never getting that chance again made Barrett sick to his stomach. It also made him angry. When he left Colorado, Barrett's anguish was tempered with the knowledge that things would work out and he'd be able to see his father again. It reminded Barrett of the time he quit smoking cigarettes as a teenager. He kept a pack in his glove compartment but never touched them. It gave him the option to smoke anytime he wanted, but instead he chose not to do it. He was in control of the situation, much like he took control when he left Colorado and then Gable in the middle of the night.

But it felt like fate was making choices for him now. Barrett was conflicted, unsure of how to move forward with his goal of surviving while knowing his father would more than likely be dead in months, maybe weeks...maybe days. He had no idea what was going on. No idea how much the cancer had spread. What was the plan of attack with treatments? How was his mother holding up? Was his brother helping out at all?

Barrett sat down on his couch and stared at his reflection in the blank, black television screen.

"Be in control," his father had told him on more than one occasion. "Don't let your emotions get the best of you."

Sometimes it's easier said than done, Barrett thought to himself. He pondered what advice his dad would give him right now.

***

"Hi, Claire," Maddison said with a warm smile. She stepped back from the door to let her guest in. "I'm so glad you could make it."

"Thanks for having me," Claire replied. "It was a nice surprise to be invited. I can always use some time out of the house."

Claire had noticed when she approached the front door that the entryway Henry had driven the truck through was fixed like new, showing no signs that any damage had occurred. She considered mentioning it as an icebreaker but decided against it. No sense in bringing that night up in conversation.

"What can I get you to drink?" Maddison asked.

"Wine?"

"Red or white?"

"Red," Claire requested.

"Coming right up," Maddison announced. "Come on. Follow me in here while I open it."

The two ladies walked into the kitchen where Maddison proceeded to open a bottle of wine.

"So how has the pregnancy been going?" Claire asked, knowing it was an easy conversation starter.

"I can't complain, really," Maddison explained. "I mean, I get tired more easily than I used to, I'm heavier, and strangely I don't seem to be eating much more than I did when I wasn't pregnant. But apparently everything is normal, at least according to my OB/GYN."

She poured two glasses of Cabernet Sauvignon and handed one to Claire before she sat down next to her at the kitchen bar. Claire glanced at Maddison's glass and then at her pregnant belly. Maddison grinned.

"It's okay," she told Claire. "It's doctor approved. One glass."

Claire flashed a nervous smile. "I guess I'm a little ignorant. I've never been pregnant before."

"Oh, I understand. I assumed I couldn't drink alcohol, too. When I was told otherwise, I was elated. Obviously, it needs to be in moderation. No shots of Jack or Jim or anything like that."

The two women laughed in unison and chatted about all sorts of things while they waited for the casserole to cook. Maddison told Claire more about what it was like to be pregnant, and Claire told her about the patrons at Stubby's and about Wilson, the cat she had inherited.

Within forty-five minutes the ladies were eating together in the dining room. Claire was starving by then as the aroma of the casserole had filled the entire house. Maddison had switched to water before dinner, but Claire enjoyed her second glass of wine while eating. When they finished their meal the two women returned to the kitchen where Maddison made a pot of coffee and poured each of them a cup, explaining that caffeine had also been "cleared by the authorities" for her pregnancy. Next, Maddison moved to the refrigerator freezer for what she referred to as a "surprise dessert" that she had "slaved over all day to make."

After grabbing two spoons from a drawer, Maddison reached inside the freezer with both hands and revealed an oversized plastic tub of chocolate ice cream. She set it on the bar between them, handing Claire a spoon.

"This is a pregnant woman's dessert," she said, slamming her spoon into the top of the smooth, untouched ice cream.

Claire looked on as Maddison took the first bite, then she placed her own spoon in the tub, pulled out a sizeable amount, and put it in her mouth. While the ice cream melted on her tongue, Claire turned to Maddison. "That's a lot of freakin' ice cream," Claire said, spinning the container. "Five quarts," she read. "My small town education tells me that's more than a gallon."

"My small town education tells me this is healthy stuff," Maddison replied, shoving in another spoonful. The two snickered and continued to dig in before they both decided they'd had enough. Maddison put the ice cream back in the freezer and the two ladies continued to sip coffee in the kitchen.

"I've enjoyed myself tonight," Maddison said. "It's nice to have another girl nearby to talk to."

Claire smiled. "I'm flattered, but you have a lot of friends," she replied.

"Yes, but not in Gable," Maddison explained.

Claire agreed. "I see what you mean. I don't really have anyone around here either, other than my mom and my aunt."

"Claire, I need your help with something."

It was almost as if Maddison hadn't been listening.

Although caught off guard by the change of direction in the conversation, Claire responded. "Um, sure. What is it?"

Maddison took a sip of coffee before leaning in closer to her guest. "This isn't easy to talk about so please bear with me," she began.

"No problem," Claire said, wondering what was coming next.

"You remember the money that Tom almost got us all killed over?"

Claire's heart skipped a beat. "Yes," she said, but the word came out at a snail's pace.

"It does actually exist."

Claire pulled her head back as she processed the information. "I don't mean to sound rude, but what does this have to do with me?"

Claire was in therapy trying to forget about the hell she had witnessed that night. She really didn't care about the money. It wasn't hers...if it existed at all.

"Well, Tom has leveled with me about it. Like I told you at the grocery store, I have ways," she elaborated while rubbing her belly. "But this place is being watched closely by the police and Tom is being followed everywhere he goes."

Claire shrugged. Maddison continued.

"I know you've spent a lot of time with Sergeant Jackson talking about what happened. He's talked to me several times, too. Well..." Maddison paused briefly before continuing. "I need help sending him in a different direction...to deter him from watching this place for a while."

Claire cocked her head slightly. What was going on here? "I don't understand what this has to do with—" She stopped herself as she realized what Maddison was alluding to. "You want me to lie to Sergeant Jackson for you?"

Maddison pursed her lips together. "It's barely even a lie," she said.

"How do you figure?"

"Fact: you and I had dinner. Fact: the subject of Tom and the money came up in conversation. Fact: I told you I believe it exists. The little white lie is that I told you I think it's hidden somewhere near a Mecca Warehouse in Adler."

Claire was shocked at how well Maddison had just sold it. She looked at the pregnant woman sitting across from her and then down at her coffee mug as Maddison continued.

"Claire, I realize that even though I just minimized it for you, it's still a lot to ask. Especially since you don't owe me anything. That's why I'm not asking you to do this for free."

Claire looked back up at Maddison.

"I'll give you fifty thousand dollars once we recover the money."

Claire swallowed hard.

"I know it's not an overwhelming amount of money," Maddison lamented.

"It would take me more than two years to make that much," Claire admitted. "But it's drug money. It's not...we don't even know whose it is...do we?"

Maddison smiled. "As far as I'm concerned, it's Tom's. The other guy—Franco—he's in prison. It's out there. Shouldn't someone benefit from that money? Look, I just want it for my baby." She patted her stomach. "And you deserve something to help you out a little, too," Maddison said. "Think of it as compensation for the bullshit you dealt with that night. You're probably still dealing with it. I know I am, anyway. Two good causes, Claire. Innocent people who had nothing to do with the mess that Tom caused: my baby and you."

Claire looked away from Maddison, toward the hallway leading to the front door.

"It's just one little story stretch," Maddison added.

Claire grabbed her handheld purse and rose from her chair. "I'm going outside for a cigarette," she said, unsure how she had lasted this long without one.

XVI

Ernie Saunders unlocked the Marble Industries shipping office door and turned around to look at the parking lot one last time before entering. He found it strange that Dan hadn't made it to work yet, but last night's snowfall could've slowed him down.

He went to his desk and thumbed through the day's shipments, deliveries, pickups, and other various paperwork. After checking the fax machine for new orders, he began to check his email. As he did this, the front door opened. When he looked up, Ernie was surprised to see an unfamiliar face.

"Hey," the man said. He was about forty years old with sandy blonde hair. He glanced at a piece of paper as he continued speaking. "I need to see Ernie Saunders."

"Yeah, that's me," Ernie said helpfully. He stood up and reached for the customer pickup paperwork. "I didn't hear your truck out there. What are you picking up?"

"I'm actually here to work," the man said. "I'm not a customer."

Ernie gave the man a puzzled look and then smiled. "There must be some kind of mistake here. I didn't hire anybody. How did you wind up coming here?"

"I was sent by Tompkins Temps-To-Hire...?" The man said it with confusion of his own as he began to wonder if he had misunderstood the instructions.

"Okay, just let me make a quick phone call and we'll get this sorted out. Hang tight for a second," Ernie told the man. "What's your name?"

"Stanley. Stanley Bundy."

Ernie picked up the phone and turned his Rolodex to the business card he had for Tompkins Temps-To-Hire. His representative's name was Jerry Heimgartner. He dialed the number. After two rings the line was answered, coincidentally by Jerry.

"Hi Jerry. This is Ernie at Marble."

"Yes, Ernie. I've been expecting your call," Jerry said.

"You have?" Ernie replied.

"You're probably wondering why Stan is there, reporting for work that you didn't authorize."

"Yeah, that's exactly why I'm calling. What's going on? What happened?"

"Ha. Great question. Let me tell you a quick story. I think you'll appreciate this one," Jerry teased.

"I'm listening," Ernie said.

"So I'm lying on my couch watching television with my wife last night," Jerry began, "and there's a knock at my front door around eight thirty. Normally I wouldn't answer it at all. You know, that's kind of creepy these days. I mean, it was frickin' snowing outside. But something told me I should answer it. So I did. And it's this guy who works for you, Dan Scotwood."

"Dan?" Ernie clarified. He looked out the glass door, still waiting for his forklift driver to walk through it.

"Yeah, weird, isn't it? So before I have a chance to say much of anything he tells me that he needs to take off but doesn't want to leave you in a bind. He asked me—actually begged me—to fill his spot with the best person I had available."

Ernie didn't like what he was hearing. "What? Come on. This has to be a joke, right?"

"No. No it's not. And it gets better. He paid me for the first two months—in cash. And I have to be honest with you, Ernie. He even tipped me, if that's what you want to call it."

"Come on..." Ernie began another objection.

"I'll give it to you if you want," Heimgartner offered. "I mean, it kinda made me feel cheap."

Ernie paused, realizing Jerry wasn't playing a game. Dan had replaced himself. "No, Jerry," Ernie said, "you earned it."

"If you don't like Stan all you have to do is tell me. We'll try someone else. It's paid for. But I really feel he is the best we've got at the moment."

"Okay," Ernie said, still staring out the door.

"Just let me know what you think," Jerry added.

"Yeah," Ernie said, but he wasn't really listening as he hung up the phone.

***

Chase sat at the hotel bar sipping his third gin and tonic. There were times in his short career with the FBI that he wondered what the hell he was doing. Why was he here in Denver? Nothing had been accomplished. The Greysons hadn't given him anything to go on and the old man had cancer. This entire investigation was a lost cause.

Chase's phone rang, startling him. Normally he turned off the ringer while in a public place, but he had forgotten to do so when he sat down at the bar.

"Sheehan," he answered.

"Agent Sheehan, this is Ta Nguyen at the lab," the voice said.

"What do you have, Nguyen?" Chase's brain was buzzing pretty good.

"Not much, I'm sorry to say. We did finally find some specks of DNA amidst the samples we collected at Barrett Greyson's condo. The problem is, it's inconclusive. What we've got is similar to the DNA found at the scene, but it's nowhere near definitive."

Chase processed the information while sipping his mixed drink. "So you're telling me this isn't going to cut it in court?" He knew the answer, but he had to ask.

"I'm sorry, Agent. Not a snowball's chance," Nguyen confirmed. "A defense attorney would rip it to shreds with his own expert if we even tried."

"So that's it."

"That's it."

"Goodbye, Nguyen."

Chase finished his drink in one gulp and put his glass in the air to get the bartender's attention.

***

"Don't forget to come home tonight," Caroline Jackson told her police sergeant husband. She set the bag of food from Stubby's on his desk. The couple's four-year-old daughter, Kaitlyn, walked over to her father where he was sitting behind his desk. She crawled up his legs and onto his lap, grabbing his face with her small hands.

"Will you come into my room and kiss me good night when you get home, Daddy?" she asked Jackson.

"Of course, sweetheart," he replied. "Here's one in advance." Jackson pursed his lips together and his daughter leaned in for a smack. When they were finished he pulled lightly on each of her pigtails. "Make sure you read tonight, Tyler." Jackson said, shifting his attention to his six-year-old son.

"Aw, Dad," Tyler Jackson groaned.

"You don't want to fall behind in school, do you?" he asked his boy. "You've been doing so well. Your mom and I would hate to see you blow it. Flunking the first grade would be a bad start to your future."

Tyler gave his father a confused look. "What's

'flunking?'" he asked.

Jackson smiled. "Your mom will explain it to you in the car."

"Thanks a lot," Jackson's wife said. She blew him a kiss and rallied her troops. "Come on, kids. Let's get a move on."

"Thanks for the food!" he said as he watched his family move through the door of the police station. Thankfully he wouldn't be long, tonight.

Less than five minutes after the door had closed Jackson was caught off guard when it opened again. This time it was Claire Mathison. He greeted her with a warm smile.

"Hi, Claire! Haven't seen you in a while. How've you been?"

Claire walked up to Jackson's desk. "I'm doing good."

"Please, sit down," the sergeant said.

"I can't stay long. I just got off work. I wasn't sure I'd find you here this late," she commented. "But when I saw your wife and kids at Stubby's getting some food to go," she touched the sack on his desk, "I figured I might be able to catch you."

"The more time I spend out in the field the more the paperwork piles up here," Jackson explained. "I'm impressed by your detective skills. You just missed the family dropping off my dinner."

"I won't keep you long. I just wanted to share a few things with you," Claire said.

"Sure, go for it."

She took a deep breath before continuing. "I had dinner with Maddison Chumansky the other night."

"Oh really?" Jackson said.

"Yeah, it was a nice surprise to be invited to her house."

"She's still got a few months before that kid comes,

right?"

"Yes, yes. Several."

"Too bad about the divorce and all."

"It's funny you bring that up," Claire said. "She made a comment that I thought you might find interesting."

"Oh?"

"Yes..." Claire paused before elaborating. "She mentioned Chum and how she believes there is money hidden somewhere."

"I guess that's not a big shock," Jackson said.

"Probably not," Claire agreed. "It was an epiphany for her, though. I think throughout the divorce she struggled with wanting to believe he wasn't as bad of a person as it looked. She's just now figuring out from things he has said that the money does exist."

Claire had no idea where those words came from. She was making it up, word by word.

"Makes sense," Jackson said "Denial..."

"Exactly," Claire agreed. "She also said she thinks..."

A sudden tickle entered Claire's throat and she began to choke, coughing momentarily. Jackson stood up.

"Let me get you a drink," he said, walking over to the water dispenser. He filled a cone-shaped paper cup and brought it to her as she was recovering.

"Th-thanks," Claire said as she took the cup and swallowed it all in one gulp. Her eyes had teared up during the spell. She reached for the Kleenex on Jackson's desk and wiped her eyes. She took another and blew her nose. After recovering, she continued to speak. "Sorry," she said. "Don't know where that came from."

"No problem," Jackson said. "If you're ready to continue, I think you were saying something about Maddison and the money."

"Yes. I was saying that Maddison seems to think the

money is hidden somewhere in Adler near one of Chum's stores." There. She said it. But why didn't she feel any better?

Jackson leaned back in his chair. "Really? Interesting. I guess we hadn't thought about that. But we have been keeping an eye on him everywhere he goes."

"Sure, that's what I figured. I just didn't know if it would mean anything to you or not," Claire explained. Maybe he wasn't going to buy it, after all.

"Well, I appreciate it. We'll take a closer look into it. I mean, finding that money might mean finding some narcotics, too. That would certainly help us finally get something on Chum."

Claire stood up from the chair. "Well, that's all I have. I'll let you get back to work," she said.

"Thanks for stopping by, Claire. I appreciate your thoughts. We'll definitely focus a bit more in Adler and the Mecca Warehouse locations," Jackson said.

Claire smiled.

"By the way," he added, "did Maddison say why she suspected this location for the hidden money?"

Claire had started to turn toward the door but stopped short when she heard Jackson's question. Slowly turning back in his direction, she answered. "No, not really. She just said it was a hunch due to some of the things Chum had recently said to her."

Jackson nodded. "Got you. Just curious," he said. "Take care of yourself, Claire. Thanks again." He smiled and gave Claire a wave of the hand as she turned toward the door again.

As she began opening it, she suddenly had the urge to stop. Claire turned around and spoke, though this time she almost felt as if she weren't in control. As if an immovable force were compelling her. "Sergeant Jackson?" she said.

Jackson's head perked back up from his paperwork.

"Yes?"

Claire's mouth began to open.

What are you doing, she scolded herself.

"I..."

She swallowed hard.

"I just wanted to say thanks for all you've done," Claire finally spit out.

Jackson smiled. "It's my pleasure. It's my job and in my nature to care," he said. "You need anything you just let me know."

Claire mustered up a half-hearted smile of her own. "Okay," she replied, then left the police station.

***

"How much you want?" the thin, young black man asked Barrett.

"I know what you should be able to get for it," Barrett said. "I want fifteen hundred."

"What?" the man bellowed. "Man...come on..."

Barrett had assumed a town called Michigan City would be a good place to sell a car. Maybe he was wrong. One thing he already knew from experience: you can buy or sell a car without proper paperwork and identification; you just have to find the right buyer.

"You'll get more than two grand for it," Barrett argued.

"Man, and what if I don't?"

"You will."

"Besides, she's got one forty on her," the young man said.

Barrett looked at him blankly and said nothing. He knew the next person to speak would lose the negotiation. Of course, at this point it wasn't even a negotiation. All the man was doing was talking.

"Nine hundred," the man said.

"Twelve fifty," Barrett said immediately while sticking his right hand out.

The man hesitated before reciprocating, shaking his head the entire time he shook Barrett's hand.

Barrett allowed himself a wry grin. In a perfect world he would've sold the car in Chicago or even Des Moines or Omaha. But he found what he believed was a good spot and went with his gut. At least now he had recovered some of the cash he'd wasted prepaying Floyd. Once Barrett's head had cleared, it was an easy decision to forgo his escape to The Great White North and return to Colorado instead. In theory, a bus trip from Michigan City, Indiana, to Denver would cost a fraction of what he'd just made selling the Taurus, not to mention the money he would save in gas and an occasional hotel. But Barrett's plan was to only take the bus to Chicago, which was a mere seventy miles away. From there he would figure out the best mode of transportation for the remainder of the trip.

Barrett had already planned to spend the money to replace himself at Marble when he thought he was heading to Canada. That expense didn't bother him. Ernie deserved it. But the four grand he blew on the idea of smuggling himself into Canada stung. Barrett believed this all had to be happening for a reason, though at this point he was struggling with exactly what that reason was. Had he only known about his father's condition a day earlier he'd have forty extra hundred-dollar bills in his backpack right now. But he absolutely had to go see his dad, no matter how much money he had lost. And no matter how much of a risk it was to his freedom.

After taking a cab to the Greyhound station, Barrett purchased a ticket to hitch a ride to Chicago. Knowing how slow the bus traveled, he figured he'd have at least two and a half hours to formulate a plan of action once he arrived. It would not be an impossible task to see his father again, but it would be a difficult one. At least that's what Barrett kept telling himself as he sat in his seat and waited for the Greyhound to take off.

Traveling by bus, Barrett had discovered, was not unlike flying. It took a lot longer to get where you wanted to go, but it was less expensive and, most importantly, required far less verification. These days Greyhound was requiring a show of identification, but there were no TSA officers examining it for authenticity. The biggest problem with the bus was its lack of flexibility. Barrett liked being in control of his traveling, which is why he had continued to buy, sell, and drive cars more often than not. In addition, riding a bus was not glamorous. The biggest difference between flying and bus riding aside from the cost and travel time was the passengers. People who couldn't afford to fly rode the bus. Barrett had hoped this would camouflage him after he left Gable and traveled across the country. The bus riders were tolerable despite their varying aromas of body odor being more excessive than those you'd find on a plane. The people were, in general, pleasant and easy to deal with. Barrett had no choice but to check his two duffel bags, but they only contained clothes and a few essentials. His backpack would stay with him at all times. This was protocol even when he traveled in a car by himself. Without the money in that backpack his ability to move at will would be stifled.

The bus took off at seven o'clock that evening. Barrett had already done his best to erase the memory of his couple of months in Caribou. So much so that he fell asleep within minutes. There was no point in dwelling; he had done his best to do right by Ernie. Other than that, Barrett had no commitments in Maine.

Within an hour he was rudely awakened by the driver's voice over the speaker system informing the passengers that they were about to make a stop for food and other essentials. Barrett knew from past experience that the bus made frequent stops, mostly for cigarette breaks. They were announced as stretch and food breaks, but it always seemed to Barrett the driver was the first one out the door with a Winston and a Bic. The stops were another reason Barrett decided not to ride the bus all the way to Denver. He'd get virtually no sleep, and it would take forever to get there.

"Hey, you gettin' off?"

Barrett looked across the aisle at a man twice his size. He had shoulder length blonde hair and a beard. His stomach and chest were massive. The man was in his late forties to early fifties and overweight, but his build revealed plenty of strength, as if he lifted weights regularly and then went out for pizza.

"I was thinking about it," Barrett said.

"Can I bum a smoke?" the man asked him.

"I don't smoke," Barrett explained. "I just thought I'd go out and get some fresh air. It's unseasonably mild out there for December."

The man looked at Barrett's backpack and grunted. "I thought everyone on this thing smoked," he replied.

Barrett began to get up from his seat, assuming the conversation was over.

"Hey," the man said, sticking his arm out in front of Barrett. "It's not for me."

Barrett gave the man a puzzled look.

"The cigarette. It's not for me."

"Okay," Barrett said, looking down at the man's mammoth forearm extended in front of him.

The man pulled back his arm bar as he continued speaking. "You see that old woman up front in the wheelchair?"

Barrett gazed toward the front of the bus as he sat back down. "Yeah."

"That's my mom. It's for her," the man said.

Barrett looked at the man and then back up front. He began to think taking the bus to Chicago had been a terrible idea. "Okay."

"I don't smoke," the man explained. "I just didn't want you to think I was a smoker."

"Well, I am. Would you mind letting me out?" The voice came from Barrett's right as the woman next to him leaned into the conversation.

"Of course," Barrett replied. He felt like hugging her for rescuing him from the awkward discussion. He got up from his seat and headed to the front of the bus. As he walked past her, Barrett glanced at the old woman in the wheelchair. She looked back at him as he trotted down the stairs and off the bus.

After a brief stretching of the legs and the purchase of a bottle of water, Barrett returned to the bus. This time as he entered he noticed both the old woman and her oversized son were gone. But this was nothing unusual.

Probably outside smoking, Barrett thought.

Sure enough, a few more minutes passed before the mother-son duo returned. Barrett could see the large man wheel his mother into her previous spot behind the driver. This time, though, the man chose a seat close to her and near the front of the bus, far away from where he had been sitting across the aisle from Barrett.

"Okay then," Barrett said under his breath.

He let the woman who had been sitting next to him back into her seat and then sat back down himself in preparation for what would be another one-hour drive.

Shortly after the bus started moving again, Barrett began drifting off to sleep. While doing so, he contemplated his plan of action once he reached Chicago. Flying was out of the question. His fake identification would never make it past security. The bus had already proven to be an experience he never wanted to have again unless he had no alternative. His previous trip from Pittsburgh to Maine had taken too long and was full of unnecessary stops and excessive body odor. He had considered taking a train this time but was uncertain of the identification requirements. And since hitchhiking was almost a worse idea than flying, Barrett settled on searching for a cheap car. He only needed the vehicle to make it a thousand miles.

Once he reached Denver he could figure something else out for transportation, if necessary. If he couldn't find a good deal on a car in Chicago, he'd locate a library and search the Internet for more information about traveling by train.

Around nine thirty Barrett was again aroused by the bus driver addressing the passengers. Talking through the speakers, he let everyone know the bus had arrived in Chicago and would be stopping at the Greyhound station on West Harrison Street within ten minutes.

As Barrett put his coat on in preparation for the dropping evening temperatures, he wondered how his father's health was at the moment. He had no idea when the *Dateline* episode had been taped or when the press conference his father spoke at had taken place. The only thing he could hope for now was that he wasn't too late.

When they left the interstate, Barrett noticed the Amtrak station was close by. Maybe fate was trying to tell him something.

Might as well check it out first, he thought.

When the bus came to a stop, he waited his turn to climb off and then immediately made his way to the baggage area to claim his two checked duffel bags. One of them had been free. The second had cost him ten dollars. Fifteen minutes later, with his backpack slung behind him, Barrett carried his two duffel bags in the direction he believed the train station to be. The weather was calm and the temperature was above freezing. Compared to Caribou, Chicago felt like spring break in Cabo. After walking about fifty yards, he heard a voice behind him. At first he didn't think anything of it, but the second time he heard it he turned his head and looked over his right shoulder, past his backpack.

"Hey, man!"

It was the large, blonde, bearded man from the bus, wheeling his mother in Barrett's direction.

"You've got to be kidding," Barrett said under his breath.

As the two approached, even the wheelchair-bound mother looked eager to reach him.

"Hey, man," the giant said again as he stopped the wheelchair in front of Barrett, who had now completely turned around. The man was out of breath from the rapid pushing of his eighty-pound mother.

"I still don't have a cigarette," Barrett said in a somewhat snarky tone. He looked down at the old woman when he said it. She was staring at him.

"Ha!" the man said. "Mom got her fix earlier at that stop."

Barrett nodded and looked down at the old woman, who was still staring at him. There weren't a lot of people who could make him feel uncomfortable by looking at him, but Granny Clampett was doing a superb job. Barrett turned his gaze back up to Goliath, hoping to answer his next dumb question so they could all move on.

"Nah, I just have one more question for you," the man said. He flashed a wide grin, bearing a gold tooth.

Barrett shrugged in response.

The man reached a hand in his coat pocket. As he did, he asked Barrett the burning question: "Are you Barry Grey's son?"

Caught off guard, Barrett could not control the horrified look on his face, despite the butchering of his name.

The instant the man posed the question he saw the expression and pulled a Ruger SP101 .357 Magnum short barrel from his pocket. Pointing it at Barrett, he spoke again. This time his tone and pitch were different.

"I think you better come with me," he instructed.

***

Jackson plopped down in his squad car after another late Friday. He answered his phone from an unknown number in one ring without thinking twice. This was nothing out of the ordinary for a policeman. He received calls from all over the place, all the time.

"Jackson."

"Officer Jackson, hello," a male voice said.

"Uh, actually it's Sergeant Jackson." He didn't recognize the voice, but figured it wouldn't hurt to correct the guy.

"I have a job for you, Señor Jackson."

It was now clear that the man was Hispanic.

"I'm not looking for work," Jackson answered. The man pretended not to hear.

"You need to get the money that Tomás Chumansky stole and bring it to me."

"What?"

"There might be coke with it. Bring this, too."

"Who is this?" Jackson's head was spinning. Was this a practical joke?

"Who I am is not important right now. You listening to what needs to be done is," the man explained.

Jackson chuckled, but he was nervous. He didn't know if he should play along or hang up. "I'm not doing anything for you, whoever you are."

The man on the other end of the phone paused.

"Señor Jackson, I'm sure you're wondering by now if I am bluffing or maybe joking. But let me ask you one question. If I was your friend and playing a joke, would I tell you that I know your little daughter goes to preschool at William Tell Pre-K? Her hair has been in pigtails every day this week. Today she was wearing a navy blue skirt with a pink and white polka-dot top. Your wife dropped her off. Your address is 1478 Underwood Drive, and judging by your yard, you vote Republican. The election's over, Señor. You can take down the sign."

"Who the hell are you?" Jackson snarled.

"Shall I continue? Your son goes to Highland Elementary School in Adler. Your wife drops him off every day at—"

"I get it, asshole. You're threatening my family."

"I like to think that we both have things that are important to us. You do what you're told and we both win."

Jackson remained silent. The man continued.

"Señor Jackson, I'm not playing games. Not only will your wife and children die, but they will be slaughtered. It will be a bloodbath. I'm not asking you, I'm telling you. From this moment forward, if I think you are veering off course, it will be done. And then you will live the rest of your life knowing it was your fault."

"How in the hell am I supposed to find the money?" Jackson asked the man.

"You are in luck. We have reason to believe Tomás will lead you to it tomorrow evening."

"How would you know this?"

"Just follow him tomorrow night."

"Well, that won't be difficult. I was already going to be doing that."

"Just be sure you follow him wherever he goes. Do not assume you know where the money is based on other things you might have heard," the man insisted.

"What are you talking about?"

"Don't veer off course, Señor Jackson."

Jackson sighed. "Anything else?" he asked.

"Sí, there is. You need to dispose of Tomás Chumansky."

"What? You want me to kill him?" Jackson cried out.

"I can't do that!"

The man said nothing for several seconds.

Worried that his extortionist might have hung up, Jackson spoke again. "Hello? You hear me? You still there?"

"I'm still here. And I heard you. But did you hear me?" the man asked. His tone remained calm. Jackson wondered if all Latin henchmen were like this.

"Come on, man," Jackson pleaded." I can't kill an innocent guy. I'm a cop."

"He's not innocent, Señor. You know that already."

"Yeah but—"

"It's very simple. Follow Tomás, get the money, take care of him. I will call you in about thirty six hours. If you haven't completed the task by that time, your family will be cut up into little bite-sized pieces."

The statement made Jackson want to reach through the phone and rip the man's tongue out of his head. Instead he held back his anger with silence.

"This is no joke. Do not test us. You will be sorry."

The man hung up.

XVII

"Can you please tell me why I'm here?" Barrett asked his captors, trying to look as perplexed as possible. He sat inside the kitchen of a small apartment near Greektown in Chicago. The chair was hard and uncomfortable, and the table in front of him sported a loaf's worth of bread crumbs. Barrett decided he'd rather be standing, but he also figured the big guy wouldn't let him. It was embarrassing to be led at gunpoint by a man pushing his mother in a wheelchair. But Barrett was playing it smart. The chance of him making a run for it with his three bags in tow and not taking a bullet in the keister would be slim.

"You know exactly what's going on," the old lady said, pointing a burning cigarette at him.

"You were on TV last weekend," the big guy said, as though he had a celebrity in his home.

Barrett shrugged and shook his head. "I was?"

"Yeah, and there's a reward for bringing in your murdering, blood-stained soul," the old woman croaked. "Keep that gun on him, Randy!"

Barrett continued to play dumb. "TV? Reward? Murderer? Me? This is all crazy."

Randy moved forward as he offered more information. "Mom is an avid watcher of the tube," he said. "She saw an episode of one of those news shows that had you on it and they said you were a murderer."

"And at the end they flashed a thingy-muh-bob on the screen that said there was a one hundred thousand dollar reward to bring you in," the old lady added with a grin and a nod of her cadaverous head. She took a puff of her cigarette.

Barrett didn't recall seeing anything about a reward on the show, but by the end of it he was admittedly shaken and a bit inebriated.

It's probably true, he thought.

"So you think I look like a killer?" Barrett asked them. "Come on. I've got somewhere I need to be. You've got the wrong guy."

Barrett began to gather his bags from the chair, but Randy walked to the table and pointed the gun at his prisoner.

"If you're not the right guy then you won't mind me calling the police over here right now," he suggested, reaching to the table and picking up an older model cellular phone.

"Does that thing even work?" Barrett asked with a chuckle. He didn't really want to find out.

Randy looked at his mother and then back at Barrett. "Tell you what," he told Barrett. "I'll even prove to you that it works before I call them."

Randy opened the old flip phone, dialed a number, and turned the speakerphone on. The line rang out loud, echoing through the kitchen and the small apartment. After three rings, a man's voice answered.

"Yeah?"

"Hey, Charlie. I want to introduce you to someone," Randy said.

"What? What are you—am I on speakerphone?" the man's voice growled.

Randy put the phone in front of Barrett's face while holding the gun with his other hand.

"Say 'hi' and tell him your name," Randy told him.

Barrett hesitated briefly but realized it was a harmless request. He was already convinced the phone worked.

"Hi, my name is Bob Barker," Barrett greeted the man

on the other end.

"Bob Barker? What the hell is going on there, Randy?" the man demanded.

"Thanks, Charlie," Randy said and closed the phone, hanging up on him. "So now that that's out of the way, I'm going to call the police and we'll sort this all out."

Opening the phone back up, Randy looked down at it and presumably began to dial. Barrett spoke quickly but confidently. "You're sure there won't be any repercussions for you, you know, kidnapping me at gunpoint?"

"Not if you're Barry Greyson. Cops won't care," Randy countered, continuing to dial.

This guy is smarter than he looks, Barrett thought. Time for Plan B.

"Okay, stop," Barrett said. "Stop a minute."

Randy closed the phone and looked at his mother, who tapped her smoke into the ashtray on the table.

"How would you like the chance for more than a hundred grand?" Barrett asked, giving them both a glance. He found the irony of the inquiry hilarious after telling some guy named Charlie he was "Bob Barker."

"Oh yeah? How's that?" Randy asked, his interest piqued.

Barrett leaned forward in his chair. "I need to get to Colorado," he began.

"No you don't," Randy responded.

"No, really. I do. Hear me out."

"Wait a minute, Bucko," Granny squawked. "Why would you want to go back to Colorado? That's where you're from. They're looking for you there."

Barrett decided to stop playing the game of "I'm not him but if I were him..." and instead elected to speak frankly, without actually admitting his identity.

"My father is sick. He has cancer...and I want to see

him before—"

"Yeah, I saw that on the TV too," the old lady interjected in an almost considerate manner, saving Barrett from having to finish his sentence.

"Go with me to Colorado," Barrett said to Randy. "Follow me everywhere I go. Let me see my dad. When I'm done, you can turn me in and collect."

Randy stared at Barrett. "I'm still waiting to hear how this is going to benefit me. Something about extra money?" he said.

Barrett stroked his chin before answering. "I'll pay you to let me do it."

"How much?" Randy asked.

"Ten thousand," Barrett responded immediately.

"When?"

"Three now, the balance after I see my father."

Randy rubbed his cheek in deep thought. "Five now," he countered.

"What makes you think I have that kind of money with me?" Barrett asked with open arms.

Gun still drawn, Randy moved forward and grabbed Barrett's backpack, tossing it on the table in front of them.

"Hey!" Barrett cried out, but Randy was not fazed. He unzipped the backpack and dumped the cash on the table.

"Because if you have three to offer, there's probably more," he explained. Barrett bit his lip and shook his head in anger as Randy began to organize and count the money.

"Fourteen thousand, four seventy-two," Barrett divulged, dryly.

"I'm keeping this," Randy declared. "And I want ten thousand more before I take you in."

"What the hell, man!" Barrett barked back. "You think I have money to burn?"

"I think you'll figure it out," Randy said. He waved his

gun in the air. "You're not exactly in a bargaining position right now."

Barrett placed his elbows on his knees and dropped his head forward into his hands. His voice was muffled when he spoke. "Fine. Whatever."

"So we have a deal?" Randy asked.

Barrett looked up and refocused his eyes on his captor. "Yeah, yeah. So, how are we going to get there?"

"Got that covered, too!" Randy said. "We'll leave in the morning."

***

Jackson opened the shower door and stepped inside. This was his alone time—away from the kids, wife, dog, TV, and various household noises. He tried to do it twice a day, and today he needed that second shower more than ever.

If he had been given more time, Jackson believed he could've devised a plan that would keep everyone alive. As it stood, things didn't look good for Chum. What choice did Jackson have? These Mexicans seemed to have a handle on everything, and there was little doubt that they would follow through with their threat if Jackson didn't deliver. Or if he tried to pull a fast one. Telling Perkins? Forget it.

Getting the money was one thing, but killing Chum? It was an off-the-chart demand. Jackson wasn't even sure he could do it. Aside from target practice, he hadn't fired his gun since coming to Gable. In fact, it had been ten years since he had shot at a human being, and that was in Bosnia while serving his country as a federal protective service agent. And he didn't actually shoot anyone that time. He missed.

Faking Chum's death would almost certainly result in the massacre of Jackson's family. He couldn't take that risk, or any risk for that matter. This was serious. The only question was whether or not Jackson could do the task. The man on the phone made it sound like finding the money or drugs or whatever was out there would be easy. But Jackson had never killed anyone. He briefly wondered if it would be easier to not use a gun. What other possibilities did he have? Strangle, stab, suffocate, sleeping pills—no, the other options would take too much energy, thought, and effort. He was liable to hesitate or change his mind. Jackson would only get one chance, and it was clear to him that a gun was the only way to do it. One pull of the trigger and there was no turning back. Now he just needed to figure out how to actually pull the trigger.

When he was eighteen, Jackson found himself in the middle of Operation Desert Storm as a private in the US Army. After spending three months in the thick of the Gulf War he came back a different person, but it wasn't because of post-traumatic stress. He had been forced to grow up in Saudi Arabia, and it all happened too fast. Upon arrival, Jackson learned to cope with his call of duty by reinventing the extreme environment in his head. In a sense, he repeatedly lied to himself that his situation was worse than it was. This forced him to keep his guard up at all times, in turn making him feel safer. Although to his knowledge he was never near Saddam Hussein, Jackson actually began to believe that all of the locals he came in touch with were as crazy and evil if not more so than the Iraqi president. At the time it seemed like a harmless method of dealing with the circumstances – bullshitting himself – not unlike an NFL linebacker pretending the opposing running back had just insulted his mother. But in Jackson's case there were moments when other soldiers in his troop would have to talk him out of his private world. One time in particular, near the end of his tour, Jackson drew his firearm on an innocent civilian. In his defense, the man did look a lot like Hussein, but there was no reason to threaten him. By then, Jackson was mentally exhausted, and his return to the United States could not have come at a better time. After a month of mandatory counseling, Jackson was himself again. Only now he was more mature and better equipped to deal with extreme situations. When he worked protective service he was able to handle the job without the need to develop an alternative reality. This continued with his various security jobs as well as with his current career as a police officer. It was as if he had spent three months addicted to drugs or alcohol but was able to lick it before it affected the rest of his life. He had been "clean" for more than twenty years.

But now, Jackson believed the only way to save his family was to take a flying leap off the wagon. He absolutely had to fulfill the request. If he tried to pull a fast one on the cartel and wound up causing the death of his wife and children…Jackson couldn't comprehend taking that risk.

***

Agent Delia DeMarco sat in the snow in the wooded area behind the large Chumansky house. She was grateful she'd had the wisdom to bring snow pants on her latest trip to Gable. Even though she believed she looked like a little girl in them, they were a heck of a lot warmer and dryer than the alternative.

The Gable and Adler Police surveillance of Tom Chumansky had hardly been acceptable. Parking in plain sight of the suspect in a squad car was closer to stalking than anything else. Delia knew before she arrived that she would have to get down and dirty for this assignment. She didn't want to spook Chumansky into lying low, she wanted to catch him doing something. To do this she would have to be invisible. So far, Delia had managed to do just that. She had followed Chumansky from his store in Adler to where he was now, inside the house he'd built and no longer owned, presumably speaking to his ex-wife. Delia would have found this behavior strange if not for Maddison Chumansky's pregnancy. There was obviously still a connection between the former husband and wife. Maybe there always would be.

She had parked her rental car a half mile up the county road that ran in front of the Chumansky driveway. Once she was convinced it was hidden, Delia jogged the half mile back to the property and the quarter mile down the driveway that lead to the residence. She crept along the trees on the north side of the house, staying out of sight but confirming that Chumansky's car was indeed parked near the garage.

When she'd arrived in town, Chief Nathan Perkins was, at first, reluctant to let go of the investigation. This wasn't anything unusual for Delia to deal with. She had witnessed it dozens of times. The smaller the town, the stronger the resistance to outside government forces taking over a case. But after a brief discussion, Perkins let go of his reluctance and expressed a desire to remain helpful in whatever manner Delia needed.

For now she preferred to work alone. She had only been in town for twenty-four hours and figured she needed to get a better feel for the situation before making any broad assumptions or bringing in reinforcements.

It was now eight thirty in the evening, and Delia's only light came from the moon and her mobile phone. A couple of times while camouflaging herself in the trees she had taken branches to the face. Now that she was stationary and sitting, Delia had nothing left to do but wait.

No sooner had she decided that tonight would wind up being a fruitless endeavor than she heard a noise coming from the back side of the house. Staying low, Delia moved thirty feet to her left in time to see Tom Chumansky walking out the back door. He was alone and speaking on his cell phone. Thankfully, Delia was within earshot and could make out some of the conversation.

"Where are you right now?" Chumansky said as he stared off into the distance through the wooded acreage behind the house. There was a pause as he listened to the person on the other end of the line.

Concerned she'd be out of range once Chumansky went on the move, Delia continued to move quietly in the direction Chumansky was heading.

"There's nobody here," he said into his phone.

A short pause.

"Because there's no cop car parked outside my house, that's how," Chumansky responded gruffly.

As Delia had hoped, Chumansky assumed he was no longer being watched. It would be ironic if the sloppy surveillance of the Gable PD actually helped solve the case.

"Just get here. I might need your help."

He ended the call but continued to move his fingers on the screen for another fifteen seconds. When Chumansky began moving again it was briskly, as though he now had a better idea where he was going.

He's using a GPS or a map or something like that, Delia thought as she shuffled through the woods. Were it not for his use of the mobile phone as a light, she wasn't sure she'd be able to continue trailing him. As Chumansky crept in and around the trees, Delia could no longer see him. She was merely following the light of his phone.

The hike continued for fifteen minutes as the December evening's temperature continued to drop. Delia's snow pants were getting a more extensive workout than she had expected on the first full night of surveillance. Her knees occasionally touched the ground as she dodged tree branches and sometimes entire trees in the black of night. As she went deeper into the forest, the moonlight was obscured by hundreds of barren tree branches. Delia now had to rely on all her senses and her outstretched arms to move safely through the woods.

Suddenly, Delia lost sight of the light from Chumansky's phone. She stopped cold in her tracks. Without the light to follow she wasn't sure she'd be able to pick up Chumansky's trail again. She wasn't even certain she could make her way out of this mess of trees, though thankfully she did have her phone and a GPS of her own.

There were only two reasons that light would've disappeared, Delia reckoned. He either found the spot he was looking for or he knew he was being followed.

Was he that smart?

Delia pulled out her Glock 19 from inside her winter jacket. Holding her breath as best she could, she listened intently for any sound that might tell her where Chumansky was. After a minute she heard a noise directly in front of her, near where she had last seen the light. Then she heard the noise again. And again.

She guessed it was coming from approximately one hundred feet in front of her. Thanks to the repetitive noise she was able to move forward more freely and closer to the area it was coming from.

Clank! Crunch! Clink! Crunch! Clink! Crunch! Clank!

Closer now, Delia could hear gasps of breath and thuds between each noise.

Chumansky was digging with a shovel.

***

Despite the fact Chase was feeling pretty sauced after six gin and tonics (the first one, a double) he was still inclined to plow through the case files from Otto Clevinger's murder. After meeting Clevinger's son, Boyd, Chase was beginning to wonder why the jerk wasn't still a suspect. He fingered through the colorful folders, unconcerned about the taco sauce he was leaving behind from his room service dinner.

"What was the Golden Child's alibi?" Chase asked the folders out loud. "Golden Child" was a nickname he had come up with during his internal therapy session at the hotel bar as he realized just how privileged Boyd Clevinger was.

Chase opened the file on Boyd and skimmed through it. He squinted and turned his head as if it would give him the answer he was looking for. When it did not, he picked up the phone and dialed a number.

"Hey, it's Sheehan. Sorry, I know it's late."

"It's no problem," Assistant Special Agent in Charge Nolan Reed replied. "It must be important if it's you calling."

"Sarcasm will get you everywhere," Chase said. Not missing a beat, he continued. "I'm trying to figure out exactly what Boyd Clevinger's alibi was the night of his old man's murder. All it says here in the files is 'cleared.' What the hell is that?"

His boss sighed through the phone. "I can't tell you much."

"Why? Because it's classified? Don't pull that bullshit with me, Nolan. We've known each other too—"

"Hey, hey. Easy there, Captain Morgan. It's because I don't know much, but I'll tell you everything I do know."

"My bad," Chase recovered. "Shoot."

"He was banging the receptionist that night," Agent Reed explained. He paused and waited for Chase's reaction.

"Wow. Good for him," Chase said with sarcasm. "Why the hell isn't it written in the file?"

"That's the part I don't know for sure. Even *Dateline* tried to get more information from us and couldn't."

"So it might not be true," Chase hypothesized.

"Oh, I think it's true," Reed confirmed. "I mean, you're welcome to check it out while you're there, of course. But I don't have any reason not to believe it. This seems more like a cover-up."

"What, so his wife doesn't find out?"

"You'd think so, wouldn't you? But she knows about the affair. If you read a bit further you'll see that Junior didn't have an alibi at first because his wife couldn't vouch for his whereabouts."

"Junior? That's funny," Chase said.

"Yeah, if we keep referring to him as 'Clevinger' around here no one knows if we're referring to the dead one or the one who should've died."

"He's kind of a prick, isn't he?" Chase commented.

"Yes. Yes, he is," Reed agreed.

"So when you say 'cover-up'..." Chase said, pulling the subject back to the forefront.

"I think—though I can't be sure—someone higher up was paid to sign off on the alibi," Agent Reed explained.

"But why, I mean, if he really was banging her. Why the need to keep it secret?"

"I don't know. I just...I don't know," Reed said. "I don't think it really matters in this case, though, Chase."

"Only if the alibi is true. Come on, Nolan. There might be something there!"

"It's slim, man. Slim."

"Someone's taking money for this crap?" Chase said, making sure he'd heard correctly.

"I don't know that for sure, Chase. You gotta keep this quiet. Talking trash like that could get your ass bounced. I'm only telling you what I think might've happened so I can help you. We're friends."

"I guess I didn't realize this stuff happened inside a federal agency," Chase replied.

Reed paused before responding. "It happens everywhere, Chase. People get...desperate."

"I'm gonna check things out here."

"Of course. Absolutely!" Reed agreed.

"One more thing," Chase added.

"Yeah, what's that?"

"It was Tanqueray tonight, not Captain Morgan."

Reed snorted. "Only the finest for my drinking buddy, right?"

"I haven't decided yet if I'm going to expense it or not," Chase joked, and hung up.

***

Delia kept her gun drawn and continued to listen to

Chumansky dig. She wanted to move forward fast in order to see and hear more, but she knew if she did she might compromise the situation. She had the suspect right where she wanted him. It was a textbook situation, just like she had been taught in training. Instead of rushing to the scene, Delia methodically stepped in the direction of the digging. She was moving so slowly she felt like she'd never make it there.

After fifteen minutes, still hidden behind some trees, Delia found herself thirty feet from Chumansky. She could view the silhouette of the small man digging with a large shovel, thanks to the light of his cell phone shining behind him from the ground.

Delia knew she still needed to wait.

Chum continued to dig, grunting with every move. Delia was surprised the ground had thawed enough for him to do this, but she knew he had to be tiring. This would play to her advantage when she took him by surprise.

Clank! Crunch! Clink! Crunch! Clink! Crunch! Clank!

Delia yawned.

Clank! Crunch! Clink! Kah-chink!

A grunt from Chum.

He found it, Delia thought.

Kah-chink!

Oh yeah. He found it, she thought.

Clank! Crunch! Kah-chink! Crunch! Clink! Kah-chink!

Delia assumed he was now digging around it. Whatever "it" was, she hoped it contained a large amount of cash and hopefully illegal narcotics. If the drugs were missing, her bust was going to be lacking some important evidence.

Ten more minutes passed as Delia continued to be patient. Every so often she edged closer to Chumansky. The noise of his digging was disguising any sound she made while she crept into position. At one point she thought for sure he had heard her break a large twig beneath her boots. But luck was on her side as Chumansky didn't miss a beat.

Clank! Crunch! Kah-chink!

She was now a mere twenty feet away.

Suddenly, the digging stopped. Delia watched Chumansky drop to his knees and groan as he pulled what appeared to be a large metal case from the hole he had just finished digging. He reached behind him and snagged his phone. As he did, the light glowed on his face and Delia could see his bulging eyes. He was excited, this much she could tell.

This isn't a box of Playboys, Delia thought.

Chum put the phone in his lap and appeared to begin working the combination of a padlock. After his first attempt failed, he took more time and successfully opened the lock on the second try. He pulled the top of the hinged box open and gazed inside. Delia could see the excitement on his face as his eyes lit up, a slight smile appearing.

Chumansky fiddled with something in the box and grinned again. Bringing his index finger to his face, he stuck the tip into his mouth and took a taste.

"Wanna share?" Delia shouted, breaking the silence in the quiet of the night and appearing from behind the trees in front of him. In a knee-jerk reaction, Chum began to return the metal box to its spot beneath the earth before realizing the point was moot. "I can't say you've made this easy," Delia continued.

She had met Chumansky many times during the early days of the investigation. Chum immediately put his hands in the air and stood up. "Agent DeMarco. I've missed our talks," he said.

Delia continued to move toward him gradually, gun drawn and aimed in Chumansky's direction. "I'm just happy we've met again under these circumstances," she replied.

"I'm sure you are," Chum said, realizing what was ahead. "How'd you find me?"

"Patience," Delia explained. She stepped next to Chumansky. "Back up," she commanded.

Taking two steps backward, he continued to speak. "No one was supposed to be watching the house."

"Who said that?" Delia asked, bending over and taking a taste of her own. The bag clearly contained cocaine as her tongue immediately went numb. "Wow. Good stuff," she said. "No wonder you almost got your wife killed for it."

Chum took an extra step back. "Hey, it wasn't really like that," he claimed.

"Sure it was," Delia responded immediately. She moved five bags of coke aside to reveal a large sum of cash. "Who told you the house was clear? Your wife?"

"Ex-wife," Chum corrected her.

"So was it her?"

Just then another male voice echoed through the silence of the night from the surrounding trees. Delia's instinct was to move her Glock from Chum to the area where the voice had come from. She relaxed, though, when the man became visible.

"No backup out here, Agent DeMarco?" Jackson commented. His own gun was drawn and pointed at Chumansky.

"Apparently I've got you," Delia replied. "How did you end up out here?"

Jackson made his way to the box full of narcotics and money. "I followed him here from Adler," he explained as he gave the coke his own test and riffled through the money. "Looks like we've hit the jackpot here."

"You followed me, too?" Chum said. "How did I not notice either of you?"

"I don't know. Overconfident? Does it really matter?" Jackson asked him. "Maybe you're not as smart as you think you are. She caught you with both hands in the cookie jar, regardless of whether or not I made it here."

Delia noticed Jackson seemed surlier than she remembered him a few months ago. Maybe he's just fed up with the shenanigans in his town, she thought.

Chum shifted gears and began his sales pitch. "Look, I realize what this all looks like but it's not difficult to work something out between us. Something where we can all walk away from this and still get what each of us needs..." Tom Chumansky announced. He swallowed quickly before finishing. "...or wants."

"No thanks," Delia declared. "Forgive me for sounding cliché, but I just want justice."

She pulled out her handcuffs and began to walk toward the criminal.

"Hang on a second," Jackson said. "Don't you at least want to hear him try to weasel his way out of this?"

Delia turned to the police sergeant. "Not really."

"I've known this guy for a long time," Jackson explained. "He's a snake and I'd love this last chance to hear him beg for our mercy and not get it. It'll make for some great conversation at the station."

"Forgive me for sounding cliché, but you know I'm still here and listening, right?" Chum interjected.

Jackson ignored him and looked Delia in the eyes. "It would really mean a lot to me," he added. She stared back at Jackson and noticed something indefinable behind his stare.

Delia sighed. "Fine, but let's keep things moving. I'm cold and hungry," she said.

Jackson smiled and turned to Chum. "Well?" Jackson said.

"Are you kidding me?" Chum asked him. "I'm not playing this game."

"Sure you are," Jackson said, positioning himself in front of Chum. His gun was still drawn and pointed directly at the smaller man. "Hypothetically, how would you get yourself out of this situation?"

Chum's hands went above his head again as the barrel of Jackson's firearm pushed against his chest through his winter jacket. "Come on, Jack. Jesus…just take me in. I give. Uncle," Chum pleaded.

"This is pitiful," Jackson snarled. "You've lived your life fast-talking people, pulling the wool over their eyes, selling them a song and dance, and always getting your way. Now you've made it to your final hurrah, the granddaddy of opportunities, and you shrivel up and chicken out?"

Chum glanced at Delia and then back to the police officer who was sticking a gun in his chest. The look on his face begged for mercy.

"Please?" Chum whined.

Jackson's intensity increased. "I want a goddamn sales pitch now!"

"Sergeant Jackson!" Delia protested. She could tell he was beginning to come unglued, for what reason she was not sure. Jackson's hand appeared to shake as he kept his gun pressed against Chum. Was it nerves? Or was it fear? Delia sensed something was not right. Before she had the chance to evaluate further, Chum gave in.

"Okay, okay," he said. "It's not that big of a deal."

Jackson gave Delia a look and a nod. "I'm listening," he said.

"Could you give me some breathing room, maybe let me put my arms down?" Chum requested.

Jackson took three steps backward and pulled his gun down to his side. "I'm waiting," he said. "Agent DeMarco is hungry."

Gazing into the trees past Jackson, Chum spoke to both law officers, slowly, as if in a trance. "If you two don't take me in...you can keep the coke and the money...there's over a quarter million in there...take it. And I'll never tell anyone this happened. We can just all move on."

Delia was not impressed and immediately began her objection. "Yeah, I don't think that's—"

She was cut off by Jackson.

"Deal!" he said and drew his gun, firing a bullet into Chumansky's chest.

XVIII

"What the hell are you doing?" Delia shrieked. She ran over to Chumansky and knelt beside him, unzipping his jacket and ripping open his shirt. It was immediately clear to Delia that the bullet was lodged in or near the heart and Chumansky was already bleeding out. "My God, Jackson!"

She pulled out her phone and began to dial.

"Put the phone down, Agent DeMarco," Jackson commanded her sternly.

Delia looked up and saw Jackson's gun now pointed in her direction. She looked back at Chumansky, who was already fading away, an agonized look on his face as he stared into space.

"He's going to die!" she pleaded.

"I know," Jackson confirmed. "Slowly toss your phone in my direction, Agent."

"What are you doing?"

"I'm not going to ask again," Jackson said in a more relaxed voice. "As you can tell by Chum's condition, I'm pretty unstable right now."

Delia threw her phone underhand in the direction of the police sergeant. It landed two feet in front of him. She looked at her gun that was now lying beside her. She had set it there when she knelt beside Chum.

"Now your piece," Jackson ordered. "Slide it over here. Slowly."

Delia began to reach for her Glock. She knew she had made a big mistake when she rushed to Chumansky instead of drawing on Jackson.

"Don't pick it up," Jackson instructed her. "Push it."

"It's not going to make it to you," Delia said.

"I don't care. Do it."

She pushed the gun in his direction, feeling hope slip away. The gun moved about four feet from Delia through the grass, dirt, sticks, and snow. Jackson moved to it and squatted, picking up both the gun and the phone, all the while keeping his own gun pointed at the DEA agent.

"Hands up, stand up," he told Delia.

She obeyed but also spoke again. "What's going on here?"

"You have any other pieces?"

Delia remained silent.

"Of course you do," Jackson said as he moved toward her. "Do not move," he told her. He began to frisk her in a professional manner as Delia, herself, would do to any common criminal. He checked every nook and cranny that could hold a gun or weapon. When he found her .38 Special tucked in the back of her jeans underneath her snow pants, Delia's heart sank. She looked down at Tom Chumansky. He was already gone.

"Why did you kill him?" she asked Jackson. "He wasn't a threat. He was only a mule. We needed him to get further up the chain."

"I don't have time for a press conference, Agent. Hands behind your back. But I will tell you this for now: I don't want you to end up like him. So please cooperate."

"What are you going to do with me then?" Delia asked as he secured her with her own handcuffs.

"I don't know," he replied, and spun her around so they were face to face. "Have a seat."

He motioned toward the ground. Delia obeyed instantly, realizing there was no alternative at the moment. The admission that Jackson wanted to keep her alive was a sign she would have future opportunities.

After moving the metal box and its contents from the hole, Jackson grabbed the shovel Chum had been using earlier. He glanced at Delia and gave her what almost resembled a look of apology before hastily beginning to dig a larger hole.

Clank! Crunch!

How ironic, Delia thought. Chumansky dug a portion of his own grave.

Clink! Crunch! Clink! Crunch! Clank!

Delia sat and watched Jackson dig for thirty minutes while, unbeknownst to both of them, another figure lurked in the shadows and watched.

***

"You know, when you said we were taking a bus this was not what I pictured," Barrett said as he drove the mini-sized yellow school bus on the interstate. The engine was loud, causing him to keep his eyes on the road and speak with a raised voice.

"I needed something cheap and handicap accessible," Randy replied. "Couldn't leave mom at home alone." His massive body was planted in the front seat, next to the entrance steps so he could keep an eye on Barrett. His mother sat in her wheelchair, parked in the aisle next to her son.

"I don't have a license to drive this thing," Barrett continued. He knew his objections wouldn't amount to much, but it made him feel better to tell Randy how bad of an idea this was.

"Neither do I," Randy explained. "That's why you're driving."

Barrett thought about this for a moment and realized that, once again, the big oaf was making sense. Randy and his mom could play dumb if they were pulled over. Barrett, with no commercial license—no driver's license at all—would have the police focusing on him instead of his kidnappers. His only hope would be to get the cops to find Randy's gun. But even then Barrett would end up in trouble. The only identification he had was a fake Pennsylvania state card he had bought in Pittsburgh as "Dan Scotwood." If he showed it to the police, it wouldn't take them long to discover it wasn't legit, and they might decide to run his fingerprints. Then all hell would break loose and it would happen before he had the opportunity to see his father. No, intentionally getting pulled over would not be a good idea. But it couldn't hurt to throw out some scenarios to Randy.

"This thing sticks out like a big banana on the interstate," Barrett announced. "Getting pulled over just because some highway patrolman wants to do a check wouldn't be good for either of us. They'd find your gun, I probably wouldn't get to see my dad, and you wouldn't get your extra money from me. Who knows if you'd even get that reward."

"As soon as we get outside the city limits we're going to start taking the back roads," Randy explained.

"That'll make a fifteen- or sixteen-hour trip about twenty-four," Barrett protested.

"Do you wanna see your old man or not?" Randy snarled. "If you don't stop your bitching soon I'm gonna turn you in right now."

Barrett pursed his lips. He was aggravated, mostly with himself, for being vulnerable enough to let this happen. It was bad enough he was being forced to drive a short bus a thousand miles across the middle of the country. Now it would take even longer. He decided the best use of his time was to think of ways to ditch Randy.

The trio kept quiet as the bus headed west out of the Chicago metro area. After an hour, Randy broke the silence by giving Barrett new instructions. "Take the exit coming up," he told him. "Turn left on the highway."

Barrett said nothing in response. He wasn't going to change Randy's mind and he couldn't argue with the plan. The real problem was driving a school bus in the first place. It wouldn't have been Barrett's first choice, or his last for that matter. He'd have been better off calling Floyd the bartender and asking for advice. After the profitability of their last transaction, Floyd would probably be inclined to help his old pal, "Cody," again.

But now Barrett didn't have a dime available to him. Even if he was able to give Randy the slip, he'd have a difficult time getting very far. At least Randy had brought Barrett's backpack of cash with him on the journey. Maybe it was because he felt safer keeping it with him rather than in a dumpy apartment in Chicago. It was also probably the only money Randy had to his name. Whatever the reason, it gave Barrett hope that he could reclaim his savings and make a break for it.

When he turned left on the highway, Barrett nearly killed the engine but was able to recover, keeping the bus moving. It had been a process to learn how to drive the vehicle in the first place. Randy hadn't realized how much different driving a bus was than a car. As soon as he discovered this, he nominated his hostage as the chauffeur.

Thankfully, Barrett had learned to drive a manual transmission automobile years ago. There were subtle differences when it came to driving a school bus, but he was able to put his knowledge and understanding of how a motor vehicle works to the test and figure the process out.

"I need a cigarette," the old woman announced.

"Already? Jesus, Ma." Randy said.

"I can't help it. I got needs," she croaked.

"Here," Barrett heard Randy say. "We're not stopping right now."

"Do you know how hard it is to chew gum with

dentures?" she said to her son.

"No, but I'll bet you're gonna tell me."

"Maybe you oughta move a little closer so I can make room in your mouth for your own set," the old lady hissed. Randy did not reply.

Never a chatty driver under the best of circumstances, Barrett decided to remain silent for a while. The trip would be a long one without something to pass the time.

Thirty minutes ticked by without much being said. Occasionally, Barrett would swear he heard someone pass gas, but he never smelled anything. There wasn't much he could do about it, anyway.

Another half hour passed before any additional words were uttered. When they were, to Barrett's surprise, they were sung.

"He was four and I was, too," Randy's mother sang out loud.

"Ma!" Randy exclaimed, embarrassed by her sudden need for song.

She ignored his objection and continued her concert. "We played some doctor then we went to the zoo," she continued, adding volume to her vocals.

Barrett recognized the tune and was almost inclined to sing along. Not so much because he liked the song, but because of how much it apparently annoyed Randy.

"And that's how he learned about the birds and the bees," she sang. "The facts of life."

"Oh God," Randy protested.

"He really knows his stuff," she continued. "He's really had it rough."

"So this is what hell is like," Randy commented as his mother began singing the next verse.

***

"You can honestly look me in the eye and confirm, without a doubt, that Boyd Clevinger was with you on the night of August eleventh of this year between the hours of ten and eleven thirty in the evening?"

Chase took a drink from his coffee cup as he stared across the table at Julia McGregor, the front office clerk at the Clevinger Group.

"Oh, yes. Yes, I can," Julia said with a nod. "I realize you're not asking my opinion, but I'll go ahead and give it anyway. Based on what I know about what happened that night, the only way Boyd could've been involved in his dad's death would be if he had someone else do it."

She took a drink of the vanilla latte Chase had bought her and waited for his reaction.

"I appreciate your assessment, Ms. McGregor," he began. "Truthfully, I tend to agree with it. I invited you here this morning so I could ask you a few other questions."

"Okay," Julia replied. "You don't need to call me 'Ms. McGregor.'"

"I prefer to keep things formal," Chase explained. It wasn't an entirely true statement, but he figured a seemingly promiscuous woman didn't need to feel at home while speaking to an FBI agent about a homicide.

"I understand," Julia said, though Chase didn't believe her.

"Can you tell me about Boyd's relationship with his father, Otto?" Chase asked.

"He treated his dad like shit, for starters," Julia remarked.

"How so?"

"He was constantly yelling at him, telling him how stupid he was and how he wished he'd just go away."

"He said that?"

"Yeah, but it was more in a 'just retire already' kind of way, not..." Julia swallowed hard before finishing her sentence. "…murder."

"What makes you think that?"

"Because despite Boyd's horrible treatment of his dad, I don't think he's capable of killing him," she explained.

"What about hiring someone to do it?"

"I don't know," Julia said as she stared out the window of the coffee shop. "I want to say he wouldn't do that because..."

"Because why, Ms. McGregor?"

"Well, because Boyd's not exactly fit to run the business," she explained. "If you think back to the conversation I had with him when you were leaving the office a few days ago, he didn't know overtime meant paying employees more money per hour. I barely graduated from high school and I know that. I mean, come on!"

"I see your point," Chase agreed. "And to top it all off, he's now in charge of an accounting firm."

"He has no idea what he's doing, Agent Sheehan," Julia informed him with a shake of the head.

"Boyd mentioned that he felt like Barrett Greyson was the son his father always wanted," Chase revealed.

"Oh, that's probably accurate," Julia said. "Barry and Otto were close. They talked numbers and business all the time, went to lunch often; they knew each other well."

"Do you think Barrett Greyson killed Mr. Clevinger?" Chase blurted out.

"If it wasn't for all the publicity telling me it was Barry, I wouldn't think it was possible," she admitted. "I still have a hard time with it. And now with both Barry and Otto gone, there's no one here with any business sense running the Clevinger Group. It's awful."

Chase decided it wouldn't be wise to let Julia know there wasn't any solid evidence that Greyson was the killer. He didn't want to compromise the investigation.

"So if Boyd were to orchestrate his father's death, he'd still have someone to run the company for him in the form of Barrett Greyson, correct?" he asked.

"Yes, I guess that would be true."

"I mean, assuming Boyd realizes his limitations, it wouldn't make much sense to get his father out of the way and frame his only asset," Chase continued. He watched as Julia McGregor processed the hypothesis while continuing to stare out the window.

"Yes. I guess that would be true."

"You seem unsure, Ms. McGregor," Chase observed.

"It's just that I hadn't given it much thought. Now I'm starting to wonder about Boyd, myself."

"But like I said, it wouldn't be smart for him to—"

Julia cut him off. "He's not the sharpest guy, Agent. I think you know that."

"How long has he worked for the company?"

"A few years, I guess. Like three, maybe."

"What did he do prior?"

"Sucked on the family tit," Julia snorted.

Chase raised his eyebrows and chuckled. "Makes me wonder how...why the two of you hooked up," he said, correcting himself.

"Tell me about it," Julia said with a hand wave. "I should clarify that Boyd is still a helpless little boy even with a job. He has a silver spoon shoved so far down his throat it's coming out his ass."

Chase allowed another grin to surface. Julia wasn't pulling any punches. It was kind of funny, too.

"That analogy paints quite a visual," he commented.

"Sorry," Julia said. "Sometimes I can't help but be brutally honest."

"No problem. That's why I'm here. I need the truth,"

he explained. "What was Boyd and Barrett's relationship like at the office?"

"Well," Julia began, "at first it wasn't good. They argued loudly a few times behind closed doors."

"Any idea what they argued about?"

"It sounded like a power struggle. Actually, that's what Otto told everyone. I think he felt like he needed to make excuses for Boyd, so he was always trying to explain away his son's behavior to other employees."

"Power struggle, eh?" Chase confirmed.

"Yeah, which is strange since Boyd had absolutely no power around the office. Still doesn't. Because no one likes him. That's the problem."

"Barrett did, though?"

"Barry was respected by everyone at the Clevinger Group. He treated the staff well and genuinely cared about the business and its success," Julia explained.

"He must've been pretty upset when the Golden Child slid in above him like that," Chase suggested.

"Golden Child? That's funny!" Julia said with a quick laugh. "Yes, I think Barry was pretty hurt by it. But I also think he eventually saw the writing on the wall and realized that fighting with Boyd wasn't going to fix things. He started to become more submissive, bit his tongue a lot."

A thought jolted inside Chase's brain.

"Have you ever had a sexual encounter with Barrett Greyson?"

The horrified look on Julia's face told him all he needed to know.

"No," she protested. "God, no!"

"I had to ask," Chase assured her.

"Agent Sheehan, I know you're just doing your job," Julia said. "And I'm sure I look like the office slut to you. But I'm far from it. I made a mistake with Boyd. Barry was someone I liked too much to ever consider sleeping with."

"Okay, okay," Chase said. "I believe you."

Julia began to gather her things.

"I don't mean to rush you, Agent, but I need to get to my mother's house and pick up my son. She's leaving for church soon and I really don't want my little boy to be subjected to that nut house she goes to. Is there anything else I can tell you about? Or maybe we can schedule another meeting?"

Normally, Chase might've found her eagerness to leave a sign he had suddenly struck a nerve, but he truly did believe she needed to go. And she had, after all, offered to continue the conversation.

"I totally understand," Chase conveyed. "The only other thing I'm wondering is whether or not you were aware that your affair with Boyd is not listed as such in the case files."

"Huh? How would I know that?"

"Has anyone come to you and told you to forget it ever happened?"

"Besides my conscience?"

"Paid you money?"

"God, I wish."

"Nothing?"

"I wasn't even allowed to speak to the *Dateline* people, which was fine by me because I didn't want the world to know," Julia explained.

"Yeah, that makes sense," Chase agreed. "The Clevingers didn't want the world to know either."

The two said their goodbyes and Chase gave her another business card, telling her to call if she thought of anything else that might be important. After watching her walk out the door of the coffee shop, Chase looked down at his phone and wondered if his sister was ever going to return his calls and text messages.

***

Jackson pulled his personal vehicle parallel to the abandoned warehouse. He grabbed the case full of coke and cash and walked through the only door he could find. As he stepped inside, he immediately noticed the warehouse was empty with the exception of three Hispanic men standing in the center.

The overhead lights inside were dim, but Jackson could see that two of the men were armed and he assumed the third—the one in the middle with a goatee—was also packing. Jackson meandered in their direction, pretending to scout out the warehouse as if he were interested in buying it. When he reached them, the man in the middle spoke.

"You brought what was asked?" he inquired.

Jackson held the case out, but said nothing. He was fairly certain from the voice that this was the man who had called him and threatened his family. One of the visibly armed men stepped forward and took the suitcase. He opened it up and examined the contents, allowing the man with the goatee to observe it as well.

"How much did you keep for yourself?" the middle man asked the small town police sergeant.

Jackson glared at the man. "Are you kidding me?" he snarled. "You threaten my family and you still think I'd steal from you guys? Stop being so goddamn paranoid."

The man shrugged. "I'm just doing my job. Was told to ask," he explained.

"Who is your boss?" Jackson quipped.

"Uno momento, friend," the man said. "I have more questions."

"Fine," Jackson said as he crossed his arms.

"Did you take care of our other problem?"

"Chumansky? Yeah, he's out of the picture," Jackson said.

"Will his body be found?"

"Maybe, but it's within the Gable city limits," Jackson explained. "If he's found I'll be able to control the investigation. Not that it will matter much. It'll just be assumed that one of your guys took him out. Most people will feel like he got what was coming to him, anyway."

" Sí," the man agreed. "He did."

"Why couldn't you guys just do it yourselves?" Jackson asked him.

"I'm not done asking you questions, but I'll answer this one out of good faith," the man replied. "The answer is simple. Your town and the surrounding areas would be suspicious of a bunch of Mexicans hanging around waiting for Tomás to screw up."

Jackson rolled his eyes, threw his hands up, and nodded. He couldn't argue with that assessment.

"And that reminds me," the goateed man continued. "What's going on with Eduardo? What about Tomás's wife?"

"What about them?" Jackson said with a puzzled look. "They'll assume what everyone else will. That Chum screwed with the wrong people. Besides, all I have to do is plant that seed with a TV station, and they'll handle the rest. The public believes whatever the media tells them."

The man nodded.

"So who's your boss?" Jackson asked again.

"I can't give you that información," the man said with a grin. "But I assure you there are higher levels within this organization."

"Cartel," Jackson added.

"Whatever you want to call it," the man conceded. "I'm Pablo, by the way."

Jackson didn't offer a hand and neither did Pablo.

"You tell me that like we're going to see each other again," Jackson stated.

"I believe we will," Pablo said.

"Why?" Jackson asked. "I did what you guys wanted. I took Chum out. I got you your shit and money back. Now how about leaving me alone?"

"Señor Jackson, I should say no more," Pablo said. "But I will tell you this. Business has been down and it's because of Tomás and the arrest of Rafael. I think we will need further assistance from you."

Jackson's blood had reached a boiling point. "You tell your boss, no!" he shouted. "Better yet, you tell him, fuck no! You got that, Pablo? I'm not his bitch! I'm a goddamn cop and I will not risk my reputation for you assholes any more than I already have!"

Pablo stared at Jackson. "I said too much," Pablo said. "Go home, Señor Jackson. Go home and hug your family."

Pablo turned and began walking toward a back door that Jackson had not noticed until now. As he did, the two armed men walked backward, keeping their eyes fixed on Jackson, insuring Pablo's safety as well as their own.

Jackson stood and watched as the men left through the door, closing it behind them. He listened as the roar of an engine echoed through the empty warehouse and then faded into the early, winter morning.

Christmas was just around the corner, and this mess was not on John Jackson's wish list. He got into his car and began his short drive home from the warehouse. He breathed several sighs of relief while at the same time realizing his personal nightmare was nowhere near finished.

XIX

Barrett walked into the men's room with Randy following closely behind. He went to the urinal and began unzipping his jeans. When he realized Randy was standing behind him and leaning against the sink, he stopped what he was doing and turned his head around.

"You don't have to go?" he asked.

"Not really," Randy said.

"Not even a little?

Randy gave Barrett a dirty look.

"Seriously, just get up here and go. What am I going to do, run?" Barrett said, motioning toward the restroom door.

The big man ambled forward to the urinals.

"Just make sure you use a buffer," Barrett added.

"A what?" Randy asked, stopping short.

"A buffer space. You know. So we're not standing ankle to ankle while touching ourselves," Barrett explained. He was only half serious, but after Randy's mother's concert a couple of hours earlier, Barrett was beginning to get a kick out of watching his reactions.

"You're weird," Randy commented as he parked himself in front of a urinal that was three spots away from Barrett. "This far enough?" he asked.

"Perfect," Barrett confirmed.

The two men finished their business and headed back to the convenience store portion of the gas station. After grabbing some snacks, they headed back to the bus. Just before entering, Barrett stopped short.

"What about your mom?" he asked Randy. The old lady had remained seated inside the warmth of the school bus.

"What about her?" Randy countered.

"Doesn't she have to...go?"

"Why are you so concerned about everyone's bodily functions?" Randy snapped at him. "Do you really want me to explain how things operate with an eighty-year-old woman in a wheelchair? Use your imagination!"

It took Barrett only a few seconds to realize what Randy was hinting at. The adage about role reversals and how the parent eventually becomes the child came to mind, and that was as far as Barrett was willing to let it go in his head. He was just looking for an opportunity to escape.

"I guess I see your point," Barrett acknowledged as they climbed the steps of the bus.

"Christ, Mom. Give me the lung dart. You're done." Randy bellowed. The bus was filled with smoke. Randy had allowed her to have a cigarette inside the vehicle while they used the restroom, stating it was easier than taking the time to lower the wheelchair ramp in the back of the bus and wheeling her outside.

Randy confiscated the remainder of the cigarette from his mother and trounced back down the steps of the bus to discard it.

"Hey," Barrett called to him as he turned around and re-entered the bus.

"What now?"

"How about giving me a break from driving?"

"Not a chance."

"Why not?" Barrett asked.

"Because I said," Randy snapped back. "And because I have the gun."

"And because he's a scaredy cat," Randy's mom added with a cackle.

"Knock it off, Mom," Randy said.

"What? It's true. I knew right away why you made him drive. You're afraid you can't do it," she snickered at her son.

"I kind of assumed the same thing," Barrett added, deciding to join the fun.

"You shut up!" Randy barked with a vigorous point of the finger at Barrett.

"Come on, I need a break," Barrett pleaded. "I'll show you how. It's not that difficult."

He didn't really need a break yet, but Barrett figured he would create more escape opportunities if he could get Randy to share the driving duties. Thankfully, the old woman had helped pave the way.

"Come on, Randy Ringer. You can do it!" she exclaimed with sarcastic encouragement to her son. Barrett watched as the big man with long blonde hair stood up.

"Fine, have it your way," Randy declared as he gave both of them an annoyed glare. "And don't call me that," he said with a final look to his mother.

***

Fast Eddie Clark sat on the floor with his back against the couch and looked down at his cell phone ringing on the glass coffee table in front of him. The caller ID told him it was Maddison Chumansky. He knew exactly why she was calling. The problem was, he didn't know what to tell her. After watching his best friend take a bullet to the chest, shot by the town police sergeant, Eddie didn't know whom he could trust anymore. For all he knew, Maddison was involved with Jackson and had orchestrated the entire thing. It wasn't like Jackson had provided any answers while apprehending the DEA agent and burying Chum's body.

Eddie hadn't slept the entire night after slipping away

from the scene through the trees and shrubs. He was supposed to meet Chum at the GPS coordinates they both had saved in their phones. They had finally been given the opportunity to dig up the money and coke they buried months ago. The thought of what might have happened to him had he not been running late made it impossible for Eddie to sleep or relax. He was, in fact, a mess right now.

His phone ceased ringing as Eddie continued to stare at it. He snagged the last cigarette from his pack, lit it, took a massive drag, and held his breath. When his phone beeped, informing him of a new voicemail, he finally exhaled.

Holding the cigarette between his lips, Eddie picked up the phone and listened to the message from his dead boss's ex-wife.

"Eddie, it's Maddison. Where are you? Where's Tom? Did you meet up with him last night? He's not answering his phone. Neither are you. What the hell is going on, Ed? We had things all worked out. Call me as soon as you get this. You guys have me freaked out."

Eddie desperately wanted to call her back even though he knew it would break her heart to hear what he had witnessed. Or would it? Maddison had, after all, divorced Chum. Sure, she was pregnant with his child. But she had also basically blackmailed Chum by keeping her mouth shut during the divorce and making him gather the money so they could split it. Maybe she was in cahoots with Jackson and he'd told her there had been no sign of Fast Eddie Clark. What if Eddie was to then call her back and tell her what he'd seen? He could always tell her he knew nothing, had seen nothing. But that, too, could always implicate him down the road.

It was a simple answer, really. Eddie didn't like any of the options racing through his mind. He pulled himself from the floor, cigarette still in his mouth, and walked to his bedroom. He opened the double doors of his closet and grabbed a duffel bag with the Mecca Warehouse logo on it. There was only one thing Eddie could think to do at this point that would guarantee his safety, at least for the short term.

***

Despite the substantial stress of the past several hours, Delia was still able to fall asleep on the California king bed in the locked room where Jackson had stashed her. He had even been gracious enough to handcuff her to the headboard allowing her to have one hand free and making it more comfortable to doze off.

But Delia had no idea where she was being held. Jackson had blindfolded her before driving to the destination. She knew it was at least an hour to ninety minutes from the Chumansky property. There was a narrow window, but it was covered by curtains and what appeared to be a shade. Unable to hear any sounds from the window or from outside the door, Delia began to assume she was underground.

Now that she was awake, being attached to the bed by one arm was becoming increasingly uncomfortable. She was also hungry and thirsty, but at least she wasn't cold. She wasn't able to tell for sure but she concluded a furnace must be turned on, silent as it was.

Though she doubted it would help, Delia was just about to begin yelling to see if there was anyone within earshot when the door to the room was unlocked from the outside.

Jackson walked in. He was dressed in the same clothes as when Delia last saw him. The knees of his jeans were still dirty and looked damp.

"Well, look what the cat dragged in," Delia announced. "Could you..."

She attempted to raise her secured hand but instead grimaced in pain as the cuff bit into her. Jackson strolled forward. He kept one hand on his holstered gun as he unlocked the handcuff.

"Thanks. I was really hoping you would forget I had the key before you left me here," Delia admitted as she rubbed her wrist. Jackson had searched her and found the key in her pocket when he had led her blindfolded to her cell.

He said nothing as he backed away from the bed.

"And I'm guessing by the way you were touching your gun just now you have no intention of letting me go home."

Jackson shook his head.

Delia continued her interrogation. "What are you going to do with me? Do you even have a plan?"

"You weren't supposed to be there, Agent DeMarco."

"It's a narcotics case."

"Yeah, but aren't you supposed to check in or something?" Jackson asked.

"I did!" Delia insisted.

A puzzled look came over Jackson's face. Then, almost as quickly, it retreated. "Perkins," he said. "You told Chief Perkins."

"He answered the phone," she explained.

"Why the hell didn't he tell me?"

"Maybe he got busy. You want to tell me what's going on? What's it gonna hurt? You're gonna have to either kill me or..."

Jackson glared at her before speaking. "What's the alternative, Agent?"

Delia swallowed hard. "Let...let me help you," she suggested.

"Right. Because you won't take me into custody out of the goodness of your heart," Jackson said.

"Can I stand up, please?" Delia asked, politely.

The police sergeant motioned in agreement with an open palm and backed himself against the door. Delia stretched her arms to the sky and let out a groan full of relief in doing so.

"Let's think about this for a minute," she began. "What have you done wrong?"

"Killed a guy," Jackson said.

Delia shrugged.

"I buried him, Agent."

"Did you really kill and bury Chumansky?" she asked.

"Yes..." Jackson watched as Delia's eyebrows rose up her forehead. "What are you getting at?"

"There are ways around this. I mean, assuming you've got a good reason for all of it."

"What about kidnapping you?" he asked her.

"Didn't happen."

Jackson stroked his chin and contemplated the possibilities. "I'm not buying it."

"Good, because I haven't offered it yet," Delia snapped back. "What is going on?"

Jackson sighed and crossed his arms. "Got a call from the Mexican cartel that's behind the muling that's been going on around here."

"When?"

"Friday night."

"What did they say?"

"Find the money and coke Chum stole, dispose of him, and bring the stuff to them. Otherwise they'd kill my family." Jackson looked down during a brief silence before speaking again. "They even told me how to find the stuff. They said to follow Chum last night and he would lead me to it. He did."

"I wish they would've told me that," Delia joked. "I had to sit out in the snow for hours not knowing if I was on the right track until he started digging."

"They must've bugged Chum in order to have that kind of information."

"Probably," Delia agreed. "His car or house or something like that. Some place where he talks."

"When they put a gun to Maddison's head last summer

and that didn't do the trick, they must've realized they'd need to do something else to recover their stuff."

"Good point," Delia agreed. "How come he didn't see you tailing him?"

"I wasn't driving a squad car. Once he turned west on Main in Gable, I was pretty sure I knew where he was going. I pulled into the Corner Store to make it look like I was getting gas, waited thirty seconds, and continued following him from a greater distance. The hills and curves out there made it easy to keep track of his taillights."

"Wow," Delia said. "You were my buffer car. I was behind you following him." They both paused briefly before she continued speaking.

"So that's it? That's not so bad. You gave the stuff back to them?"

"Yeah, I did. Earlier this morning. But it ain't over," Jackson explained.

"What?"

"Sounds like they want me to do more."

Delia moved in Jackson's direction. "We can work on this together. I have the entire DEA—the government—at my disposal," Delia pleaded. "Let me help you."

"Right," Jackson replied. "Like you're just going to forgive and forget."

"Why wouldn't I?" Delia asked. "It's not like you beat the crap out of me or shot me."

Jackson moved closer to her. "Do you have any idea what it's like to have your family threatened?"

"I know. I mean...I can imagine," Delia said, trying to sound sympathetic.

"I've lived the last twenty years of my life trying to keep the bad guys behind bars, and out of nowhere they decide I need to take orders from them? This has been a living hell!"

Jackson briefly flexed his chest as he verbalized the

climax of his outburst. Delia was close enough to see his nostrils flaring.

"Let me help you, Jackson! Damnit!" Delia's frustration was beginning to burn.

"I don't know," Jackson said. "You could be pulling my chain. I know the routine."

"I can see you're telling me the truth. And what's the alternative?" Delia reminded him.

Jackson again looked down at the ground in silence.

"Come on," Delia said. "You've got to trust somebody."

He suddenly looked up, staring through Delia and shaking his head. He turned around and opened the door.

"Jackson!" Delia bellowed. But the police sergeant kept moving, slamming the door behind him.

"You're gonna get someone killed!" Delia yelled at the closed door, but she heard no response. "Damnit," she said under her breath.

Within seconds, the door creaked open again and Jackson appeared in the entryway. He was holding Delia's gun and phone.

"I swear to God if you double-cross me..." Jackson said while handing them to her.

"You just do everything I tell you," Delia replied as she holstered her gun and checked her phone, discovering the battery was dead. "You know, you could've turned off my phone and saved me some battery."

"I didn't know I was giving it back anytime soon," Jackson explained.

"I've got a charger in my rental car."

"Agent DeMarco?"

"Yes, Sergeant."

"If anything happened to my family, I wouldn't be able to live with myself," Jackson said.

"Nothing's going to happen to anyone," Delia assured him.

"I mean," Jackson continued, "I wouldn't want to live."

Delia walked closer to him. The two stood toe to toe. "Nothing," she repeated, "is going to happen to anyone."

***

The old woman sat across from Barrett. Randy had positioned her wheelchair to face their prisoner instead of sitting next to him. The gun was in her lap and she was crocheting.

"When I was growing up I would hear 'The Facts of Life' all the time on AM radio when my dad drove me to school," Barrett told her. He hoped making conversation with her might help his situation. What did he have to lose? At least he wasn't driving anymore.

"That song kind of reminds me of another song," she replied. "You ever heard 'Ukulele Lady'?"

"Ethel Merman," Barrett said.

"Among many other versions," the old lady added.

"Don't start singing again!" Randy commanded from the driver's seat. He had surprised even himself by taking Barrett's instructions well and learning to drive the small yellow school bus in a short period of time. The weather had also been cooperating. It was three days before Christmas and there had been a limited amount of snow expected throughout the Midwest before they left Chicago.

Barrett changed the subject and worked on charming the old woman. "You don't really think I'm a killer do you? Look at me. Do I really look like I'd hurt someone? Murder someone?"

The old woman stopped what she was doing and looked over to Barrett with her beady black eyes. "Ted Bundy didn't look like it, either," she squawked.

"Come on," he said, laughing. "Stereotypes exist for a reason. Besides, he was a serial killer. He had to blend in."

The lady went back to crocheting. Barrett turned his attention to Randy.

"I take it your real name isn't Randy Ringer?" he queried with a slightly louder voice so he could be heard over the noise of the engine.

"Do you ever shut up?" Randy snapped back.

"That was his rastling name," the old lady chirped. "Randy 'The Bastard' Ringer."

"Ma!" Randy protested.

"Wrestling?" Barrett confirmed. "Now that I can see. It makes sense."

"Wanna know how he got the name?" she snorted.

"Good God, Mom!"

"Sure." Barrett sat back in his seat and folded his arms.

"Well, first of all," she began, "he is."

"Is what?"

"A bastard," the old woman said, matter-of-factly.

Barrett looked at Randy, who was shaking his head and keeping his eyes fixed on the road. Barrett glanced back at the woman. Her face remained serious.

"Well, he was," she repeated. "Is."

"Okay," Barrett replied. "Shit happens...right?"

"Yeah, it sure does," she agreed.

"The best part about my wrestling name was the ringer part," Randy piped up, changing the subject.

"How's that?" Barrett asked. He wanted to be entertained, but he also wanted to get his money and get to Colorado, preferably alone.

"We did this thing where I was the ringer. You know, the guy people think is an amateur. I'd sit in the audience and wait to be signaled into the ring to help."

"But he was always in some kind of disguise. As if no one would recognize the big blonde buffoon," the old woman added.

"Some costumes were better than others," Randy admitted with an index finger in the air.

"He would crawl into the ring and rip off most of his clothes," his mother explained.

"It was part of the gimmick. Then I'd help someone to victory."

Barrett had never been a wrestling fan, the sport or the Vince McMahon kind. His younger brother, Milo, however, was a different story. He had wrestled his way through high school and was still competing at Colorado State. Milo enjoyed the WWF and other wrestling entertainment on television or watching it live at the Pepsi Center with his friends. Barrett was nearly a decade older than his brother. When he was a senior in high school, Milo was only in the second grade. Because of the age difference, the boys never had much in common other than their parents and relatives.

"Sounds like a quality act," Barrett declared. "What happened?"

"What do you mean?" Randy barked with a swift glance to his right.

"I mean, why aren't you doing it anymore?"

The old woman let out a cackle that sounded like she was choking. Randy ignored her.

"Well, for starters I'm fifty-two years old."

Barrett nodded in understanding.

"Yeah, tell him the truth, big boy," his mother said.

Randy shook his head in disbelief, but said nothing in return. Barrett was willing to let it go, but the old lady had other ideas.

"First of all, he never got very far with the rastling thing," she began. "Never made it past the local scene."

Randy sighed extra loud so his disapproval could be heard over the noise of the bus engine.

"But where he really hit rock bottom was when he met Toots," she continued. "That's just my nickname for her. What was her real name again, Randy? I always forget."

Randy visibly gripped the steering wheel tighter, yet he still said nothing.

"Anyway, Toots really screwed up Goldilocks here," she explained, pointing a bony finger in Randy's direction.

Barrett continued to listen, figuring the old woman didn't need any encouragement. She was able to belittle her son just fine on her own.

"She talked him into quitting the rastling. Told him there was no money in it. That the odds were a million to one. By then she was already stealing what little money he did have, and soon she started talking him into stealing money for her. Then she got pregnant. Well, the first time she lied to him about it. Or maybe it was a false alarm or maybe she wasn't sure who the father was. But then she really did get pregnant. That's when the shit really hit the fan."

Barrett thought he felt the bus pick up speed as the woman continued her story.

"Come to find out, Toots was only sixteen. And when she got pregnant she left Randy high and dry when she realized he wasn't going to be able to support her and a...well, a baby bastard. You know, like father like son."

The woman didn't have a filter. Barrett hoped he had more class left in his arsenal than she did by the time he was her age.

"But the story doesn't end there," she announced. "Toots moved in with her parents and told them who the father was, the stupid bitch. And just like that Randy was sentenced to seven years in the big house."

The bus was moving faster. Really fast.

"Hey, uh, Randy?" Barrett called out. "Slow down."

Randy's face and hands were red. He looked as if he were about to pull the steering wheel off the dash.

"Randy, slow it down!"

This time Barrett yelled and stood up while holding on to one of the bars separating the stairs and his seat. The old woman paid them no mind as she went back to crocheting. Barrett stepped up to Randy's side and put a hand on his shoulder. Randy swatted it away. In doing so he briefly lost control of the speeding vehicle. The yellow bus swerved into the oncoming lane of traffic. As Randy abruptly pulled the steering wheel and the bus back into position, he also stepped on the brake. The extra motion threw Barrett off balance, thrusting him into the stairwell. As he fell backward he reached out for the bar to brace his fall. This swung him around, smacking his back against the bars, but slowing his fall down the steps.

As Barrett gathered his bearings from the bottom of the stairs, Randy drove the bus to the shoulder of the two-lane highway and parked. He unbuckled his seatbelt and stood up in front of his mother. Grabbing the .357 from her lap, he pulled the hammer back and stuck it in front of the old woman's head. Her eyes stayed glued to her crochet project as her enraged son spoke.

"You don't have a pot to piss in and you're telling him how worthless I am?" Randy bellowed at her. "I do the best I can as an ex-con and registered sex offender and I have to support your bony ass in the process!"

Pulling himself up silently, Barrett viewed the scene from the stairwell. He was shocked to see the old lady still crocheting, head down. Barrett could only see Randy from the back, but his voice roared through the bus and his yellow hair shook like the mane of an angry lion.

"I made some mistakes, so what? You did, too! And yes, I'm one of them! We aren't the first two people in this world to bump uglies without thinking! But I've had it with your condescending, bullshit attitude toward me when all I'm trying to do is keep you alive! I'd rather not have to steal your diapers, old woman! But it's a hell of a lot better than the alternative of having to clean up after you! You're so nasty it's a wonder someone didn't put you out of your misery a long time ago!"

Randy paused to take several deep breaths. Barrett wasn't sure what would happen next. He hoped it didn't involve a giant man having a heart attack and falling on him. This whole thing was getting ludicrous. All he wanted was to get to Colorado and see his ailing father.

"In fact," Randy continued, this time with a lower volume, "I can't think of one good reason to not take care of my biggest problem right here, right now. Can you, Nora?"

This was the first time Barrett had heard the old lady's name. He wanted to speak up in an effort to stop the confrontation, possibly even save the woman's life, but an immoveable force held him back. Instead, Barrett watched the exchange take place as if he were watching a movie. He still couldn't see the expression on the big man's face, but Barrett could tell by his tone that he was not playing games.

Randy moved the gun closer to his mother's face.

"Give me one good reason not to pull the trigger, Mom."

Slowly, Nora raised her head and looked up the short barrel of the gun at her son. Completely unfazed by the words and the threat against her life, she spoke quietly. "Aubrey," she said. "Her name was Aubrey."

And with that the elderly woman once again lowered her head and traveled back to her creative zone. Barrett looked on as Randy "The Bastard" Ringer uncocked the gun and lowered it back to its place in his mother's lap. He sat back down in the driver's seat and turned the key.

"You wanna fall again or are you going to get back up here?" he asked Barrett.

XX

Claire opened the screen door to Stubby's and zipped her coat. She looked both ways before crossing Main Street and entered the passenger side of Maddison Chumansky's car.

"Hey, sorry," Claire apologized. "I came out as fast as I could, but as soon as you called it seemed all of my tables needed something."

"Tom is missing. So is Eddie," Maddison said. She continued to look straight ahead through the windshield as a train passed on the railroad tracks fifty yards in front of them.

"What?"

"No one has seen or heard from them since last night. Neither of them are at work. No call, no show," Maddison explained.

"What are you saying? What am I missing? Start from the beginning."

"Tom came to the house last night," Maddison said. "The coast was clear. He went into the woods behind the house. Eddie was supposed to meet him out there. They were going to get the money...and the...coke. He didn't come home and didn't answer his phone. Eddie didn't answer his either."

Maddison turned to Claire with a worried look on her face.

"What about their homes?" Claire asked.

"I have a key to Tom's. No one's there. Eddie didn't seem to be at his place either from what I could tell. I just got back from there."

"What do you think happened?"

"I haven't stopped thinking about it," Maddison said. "I didn't sleep all night. There are only two logical things it could be."

Claire swallowed hard as Maddison continued.

"They could've taken off and split the money. But that doesn't make a lot of sense. The money really isn't enough for Tom to run away and start over with, not even if he kept it all for himself."

"Maybe it was more money than what he told you," Claire suggested.

Maddison considered this for a moment. "I hadn't thought of that. I suppose it's possible. I just think it would have to be an awful lot of money. And he'd be leaving behind his unborn child. He's given me every reason to believe he wants to be a father and a part of our baby's life."

"And there's the drugs, too," Claire reminded her.

"True," Maddison agreed. "He did admit to me last night—the last time I saw him—that there was cocaine left, too. I told him we were going to flush it down the toilet together."

"What's the other thing you think could've happened?" Claire asked, beginning to realize her fifty-thousand-dollar payday was slipping away.

Maddison had gone back to observing the train. She paused a few seconds before responding. "You know how when a train stops on the tracks and blocks traffic for long periods of time?"

Claire raised her eyebrows. "Sure," she answered.

Maddison continued to look straight ahead, her hands on her pregnant belly. "It drives me nuts. I'm impatient when I'm driving. I want to get to where I'm going and spend as little time as possible in the car. I need to be moving forward all the time. So I find a way to drive around the train...and you know what?"

Instead of answering, Claire shook her head.

"By the time I get to the other side of the tracks, the train has cleared," Maddison said. "I could've waited for it and I would've gotten to my destination just as quickly."

"It was a waste of energy," Claire added.

"But it wasn't," Maddison said, finally turning her head and looking at the young woman next to her. "I do it every time even though I know what the results are going to be. The feeling of moving forward and accomplishing something is more important to me. I could do less and accomplish the same thing, but I don't."

"I'm not sure I understand how this is relevant," Claire said. She pulled a cigarette from her coat pocket. She had no intentions of smoking it in a pregnant woman's car; it simply calmed her nerves to hold one.

"I'm not either," Maddison said as she watched the final cars of the train pass. "But it is, somehow."

The red lights on the train crossing ceased flashing. The warning bells stopped ringing. Maddison turned to Claire once again and gripped her left hand with both of hers.

"I'm afraid something awful has happened to Tom and Eddie," Maddison revealed, her eyes beginning to well up. The fear and concern on Maddison's face caused Claire to feel a sickness stirring in her stomach.

This shouldn't surprise me, Claire thought. Not after what she had witnessed first-hand last summer. She had spent so much time with Dr. Hammond trying to suppress the feelings of the experience that it had started to feel like it was all a bad dream. But the emotions were coming back now, and quickly. The reality of the situation was smacking her in the face. With tears in her own eyes, Claire returned the hand squeeze and spoke.

"What are we going to do?"

***

It had been too long since he'd heard from Delia. Chase didn't need to be a federal agent to know his twin sister was in some type of trouble. He could sense it. When Chase called Agent Reed and told him he planned to fly to Iowa, Reed's displeasure was immediately apparent.

"What the hell do you think you're doing, Sheehan?" Reed said. "You have a job to do—for the F.B.-friggin'-I. You're not a DEA agent! You know that, right?"

"It's my sister, Nolan. I think she's in trouble."

"I understand you're concerned about your sister, but what about the case in Colorado? Let me make a couple of calls," Reed suggested. "I'll get the DEA to send an agent to check up on your sister."

"I have a better idea," Chase countered. "Make a call and send another F.B.-friggin'-I. agent to Denver. I've hit a dead end, anyway. Nothing's happening."

When Reed didn't respond right away, Chase knew he had him.

"Come on, Nolan," Chase pleaded. "Just this once. I have vacation time. Do this for me and I'll owe you big time."

Chase heard a sigh through his phone.

"Fine," Reed agreed. "But keep me posted."

"I will," Chase said. "Thanks, Nolan."

He was heading to Gable, Iowa, with or without permission, but having Nolan Reed's blessing helped ease Chase's conscience, if only a slight bit. Family came first for the Sheehans, before careers or money or anything else. Chase had been there for Delia in the past, and he wasn't going to let work stop him from helping her again. Besides, her investigation was connected to his. Maybe he'd learn something vital in the process.

Chase tucked his phone in the inside breast pocket of his jacket. Then he picked up his carry-on bag and threw it over his shoulder as he found his place in line to board the airplane. He wondered if he'd get a nap in before the flight screwed with the pressure in his ears like it usually did.

His plane was scheduled to land in Omaha in less than two hours. He'd then travel by rental car another two hours or so to make his way to Gable. It would be late by the time he arrived, but Chase hoped to get an early start the next morning. His real hope was that when he landed in Omaha he would turn his phone on and find a message from Delia. But deep down he knew that wouldn't happen. Something was wrong.

***

"Hand me the ketchup, will you?"

Barrett reached with his left hand to the back corner next to the napkin dispenser. He picked up the red bottle and handed it across the table to Randy.

"Thanks, man."

Randy squirted a third of his plate full of the sauce and began to eat his fries. Every so often he would also dip his burger in it and take a bite. Nora sat to Barrett's right in her wheelchair. She sipped her coffee and occasionally took a bite of her grilled chicken salad while reading the *Des Moines Register.*

It was if nothing had happened an hour earlier when Randy nearly drove the bus off the road and threatened to put a hole in his mother's head. Barrett assumed the outburst was not the first between the two and that their entire existence of living with each other revolved around the constant disappointment of the past. In fact, their present and future didn't seem so wonderful as far as Barrett could tell. The prospect of having some money for a change almost assuredly was the driving force behind the current situation Randy had put them in.

Because money solves everything, Barrett thought sarcastically.

Randy had pulled into a truck stop thirty minutes

earlier, just outside of Des Moines, Iowa, when it became apparent that Nora needed to stop. As far as Barrett could tell, she had already relieved herself, but he pushed the notion out of his mind in favor of stretching his legs and getting something to eat. Randy had other ideas, though.

"You're coming with us," he said.

"What? Why?"

"Because I'm not leaving you alone," Randy explained.

"You've got the keys and my money. What am I going to do, take a cab and pay for it with my good looks?"

The truth was, Barrett wanted his money back almost more than he wanted his freedom. He had saved and stashed it away for years in case of an emergency. Every time Randy filled the gas tank of the bus Barrett watched his future fade away a little more. That money was the key to his freedom. While Randy thought it would buy him happiness, Barrett knew it was a key factor to his own survival.

"I'm not taking any chances. Come on," Randy commanded.

The blonde hulk had enough couth to not force Barrett completely inside the restroom while he helped his mother. Instead, he told Barrett to stand outside the door and keep others from entering. The only stipulation Randy made was that Barrett's foot remain inside the restroom door, propping it open slightly and assuring the former wrestler that his hostage hadn't fled.

Barrett welcomed the two men who attempted to enter the men's room during that ten-minute period. They served as a distraction from overhearing anything that was going on inside.

"Got a little emergency going on in there," Barrett told them. "Would you mind waiting just a few minutes?"

Thankfully, the men didn't ask any questions. Barrett was prepared to tell them the truth if he had to, but they probably assumed there was a sick child inside. In a way, there was. Two of them.

Now the threesome with a school bus parked outside sat together at a table in the truck stop's restaurant like a family—eating, reading, and chatting.

"Listen to this," Nora said from behind the newspaper. "Fast food restaurant's hamburger contained THC, a substance found in marijuana."

Randy investigated the cheeseburger in his left hand before taking a bite and speaking with his mouth full. "I think I got ripped off," he commented.

Barrett had to give the old woman credit for the subject matter she elected not to mention. He could view the front page of the newspaper from his position at the table. It read: Caretaker Accused of Sexual Abuse at Special Olympics.

Nora lowered the paper and spoke to her son. "I bet that cow you're eating was born and bred right up the road from here," she declared.

His mouth still full, Randy answered back. "Besides farm, what do people do in Iowa?"

Nora didn't respond. Her newspaper still lowered, she and her son looked to Barrett for an answer.

"I don't know," he said, raising his water glass. "I've never been here."

It was a half-truth. He'd never been to Des Moines.

"Liar," Nora stated. She put the newspaper back in front of her face and returned to her reading.

Randy snorted. "Mom has spoken," he said.

"You do realize I'm not the person you think I am, right?" Barrett protested. He figured it might be worth another try, but guessed the effort was futile.

"Yeah, you told us," Randy said.

Barrett didn't know where to take the conversation from this point, so he kept his mouth shut. The waitress came over and asked if everything was okay. It was, and Randy told her so. She gave Barrett a glance and a smile as she walked away.

The newspaper came back down and Nora picked up where she had left off. "Wait a minute," she said. "Not only were you in that small Iowa town awhile back, but you were involved in some kind of drug heist. There was some missing money."

Randy looked at Barrett and then at his mother. "What are you saying?" he asked her.

"What I'm saying is this guy might know where the real loot is."

Randy wiped his face with his napkin. "That true?" he asked Barrett.

Barrett didn't like where this was going. He decided to tell the truth for a change. "No. No it's not," he replied.

"The TV show said there were murders committed over some missing money and drugs," Nora recalled. "They thought this guy might know something, and that's probably why he took off."

Barrett could barely contain himself. He put his right elbow on the table and stroked his forehead with his hand.

"You have anything you want to tell us?" Randy asked him.

Barrett said nothing as he weighed the pros and cons. He shook his head while looking down at his plate. His motives hadn't changed. If he couldn't get his backpack full of money and break away from Randy and Nora, the only other thing that still mattered to him was getting to Denver to see his father before it was too late. At this point, telling the truth wasn't going to harm anything.

"Fine, you got me. I'm Barrett Greyson."

"Jesus," Randy responded. "It's about time."

"But that doesn't mean I know anything about the missing money and coke," Barrett added. "The money you have of mine is my savings. It's all I have with me. That's an obvious truth."

"You've gotta know something," Randy countered.

Barrett was telling the truth, but he knew the best way to convince Randy and Nora was to tell them the entire story beginning with his first day in Gable. He told them about his job and about meeting Chum and living in his old farmhouse. He told them how he was blindsided by Franco and his men and how he devised an impromptu plan to overtake the men at the Corner Store.

"So you conked that Chum-guy in the head and left him in the cooler with the Mexicans?" an intrigued Randy asked.

"I actually used a choke hold on him. He only passed out for a half minute or so."

"Choke hold, eh? I like it." The former wrestler smiled and mopped up the balance of the ketchup on his plate with a cluster of fries.

"So then you just left town?" Nora asked.

"For the most part, yes," Barrett said.

Nora looked at her son then back at Barrett. "So what do you think was really going on with the missing loot?" she continued. "It was a couple hundred grand, right?"

"Like two fifty, supposedly. The way things transpired that night I think Chum knew where it was all along; probably still does," Barrett suggested.

"Why would he risk the lives of all those people that way if he knew where the stuff was?" Randy inquired.

"Because he's an idiot!" Nora exclaimed.

Barrett nodded in agreement. "That's what I've been thinking."

"And the asshole got the wise idea to try and make it look like you stole it while living in his house," Randy said.

Barrett nodded. "I'm not sure the money was ever there, either."

"I think we need to make a detour," Randy proclaimed, wiping his mouth with his napkin.

"What? What are you—"

Barrett stopped short when he saw the smile on Randy's face; it told him everything he needed to know.

"Aww, no!" Barrett cried. "I can't go back there! I'll never get to see my dad!"

"Maybe not, maybe you will," Randy teased.

"No, no I won't. As soon as I'm spotted it's all over with," Barrett reminded him. "And you won't get your reward."

"Sure I will," Randy argued. "I'll collect the reward for turning you in and I'll also find this guy and his money and blow. It'll be a double payday."

Barrett looked at Nora who seemed to hold no objections. He turned back to Randy. "I'm not going back to Gable," Barrett protested.

"Wanna bet?" Randy countered.

"What are you going to do, shoot me?" Barrett stood up, pushing his chair back from the table. "Go ahead," Barrett said as he put his coat on. "Stop me from walking out of here."

"I've got your money," Randy reminded him.

"I don't care," Barrett replied. "It's more important to me that I see my father." He got up, walked past Nora, and headed toward the door. "Good luck, you two," Barrett said, bidding the mother-son duo farewell.

Turning his back to them, he moved to the cash register and put his hands on the front door. Pushing it open he felt the brisk, Iowa wind kiss the glass and shove it closed again. At the same moment he heard what sounded like a firecracker explode behind him, followed by gasps and screams from the restaurant and convenience store's customers.

Barrett spun around and saw Randy, standing up beside his seat at the table, pointing his now smoking gun in the air. Above him, the ceiling was crumbling where he had fired off a round.

"Get back here!" Randy commanded.

***

"Damnit!" Delia growled, realizing her phone would not make a call until it was charged to at least ten percent. She was driving her rental car and following Jackson on the highway in front of the Chumansky property. They had agreed to meet at the police station. Both would make phone calls on the way—Jackson to his wife, telling her to gather the children and head to her mother's house in Minnesota. There was no telling what was about to happen, and Jackson and Delia agreed it was better to play it safe. Delia needed to call Devling in Chicago and brief him on the latest happenings, or at least some of the details. Enough that he would send protection to Jackson's mother-in-law's house. She also wanted to call her brother. As she drove the Chevy Malibu along the winding back roads of Gable, a light snow began to fall. The wet flakes smacked the windshield with a vengeance as the vehicle accelerated through them.

Delia wasn't even sure if what she was doing was the right thing, but at the time it was her only way out of the basement of Jackson's fishing cabin. She looked down at her phone again:

Two percent.

She thought back to the drive away from the cabin.

They had driven for an hour and fifteen minutes together from Blackbird Lake, mostly in silence. It wasn't until the final stretch that Jackson had said anything of substance.

"I'm sorry," he said.

"You mean for kidnapping me?" Delia asked him.

"For all of it. For shooting Chum, for kidnapping you," Jackson explained. His voice cracked slightly, expressing a sincere regret Delia had yet to see from him until now. "The only thing I could think of was protecting my family. I didn't know what to do."

"You did the right thing by letting me go so I can help you. That was a good start," Delia told him.

"Yeah," Jackson said under his breath without taking his eyes off the road.

"Look, I'm the last person in the world to condone shooting an unarmed person even if he was a slimeball and a criminal," she began. "But I can't say I would have handled it any differently. How do I know what I would've done if I've never been in that same situation? I'm not going to beat you up over this, Jackson. I'm really not."

Five percent.

Jackson continued to watch the road. "He was going to be a father soon," he said, shaking his head.

"Yeah, and there's a couple of different ways of looking at how that was going to work out for the child. Divorced parents, drug mule dad." Delia couldn't believe the words she heard from her own lips. She didn't know if she really believed what she was saying, and she sure as hell didn't know if she would really protect him with the secret of the last fifteen hours. At that moment, Delia was hell-bent on getting Sergeant Jackson to snap out of his funk of regret, let her help him protect his family, and hopefully throw some more bad guys in prison.

Seven percent.

"Agent DeMarco, I appreciate what you're trying to do for me here, but have you considered I might want to be beat up?" Jackson asked, turning to her slowly as he spoke. The desperate look on his face told Delia he wasn't joking. He pulled his vehicle behind her rental car and parked on the shoulder of the county highway.

"I can't help you with that right now," she told him when she opened the passenger door. "Let's continue to keep our goals in line. Protect your family; figure out how to handle these shitbags from here on out."

Delia granted Jackson a four-minute head start for his

drive to the Gable Police Station as she struggled to get her bearings and locate the phone charger in her rental car.

Nine percent.

Maybe that's charged enough, Delia thought.

She pushed the gadget's main button with her right hand while maintaining the steering wheel with her left. The phone lit up—it was working!

Delia pressed the speed dial button and the number one. The phone rang. Two times. And a third time. Finally, a click.

"You've reached the desk of Special Agent in Charge David Devling," the recorded voice said on the other end of the line.

"Damnit!" Delia yelled at her phone as she hung it up. She made another attempt with the speed dial button, pressing the number two. This call went straight to Chase's voicemail without even ringing.

"This is Chase Sheehan. I can't take your call at the moment, but if you—"

Delia hung the phone up again.

"He's got it turned off?" she questioned out loud. Delia wondered if Jackson was at the station yet.

All of sudden, from the ditch to her right, a black pickup truck pulled in front of Delia and onto the two-lane road. When it hit the asphalt it stopped abruptly across her lane. Delia slammed on the brakes to keep from T-boning the truck. The tires screeched as the Malibu fishtailed to a stop, bringing it parallel to the pickup.

Delia reached for her gun. She knew this wasn't an accident. Opening the driver's side door slowly, she backed her way out of the vehicle, keeping her gun drawn and eyeing the black truck through the windshield.

Remaining on her haunches, Delia shouted out. "I'm a federal agent! Come out of the vehicle with your hands on top of your head!"

The driver's door opened and a medium-sized Hispanic man stepped down from the pickup with his hands on his head.

Delia stood up with her gun drawn and slowly moved toward the man. "You lost?" she asked him.

The man did not respond.

"I'd ask you in Spanish if you speak English, but judging by the way you got out of the truck with your hands up..."

Again, the man said nothing. He was staring right through her. Something was wrong.

Is someone behind me? Delia asked herself.

By the time the question was fully formed it was too late. Everything went black.

***

On his drive to the police station, Jackson called his wife and ordered her to Minnesota with the children. It was a discombobulated phone conversation that frightened his wife to near hysterics until Jackson promised her everything was going to be fine. He hated lying to her, but it was the only way he could get her to head out of town without taking the time to fill her in. Besides, he wasn't even sure he wanted to tell her the truth.

Next, Jackson poured himself a cup of coffee and sat down at his desk to wait for Agent DeMarco. When twenty minutes had passed, he began to worry. He stepped outside the station and into the parking lot, hoping DeMarco had arrived and was simply still on the phone in her car.

Nothing.

Jackson was deep in thought when his cell phone rang. He didn't recognize the number on the screen, but he answered it with the hope it was DeMarco.

"Jackson," he said.

"Señor Jackson," a male voice said, "do you know who this is?"

Jackson recognized the accent and the voice. It had to be Pablo. "Yeah."

"You can go home now, Señor Jackson," Pablo instructed him. "There's no need to wait around for your little helper. You won't be seeing her again. Ever."

"What are you talking about?"

"You know what I'm talking about," Pablo said. "Go home to your empty house and enjoy the peace and quiet while you can. We will let you know in a few days what your next assignment is."

"Bite me," Jackson snarled.

"Let's try to keep our relationship professional," Pablo suggested. "Besides, you need to be a better listener. I'll say it differently to you this time."

"Say what?" Jackson said. He was growing tired of being spoken to in riddles.

"Your wife and children are already on the road going north. They are probably on their way to your mother-in-law's house. Does the address fourteen twenty one South Lawton Street in Otsego, Minnesota, sound familiar? Just outside of Minneapolis, no?"

Jackson could feel his face lighting on fire. "You sonofabitch!"

"Don't worry, Señor. We'll keep an eye on them, keep them safe. I'll be in touch with instructions."

The line went dead.

Jackson hit the call back button. It rang straight to an automated voicemail announcement.

"This voice mailbox has not been setup. Goodbye."

Book 3
The Wrong Side of Right

XXI

"What the hell are you doing?" Barrett shouted across the restaurant.

"Calling your bluff!" Randy hollered back. He ended the exclamation with what almost sounded like a question mark. Barrett watched Randy closely as he held the gun in the air like an Old West outlaw who was staring down his nemesis.

The restaurant was full of gasps, tears, and shrieks. Barrett remained frozen near the exit.

"Shut up!" Randy screamed, shaking his head back and forth like a father who had reached his limit with his children. "Not a peep! No one move!"

Barrett wondered if he was speaking to the people in the building or the voices in his head. He didn't care enough to stick around to find out, so he made another move for the door. This time, before he was able to push the door open, Barrett heard gunfire and more screams. Turning his head ninety degrees, he witnessed Randy holding the gun out away from his body. A middle-aged woman was on her knees about twenty feet from the big man. She was crying and begging for her life.

"Don't kill me," she said, sobbing. Randy ignored her and refocused his attention across the restaurant on Barrett.

"I was aiming for her shin," he explained, "but I missed."

Still stunned at Randy's disregard for drawing

outrageous amounts of attention to himself, Barrett did not respond. Instead he glared at the giant Goldilocks. He could see Nora observing the scene as if she were sitting in a theater, watching a play.

Without warning, Randy grabbed a small boy from his seat next to his family. The toddler immediately began to cry. The boy's mother screamed hysterically and his father stood up and began to make a move towards Randy.

"Sit down, Papa Bear," Randy instructed him, poking the gun in the little boy's ribs He held the child with his left arm, wrapping it around his waist. "Do you want to see how far I'll go?"

Randy glanced at the door again, making sure Barrett could see the gun.

"Put the kid down," Barrett urged.

"Get over here," Randy retorted.

"Why? So we can pay the bill before we leave? Put the kid down and let's go."

It wasn't ideal. But there hadn't been much lately that was. Going back to Gable hadn't even been on Barrett's radar. The only saving grace he could think of was that he'd have a couple of hundred miles to think about how to work it to his advantage.

"Fine," Randy replied. He handed the boy back to his parents, keeping the gun in a defensive position.

The poor kid couldn't be more than two years old, Barrett thought. Now he might be scarred for life.

"Come on, Mom," Randy told the old woman. He pushed her wheelchair away from the table as Nora grabbed the newspaper, never once letting his eyes stray from Barrett. It was hard to believe they had been eating and chatting only moments earlier.

As Randy and Nora approached the front door, Barrett spoke again. "Have you given any thought to how we're *not* going to get spotted driving a big yellow school bus through the Midwest? You know, now that you've made us stick out like a sore thumb?"

Randy stopped pushing the wheelchair. Without completely turning around, in an effort to keep an eye on Barrett, he strolled back to the father of the boy he had briefly snatched.

"Give me your car keys," Randy told him.

"What?" the man asked.

"Jesus Christ, man. Do I have to shoot someone to…?"

Randy fired the handgun. The restaurant patrons gasped and screamed again. The kid's father looked down at the floor.

"Sometimes my body gets ahead of my brain," Randy explained. "You're lucky; I missed again. Looks like you were close to having one of your little piggies go to market. Now give me your keys unless you want me to turn your entire foot into a slab of bacon."

The man obeyed and handed Randy his keys. He looked back down at the hole in the floor, next to his left foot.

"Here," Randy said. He dangled the bus keys in front of the man's face. "It's the least I can do. A trade-in."

***

The house was dark with the exception of one dim lamp on an end table. In the reclining chair next to it was Jackson, flat on his back and staring at the ceiling. He held his gun in his right hand. It rested over his heart, making it look like he was pledging allegiance to…something.

After receiving the phone call from Pablo, Jackson had called his wife to check on things. Not wanting to alarm her any more than he already had when he sent her away, he mentioned nothing about the latest events. Even so, Caroline Jackson knew something was going on. This kind of stuff didn't happen to a small town police officer every day.

When Jackson had told her to pack up and take the kids to her mother's in Minnesota, he was elusive as to the reason. But his wife hadn't objected. Within thirty minutes, Mrs. Jackson was on the road with their children.

He thought they were safe. Until now.

What the hell did I do to deserve this? Jackson thought.

Worse yet, what was he going to do now? Killing Chum was one thing. He did what he thought he had to do to protect his family. And Chum was dead any way you sliced it. That's how Jackson justified it to himself, anyway.

But now DeMarco was gone. She was dead as far as he knew. And these guys already knew where his family was. For this, Jackson could blame no one but himself. He should have been more careful. He could've swept the car for a tracking device or made sure they weren't followed. But he had been so wrapped up in the entire predicament and getting them out of town, he plumb forgot what the protocol should've been. Not that he was accustomed to acting like a special agent, but his protective service training in the military had taught him how to do it all. Instead, Jackson had neglected to recall or use any of it.

And now what was going to happen? What were these guys going to try to get him to do next? Whatever it ended up being, how could he *not* do it? They'd kill Caroline and the kids. He couldn't go to Chief Perkins. All he'd want to do is call the FBI and DEA. Besides, going to his boss would mean he'd have to tell him what had happened. Everything. It just didn't seem like a good idea right now. While Jackson wanted all the help he could get to protect his family, he wasn't ready to confess those sins right now: murder and kidnapping a federal agent, then allowing her to be abducted by the cartel, who did God knows what to her.

No, there wasn't much more Jackson could do right now other than wait. Wait for further instructions and sink deeper into the muck he hadn't asked for.

Jackson continued to contemplate his limited options while his brain fired but his body went numb. He felt as if he'd fallen asleep for the night with his eyes open. Before he knew it, the ceiling he'd been staring at for hours was flooded with light from a cold winter sunrise. It was time to go to work.

***

Chase had rented a car after his plane landed in Omaha and driven as far as Adler before settling down at a hotel for the night. Following a continental breakfast the next morning, he checked out and drove another twenty minutes north to Gable.

His original intent was to drive into town and scope things out, inconspicuously. But before he made it there he noticed the police station along the highway. Chase pulled the white sedan into the lot and walked through the door.

"Morning, stranger," Chief Perkins called from his desk. "What can we do for you?"

"I'm looking for someone," Chase said.

"Okay," Perkins replied, waiting for more information.

"My sister," Chase explained.

"Your sister, got it," Perkins confirmed. "I didn't catch your name."

"Sheehan. Chase Sheehan," Chase stated, moving forward to the man's desk. Perkins stood up and offered his hand.

"I'm Chief Nathan Perkins," he said. "And around here somewhere is my lone wolf sergeant. Excuse me a second."

Chase nodded and took a step back. Chief Perkins turned and hollered down the hall towards the restrooms.

"Jack! Company!"

Jackson appeared from around the corner. Chief Perkins had given him grief when he arrived late for work and looking like he had tied one on the night before.

After the introductions, the conversation continued.

"You said you're looking for your sister," Perkins reiterated.

"That's right," Chase confirmed, reaching into his pocket. "I should also mention I'm with the FBI."

He handed his credentials to Perkins, who glanced at them before handing them back. Jackson didn't seem fazed. He was still in a daze following a sleepless night of spinning wheels and lucid nightmares.

"Welcome to Gable, Agent Sheehan," Perkins greeted him more formally. "How did your sister go missing?"

"Well, I didn't say she was missing," Chase elaborated. "I just haven't been able to reach her, which is kind of strange. She's supposed to be here in your town."

"Sorry about that. I just assumed since you were a fed and—" Perkins interrupted himself. "What's her name?"

"Delia. DeMarco. Delia DeMarco."

Jackson's heart skipped a beat.

"Agent DeMarco?" Perkins confirmed. "Well, yeah. She's here. She's working on the — the Chum — err — Tom Chumansky case. He's slippery."

Chase nodded. "Any idea where she is now? When was the last time you had contact with her?"

The chief massaged his chin. "As I recall," he began, "she arrived late the other day."

"The other day?" Chase asked. "Which 'other day,' exactly?"

Perkins looked to his sergeant for help.

"I didn't know she was here, Chief," Jackson informed him.

"Oh? I guess I didn't get around to telling you," Perkins said. "Yes, that's it. I apologize for the confusion, Agent Sheehan. She showed up late Saturday and contacted me. Because it was over the weekend, I got sidetracked and never got around to telling anyone else."

"How did your conversation with her go? What did she say?" Chase asked.

Perkins sat down at his desk as if it would help him recall his phone call with Agent DeMarco. "She called me on my cell phone," Perkins elaborated. He picked up his phone from his desk and began scrolling through the history.

"It was eight fifteen Saturday night," he said. "She said she had come to help with the investigation and that she'd be in touch. She also said she was staying in Adler at the Stone Creek Inn."

Jackson listened but remained silent.

"I assume you gave her an update?" Chase inquired.

"Yes, of course," Perkins agreed.

"What did you tell her?"

"What's going on here, Agent Sheehan? I feel like I'm being interrogated."

The chief opened his hands on the desk, indicating to Chase he had nothing to hide.

"My sister and I are very close. She hasn't responded to any of my attempts to contact her in over twenty-four hours. That never happens."

"I see," Perkins said. "Well, I think I've told you everything I know. But we're here to help. I'm sure she's around here somewhere. Maybe in the middle of some surveillance?"

"Maybe," Chase said. "But it's highly unusual that she hasn't even returned a text message."

"There are a lot of reception gaps out here in rural Iowa," Jackson added. "Depending on her service provider and location, it's possible she hasn't even received your messages yet."

Chase thought about this.

"That's always a possibility," Chief Perkins agreed. "But we still want to help. We'll figure this out together, Agent."

"So what *is* the latest in the ongoing investigation? What did you tell her?" Chase asked.

"Well, there wasn't much to tell," Perkins said. "We follow Chumansky wherever he goes. Try to follow his pal Eddie Clark, too."

Jackson jumped into the conversation. "Mostly he goes to his stores and new home in Adler and his ex-wife's house here in Gable. He hasn't done much else for weeks."

"Why aren't you watching him now?" Chase asked them.

The two uniformed men looked at each other.

"Office Hodge should be on that right now," Jackson told them.

"Does he know Delia is here?"

Perkins reacted with a puzzled look. "I guess not," he said. "I mean, unless she happened to run into him. He has met her before, so it's possible."

"So no one has seen my sister?"

"I guess not," Perkins said. "I'm sorry. I'm sure she's here somewhere. I know how determined she was to catch Chumansky in the act of…doing something."

Chase took what seemed like his first breath of the conversation before speaking again. "Would you mind getting the Stone Creek Inn on the phone? I'd like to find out if she checked in."

After confirming that Delia had, indeed, checked in to the Stone Creek Inn around nine o'clock Saturday evening, Chase decided it would be best to drive back to Adler and begin his search there. Retracing Delia's steps made the most sense. Since they were both federal agents, it was easy for Chase to do this. But being twins brought an extra edge of understanding that was impossible to explain to people. There was a shared sixth sense between the pair, something that ran so deep they rarely felt the need to talk about it because they just "knew."

Chase thanked Perkins and Jackson for their help. The men exchanged phone numbers and agreed to inform each other if they heard from Delia. As Chase drove away from the station, Perkins received a phone call. Jackson watched the departing car through the window, shaking his head.

***

"What's been going on lately?" Dr. Hammond asked Claire. "How have you been feeling?"

"Still crazy," Claire admitted. She was already lying flat on her back in the recliner.

"You're not crazy," Hammond assured Claire as she wrote something in her notebook.

"Okay. Define 'crazy' for me."

The psychologist paused. "Let's look it up in the dictionary," she suggested. Dr. Hammond pulled her laptop closer and typed quickly on the keyboard. "Google is your friend," she quipped. Claire continued to stare at the ceiling as she always did during these therapy sessions. "The dictionary defines the word 'crazy' as mentally deranged, impractical, and completely unsound. Is that you?"

Claire didn't answer

"Are you mentally deranged?" Hammond asked.

"Define 'mentally deranged,'" Claire requested.

Hammond typed some more on the keyboard. "'Derange' means to upset the normal condition or functioning of something or someone."

"There," Claire said. "That's me. I'm crazy."

"Um, no. That just means you're out of sorts."

"Whatever. I'm pretty screwed up right now."

"The term 'derange' often gets used negatively, but

when you look at the word you can see it's derived from the word 'de-arrange,'" Dr. Hammond explained. "You want to tell me why you're feeling this way?"

Claire thought about this before replying. "I can try."

"I'm all ears," Hammond said, pushing her laptop away and returning to her pen and notebook.

"This is all in confidence, right?" Claire asked. She considered sitting up but didn't want to run the risk of losing her train of thought by seeing Dr. Hammond's nervous eye tic.

"Of course," Hammond replied.

"Okay," Claire said with a big sigh as she began to tell the story of the past several days. She detailed how Maddison had invited her to dinner and how she had asked for Claire's help getting to the hidden money. She told the therapist how she had lied to Sergeant Jackson for money and how now it seemed Chum and Eddie were both missing. Dr. Hammond did not ask questions as her patient spoke. Instead she only scribbled notes and glanced in her direction. When Claire was finished, Dr. Hammond set her notebook and pen down.

"That's quite a story," she uttered. "How does that make you feel?"

Claire bolted upright in the recliner without using the lever, causing the back of the chair to smack her even farther forward.

"How does it make me feel?" she exclaimed, regaining control of her body. "How do you *think* it makes me feel? This crap hasn't gone away. It's still hanging around. It won't leave me alone. I don't want to be here. I never asked for this. I haven't done anything to deserve this!"

"Deserve what, Claire?"

Claire reached down one side of the chair and grabbed the lever to bring it upright. She pulled the band from her ponytail and let her hair fall to her shoulders. When she finally spoke, she said, "Feeling like a victim."

Hammond leaned forward. "Are you a victim or are

you just feeling like one?"

"What's the difference?" Claire snapped back.

"The difference lies in what happened, Claire," Dr. Hammond said forcefully. She got up from her chair and took two steps in her patient's direction. Before she continued speaking, she put her hands on her hips. "Who are the victims in all of these events we've discussed during our sessions? Think about that for a minute."

Claire did as she was told. Leaning forward and looking at the floor, she considered the circumstances of the past few months.

"A strong person knows she is not a victim," Hammond said. "The word isn't even in her vocabulary. She pushes forward and perseveres."

Claire looked up at her therapist but said nothing. She didn't even worry about seeing Hammond's surprise eyes.

"Eddie was shot in the leg. Marty was murdered. Maddison found out her husband was a criminal. What makes you such a goddamn victim?" Dr. Sherrie Hammond was clearly annoyed by her client's pity party.

"Am I really paying for this kind of treatment?" Claire protested.

Hammond retreated a step before saying more. "I'm sorry, Claire," she said. "But you're paying me to help. And I'm trying to do that by telling you the truth."

Doctor and patient took a moment to gather their composure.

"You're not a victim in this," Dr. Hammond said.

Claire looked up and made direct eye contact with her psychologist for the first time in a long time.

"Then what am I? What am I feeling?" she asked in desperation.

Dr. Hammond reached for her desk chair and wheeled it to where Claire was sitting. She sat down directly across from her before speaking again. "I think you're feeling overwhelmed," Hammond said. "And I also don't think Chum and Eddie were killed or abducted or anything like that."

"You don't?"

"No," Dr. Hammond continued. "It seems far more logical to assume they skipped town with the money."

Claire thought about this while stroking her forehead. "I'd agree with you if I hadn't witnessed the violence I did. It was all about that money."

"That is true," Dr. Hammond agreed. "And aren't those criminals in prison now?"

She had a point and Claire knew it. "Am I just a drama queen?"

Hammond shook her head and answered. "No. You're just in a funk right now and still processing what happened this summer. The entire arrangement with Maddison and the money and the missing guys? It's just compounding things and making it difficult for you to get past it all."

"How am I supposed to deal with Maddison?" Claire asked. "She's not going to leave me alone. I'm the only other person who knows what happened. Am I supposed to tell her I think her husband and his buddy are lovers and ran off together?"

Dr. Hammond smirked at the thought. "Now *that's* kind of dramatic," she said. "Just leave it open. Don't tell her you agree and don't tell her you don't."

"That works — because I don't know what I believe," Claire remarked.

"There is one more thing to consider," Hammond said as she got up from her chair and began to move it back to her desk.

"What's that?" Claire asked.

"You could go to the police."

"Wait a minute. I thought you didn't believe anything bad has happened."

"I don't," Hammond agreed. "But if you need a way to deal with it because Maddison is upset, it might be best to let the pros investigate things."

"But we lied to the police," Claire reminded her. "I could go to jail."

Sherrie Hammond stood next to her chair and crossed her arms. "I'm a psychologist and don't know anything about the law," she said. "But I've watched enough episodes of *Boston Legal* to know how you should handle this."

"Great," Claire said. "I'm listening. Should I take notes?"

Hammond shook her head.

"Wait a minute. Is this covered by my insurance?" Claire asked. "Are you going to charge me extra?"

"I should," Dr. Hammond replied with a comforting smile. "But I won't."

XXII

The heavyset hotel manager swiped the master key card for room 104. When the light turned green he pulled the handle down and pushed on the door just enough to keep it open. He turned to Chase.

"It's all you from here, Agent." The manager looked as if he had just woken up. His black hair was tousled and his white shirt was untucked in the back. Even his gold name tag was hanging sideways from the pocket of his shirt.

Chase reached for his gun and took control of the door. "Thanks...Norman," he said with a glance at the name tag.

The sight of Chase's firearm caused Norman to back away. "I-I'm just going to go back to the front desk and make sure everything is okay," he said.

Chase grinned. "I'll let you know if I need backup."

Norman's big body hustled down the hall in a brisk walk and disappeared around the corner. Chase didn't know what to expect inside. The chance of there being any danger behind the door was slim. His biggest concern was about what danger had already happened in room 104.

He held the heavy door open with one hand while keeping his gun drawn with the other. As he entered the room, his stomach tied itself in a knot with worry of what he might discover. From his position in the doorway Chase could see nothing on the bed or desk that showed evidence of foul play.

He let the door slam behind him and flipped the bathroom light switch. The shower curtain was open, revealing a dry and empty bathtub. The sink was also dry and the counter area surrounding it still contained his sister's travel essentials including a curling iron, toothbrush, and makeup.

Chase moved to the living area of the hotel room. The bed had clearly been slept in. Delia's small suitcase lay on top, open. He reached inside and shuffled the clothes and other items around, looking for a sign that might tell him where his twin sister was now.

Before arriving at the Stone Creek Inn, Chase had stopped at the two Mecca Warehouse locations in Adler. His first thought was to possibly find Delia conducting surveillance on Tom Chumansky. When that hunch turned up nothing at the first location, Chase decided to go inside and speak to Chumansky. But no one had heard from or seen him all day. After receiving the same information at the other store, Chase inquired about Chumansky's right-hand man, Eddie Clark, only to discover he had not come to work either.

Suspicious as it seemed, Chase hoped his sister had simply hit the jackpot and placed both men in federal custody over the weekend. After making a couple of phone calls and doing some quick research on his phone, Chase found this theory to be another lost cause.

He sat down on the edge of the hotel bed and began crunching the facts. Three people were missing, two of them were tied to organized crime, and the other was a federal agent. The fact that Delia had gone this long without making contact with Chase only reinforced his belief that something was wrong. She would never go this long without communicating. It was all tied together — Chase was almost certain of this. But what should he do next? Where was he going to find the answers he needed?

Clark wasn't married, but Chumansky had a wife, or ex-wife. Chase couldn't recall for certain the couple's current status. Heading back to Gable seemed like a good idea. He didn't have a lot to go on, but he certainly had more information now than what he'd received from the police department earlier in the day. There was no doubt in Chase's mind that Devling had made the right call by sending Delia to Gable. The investigation by the locals was a disaster, and at this point Chase wasn't sure whether he should continue to involve them or not.

He took one final glance around the room before closing the door behind him. He was disappointed that the search had yielded minimal results, but he was confident a refueling of his body would help him think more clearly. On the way to Gable earlier that morning he had spotted a restaurant that served authentic Mexican cuisine. At the moment, it sounded perfect.

After retracing Norman's path down the hall, he turned left and headed out the lobby door. As he passed the front desk he saw that it was empty. Chase assumed the manager was hiding in the back office, more than likely with his fingers on the phone, ready to dial 911 if necessary.

Like that would help, Chase thought. He strolled across the parking lot to his rental car and jumped inside. As he drove away, a blue minivan pulled into the lot from the other side.

***

Barrett sat in the uncomfortable lounge chair in the corner of room 105 inside the warm comfort of the Stone Creek Inn. It was now five o'clock in the afternoon and snow had started to fall in the area. Trying to go to Gable now to find the money would be a worthless move, according to Randy. Instead, he spent more of his prisoner's money on a hotel room for the threesome. Nora was in her wheelchair in the short entryway by the door. She held the gun tightly in her lap as Randy used the bathroom.

"Do you like this?" Barrett asked her.

"What are you talking about?" Nora squawked back.

"This," Barrett said. "Traveling around the country at your age confined to a wheelchair."

Nora snorted. "I do okay."

"You do. But is this how you want to spend your —"

"Just knock it off right now, bub," Nora snarled. "I'm not going to be your ticket out of here. I'm in this for the long haul."

Barrett shook his head. "I believe it," he said.

Just then the volume of a toilet flush increased as the bathroom door opened and Randy entered the room.

"What's going on in here?" he asked. Barrett couldn't tell if he was mad or just talking louder so he could be heard over the running water.

"Nothing," Nora replied. "Just the usual poo-poo."

Randy took the gun from his mother and sat on the edge of the twin bed furthest from Barrett. He tapped the gun in his empty hand repeatedly. It was as if Randy were applauding himself.

"Are you finally done underestimating me?" he asked Barrett. They had hardly spoken since screeching off from the truck stop in the dark red Nissan Altima Randy had received as a "trade-in" for the bus. Despite being fed up with his captor, Barrett was impressed with Randy's understanding that he needed to ditch the new car fast. The authorities would be looking for it by make, model, and color. After driving the Iowa back roads for several hours, they finally parked it in a secluded lot in Charles City. From there they wheeled Nora several blocks through the snow- and ice-covered sidewalks to the center of town. Randy had called a local taxi service on the way. The cab met them on a corner, and Randy gave the driver five hundred dollars from Barrett's money to drive them fifty-five miles south to Waterloo. Once they were dropped off it took Randy another ninety minutes to score a blue Dodge minivan at a local pub. Barrett wasn't sure if Randy had stolen it or bought it, and he didn't really want to know. The thought of how much of his money was being wasted away right now was not pleasant. Although fifteen years old, the minivan was in decent shape and drove well. Randy made Barrett drive the back roads until late in the evening when they stopped at a hotel in Iowa Falls.

That was the first night the trio had slept outside of a moving vehicle. Barrett had considered trying to escape while Randy and Nora slept, but he was tired. If he was going to break away it would need to be when he was more focused. The next day they drove all the way to Adler. It only took three and a half hours of drive time to get there, but they had a late breakfast before leaving and stopped for lunch along the way. When they finally arrived in town it was late afternoon and snow flurries were beginning to accumulate. Barrett was surprised Randy had stopped, but figured any delay in getting to Gable was a plus in his book.

"Did you need to go batshit crazy the other day?" Barrett snarled. "What the hell is your problem? There's probably a multi-state APB out for you now."

Randy chuckled. "You did that, pal."

"Right. My bad," Barrett said sarcastically. He sat back in the chair and slouched. "So what do you have planned next? Blow up a building in front of an audience in broad daylight and then spend some more of my money to disappear? Maybe we can just go in circles until we run out of money."

Randy stood up and stretched as he answered. "First of all, it's *my* money now. And I was going to ask you the same question. You're the expert around here. Where do I find that money? How should we handle this?"

"We?" Barrett bellowed. "There's no 'we' in this, Randy. This is your expedition."

"You'll help if you want to see your old man in the hospital before I turn you in for that reward," Randy reminded him.

"You can't turn me in now, you big dummy. They'll arrest you. You won't get a dime of it."

"Again," Randy said, "stop underestimating me. The reason I did what I did at the truck stop was because of you."

Barrett shook his head. "You really think they're gonna buy that bullshit?"

Randy smirked. "Barry. Buddy. This ain't my first rodeo. I know what I'm doing. You're wanted for murder. I was under duress, but I didn't kill anyone. I can sell it. They will buy it." Randy began applauding himself again with the gun. Barrett wanted to smack the smug look from his face. "And that reminds me of another question I've been meaning to ask you," Randy continued. "Did you kill that guy?"

"Of course he did," Nora croaked from behind her son. "Ain't you ever watched those mystery shows? They don't feature people who are innocent. They *always* go to jail at the end."

Isn't that the truth? Barrett thought. He could count on one hand the number of times he had watched an episode of *Dateline* or *20/20* or *48 Hours* where someone had not gone to prison.

"It's possible," Randy replied. "So what's the verdict, man? Did you do it?"

Barrett couldn't decide whether he should tell him the truth or not. "What do *you* think?" he asked.

"I don't think you did it," Randy admitted. "You're too smart. You're like me. I've never killed anyone."

Barrett cringed. Being compared to a thief and registered sex offender wasn't exactly high praise. "Goes to show what you know," Barrett scoffed.

Randy's bushy eyebrows shot up in surprise. "Come on," he said. "Really?"

Barrett stood up as tall as he could and took a step forward. He gritted his teeth and shook his head as he responded in a low growl under his breath. "I strangled the shit out of that sonofabitch."

Randy shrugged. "Well, what do you know?" he said,

turning and glancing at Nora. "You hear that, Ma? I didn't think he had it in him."

"Never put anything past *any* man," Nora replied.

"You just seem too submissive to me," Randy said. "You haven't even put up a fight with me. I mean, what you did at the truck stop? That wasn't a fight. That was miserable."

Captor and captive were standing three feet apart now. Barrett didn't get the feeling Randy was being confrontational, and he didn't want the big oaf to get the wrong idea.

"You've had a gun the entire time," Barrett said, taking a step backwards and throwing his hands up. "What am I supposed to do?"

"Good point," Randy replied.

"But make no mistake," Barrett continued, this time returning to the threatening tone he'd used moments ago when confessing. "I will have my moment. This is not going to end well for you."

Randy roared with laughter. "I'll keep that in mind," he said. Still chuckling, he added, "You should be a comedian."

"I understand your disbelief," Barrett said. "You'll see, though. And when you do it will be too late. But if it's any consolation to you, none of this is going to end well for me, either."

"Yeah, yeah. I know. You're going to prison," Randy said. "Let's get back to the plan. Where do we find this guy, Chumley?"

"Chum," Barrett corrected him. "Tom Chumansky."

Randy nodded. "He Polish? Jewish?"

"Russian." Barrett snorted. "Give me a break. How would I know? We weren't exactly tight. Things kind of went sour when he tried to get me killed."

"Just wondering," Randy said. "I don't have much of a filter. Something pops into my head and before I have time to think about it, I've already said it."

"I hadn't noticed," Barrett replied dryly. Without taking a breath he changed the subject back. "So Chum has two retail stores here in Adler — Mecca Warehouse. It'll probably be best to scout them out tomorrow and see if you can find him there. It's hard saying where he lives now. I mean, unless you just want to go into the store tomorrow and start shooting it up in order to get him to take you to the money."

"I'll sleep on that idea," Randy retorted.

***

"Honey, I know you're scared," Jackson told his wife. He held the phone between his chin and shoulder as he moved through the kitchen and made himself a quick breakfast. It was Christmas Eve morning and his family was hours away. The entire fiasco was officially worse now.

"I'm not sure what I'm more scared about," Caroline Jackson whispered on the other end of the line. She was keeping her voice low so the children and their grandmother couldn't overhear.

"What do you mean?" her husband said as he pulled a dozen eggs from the refrigerator and dropped some butter in a pan.

"I mean, I don't want anything to happen to any of us. And since you won't tell me what's going on, I'm not sure who's in more danger."

"Caroline," her husband said in a soothing tone, "I sent you away for a reason. Do you think I'd send you *into* danger?" The irony of the comment made Jackson want to vomit.

"So you — you *are* in trouble!" She began the sentence in a loud voice but caught herself.

"I didn't say that," Jackson corrected her. "It's just that things are complicated around here right now, and I think it would be best for you and the kids to stay away for a while, just in case."

"In case what?"

"I don't know, honey. What do you think?" he snapped at her. "In case the shit hits the fan!"

There was silence for a moment.

"I'm sorry," Jackson said, gently massaging the egg he was holding.

"Me, too. I know you must be under a lot of pressure with whatever is going on. We just miss you. It's Christmas, John."

"I know, I know. But you've got to believe me when I tell you that's the best place for you. Even Perkins agrees."

Two lies in one sentence, Jackson thought. I'm getting too good at this.

Caroline Jackson sighed. "Okay. Will you call us later?"

"Of course."

"I love you, John. *We* love you. Be careful."

"I love you guys, too. Have a nice time and don't worry about me," he assured his wife of twelve years.

After hanging up, Jackson set his phone on the kitchen counter and moved to the stove. He took the egg he had been holding and cracked it on the edge of the pan. The instant he did this, the doorbell rang. The sudden sound caused him to drop the egg into the pan, shell and all. He looked down at the mess and saw that the inside of the egg was filled with blood. Jackson felt his stomach turn again as he moved to the front door and looked through the peephole. When he saw who it was, he quickly opened the door and ushered Claire Mathison inside.

"Merry Christmas," she greeted the police sergeant.

"Merry Christmas to you as well, Claire. What brings you to Adler so early in the morning?" Jackson asked her. "It's cold out there."

"And it's starting to snow again, too," Claire added as

she wiped her feet off on the mat in the doorway and took her stocking cap off.

"Great. Everyone will be driving like idiots on the highways," Jackson said with an eye roll. "Have a seat. Can I get you anything?"

"No, thank you," Claire said as she sat on the sofa.

"I'm here for a couple of reasons," she began, "but I guess I'll start with the most urgent one."

"Okay..." Jackson said as he leaned forward in the chair next to her.

"Chum hasn't been seen or heard from since Saturday night," Claire explained.

Jackson did his best to look surprised. This wasn't too difficult to do since he hadn't expected to hear this from Claire. "What?"

"Maybe it would be better if I started the story from the beginning," Claire suggested.

"I suppose so," Jackson agreed, still perplexed.

"When I came to you and told you that I thought Chum had hidden the drug money near the stores," Claire said, "that was a bit of a misdirection."

Jackson responded by giving her a confused look. "So, you lied to me?" he clarified. Claire looked to the floor. "Can I ask why?"

"If Maddison were here she'd probably say it was her fault. But I did what I did of my own free will. Maddison was trying to help Chum recover the money. He went out into the wooded area behind the house on Saturday night to dig it up, but he never came back. They were going to split the money up and Maddison was going to use a good portion of it to put the baby through college. She didn't mean any harm," Claire pleaded.

"You're defending Maddison. What about you? Why did you get involved?" Jackson asked.

"She was going to give me a cut," Claire said with a

frown.

"Wow," Jackson responded. It didn't disturb him as much as it could have, given the circumstances. He had bigger fish to fry right now.

"I'm telling you because I think something went terribly wrong. I'm hoping you can help clear things up."

Claire looked at the floor again. Jackson knew he had to play along. He was doing double-time between his family, Agent DeMarco, and now Chum's disappearance. His head was pounding. All he could do now was take it one moment at a time. He had to react based on what was in front of him in order to survive, no matter how many lies he had to tell.

"Yeah, I'd agree that something went terribly wrong," Jackson said as he stood up and moved away from where they were seated. "You lied to me, and because you lied to me Chum slipped out of our sight. And now he has vanished. You and Maddison are what went terribly wrong!" As he continued to speak, the volume of his voice increased and his rage became evident. "Do you realize I could take you in right now? I should arrest you. It's called obstruction of justice, Claire!"

Claire hadn't looked up from the floor during Jackson's rant. Now that he seemed to be finished, she picked her head up slowly, as if it weighed a thousand pounds. "No. No, you couldn't," she told him.

Jackson turned back in her direction. "Excuse me?"

"I'm sorry," Claire said honestly. "You don't have anything to arrest me for. It wouldn't hold."

"You just admitted that you intentionally gave me misinformation with the hopes of benefitting from it," Jackson reminded her. "I know what I heard."

"Are you sure you heard that?" Claire asked him. "I don't think I said anything of the sort. I came here to tell you that Chum is missing. That's all."

Jackson could tell she was embarrassed to say these things to him. What was going on? "Did someone put you up to this?" He sat down next to her on the sofa. "Did Maddison send you here to tell me the truth and then deny it?"

"God, no!" Claire gasped. Jackson could tell she was telling the truth. "She doesn't know I'm here. She'll probably kill me when she finds out I told you."

Jackson saw an opportunity to send some misdirection Claire's way. It was time to do everything in his power to keep everyone off his trail. "Be careful, Claire. Maddison could be involved with Chum's disappearance," he told her.

"I really don't think so," Claire assured him.

"You can't be too sure," Jackson said. "Think about it. She tells you to lie to me so her husband can get to the hidden money. She was going to pay you for doing it. Now her husband is gone and so is the money…supposedly. I'm just saying it's a likely story. She doesn't have to pay you now because the money is missing."

Claire stared straight ahead and thought about it for a moment. "It was only fifty thousand dollars. It's not like she was going to pay me a fortune."

"You see my point though, right?" Jackson knew he needed to sell it hard.

"I guess it's possible, yes," Claire admitted. "But what are you saying you think happened to Chum?"

"I don't know," Jackson said. Let her come up with it on her own, he said to himself.

"You don't think…" Claire began then paused. "Could Maddison have done something to him?"

There we go, Jackson thought. "A few months ago I wouldn't have thought it was possible," he told her. "But after the tragedy last September…"

"God, I just don't know," Claire said. "She's pregnant and—"

"Look, don't think about it so much right now. Just be careful. Be alert. Be careful what you say to her." Jackson doubted Chum himself could've pitched a better sales job than he just had.

"You're not going to arrest me?" Claire asked him. The look on her face told him the question was just a formality; he knew she knew better.

"No, I'm not." Jackson told her. "But I am going to begin an investigation."

"Thank you for your help, Sergeant," Claire told him as she stood up to leave. She stepped forward and gave him a quick, unexpected embrace.

He walked her to the front door and opened it. The snowflakes were larger now.

"At least it's not windy," Claire observed as she put her cap on. They said goodbye, and Jackson added another reminder to proceed with caution. He walked back through his house and into the kitchen. Before he made it back to the stove, his cell phone rang. It was Claire.

"Hi again, Claire. Did you forget something?" he asked.

"Yes, I did. I got out here to my car and realized I forgot to tell you something."

"What's that?" Jackson asked. He moved to the stove and looked down at the bloody egg still sitting in the pan he had left on the burner.

"Eddie Clark is missing, too," Claire said.

***

After searching his sister's hotel room and coming up empty, Chase grabbed a burrito at El Sombrero Grande, the Mexican restaurant he had seen earlier. He took his time while he ate but stayed productive, sending emails and making a couple of quiet phone calls. The first thing he did was make a special request to the DEA to acquire Delia's cell phone records. Finding out where her phone was last pinged would be a great start. But he also hoped to find valuable information from the calls she had made since arriving in town.

At this point Chase would not allow himself to consider the worst had happened. He buried the notion deep inside. The likelihood was small. It had to be. This was Iowa. What could possibly go wrong in Iowa?

Chase also checked into Delia's credit card activity to see if any of her cards were being used. Unfortunately, the last charge she had made was when she prepaid for her hotel room at the Stone Creek Inn.

The answer has to lie with the people, he thought. The fact that neither Chumansky nor Clark were at work today made Chase curious. It could be a coincidence. People are allowed to take days off from the job. And those two men were friends, according to the files, so the notion of them being gone at the same time was not that strange. But still, he needed to talk to them.

Chase paid his bill and began thumbing through his phone to find Chumansky's current address as he walked to the parking lot. It was now snowing in Adler, making him wonder why he could never get any assignments in warmer climates. He was still searching for the address on his phone when it rang, startling him. As he answered it, Chase thought how ironic it was to be caught off guard by a phone call while using a phone as something other than a phone.

"Sheehan," he announced.

"Agent Sheehan, this is Chief Perkins."

"Yes, Chief. Have you found my sister?"

"No, son. But I do have a development you need to hear about. For all we know, it might have something to do with your sister."

"Okay, good."

"Are you far away? Might be good to come back to the station, so I can fill you in."

"I'm in Adler," Chase told Perkins. "Give me twenty minutes. I'm on my way."

***

"You did *what*?" Maddison blurted. Claire sat down at the kitchen table, where the two had enjoyed dinner just a few days earlier.

"It's okay, Maddison. He's going to help figure out what happened. What's the matter with that? What else were we going to do?"

"What if Tom is okay?" Maddison suggested. "What if the money is still available to all of us? Now we'll never get it with the cops involved."

Claire hadn't considered this. "But if he's okay, where is he? Why did he and Eddie both disappear?" She wondered if this would be a good time to throw out the idea of the two men being lovers. She decided against it.

"I don't know," Maddison replied. "I just…I don't know anything, anymore." Maddison waddled to the refrigerator and pulled out a jug of water. She placed two glasses on the table and sat across from Claire. After filling them, she slid one glass to Claire and spoke again. "What did he say when you told him you lied to him?"

"He was kind of pissed at first," Claire told Maddison. "But he didn't stay mad long."

"That's weird."

"Well, he threatened to arrest me," Claire continued.

"Oh my God!"

"Yeah, but he backed off when I reminded him that he had no cause to arrest me. No proof that I had 'obstructed justice' or whatever he called it."

"Wow. That was clever," Maddison said as she took a drink. "His only evidence was the private conversation you had."

"Exactly."

"So he calmed down after that?" Maddison asked.

Claire sat silently as she recalled Jackson's warnings

about Maddison's possible involvement. She rubbed the tip of her thumb along the condensation on her water glass. "Pretty much."

"So you told him everything?" Maddison seemed to be asking a lot of questions.

"Well, yeah. I guess," Claire said. "Is there something in particular you're wondering about? I almost forgot to tell him about Eddie being missing, too." When Claire had called Jackson to add this detail, she asked him if he thought it was possible that Maddison had disposed of both Chum *and* Eddie. But he didn't answer the question. Instead he verified what he had heard, thanked her, and told her he'd be in touch. Then he hung up. "Jackson's going to begin an investigation," Claire continued.

"Great. Of course he is," a frustrated Maddison replied.

"What? Don't you want to know what's going on?"

"I do," Maddison admitted, "but I don't. I'm just sick of investigations and…I'm scared. I'm scared to find out what happened."

The look of agony on Maddison's face made it difficult for Claire to believe she was capable of ending a life, or possibly two. But Jackson was adamant about being careful. Claire knew it was best to leave the investigating to the professionals.

The sound of the doorbell playing the Mecca Warehouse jingle interrupted the deep thoughts of both ladies.

"Could that be Jackson already?" Maddison wondered out loud as she pulled her pregnant body from the chair and moved to the front door. Claire followed. As Maddison peered through the peephole she quietly announced what she was seeing. "Looks like Hulk Hogan with more hair," she said.

"Who?" Claire asked.

"Never mind. Before your time," Maddison said. "I'm going to see who it is. He looks like he could be a friend of

Eddie's. Maybe we can learn something."

"But—"

Claire began to object but Maddison was too fast. She opened the door and there stood a man who was easily a foot taller than either of them.

"Hi," Randy greeted them. "Is Chum around?"

XXIII

Barrett had convinced Randy that the only way to proceed without raising suspicion was to approach the Chumansky house alone. Wheeling Nora to the front door would be awkward and strange. Forcing Barrett to do it would cause more questions and commotion than Randy wanted. The only problem with Randy doing it by himself was the dilemma of who would get to keep the gun. Nora won that argument easily. Without her keeping the gun on Barrett there was nothing to stop him from making a run for one of the wooded areas near the house. She sat behind the driver's seat with the gun in her lap, two hands tight on the grip and her index finger wrapped around the trigger. Barrett sat in the passenger seat with most of his hand shielding his face. Due to the angle of the driveway it was doubtful he could be spotted from the front door. But he wasn't taking any chances.

Earlier the trio had made stops at both Mecca Warehouse stores in Adler only to discover that Chum was not working at either today. When they arrived at the large Chumansky house outside of Gable, there was a familiar green car parked in the wide driveway, but Barrett couldn't place it. He also remembered that Chum and Maddison were getting or had gotten a divorce recently, according to *Dateline.* He couldn't remember which for sure thanks to the beer buzz he'd had while watching the show. This might have been relevant information if Barrett actually wanted to help Randy succeed in his quest for the money. But in the long run, Barrett didn't care. He still had only one goal: to see his father. As far as any of them knew, Chum still lived here.

Shortly after Randy rang the doorbell the door opened. It wasn't easy to see around or over Randy from his position in the van, but Barrett thought he saw a woman's hair. He assumed it was Maddison. It was at that moment that Barrett hoped Chum *was* in the house, just in case things went south. Maddison versus Randy would not be a fair fight. But there should be no reason for problems as far as Barrett could tell. If Chum wasn't there Maddison should simply give suggestions as to where he might be and Randy would be on his way. But if Chum *was* there…

God only knows what will happen, Barrett thought.

The falling snow landed gracefully on the windshield in front of him, flake after flake. Barrett watched the back of Randy's head bob up and down and from side to side as he spoke to whoever had opened the door. Randy threw his arms in the air. Another time Barrett could see him shrug. He could observe body language, but it was difficult to tell what was being said. Barrett pushed the button for the automatic window and began to lower it.

"What are you doing?" Nora cracked from over his left shoulder.

"Shhh," Barrett hushed her. "Listening," he whispered. Leaving the window open only a crack, he strained his neck towards the opening. To his surprise, instead of making out any of the exchange that was happening in front of him, he heard the telltale sound of snow and gravel crunching behind him. There was a car coming down the drive!

Barrett whipped his head around and tried to look out the dirt and snow-covered back window.

"Someone's coming!" Nora whispered abruptly. "Get down!"

"Get down?" Barrett said, raising the window. "There's no room to get down up here!" He looked to the driver's side of the front seat and tried to imagine jamming his head under it and squeezing his six-foot frame on the floor. It would never work. "Get out of the way. I'm coming back there!"

"What? Don't get cute, sonny. I'll shoot you so fast - "

"Shut up and get your bony butt out of the way!" Barrett barked as he threw himself headfirst into the backseat next to Nora. After a glance behind him, he crawled into the third-row seating area. Thankfully, whoever had previously owned the minivan had been driving it with the extra seats folded down. There wasn't a lot of room, but Barrett did his best to pull a blanket that had been left behind over his body as he curled into a ball. The back windows of the van were almost completely snow-covered. He wasn't worried that someone would spot him back here, not in this position. He didn't even know for sure that it was necessary to hide. But he wasn't willing to take the chance.

"Holy crap, it's the cops!" Nora said.

"Shhh. If they see you talking, they're gonna wonder who you're talking to," Barrett whispered.

"It's two cars. A police car and a regular car," she continued.

"Shhh," Barrett repeated.

"I'm talking with my mouth closed," Nora demonstrated.

"They have ears," he whispered again. "Be quiet. Look natural."

I wonder why the police are here, Barrett thought. As badly as he wanted to get away from Randy and Nora, he hoped the police hadn't tracked the minivan to the Chumansky house. That would be another wrench thrown into Barrett's plan to get back to Colorado to see his dying father. Much like the earlier possibility of getting pulled over on the interstate while driving an empty yellow school bus, it didn't seem worth the risk.

Barrett could hear the doors of the vehicles close.

"Two men," Nora whispered.

"Shush!"

The snow on the driveway and sidewalk crunched as the men walked the path to the front door.

"They can't see me now," Nora said. "Can I talk now?"

"Do you have something important to say?"

"They walked around behind us. I assume they didn't see you. I think they saw me."

"Hopefully they didn't see your gun," Barrett said.

"I hope Randy gets back here soon."

"You better hope they're not here for him."

***

"Hi, Maddison. Claire," Jackson said from behind Randy, who was still standing outside the front door. Chase brought up the rear.

Randy turned, looked, and spoke to the two men. "Who are you?"

Before Jackson or Chase could answer, Maddison spoke up. "Sergeant Jackson, hello. I didn't recognize you in regular people clothes," she joked.

"Sergeant?" Randy said.

Jackson held out his hand. "John Jackson, Gable Police."

Randy shook Jackson's hand while looking at Chase. "Who's your shadow?" he asked.

"Agent Chase Sheehan, FBI," Chase replied, not offering his hand.

"FBI. Right," Randy snorted with laughter.

Chase pulled out his badge and held it in front of Randy's face.

The big blonde man squinted and then flashed a look

of surprise. "Man, I didn't do anything," he said.

"That's good, because we're not here for you," Chase said to him.

Randy turned to Maddison. "Thank you for your time and help," he said. Jackson and Chase moved out of Randy's way and allowed him to walk back down the drive.

"No problem," Maddison said and then directed her attention to the law enforcement officers who had just arrived. "Come on in, gentlemen."

The two men entered the house. After Jackson introduced Chase to Maddison and Claire, he explained why they were there. "We understand that both your ex-husband and Eddie Clark have disappeared and we'd like to try and figure out what happened."

"Yes," Maddison said. "Claire was just filling me in about what she told you. I must say, the FBI got here fast."

Jackson turned to Chase.

"Actually, I'm here because my sister has also disappeared," Chase told the women. "She's with the DEA. You might know her from the earlier investigation: Delia DeMarco." He handed his phone to Maddison, who showed it to Claire. It displayed a picture of Chase and Delia at a Chicago Cubs game.

"I remember her," Claire said.

"So do I," Maddison said. "It took me a while to convince her I didn't know about any of the crap Tom was involved in."

"She's a good agent," Chase said. "Have either of you seen her around in the last few days?" The women looked at each other and then back to Chase. Neither could recall seeing Delia. As he took his phone back, he changed the subject. "So, who was that guy that was just here?"

"Some guy looking for Tom," Maddison said.

"Isn't that a little strange?" Chase asked.

"Well, not really. I mean, he knows a lot of people,"

Maddison pointed out. "And knowing now what I should've known before, I can see why there are so many people looking for him."

"Did he say why he was looking for your husband?"

"He said he was an old friend from high school who had been living in Adler for twenty years and just today discovered Tom owned Mecca Warehouse. He said he had been to the stores today and they said he wasn't in so he found this address online. He obviously didn't know we're divorced and that Tom doesn't live here anymore."

"Wait a minute. How old is your husband? I mean, *ex*-husband. Sorry," Chase said, correcting himself.

"Thirty-nine," Maddison answered.

"Didn't that guy seem kind of old to have gone to high school with your husband?" Chase asked her.

Maddison's eyes widened. "My God, yes. I guess you're right."

"There was an old lady in the backseat," Jackson added.

"The license plates were Michigan," Chase said. "There was a window sticker that said East Lansing High School. The Trojans, I think it was."

"What the…" Jackson said.

"Something's not right," Chase suggested, looking at Jackson. "You need to go follow him. There's still time. Maybe run the plate." He turned to Maddison. "Did he say what his name was?"

Maddison shook her head. "We didn't get that far. You guys showed up."

"I can run out to my car," Jackson suggested. "Let me make a quick radio call to Hodge. He's supposed to be patrolling between here and Alder and north to Merchant." Jackson desperately wanted to stay and help direct the investigation, but his fear of being found out was overtaking his common sense. The instant he suggested radioing Hodge he realized his mistake. The last thing he needed right now was to look like he wasn't a team player.

"You understand what's going on here. It really needs to be you," Chase said. "I'll do this and we can get together later."

Jackson nodded. He knew what he had to do. "All right, you got it. I'm out of here. I'll keep you posted."

He said goodbye to the ladies and exited through the front door to his squad car. In a perfect world Jackson would be able to steer the disappearance of Chum in a direction that kept the rest of the world off his trail. Now that the FBI was involved, it wouldn't be as easy as he'd originally thought. But Chum's disappearance still fell in Jackson's favor. Just like he had told Pablo in the abandoned warehouse, people would assume Chum had been knocked off by the cartel. There would be no evidence to link Jackson, assuming DeMarco was dead. Or if she was alive and eventually found, he prayed to God she would stay true to her word about protecting him. If she didn't, Jackson doubted his fate would be anything other than a prison cell. And then there was the latest news he had received only a couple of hours ago: Fast Eddie was missing, too. What had happened to him?

Jackson fishtailed his car through the snow as he pushed the accelerator to the floor, pulling away from the Chumansky driveway and heading back to the highways of western Gable. Despite the fact that he was already in over his head, he was curious as hell about the guy who had just been at Maddison's door. Sheehan was right: something was wrong. And the more Jackson thought about it the more he wondered if this guy driving the minivan was tied to Eddie's disappearance.

He slowed his squad car down as the highway turned into Main Street and he made his way into town. He didn't know for sure which direction to go from this point. He quickly called Officer Hodge on the radio to confirm his location. After learning that Hodge was north of Gable and had yet to see a minivan, Jackson turned right and headed south on Highway 57, ordering Hodge to keep his eyes peeled and to run the plates if he spotted the vehicle. He put the accelerator to the floor, and the Crown Victoria raced down the highway. After five minutes of driving at a seventy-five-mile-an-hour clip, Jackson was able to make out the minivan from a short distance of about a half mile.

Slowing down his vehicle, but still allowing himself to get closer at a more gradual pace, Jackson reached for the two-way radio, ready to call in the plate number as soon as he was close enough to read it. Before he was able to do so, however, his cell phone rang. Jackson could tell by the caller ID this was another call he didn't want to take. He hit the answer button and remained silent.

"Hola, Señor Jackson," Pablo greeted him. "Are you ready for your next task?"

***

"Just stay back there," Randy said as he drove the van south on Highway 57, out of Gable. "I like having your mouth as far away from me as possible."

Barrett stayed silent.

"What did they tell you?" Nora asked. "Where is he?"

"I didn't get very far before the cops showed up. But he's not there at the house."

"One of them was FBI?" Nora confirmed.

"Yeah. For a second I thought they were after me, maybe the van," Randy said. "When I found out they weren't, I split."

"So why are we going back in this direction?" Nora asked.

"Because someone at one of those stores of his is bound to tell me something." Randy said this firmly, letting his passengers know the decision was not up for discussion.

As Barrett remained seated in the third row listening,

the storage compartment behind him caught his eye. It was bulging and not completely shut. Curious, he quietly shifted around in order to lift up the compartment's door just enough to see what was inside.

It was his backpack!

Remaining composed, Barrett set the door back in place and tried to refocus his attention on his captors. It was difficult to keep a smile from taking over his face. He was ecstatic to know his patience was beginning to pay off. The bad news was the back door probably couldn't be opened while the vehicle was moving. Barrett's next task was to figure out how to get out of the van with his money. This would more than likely need to happen through the back. If he had only spotted the backpack while Randy was at the Chumanskys' front door, he might be free by now.

"What did the cops say?" Nora asked.

"Like I said, one of them was FBI. His name was like Chad Sheeran or something like that. The other guy was local. Jackson, was his name."

Barrett's ears perked up. It was a good thing he had taken cover. Jackson would've recognized him immediately.

"I don't want to invite them to dinner," Nora quipped. "I asked you what they said to you."

"Yeah, yeah," Randy said. "They didn't say much. I joked that I 'didn't do it' and they said they weren't there for me, so that's when I took off."

"I wonder if they were looking for our friend back here," Nora said, pointing over her shoulder with a bony thumb.

"Good point. I hadn't thought of that. Maybe I should've turned him in right then and there." Barrett didn't respond. He figured it was possible they were still investigating things that happened months ago. Or maybe Chum had done something again. You never could tell about that guy.

"There was another woman there with the wife,"

Randy continued. "Don't know who she was. Not that it matters. I think she was too old to be a daughter. Didn't look anything like the wife, either."

The green car Barrett had seen in the driveway — it was Claire's!

It wasn't until Randy mentioned another woman being present that Barrett remembered seeing Claire's green car the night of Chum's party. She had met Barrett at the farmhouse in the early evening and parked the car out front. Then they had walked to the Chumansky house for the get-together. The next time he saw the car was in the black of night, shortly before he left town.

Now that he was this close to her again, Barrett realized Claire was the one person in Gable he wanted to explain himself to. The reason he left when he did, the way he did. The reason he was in Gable at all in the first place. Getting that chance would be a long shot, especially now that he was traveling in the opposite direction. But as Barrett continued to contemplate the possibilities of slipping away from Randy and Nora with his money, he began to wonder if *getting caught* might be his best bet to get back to Colorado.

***

"So you're confirming to me, on the record, that your husband has always known where the money was," Chase stated.

"Ex-husband," Maddison reminded him. "Yes, that's correct. He told me it was in the farmhouse until he rented it out to Henry — or whatever his name really was. Tom put it in a different spot shortly before he moved in."

Claire touched the hollow of her throat at the mention of Henry's name.

"And he buried it out here somewhere," Chase confirmed with a hand motion.

"Yes. I can't say for sure where, but it was in the

wooded area here by the house. I think he had information in his smartphone about exactly where."

"Eddie Clark," Chase continued. "You say he's missing, too."

"I believe so," Maddison said. "I haven't been able to contact him either. I've left him voicemails and been to his house. He seemed to not be there."

"And he was supposed to meet your ex-husband out there to recover the money, correct?"

"The last thing he said to me was that he was going to call Eddie and get him to help," Maddison remembered. "He had his phone in his hand when he left through the back door." Maddison pointed in the direction of the kitchen where the door was located. Her arm lingered in the air, pointing. Chase assumed she was envisioning the last time she had seen him.

"Ladies," Chase said, making eye contact with each of them. "As I mentioned when we first sat down, the authorities aren't interested in pressing charges for obstruction. You're both safe." The women nodded. "We're more interested in what's still going on around here. And your help and information is far more important than making you pay for one bad decision." Claire looked down at the floor as Chase continued. "Like I said before, I'm not even here on official FBI business. I'm really on vacation and looking for my sister. But the longer I'm here the more I think the three disappearances are related: Chumansky, Clark, and Delia."

Chase let out a big breath of air. He was extremely anxious about his sister. This was not looking good.

"So what else can we do to help?" Claire asked.

"Be available," Chase said. "We might have more questions soon. The first thing I want to do is get inside both of their residences. You say you've been in your ex-husband's place, but we should check it, anyway. And Clark's, too, of course. The other thing we're going to do is get some K-9's out here in your woods and see what they can find."

Maddison shuddered as if a chill had just passed through her.

"I know," Chase said empathetically. "It's frightening to think what the dogs could turn up out there. But it might be the only way we're going to figure out what happened."

"Speaking of dogs, I suppose I should go to Tom's and get Millie and Hazel. They're his dogs. He kept them in the divorce," she explained to Chase. "With him…um…not around right now, someone needs to take care of them."

"If you wouldn't mind, I'd like to go with you," Chase said. "It'll give me a chance to search his house."

"Sure," Maddison said.

"I should head out then," Claire said. "I need to be to work by eleven."

The ladies exchanged phone numbers with the agent and parted ways.

***

Jackson tried to block out the call from Pablo. At the same time he knew he better damn well not forget about it lest he be burdened with the deaths of the three most beloved people in his life.

He picked up the two-way receiver again and called dispatch. It didn't take long to discover what Jackson had already suspected: the blue minivan he was following had recently been reported stolen in Waterloo. To make matters worse, it had been stolen at gunpoint by a large blonde man. This meant there was probably at least one firearm inside the vehicle.

Just what I need, he thought. More crap to deal with around here.

After requesting backup from Hodge, Jackson flipped the lights and siren on and attempted to pull the van over. After ten seconds it was evident the driver was not going to give up without a fight.

But what the driver didn't know, Jackson realized immediately: the minivan's engine was small and would not be able to outrun a police car, especially not on a highway where it had nowhere to go but into a ditch. Jackson picked the receiver up once again and attempted to make contact with the driver.

"This is the Gable Police Department — pull over now!" he ordered.

Another fifteen seconds went by before the minivan finally began to make its way to the shoulder. When it had come to a complete stop, Jackson put his police coat on and opened his door. As he moved to the driver's side of the vehicle, he observed what he could about who was inside and what they were doing. As he had assumed from seeing the van earlier in the Chumansky driveway, there were two occupants: the driver and the old woman in the backseat.

Snowflakes repeatedly spit in Jackson's face as he made his way to just behind the driver's side door. He rapped on the window.

"Merry Christmas, officer," the driver said as he lowered the window. "Hey, I know you!"

Jackson had forgotten it was Christmas Eve day until now. He kept his body behind the driver as he had been trained to do. His right hand remained at his side, near his holstered gun.

"License and registration," he said.

The large blonde driver stared at the police officer blankly. "This is going to sound crazy," the man said. "But I don't have either of them with me. It's a long story. I realize I'm probably going to—"

Jackson knew he should wait for Hodge to arrive, but he had other things to do. "Put both hands on the wheel, sir," he commanded.

"I don't understand," the man said.

"Oh, I'm sure you do," Jackson replied. "I'm not going to ask you again." The man obliged. "Now slowly use your left hand to open the door and get out."

The man once again did as he was told and stepped out of the minivan. Leaning him against the hood, Jackson frisked him. After finding no weapons, he pulled the man's arms behind his back and hooked his wrists with his handcuffs.

"You're under arrest for being in possession of a stolen vehicle."

The man turned around. "What? This thing is stolen?"

"Yes, I know. Shocking, isn't it?" Jackson said. "Don't move." He took two steps to the passenger door on the driver's side and slid it open.

"Ma'am, can you get out of the—"

"No, I can't," the old woman interrupted Jackson, pointing a .357 Magnum at him.

Jackson slowly put his hands in the air and began to back away from the open door. "Okay, wait a minute. I don't know what's going on here, but this is not a good idea," Jackson said. "I have backup coming." He turned his head to the right, hoping to see Hodge's squad car. "Any minute," Jackson added.

"Then I guess I better hurry up," she said, holding the gun steady in his direction. "First, I need you to unlock my son's handcuffs and give him your car keys. Then I'm going to have you move your buns across the highway and start walking," the old lady said, pointing south. "Away from us and your car and your backup."

Jackson shook his head in frustration. This was not good, but all he had to do was take his time with the woman's tasks. Hodge should be arriving any minute. They had no idea how close he was.

"Get going," she instructed. Jackson reached into his pocket to get his keys and moved towards the big man.

"Easy there, Smokey," the woman warned him. Jackson turned to make eye contact and assure her of his intent to comply. As he did, he noticed a figure moving in the extra seats behind the old lady. Snowflakes teased Jackson's face and nose and landed in his eyes. He wasn't sure what was going on until it happened, and when it did it happened quickly, with lightning precision.

The silhouette of a second person inside the van reached around the old woman with both arms and grabbed the hand holding the gun. The sudden impact caused the firearm to discharge, but the attacker had been able to change the position of the gun before it was fired. Instead of hitting the policeman, the bullet lodged in the back of the driver's seat. Jackson could now see that the figure who had taken the old woman by surprise was a man, and he wasn't finished. He kept her head locked between his elbows as he continued to swing her frail body back and forth until she released the gun from her hand into his. Simultaneously, Jackson unholstered his weapon and aimed it inside the van.

The old woman began coughing in an effort to catch her breath after being tossed around.

"Throw that piece out here," Jackson called to the man in the far backseat as he took two steps backward onto the highway. He glanced at the big blonde man, who still stood handcuffed near the hood of the van.

"Mom?" Randy called out. "Are you okay? What happened?"

"She's fine," Jackson quipped. "Shut up." The .357 Magnum flew out the open door and to the ground. "Both of you get out of the vehicle."

"I need my wheelchair," the old woman cried between coughs. Just then Officer Ryan Hodge pulled up in his squad car. He parked behind Jackson's vehicle and, noticing his superior officer's weapon drawn, pulled his own gun out as he jogged to the scene.

"What the hell?" Hodge commented as he glanced inside the van and saw the old woman.

Jackson first instructed Hodge to get the big man inside his car. The police sergeant kept his gun on the old woman and the other man, who was still barely visible in the third-row seats. When Hodge returned he opened the rear door of the van with his gun drawn.

"Come here," he told the man. "Slowly." The man scooted to the edge and put his feet on the ground.

"Hands up," Hodge told him.

"This isn't what it looks like," Barrett pleaded. "Let me talk to Jackson."

Hodge turned him around and lowered his arms behind his back, placing handcuffs on them. Then he turned Barrett around to face him. "What?"

"Let me talk to Sergeant Jackson."

"What's going on back there, Hodge?" Jackson shouted, his view blocked by the open back door. Barrett gave Hodge a nod.

"This guy wants to talk to you," Hodge replied. "He knows your name."

This wasn't the first time Jackson had heard something like that. Usually it was someone who had a prior or two and thought they could talk their way out of another one.

"Switch with me," he told Hodge. "Get her wheelchair out and put her in my car. We'll keep her and the big guy separated." Jackson moved to the back of the van with his gun pointing upward. When he saw Barrett he holstered it.

"Superhero strikes again," Jackson greeted him.

Barrett shook his head. "I'm sure you're wondering why I'm here."

"Not really," Jackson replied.

"I had nothing to do with any of this," Barrett explained. "They kidnapped me."

"Kidnapped?"

"Whatever you call it," Barrett said. "They brought me here against my will."

Jackson looked at Barrett and then at Hodge as he

wheeled the wrinkled woman to the backseat of his squad car.

"Come on," Barrett continued. "If I was with them do you think I'd have grabbed the gun from her? I *helped* you."

Remaining silent, Jackson closed his eyes and tilted his head to the sky before moving his gaze back to the cuffed man in front of him. He had too much on his mind and he needed to focus. With a sigh, he rubbed his hands across his face before he finally spoke again. "What is it with you, always finding yourself in the middle of these ambiguous situations?"

Barrett shrugged and then looked down at the snow-covered ground.

"You've got a lot of explaining to do," Jackson said as he led him by the arm. "And I have the perfect person for you to talk to."

XXIV

"I appreciate you coming over here and opening up his house, Mrs. Clark," Chase told Eddie Clark's mother, Marge. "I'm sure your son is fine, but it was important for us to look for clues as to his whereabouts."

"Did you find anything?" Mrs. Clark asked the FBI agent. She was a short, portly woman with salt and pepper hair and rimless spectacles.

"Not really," Chase said. "Did Eddie have a girlfriend?"

"Yes. She lives here in Adler. Her name is Sheila. I can give you her address. It's not far."

Chase handed the woman his small notebook and pen, and she scribbled the information down.

"Agent," she began, after returning the notebook, "I'm worried about my boy, but I'm not terribly surprised. He's always wandered to the other side of the railroad tracks."

"I understand," Chase said. "Let me know if you think of anything else that might help, and I'll keep you posted." He handed Marge Clark a card before she drove away in her gray Honda CR-V.

Chase pulled out his phone and dialed Nolan Reed. "You wanted to be kept in the loop, so here it goes," Chase said. He told Nolan everything that he had learned so far about his missing sister. Then he also added the story of the missing men, drugs, and money. When he was finished, he detailed his next moves. "I've got the K-9's from Adler on the way. Can you have Delia's phone pinged? Also Chumansky's and Clark's."

"You got it," Reed said. Chase recited the phone numbers to his boss before hanging up.

After getting situated in his car, he decided to call the Gable PD and see how Jackson had made out with the suspicious minivan. Chief Perkins answered the phone at the station and let Chase know there had been some arrests made in connection with the van and that it would be best if the FBI agent returned to Gable. Questioning Eddie Clark's lady friend, Sheila, would have to wait.

As he began the short drive, Chase contemplated the details of what he had just learned, which wasn't much. The differences between Chumansky's house and Clark's house were minimal. Neither looked to have left his residence under duress. There were no wallets or personal effects left behind. The possibility that one was involved with the other's disappearance remained. Or they vanished under the same circumstances. Something was awry, and there was a good possibility that Delia's disappearance was connected.

***

Jackson stood in the same abandoned warehouse where he had met Pablo only a few days ago. This time he had a companion.

"Man, I appreciate you helping me out but I don't understand what we're doing here," Bart Timmons said to Jackson. Timmons was an obese farm boy in his mid-twenties, dressed in blue jeans and a bright orange T-shirt, size 4X. With a CAT cap on his head he stood a couple of inches taller than the police sergeant. Despite Bart's unhealthy weight, Jackson knew the young man was as strong as an ox.

"I'd rather explain myself once," Jackson said. "So hang tight. He should be here any minute."

Before the words were out of his mouth, Pablo

entered the building with two of his men. When they realized Jackson was not alone, Pablo's guys pulled out their handguns.

"Ho, hey! What the hell?" Bart Timmons shouted, looking at Jackson and then back at the guns pointed in his direction.

"Put them away," Jackson said sternly. "He's okay."

Pablo motioned for his guys to put their guns away before he spoke. "Señor Jackson, what is going on here?"

"We need to come to an understanding, Pablo." This was the first time Jackson could remember calling him by his name. "I can't be your mule. But I can still be of service."

"Mule?" Timmons said.

"Be quiet. Listen," Jackson told him. "I'll let you know when it's time to speak." The big guy folded his arms across his flabby chest and took a step backwards.

"I'm not sure about this," Pablo said, setting down a bag he had carried in. He glanced at his men on either side of him.

"Hear me out," Jackson said. "You're going to get everything you want." He could sense the other man was uncomfortable with not being the one in control.

"Fine," Pablo agreed.

"You can use him." Jackson jerked his thumb over his shoulder at Timmons.

"How do I know I can trust him?" Pablo asked.

"For starters," Jackson said, "I'll kill him before you do if he double-crosses you."

"What?" Timmons blurted out. Jackson turned and glared at him.

"It seems he hasn't agreed to any of this, señor," Pablo said.

"You're very observant," Jackson replied sharply. He turned to Timmons, who reminded him at that moment of what Charlie Brown's Great Pumpkin would look like if it actually existed.

"Okay, Bart," Jackson began, "Here's the deal. Hodge got you last Friday for another DWI. It was your third. You're looking at up to five years in the can, a major fine, and a license suspension…it ain't good and you know it."

"Yeah," Timmons agreed, "I know." He put his mammoth hands inside the front pockets of his jeans and kicked the ground.

"But I'm going to make it all go away," Jackson continued. He looked back at Pablo and saw he was now smiling.

"That's great!" Timmons exclaimed. "I really appreciate it. It means so much to me."

The police sergeant remained silent. No one in the warehouse said a word. Jackson knew Bart Timmons wasn't the brightest bulb in the fixture, but he thought the kid would've put two and two together by now.

"I'm glad to hear how much it means to you," Jackson said, "Because you know nothing in life is free, right?"

The lightbulb just turned on, Jackson thought.

"You want me to push drugs?" he asked, wide-eyed. "Are you…you're selling drugs?"

"I wouldn't call it selling, señor," Pablo interjected. "You're just the middle man."

Bart looked at Pablo and then back to Jackson. "What's going on? Is this a joke?"

"I'm afraid it's not," Jackson confirmed. "You help out by doing this, and your latest arrest never even makes it to a judge."

"But how can you do that?" Bart said.

"It's not your problem." Jackson turned to Pablo. "You want to explain more? You good with this?"

"It's okay for now," Pablo said. "But I'm worried about what he'll be like after you fix his problem."

"You and I both know the answer to that," Jackson said. "If need be, one of us will find more leverage."

"One of us?" Pablo repeated. "You're still in, señor?"

Jackson put a finger in the air and looked back and forth between Timmons and Pablo. "First of all," he said sternly, "let's be clear that I was *never* 'in.' You left me no choice when you threatened my family."

"You always had a choice," Pablo said.

"They threatened your family?" Timmons asked.

Jackson ignored them. "Second, it's not like you were going to let me off that easy just because I brought someone to the table. You're still going to want me involved. I'm not stupid. But I expect it to be under different circumstances now. We can discuss those circumstances in a minute, but right now why don't you take the time to conduct some orientation for your new employee, Bart Timmons."

Pablo pulled a cell phone from the bag he had brought in.

"This is your lifeline," he told Bart. "You will not make outgoing calls with it. I will call you. Do not program names or numbers in it. Every time I call you it will be a different phone number listed on the caller ID. Every time it rings you will answer it."

Jackson could tell Bart was taking notes, mentally. A part of him felt bad about what he was doing to the kid. But on the other hand, Jackson felt tremendous relief knowing he finally had some power over the situation he was in.

"Inside this bag is the product," Pablo continued. "You will distribute it as instructed. You will collect payments as instructed. And once a week, you will settle up with me by bringing the cash you have collected." He handed the bag to Bart. "It's funny that Señor Jackson referred to you as my employee. In an effort to keep you from the temptation of spending the money you collect, I will be paying you for your services, weekly. Remember, I know how much money you are supposed to be bringing me. Don't try to be smarter than me, because you are not."

"Okay," the big farmer said.

"And don't get caught," Jackson added. "Especially not in Adler. I have almost no pull there."

"Okay," Bart repeated, emotionless.

"Why don't you go out to my car and wait for me?" Jackson told him. "I'll be there in a minute to take you home."

Timmons took the bag and phone with him and shuffled to the door. When he had exited, Pablo spoke first.

"You have big cojones, señor."

"I need some breathing room," Jackson said. "I can't be your distributor. It would only be a matter of time before the cat was out of the bag and then you'd be left with nothing. I'd be in the slammer. It's a bad idea. This way I can still help."

Pablo nodded. "Like I said. We can give it a try. But if there's a problem with him—"

"Then you let *me* know and I will handle it," Jackson said. "If you want this to work you need to use my brain to your advantage instead of trying to make me your errand boy."

Pablo looked from side to side at his two men again. Jackson knew the leader didn't like being told what to do in front of them.

"Think of this as a partnership. We're working together." Jackson softened the blow. "You still get what you want and need, and so do I." He paused to let it sink in before continuing. "Speaking of which, I'm not asking for money. I just want two things in return for my services of looking the other way and running interference."

"I'm listening," Pablo replied. He shifted his hips and shoulders to project a more powerful position.

"Leave my family alone. No more threats," Jackson said. "If you have a problem with Timmons or anything else, you come to me and we'll work it out together."

"Señor, that takes away my leverage," Pablo said.

"I can't help keep your operation going while I'm worrying about my family all the time. My wife already knows something's up. It's bad business for you to overwhelm me with all of that and still expect me to cooperate. Eventually, something will go wrong, and it probably will end up bad for both of us. You kill my family and you'll lose my cooperation for sure. Let me prove myself to you instead."

"You said two things," Pablo said. "What is the other?"

"No more bloodshed," Jackson told him. "Missing people and murders are only going to draw attention. Again, you have an issue, bring it to me first."

It had been a wicked couple of days for Jackson. He hadn't had much rest nor a lot of time to think straight. But during the period of disorientation and frustration, he was able to piece together a plan that he believed would keep Pablo happy and feeling like he was in control. This was the key. It wasn't ideal for Jackson, but for now it would have to suffice.

"Okay. That makes sense." Pablo said. "As long as you understand that I still have the right to—"

"You're the boss," Jackson interrupted. "You always have the right. That's my motivation, Pablo. Just know I'm trying to work with you, not against you. For the good of both of our goals."

With a step forward Pablo stuck his right hand out in front of him. The move caught Jackson off guard, but after a slight hesitation he reciprocated. As the four men prepared to part ways, Jackson spoke again.

"Can I speak to you for a minute, alone?"

Pablo raised an eyebrow at the police sergeant and motioned to his men to give him and Jackson some privacy.

"I have one more thing," Jackson said in a low voice. "A suggestion."

Pablo motioned for Jackson to continue.

"If Agent DeMarco is still alive, you might want to let her go. The FBI is already here. It's her brother, in fact. This guy is not going to give up. It's going to get messy and difficult to conduct your business. It will all lead back to me and then…"

"If she is still alive she knows your involvement," Pablo reminded Jackson.

"You let me worry about that."

"And if she's dead?" Pablo asked.

Jackson shrugged. "Then you've made all that we just discussed a thousand times more difficult."

The Hispanic man showed no emotion, but Jackson could tell by the look in his eyes that he understood. The men prepared to leave through separate doors just as they had a few days ago when Jackson returned the money and the coke. As the sergeant turned the knob, he heard Pablo call out to him.

"Señor," he shouted across the building from the doorway. "I have one more thing for you."

Jackson could sense sarcasm in Pablo's voice — he was being mocked. The thought of what "one more thing" could be caused the policeman to put his hand on the butt of his gun. What now?

"Feliz Navidad," Pablo said with a wave of his hand and a grin that was wide enough Jackson could see it from the opposite side of the warehouse. The door closed and Jackson was left alone, his fingers still touching his gun.

***

"The K-9's are on their way from Adler," Chase told Hodge and Chief Perkins as they congregated in the front office of the station. "The snow is getting worse out there but hopefully we can still learn something from the dogs. It's worth a shot. Where's Jackson?"

"He had something he had to take care of," Perkins said. "He said he wouldn't be long."

"Now?" Chase asked, frustrated.

"He's my main man around here," Perkins said. "I give him leeway. I'd rather not piss him off and lose him."

Before he could say anything else, Chase's phone rang. "Nolan, what do you know?"

"Looks like Chumansky and Clark were in the same area Saturday night," Nolan Reed said.

"Where was that?"

"Near the big Chumansky house."

"Probably in the woods. They were supposed to be back there digging up the money," Chase said.

"But here's the thing," Nolan continued. "Chumansky's phone hasn't bounced off of any towers since then."

"Nothing?"

"Nada."

"And Clark's?" Chase could already guess the answer by the way Nolan was feeding him the information.

"It hasn't stopped pinging. It looks like he went to his house or near it about an hour or so after he was in the same spot as Chumansky," Nolan said, paraphrasing the report.

"And now?"

"Still inside Adler city limits, but a couple of miles from his house."

"Could you text me the coordinates?"

"Give me two minutes," Nolan replied and hung up.

Chase turned his attention back to Hodge and Perkins and relayed what he had just learned. "I'm already getting sick of going back and forth between these towns. Doesn't anyone live here?" he asked.

"Eight hundred seventy-nine," Chief Perkins said. "You might've noticed the sign on your way in."

Chase shook his head as his phone beeped. After a few seconds of reading the text message from Reed he looked back up at Perkins and Hodge.

"We need Jackson back here," Chase said. "You've got three missing persons in a town of nine hundred. The more manpower we have working on this, the better."

"With all due respect, Agent Sheehan," Hodge said, speaking up for the first time, "there's a good chance Chum and Fast Eddie have been snorting up the evidence for the last few days and are hanging out at a casino in Nebraska."

Chase's face tensed. "What about my sister?" he growled, taking an aggressive step forward. "I know *she's* not doing that!"

"Hey, just a second," Perkins interjected. "We're all on the same side here, Agent. Hodge didn't mean anything by that. We just know these two fellas and their personalities pretty well around here."

"Apparently not well enough to know they were muling coke!" Chase shot back, his words echoing down the hall in front of him. The chief's eyes lowered to the floor as an uncomfortable silence filled the room.

"That wasn't necessary," Chase said with a deep breath. "I apologize. Just please keep in mind I'm only here because of my sister. I'm technically on vacation."

"Absolutely. Completely understood. We're gonna find her," Perkins assured him.

"Having said all that, I think we agree there's reason to believe all three disappearances are connected," Chase continued. "Do you know Clark's girlfriend, a Sheila Macon?"

Hodge and Perkins nodded.

"Don't know her well," Hodge said. "Seen her around. Not so much lately."

"Clark's mother gave me Sheila's address before I left her son's house," Chase offered. "Eddie's phone has been bouncing off a tower not far from there."

"Well, how do you like that?" Perkins chuckled.

"Granted, all this means is his phone is around there

somewhere. It doesn't mean Clark is," Chase explained.

"Well, we should go check it out!" Hodge exclaimed.

"I thought we had something special brewing here already?" Chase asked.

"Yes. Yes, we do," Perkins agreed.

"So why don't you call Jackson and tell him to get over to Sheila Macon's," Chase suggested. "See what he can find out, investigate. Clark might be there. Hell, Chumansky might be there, too, with a dead phone."

"Okay, I'll holler at him here in just a minute," Perkins said. "But first you need to hear about who we've got in our jail cells."

Chase heard Perkins, but he wasn't finished with his thoughts. "Hodge, stick around and wait for the K-9's. Check with me when they get here. If I can't leave, I'll send you out to lead the sniffing and then catch up with you. Get with Maddison Chumansky first and let her know you're there. She might be able to lead you in a general direction, but don't let her go out there with you. There's no telling what you might find, and the last thing we need is her out there seeing it, firsthand."

"Got it," Hodge said.

"Sorry, Chief," Chase said. "Now what is it you've got for me?"

***

Barrett sat on a metal folding chair up against a table in a room that looked all too familiar. He couldn't believe he had turned himself in, so to speak. But it seemed like the most sensible thing to do at the time. God knows what Nora would've done to Jackson, pointing that gun at him the way she was. Barrett's hope was that disarming the old bat would score some brownie points with Jackson. Instead, the police sergeant seemed preoccupied and left Barrett locked in an interrogation room after telling him there was someone else he needed to talk to.

At least I'm not in jail, Barrett thought as he tapped his fingers on the table. He was certain that was where Randy and Nora were right now. They had both clearly broken the law. Barrett still just wanted his money back. And his freedom.

When the door opened, a man who looked to be about Barrett's age walked in and sat across from him. He was dressed in a dark blue button-down shirt that was tucked into his khakis. The man didn't speak. Neither did Barrett. Instead, they stared at each other from opposite sides of the table. Barrett could see the man's nostrils flair with every breath he took. He had no reason to be in a staring contest with the guy, but Barrett also knew that looking away would make him appear weak.

"Barrett Greyson," the man finally said, not breaking eye contact.

Barrett held his gaze as he responded. "And you are…?"

"Chase Sheehan, FBI."

"Hmmm," Barrett replied. The sound was more of grunt: he simply didn't know what to say. Sheehan stared at Barrett. Barrett stared at Sheehan. The two remained silent for another fifteen seconds.

"What are we doing?" Barrett finally asked. This was getting old.

"I'm impressed," the FBI agent said, breaking eye contact for the first time in two minutes.

"With what?" Barrett asked, relaxing a bit.

"You kept your poise."

"You mean just now?"

Sheehan nodded.

"I figured you were sizing me up."

"I was."

"What did you learn?"

"That you're smart enough to not shit your pants when you're sitting across from an FBI agent," Sheehan said, impressed.

"I try to never do that," Barrett quipped with a smirk.

"I've been working your case," Sheehan told him.

Barrett raised his eyebrows. "Case? I have a 'case?'" Barrett said. It sounded surreal.

"Well, actually it's the Otto Clevinger homicide that I'm investigating," Chase clarified. "You just happen to be in the middle of it."

Barrett bit his lip.

"But you probably already knew that part," Chase added.

"Yeah," Barrett said. Once again, he didn't know what to say next.

Sheehan solved the issue by asking a question. "What are you doing here?"

"You mean *this* time?"

"I think it's obvious you were just trying to blend in here the first time," Chase said.

Barrett saw an opening. "Then you can also understand why I didn't want to come back here," Barrett said. "I told Jackson…Randy and Nora forced me to come here."

"Why?"

"Because they thought I could help them find — steal —the drug money Chum probably has hidden somewhere."

Chase stroked his chin in silence.

"I mean, I can't," Barrett continued. "I tried to tell them. I have no idea where it's at."

"How did you get mixed up with them in the first place?"

"*Dateline*," Barrett said simply. "They recognized me on a Greyhound bus and took me at gunpoint in the middle of downtown Chicago."

"Wow," was all Sheehan could say in response.

"Tell me about it. I'd've tried to get away from them sooner but they always had a gun on me. And they also had my entire life savings. By the way, it was in the back of the van. Where is it now?"

"It's safe. Everything inside the van is being checked in as evidence."

"Did Jackson tell you I helped him after he pulled us over? The old woman — Nora — had him at gunpoint. I got the gun from her and gave it to Jackson."

"I haven't actually spoken to Jackson," Sheehan commented, "but I will. And I did hear something about you helping out. I have to admit, everything you're saying so far matches up with what I've heard. I'm going to have to do some verifying of what went down outside of Des Moines at the truck stop, but…"

"Everything I'm telling you is the truth," Barrett interjected. "I just want to get my money and…" He stopped himself before finishing and looked down at the table between them.

"We have more to talk about," Chase said. "You know that."

"I was on my way to see my dad," Barrett explained. "He's got cancer."

"I know he does," Chase admitted.

"Is he okay? Have you seen him lately?"

"I saw him a couple of weeks ago. I didn't even know he was sick at first."

"I guess that's good," Barrett said.

There was a short silence before Chase asked another question. "I'm confused. You said they kidnapped you to come here and hunt for the missing money. How does that fit into seeing your father?"

"I saw the *Dateline* episode. That's how I found out my father had pancreatic cancer." Barrett felt a lump in his throat and swallowed hard before continuing. "I was heading back to Colorado when Randy and Nora took me at gunpoint."

"So, you were going back home?" Chase clarified. "Wouldn't that defeat the purpose of running away in the first place?"

Barrett ran his fingers through his hair. "It's complicated."

"I guess it doesn't really matter," Chase said.

"Are you charging me with anything?" Barrett asked. Time to cut to the chase, he thought.

"Not yet," the FBI agent said.

"So I'm not under arrest?"

"Like I said, not yet," Chase reiterated.

"So what's stopping me from walking out of here right now?" Barrett said.

He watched a grin come over Sheehan's face. "You want your money back, don't you?"

***

After calling his wife and telling her to come home with the children for Christmas, Jackson received a call from Chief Perkins with instructions. Sheehan's investigation into his sister's disappearance had turned up a lead on Eddie Clark. Jackson had been so preoccupied that he almost forgot about the missing motorcycle enthusiast. It hadn't occurred to him until now that it was possible Eddie had witnessed something concerning Agent DeMarco or Chum — or worse, the entire thing. That's probably what happened, Jackson decided.

Locking down an understanding with Pablo was a huge leap forward. Judging by his response to Jackson raising the question of DeMarco being alive, there was a good chance she was. If Pablo heeded Jackson's warning, Agent DeMarco could soon find herself free. That would get Sheehan out of town. Of course, Jackson also had to hope DeMarco would keep her promise about protecting him. The situation with Fast

Eddie Clark was yet another curveball the police sergeant might have to deal with.

Sheila Macon lived in a small blue house with a detached garage on Clayton Street in Adler. A brown Chevy Malibu was parked in the driveway. It was pulled up so close to the garage door that there was plenty of room for Jackson to park his squad car behind it. He rang the bell and knocked on the screen door for good measure. A dog barked and scratched at the door. Judging by its volume, the dog was small. The floor creaked from the inside as Jackson waited patiently for the door to open. When it finally did his nostrils were assaulted by the overwhelming stench of incense. The woman who answered the door held a Yorkie and stood about five foot five. She unlatched the screen door and pushed it open.

"What can I do for you?" she asked, clearly annoyed by his intrusion.

"Sheila Macon?" Jackson said.

The woman wasted no time answering. "Who's asking?" she shot back.

Jackson reached into his back pocket and pulled out his badge. "Sergeant John Jackson, Gable PD," he said.

The woman's eyes widened as she tucked a piece of unwashed blonde hair behind her ear. "You don't look like a cop," she commented with a snort.

"I'm not in uniform. But you can see…" Jackson motioned to his squad car sitting in the driveway.

"You coulda stole it."

"Ms. Macon, I'm sorry to bother you on Christmas Eve, but I just have a few questions. May I please come in, out of the snow?" Jackson could tell she was considering lobbing more objections his way. Instead, she pushed the screen door open and let him in.

As Jackson entered the small house he considered making a comment about her lovely home, but decided it would be an obvious lie. The living area was filled with smoke.

There were incense sticks lit in several corners of the room. On the coffee table was an ashtray filled with cigarette butts. One was still on the edge, burning. Sheila picked it up and put it between her lips as she led Jackson in. She put her dog on the floor and moved some laundry from a recliner to a clothes basket before motioning her guest to sit. As he did, Jackson looked down at the dirty wooden floor. He knew from experience it was a common misconception that Yorkshire Terriers didn't shed. Between the cigarette and incense ashes, dog hair, and other dust bunnies, he wasn't sure the floor had ever been swept. Jackson was also confident that cigarettes were not the only thing being smoked in the house, recently. Luckily for Sheila, it was the least of his concerns right now. Besides, he was technically out of his jurisdiction in Adler.

"When was the last time you saw Eddie Clark?" Jackson decided to get right to the point.

Sheila blew smoke from between her lips. "I don't know," she replied. "I guess it was over the weekend sometime."

"Can you be more specific?"

"What am I, his babysitter?"

"You have been dating him, right?" Jackson asked.

"Dating? I mean, what does that mean?" she said, smashing the cigarette into the ashtray. "If you're talking about bumping uglies a few times a week then, yeah. We've been doing that."

Jackson rolled his eyes. He wasn't sure yet if she was lying or just irritable.

"Is he in trouble?" Sheila asked, pulling a fresh cigarette from a green and white soft pack of Marlboro Menthols.

"Not at all," Jackson said. "He hasn't been to work in a couple of days. Seems no one has seen him. Some people are concerned."

She lit the cigarette with a miniature red Bic and took a

drag. "Who?"

Ignoring her question, Jackson asked her another. "Have you seen Tom Chumansky lately? He seems to be missing, too." He figured it wouldn't hurt to plant a seed and cover his ass. Just because he knew what happened to Chumansky didn't mean he shouldn't ask about him.

"Chum?" Sheila snorted. "Ha! No, I don't even remember the last time I saw him. He and I aren't exactly best buds. He thinks he's too good for me."

Judging by her reaction, Jackson believed she might not know what had happened to Chum. But it didn't mean she was telling the truth about Eddie.

"You mind if I have a look around your house, Ms. Macon?" The police sergeant stood up. Sheila did, too.

"Don't you need a warrant or something to do that?"

"Not if you allow me to do it." He figured it was worth a try.

"This place is a pit." Sheila waffled. "I just don't feel comfortable having someone going through it in this condition. If I'da known you was comin'…"

The Yorkie began to bark frantically. Jackson watched it scamper across the wooden floor to the side door.

"Oh, Piper!" Sheila exclaimed. "Knock it off. I'll let you out in a second. Stupid dog. I swear she wants to go outside more in the winter than she does when the weather is nice."

The dog continued to bark and was now scratching at the side door.

"She seems pretty adamant," Jackson observed.

"Nah, she's got this—" But Sheila Macon's explanation was cut off by the roaring of a motorcycle engine. Jackson bolted to the side door and flung it open in time to watch Fast Eddie Clark race by him on his Harley. If he had opened the door a split second sooner Jackson might have clotheslined him. Instead, Eddie rode his bike with precision between the house and the cars in the snow-covered driveway.

"You lied to me," Jackson said, more angry than surprised. He flashed a menacing scowl at her.

"I was just doing what he told me to do!"

The police sergeant moved to the front door and watched Clark drive away.

"Thanks for nothing, Ms. Macon," Jackson said as he rushed down the front steps to the driveway. When he reached his car he could see the open side door of the detached garage. It must've been quite a task squeezing his Harley out that way, Jackson thought.

As he backed out, Sheila hurried across the front yard in his direction, holding Piper. "What's going on?" she asked him.

"Why don't *you* tell *me* what's going on?" Jackson snapped back as his vehicle hit the street. He turned the car in the direction Eddie had fled, but kept his foot on the brake and rolled down his passenger window so he could continue speaking.

"What did he tell you?"

"Nothing," Sheila insisted. "I mean, just that some stuff had gone down and he needed to lay low. When we saw you pull up he told me to say I hadn't seen him. He snuck out the side while you came in the front." She held her dog close to her face. "I'm sorry. Am I in trouble?"

Thinking quickly under pressure, Jackson realized Eddie must have seen something the night he killed Chum. On the other hand, it seemed he had not told his girlfriend any specifics. This was good news for Jackson. It was time to plant another seed, just in case.

"Ms. Macon," he began, "did you listen to a word I said to you in there?" Jackson didn't wait for an answer. "I come to you about two people that are missing. You're aware that one of them is *not* missing, but you're not sure why he's hiding from the police at your place. Now he's running away from the police. Put two and two together, lady!"

Jackson put the accelerator to the floor and fishtailed through the snow-covered street, away from the little blue house. Sheila Macon stood motionless on the curb with her little dog.

XXV

After Agent Sheehan had made it clear to Barrett that he would be going nowhere without a longer discussion, he left the room. Frustrated but hopeful, Barrett knew he had the truth on his side. He was now one step closer to reaching his goal, and it felt good to not be making up stories or leaving intentional gaps in his explanations for a change. There was also something about Sheehan that made Barrett believe he was a reasonable person. This vibe was the complete opposite of what he had gotten during his interrogation by the Denver PD.

There was no clock in the interrogation room, but Barrett knew it had to be midafternoon. He was getting hungry, not unlike the day he first arrived in Gable late last summer. Fifteen minutes passed before Sheehan returned to the room. He handed a cone-shaped paper cup of water to Barrett and closed the door behind him. Barrett swallowed it in one gulp and looked up at the FBI agent. "I'm getting pretty hungry."

"Me, too. It's like one thirty," Sheehan said. "We've got a lot going on here today. I'd like to ask you a few more questions and then we'll see if we can get some food over here."

"Or maybe I can take it with me on the road," Barrett suggested. Chase didn't respond to the suggestion.

"I'm doing my best to not treat you like you're guilty, but you've been sending a lot of mixed signals throughout the universe over the last few months."

Barrett massaged his face with his hands.

"What?" Chase asked, as if his suspect were attempting to communicate through a foreign means.

"Nothing. I'm just getting ready for the third degree," Barrett explained. "I've done this before, you know."

"I think the obvious question to ask first is, if you're innocent why did you take off the way you did?"

Barrett wasted no time answering. "Because I'm an idiot." It felt good to say it. Not because he thought he was an idiot, but because he was beginning to accept that he had made a huge mistake when he left Colorado that night.

"Can you be more specific?"

"I panicked," Barrett said. "It's really that simple."

"But you did nothing wrong," Chase confirmed.

"Leaving town doesn't make you guilty," Barrett said. "It makes you *look* guilty, but it doesn't mean you are."

"I can't argue with you on that," Chase said. "It's why we're here talking now."

"It's ironic that I ran away because I feared being falsely accused of something because of circumstantial evidence, and then by running I caused a circumstance that made me look guilty."

Chase nodded. "I see what you mean. You really did a number on yourself, didn't you?"

"I didn't kill Otto Clevinger, Agent Sheehan. The guy was like a second father to me." It was a relief for Barrett to finally spit this out, too. He was just happy to be himself again, even if it meant having to fight to prove his innocence.

"What's weird is," Chase replied, "I believe you."

Barrett let out a sigh through a half smile. "Why is that weird?" he asked. "Not that I'm not relieved to hear it."

"Well," Sheehan said as he pulled out a small notebook, "your buddy Randy over here in the jail cell says you told him that you 'strangled the shit out of that sonofabitch.'"

The federal agent read the last seven words out loud.

"Oh, come on!" Barrett pleaded. "It's this kind of crap that made me hit the panic button in the first place!"

"Did you say it?"

"Yes, but it wasn't true! I was trying to intimidate him. Maybe get him to back down a little."

"You sure do a lot of stupid things," Chase commented.

"Well, I haven't exactly been myself lately," Barrett said.

"Am I right in assuming you're starting to realize that cooperating is the right way to go?" Chase asked him.

"It's not like I have a lot of choice at this point," Barrett said. "But yes, I'm an open book. I'll tell you whatever you want to know. I mean, I don't know what else I have to tell you but, whatever you need…"

"Oh, I have plenty more questions for you," Sheehan said. "First, you need to know that your confession to Randy could come back to haunt you. He's going to try to give you up in exchange for a lighter sentence. Oh, by the way. You said it in front of his mother, too. They're both going to try and use it to their advantage."

"Great."

"But as long as you cooperate with me, I'm going to do everything I can to squash it. I mean, assuming everything you tell me continues to corroborate your story and innocence. Being a government official has its advantages. What you allegedly said to an ex-con and sex offender and his eighty-year-old mother is hearsay."

"And it's not true," Barrett added.

"And don't do it again!" Chase bellowed.

"I understand," Barrett said. "Don't forget, they kidnapped me. That's got to count for something. Like maybe I confessed under duress or something."

"Will you stop?" Despite the request, Sheehan almost seemed amused.

"What?" Barrett said. "I'm just trying to help."

The FBI agent let a smile grow. "Don't," he said, shaking his head and chuckling.

"I think I need to eat something," Barrett said.

Chase opened the door to the interrogation room and shouted down the hall, "Chief! Is there someplace in this little town where we can get some take-out?"

***

As he rushed away from Sheila Macon's house, Jackson figured the odds of catching up to the Harley were slim. He'd never seen someone maneuver a motorcycle through snow-covered streets in traffic before, but apparently Fast Eddie Clark was good at it — he had already vanished. Once Jackson left the subdivision on Clayton Street he lost sight of the thin motorcycle tracks amidst the zigging and zagging of the hundreds of full-size automobile tires that had been driving around Adler since the snow had started to fall again earlier this morning.

It all happened so fast Jackson hadn't even gotten around to turning on his lights and siren. Now that there was time to think about it, he realized there was no point; they would only tell Eddie where he was. In fact, being in a squad car was doing the same thing. Eddie could be on the interstate and heading to Timbuktu by now.

Would it be a terrible thing if he never returned? Jackson asked himself.

By now it was clear that Fast Eddie had witnessed the murder of his best friend that night in the woods. This meant he could implicate Jackson and consequently ruin his life. Of course, so could Agent DeMarco if she wanted, assuming she was still among the living. But at least DeMarco had made somewhat of a promise or effort to help Jackson. If he caught up to Eddie, what was Jackson going to do? Kill him? Hadn't there been enough of that lately? Could he talk him into shutting up? What would be in it for Eddie to keep mum?

Jackson didn't have any answers at the moment. He only knew that his family would be home in a few hours to celebrate Christmas. At this rate, he couldn't help but wonder if it would be his last one at home with Caroline and the kids.

He picked up his cell phone and filled in the Adler PD, asking them to keep an eye out for a Harley. Jackson even went so far as to suggest that the Adler PD contact the Iowa State Patrol. He wasn't certain he wanted to find Clark, but he knew he needed to keep up appearances and make it look like he did. At this point, his best bet was to stick with the story he had planted with Sheila Macon as he left her standing at the curb: Eddie must be running because *he* killed Chum.

***

Chase flushed the urinal with his foot. He made it a habit not to touch the handles or anything inside a public bathroom unless he had to. He wasn't a germaphobe, but the nature of his job forced him to touch enough weird things already. The restroom was one place that didn't fall under the purview of federal agents. After using a paper towel to turn the faucet on and wash his hands, he used the air dryer to dry them. Chase loved it when a public restroom had towels *and* a dryer. It made keeping clear of diseases that much easier.

Sandwiches were on the way, and Hodge was at the Chumansky property with the K-9's. Jackson was checking into the lead on Eddie Clark, and Barrett Greyson was in the next room. But there was still no sign of Delia. With each tick of the clock, Chase became convinced that something dreadful had happened to her. Someone had to know something. But most of the people he had been speaking with weren't even in Gable the last time Delia was heard from. Since arriving in town, Chase had spent more time working his sister's investigation into Chumansky than his own inquiry into her whereabouts.

As providential as it was that Barrett Greyson fell into his lap here, all Chase wanted was to find Delia.

His current approach with Greyson was to stay on his good side and see what he could learn from him. Chase wasn't as sure of the man's guilt now as he had been a couple of weeks ago. There was no evidence linking Greyson to the murder. The DNA proved to be a dead end. But *someone* had killed Otto Clevinger, and Chase figured his best bet was to enlist Greyson's help instead of freaking him out by accusing him. Although it wasn't intentional, the Denver PD had probably taken things too far with their questioning of Greyson. But who would've thought the guy was going to run?

***

"Thanks for bringing these over, Claire," Chief Perkins said. "We're having quite a day here at the station. Busiest day since…" — realizing what he was about to say, he quickly recovered — "since I don't know when."

Claire smiled.

"How much do we owe Stubby's today?"

"Twenty-six fifty," Claire said as she set the two sacks on the chief's desk.

"You know what, hang on a second," he said. "Usually the feds pay for this stuff."

Claire watched Perkins walk back down the hall, knock on a door, and stick his head inside a room. She couldn't hear what he was saying, but within seconds he came shuffling back to his desk and pointing over his shoulder with his thumb.

"Here comes the moneyman," he said with a smile.

Agent Sheehan appeared from behind Perkins. "Oh, hi," Sheehan said. "You work at the lone restaurant here in town? Didn't expect to see you again so soon."

"Yes, I do," she said.

"Will this cover it?" Chase handed her two twenty-dollar bills.

Claire began to pull money out of her own pocket.

"Just keep it," he told her.

"I can't do that," Claire said flatly.

"Why? Is it against the rules?" Chase asked. He glanced at Perkins, who was already busy chewing a bite of his sandwich and not paying attention.

"It's against *my* rules." Claire said. She handed him a ten-dollar bill. "Here. Now it's within my rules."

"Whatever you say," Chase agreed with a shrug. He took the bill and put it back in his pocket. "I just need to get a receipt if I could, please."

"It's right here stapled to this bag." She reached over to one of the sacks of sandwiches, tore off the receipt, and handed it to the FBI agent. "We do that in case you forget to ask or the delivery person forgets to hand it to you."

Claire was about to leave when the door to the room Agent Sheehan had come from opened. A man's head peeked out and called down the hallway.

"Hey, is it okay if I use the—"

The man's voice stopped short, and Claire turned to look. It was Henry Fields.

***

Amidst all the chaos of the past few hours, Barrett had completely forgotten about the possibility of seeing Claire. It wasn't like he was in town for a visit. Now that he was laying eyes on her again, and she on him, speaking seemed like the next logical step. Instead of finishing his inquiry about going to the restroom, he took a step outside the door.

"Come on up here and get your sandwich," Sheehan told him. Barrett strolled to the front and eyed the sandwiches, but he could feel Claire's eyes on him. He looked back at her as he reached the desk and saw that her mouth was slightly open.

She was definitely surprised to see him.

"Hi, Claire," Barrett said.

"What are you doing here…again?" she managed to say.

"Oh, that's right," the chief said. "You two know each other…kinda."

"Agent Sheehan," Barrett said. "Since I'm not under arrest would it be possible to get a few minutes with Claire?" He was sure to mention his freedom to give her peace of mind. Chances were she wasn't going to feel as safe with him as she had a few months ago.

Sheehan finished chewing before he answered. "I guess so. But that's really up to her."

Claire looked at Barrett and then back to Chase. "It's fine," she said. "I can't stay long, anyway."

"Go ahead and use the interrogation room. Leave the door open," Chase instructed.

Barrett took his sandwich and motioned for Claire to follow him. After they sat down, Barrett spoke first. "First of all, it's good to see you again, Claire. I really mean that."

But Claire wasn't in the mood for chitchat and got straight to the point. "Your real name is Barrett?"

"Yes, Barrett Greyson. I'm sorry I lied to you."

"Did you kill that man? Your boss?" There was a look of desperation on Claire's face. Barrett could tell if he answered the wrong way, she would more than likely break down.

"No!" he replied. He didn't yell, but he was sure to use an authoritative tone. "Do you think they'd leave me in here with you alone if they really thought I was a murderer?"

Claire shrugged. She kept her hands under the table and in her lap. "What's going on? Why are you here again?"

"It's a very long story. I really want to tell you, but I doubt you have time for it." Barrett was serious. He did want to tell her. Coming clean was beginning to feel very good, almost like a high. Especially since he hadn't done anything wrong.

"Give me the cliff notes," Claire said.

"Let's see," he began, "I didn't kill my boss, and I don't know who did. I panicked when they started investigating me because I was the last one who saw him alive. I left home, ran away. It was a dumb idea. Maybe I've watched too many news magazine shows. I guess I was afraid of becoming an innocent man sentenced to life in prison. I left here in the middle of the night because I figured with all the hoopla it was only a matter of time before people realized my name wasn't Henry Fields. I went to New England and was this close to disappearing into Canada when, of all things, I saw the *Dateline* episode and found out my father has cancer. That changed my mind about a lot of stuff. I realized it was more important for me to see my father again and, if I had to, fight to prove my innocence."

Barrett took a deep breath. Claire rested her hands on the table.

"Go on," she said. "There's obviously more."

"So I took off and headed back to Colorado. I planned to lie low until after I saw him and then figure out what to do from there. It was a work in progress. On my way, in Chicago actually, some guy recognized me from TV and kidnapped me at gunpoint."

Claire's eyes widened.

"He wanted to take me in and collect a reward, but I talked him out of it and offered to pay him to let me see my dad. On the way he got this crazy idea that I could help locate Chum's mysterious money that almost got us all killed. So he detoured us here."

Barrett could tell something he said had clicked with Claire.

"Big blonde guy?" she asked.

"Yes," Barrett confirmed. "You were at Maddison's when he came to the door, weren't you? I saw your car."

"You were there?"

"Yes, hiding out in the minivan."

"If he was at the door, who was watching you?" she asked.

"I guess I skipped over that part. We were also traveling with his eighty-year-old mother, who's in a wheelchair. She was holding a gun on me."

"I really want to laugh," Claire said, "but a gun is not funny…"

She was right. At the same time, Barrett was glad to see her lighten up, even if it was only briefly.

"Yeah. It was awkward, that's for sure," Barrett commented before continuing his story. "So Sergeant Jackson figured out the van was stolen and pulled us over. Then she pulled the gun on Jackson while he was arresting Randy, the big guy, her son. I was still in the back of the van and was able to get the gun away from her. And that's how I ended up here. They're both locked up, I guess."

"Wow," Claire said. "You must be pretty good at wrestling guns away from criminals."

Barrett snickered as he realized she was referring to his altercation with Franco, Rafael, and Chum at the Corner Store just a few months earlier. "Well, I didn't want her to shoot a cop. And I sure as hell didn't want to stay with them any longer. Not the best of experiences, let me tell you. I figured helping out would put me in good graces with the cops. I had no idea the FBI was here, too."

"So you're free?" Claire asked.

"Sort of," Barrett explained. "Agent Sheehan seems to believe I'm innocent, which is good. But he says he still has a lot of questions for me and wants my help to try and figure out who did kill Otto, my boss. And because all of the cash I was traveling with was in a stolen van, it's in evidence right now and I guess I can't have it. I really don't want to leave without it — it's a lot of money. I never wanted to be back here in the first place. I need to get back to Colorado."

Claire leaned back and crossed her arms in front of her. Barrett watched her ponytail sway from side to side behind her.

"That's not what I meant," he said. "Claire, I'm sorry I left here the way I did, without an explanation, without saying goodbye. I didn't want to do that to you, especially not after what happened that night. I was only thinking of myself, my own survival. At the time, I was honestly afraid of being accused of doing something I hadn't done — something I would *never* do. But I told you the night we fell asleep on the couch together…I told you I had feelings for you. I did. And I still do. I'm happy to be here with you now and explaining things to you. I never thought I would get that chance. It feels really good to tell you the truth…and to see you again. I never thought I would."

"It's nice to see you, too," Claire said. "But you need a shave, buddy." Barrett touched his face as the small town girl snickered. "It's even nicer to cut through the crap and hear this stuff from you," she continued. "You have no idea what it's been like these last few months around here. Thinking that you were a murderer, someone I had an emotional and physical attraction to. It was unfathomable. It made me sick to my stomach."

"I know," Barrett said. "Again, I'm sorry." He slowly reached across the table. When he got to her hand he grazed it, lightly touching her knuckles with his fingers. A few seconds of silence passed between them. Before either had a chance to speak again, Chief Perkins poked his head from around the open door.

"Claire, your aunt just called and wants to know if we threw you in jail. I told her it was my fault, that I was babbling too much. You might want to get back."

"Thank you, Chief Perkins," Claire said politely. "That

was very kind of you. I'll be right out." The policeman disappeared from the doorway and Claire turned back to Barrett. "So, what do we do now?" she asked.

"I wish I knew," Barrett said. "I need to find out what Sheehan's long-term objective is." He lowered his voice to a whisper. "He can't keep me here forever. I just need to get my money and then get to Colorado."

"And then?" Claire said. Barrett could tell she wanted more, just like she did the last time he was in Gable. And she was difficult to resist. Spending this time with her had brought back a rush of emotions Barrett had been suppressing for weeks.

"Tell you what," he said. "Give me your phone number. At the very least, I won't leave town without seeing you again."

***

Chase got out of his car and moved to the edge of the woods next to the Chumansky house. Office Ryan Hodge was waiting for him.

"You got something, huh?" Chase confirmed.

"The dogs are going nuts," Hodge said. "The crew just started digging."

"In this snow?"

"We've got some ground heaters that are helping thaw things out a little right now," Hodge explained. "But honestly, I don't think it's going to be too difficult to dig up. The grave, if that's what it is, looks pretty fresh."

"I'll be damned," Chase replied. "Let's go."

Hodge led the FBI agent through the outlying trees, deep into the secluded area. The men made their way through the woods, ducking under branches for ten minutes before Chase broke the silence.

"It's going to be dark in an hour and a half. We'll want to wrap this up quickly."

"Yeah," Hodge agreed. "Not to mention it's Christmas Eve."

"Crap, I almost forgot," Chase exclaimed. He made a mental note to call his wife and daughter back home in Atlanta when he was finished. Thankfully, it wasn't unusual for his family to not hear from him for days at a time. That was the life of an FBI field agent. Gwen Sheehan knew this would be the drill even back when she was still known as Gwen Miller. Chase missed his family, but at least he knew they were safe. It was the mystery of his sister's whereabouts that was going to make this an un-Merry Christmas.

After another five minutes of hiking, the men reached the site. Chase could see three German shepherds sitting obediently off to the side. They were on leashes controlled by one uniformed police officer. Two other officers were carefully digging with shovels.

"We've got fingers!" one of the officers called out to Hodge.

"Show us," Hodge said as he and Sheehan jogged over.

"Look," the other officer with a shovel said. He bent down and brushed some snow and mud out of the way. Poking out of the surface were what appeared to be three fingers and knuckles.

"You guys know to be careful where you're digging, right?" Chase asked them. The men looked at each other and then to Hodge.

"This is Agent Chase Sheehan of the FBI," Hodge told them.

"Oh, sorry," one of them said. "Yes, sir. We know what to do."

"Great," Chase said. "Don't want to damage what's down there any more than it already is."

"At the same time, we need to be fast," Hodge reminded them. "It's getting late."

"And it's Christmas," the officer with the K-9's added.

"Yes, we all want to get home to our families," Hodge said.

Chase turned to Hodge. "I'm impressed the dogs were able to find something out here so quickly," he said.

"Well, first of all, the dogs are really good at what they do, of course," Hodge said with a nod to the officer holding the leads. "And also, I wouldn't estimate this area to be more than ten acres. And that might be pushing it."

"It looks a lot bigger from the perimeter," Chase said. After watching the men dig for fifteen minutes, Chase pulled Hodge aside. "This isn't happening today."

"I know, I was waiting for you to say something. I didn't want to be the one," Hodge admitted.

"With the holiday tomorrow…" Chase said. "Look, I think it's safe to shut this thing down for the next thirty-six hours or so. We just need to keep it under wraps. No media. Just internal. Hell, no wives, either. Assuming it's Chumansky — or no matter who it is — we don't want whoever did this to hear about it before we're finished."

"Absolutely," Hodge agreed. "Makes sense. No problem. I think everyone will be relieved. Do you want me to say anything to Ms. Chumansky?"

"Nope," Chase said. "Tell her you got nothing and will resume on the twenty-sixth."

"Will do."

"You can handle it from here?" Chase asked.

"Yes, sir. Consider it handled," Hodge said.

The men said their goodbyes and Chase headed back to his car. It was an easy task to make his way back to civilization. There was just enough light peeking through the bare tree branches to see the tracks he and Hodge had made on their way in. By the time he reached his rental car, night had fallen. It was five o'clock and Christmas Eve. The strangest Christmas Eve Chase had ever been a part of in his thirty-three years. One that he would remember forever.

The snow had petered out for the day, leaving half a foot of sloppy white wetness on the ground. Chase drove his vehicle carefully through the hills and curves of the county roads on his way back to Gable. When he reached the town limits, he decided it would be a good idea to stop and get some snacks and gas while he had the chance. Tonight had the potential of being a long evening. Barrett Greyson was waiting for him at the station and at this point there wasn't much keeping him there.

Chase prepaid for his gas with a credit card and stuck the nozzle in the tank. While the gas pumped, he went inside the Corner Store to see what kind of food and drink he could scrounge up for the remainder of the evening.

"Hey, you're a DEA agent, aren't you?" the man behind the counter asked him as he passed by. Startled, Chase looked around the store, grateful it was empty. Not that it mattered much. He just didn't want to get into a long conversation with a bunch of strangers about being a federal agent.

"FBI," Chase corrected him. "How did you know?" He walked cautiously up to the counter.

"I remember faces really well," the man said.

"But I've never been here before," Chase said, even more suspicious now.

"I saw you on TV at the end of our town's fifteen minutes of fame on *Dateline*. You were standing there with Hank's parents doing a press conference. Oops. I mean Barrett Greyson's parents. Sorry."

"Wow. That's an impressive memory," Chase said. He hadn't expected to have his occupation pegged when he walked in, but he was relieved to learn it was a harmless greeting. The last thing Chase needed right now was something else weird going on in this little town.

"Yeah, my wife says it's a gift but my kids think it's a

curse," the man remarked, holding out his hand. "Bruce Townsend. I own this joint. What brings the FBI here now? Are there some developments? Never mind. You probably can't talk about it. I'm sorry I asked. Sometimes I get ahead of myself."

Chase let out a chuckle as he returned the greeting. "It's a long story. I'm Sheehan. Chase Sheehan."

"Well, Agent Sheehan, welcome to Gable," Townsend said. Chase thanked him and wandered around the small store in silence as he searched for some snacks and drinks. He filled a handheld basket with two small bottles of Gatorade, two packs of chocolate cupcakes, a bag of sour cream and onion potato chips, a loaf of bread, and a small jar of peanut butter.

"You know," Townsend said as Chase approached the counter with his groceries, "I kind of feel bad for the kid."

"You mean Greyson? He worked for you while he was here, right?" Chase confirmed.

"Yep, an entire week."

"Why do you feel sorry for him?" Chase asked.

"I was just thinking how they mentioned on *Dateline* that his father has pancreatic cancer. That's a bad one. I just wonder if he'll regret not being there for his dad during such a crappy time."

Chase shrugged and Bruce kept talking.

"I mean, my old man had a heart attack about twenty years ago when I was on vacation in Hawaii," Townsend explained. He paused as he rang up a couple of the items Chase was buying. "I didn't come back when it happened. He had quadruple bypass surgery the next day and didn't make it."

"Wow," Chase said.

Townsend keyed in a couple more items before speaking again. "I've never forgiven myself."

Chase looked across the counter at Townsend. The man was probably old enough to be his father. He wasn't crying, but the intensity in his eyes told Chase how serious he was.

"It never leaves you," Townsend said, shaking his head. "I don't know. I just hope it's worth it. I mean, if he's guilty of killing someone, well…I understand. But if he's innocent and neglecting his father at a time like this…"

"I see what you mean," Chase said.

"But what do I know?" Townsend added with a change in his tone. "He might not even know his father's sick."

Chase swiped his credit card to complete the transaction. Townsend bagged the items and pushed them across the counter to the FBI agent.

"You enjoy your stay in our area, Agent," Townsend said. "And if I can help you with anything, just let me know."

Chase said goodbye and walked out the door.

XXVI

"They found a body already?" Jackson said to Perkins on the phone. It wasn't that he never expected Chum to be found. He just hadn't figured it would be this fast. He also assumed he'd be there when it happened, but circumstances had sent him in another direction.

"They sure did," the chief confirmed. "You sound surprised."

I do? Maybe I do, Jackson thought. "Not at all," he said, recovering. "It's just that with the snow on the ground…"

"Yeah, I guess they had some special heaters out there warming the area up," Perkins explained. "They're gonna resume digging the morning after Christmas. We need to keep this quiet. No press, no one else. We don't want it to get back to the people or person who did this while we're not keeping an eye on things."

"Got it," Jackson said. His mind began to wander but his mouth kept talking. "But they do know it's a body, right? They just couldn't get it dug up fast enough?"

"They definitely found a hand. We just don't know whose it is," Perkins said. "I didn't ask, but I assume it was too big to be the baby Jesus wishing us a Merry Christmas."

Jackson chuckled. "How crazy would it be if it isn't Chum?"

"Don't even say that," Perkins snapped. "I'd rather it was the baby Jesus. The last thing we need to do is find out there are more shenanigans going on around here than we already thought."

"True."

"Go home and enjoy your Christmas, Jack," Perkins said.

"Will do, Chief. Merry Christmas." No sooner had Jackson ended the call when his phone rang again. This time it was his wife's number.

"Hi, Daddy!" his daughter, Kaitlyn said. "Santa Claus comes tonight." Jackson could hear his wife in the background reminding the little girl to tell her father that they were home. "Mommy says to tell you 'we're home.'"

"Wow, already? That was fast! Did you put out your wings and fly?"

"No," she replied. Jackson could tell his four-year-old daughter had taken him seriously.

"I was just joking, honey," he told her. "Tell your brother hello for me. Can I speak to Mommy?" Without saying a word, she handed the phone to Jackson's wife.

"What time are you going to be home?" she asked. "Soon I hope."

"Okay, look—" Jackson began.

"That doesn't sound promising," Caroline Jackson said.

"I have something I need to do first," he explained.

"How long?"

"A couple of hours?"

"It's Christmas!" Caroline pleaded.

"I know. I promise I'll be back as quick as I can."

"Is everything okay?"

"Yes. Everything is fine. In fact, this thing I need to do is going to help make things even better," Jackson explained.

"Promise me you'll hurry," his wife said.

"I promise," he said. "It's almost four o'clock now. I'll shoot for being home by six. Hopefully earlier."

"Be careful, husband," Caroline said.

"No danger this time," he said. "But I will be."

They said their goodbyes. It was going to be tight, but Jackson would try his best to make it home in two hours. Even if he was a little later than six, it would all be forgotten shortly after he walked through the door. He was lucky that way. Caroline had always lived for the moments together as a family instead of worrying about could haves, should haves, and would haves.

Jackson turned the lights and siren on in his squad car. Ignoring the speed limit would help him get to Blackbird Lake and back much sooner.

***

"Are you and I going to be spending Christmas Eve together?" Barrett asked the FBI agent. "This is a little awkward."

Chase opened up the peanut butter and began to spread some on a slice of bread. "I haven't decided what's going on here yet," he said. This wasn't entirely true, but there were still questions Chase needed answered and he didn't want Greyson thinking it was going to be a cakewalk. He had called his wife earlier and let her know that he was tied up on a case, not mentioning that Delia was missing. She was disappointed, but not surprised. Chase knew he could make it up to her and their daughter in a few days. At least he hoped it would only be a few more days. Pushing the bread and peanut butter across the table to Barrett, he continued. "I have more questions for you," Chase said. "You ready?"

"Go for it."

"You say you didn't kill Otto Clevinger. Who do you think did?"

"It's a funny question," Barrett said. Chase gave him a

look. "What I mean is, I haven't given it much thought. I've been so busy with…other things."

"Well, you have some time to think about it now," Chase said. "Brainstorm it. Start throwing names out and talk it out with me."

"I don't even know where to begin," Barrett said.

"I do," Chase said. "Boyd Clevinger."

"Wow," Barrett said, seemingly caught off guard. "They call that a 'brushback pitch' in baseball."

"Better than throwing at you intentionally," Chase responded.

"I'm not sure there's much difference," Barrett said. "Let me think about this for a minute."

"Take your time." Chase opened a bottle of Gatorade and took a drink. Barrett took a chip from the already opened bag on the table. He crunched it loudly with the first bite before closing his mouth to finish it. Chase could tell Greyson was thinking, considering his dead boss's spoiled son as his own father's killer.

"He's a pretty messed up guy," Barrett commented. "I just don't know that he's *that* messed up."

"I've met him," Chase confessed.

"Then you understand what I'm saying," Barrett said. "I mean…"

"Spoiled-rotten brat," Chase said, finishing Greyson's sentence.

"I have no doubt he still thinks money grows on trees, even at his age," Barrett said.

"Yeah, I got that from him," Chase said. "That's what happens when someone has had everything in life handed to him on a platter."

"He didn't get along with Otto very well at all, but I can't see him killing his father."

"What about hiring someone?" Chase asked.

"I mean, it's almost the same thing, isn't it?"

"Not really," Chase explained. "Sometimes it helps a killer separate himself from the actual act so he doesn't feel like he did anything wrong. The person lies to himself to the point of believing his own lie."

"Hmmm. I hadn't thought of that," Barrett said. "It certainly sounds possible. One thing Boyd has always been is in denial. About other things, I mean. Like whether or not he actually works."

"You're not a big fan."

"Do you blame me?" Barrett asked.

"I don't know him like you do."

Greyson shrugged. "I got used to dealing with the guy. I was fully prepared to let him be 'the boss' when Otto retired. And I'd keep doing my thing."

"You were the one who was really running things," Chase commented.

Barrett shrugged again. "I'd been there long enough to know what I was doing. I knew the clients well and knew how to make good decisions. I mean, I think I did."

"At least one of your coworkers agrees," Chase said. "Julia McGregor."

Barrett smiled. "Oh, Julia. She's a nice girl. Sometimes finds herself in a pickle, but she means well."

"You mean like having an affair with Boyd Clevinger?"

"She told you about that?" Barrett asked with a smile.

"I could ask you the same thing," Chase said.

"I think the entire place knew," Barrett said. "You know how rumors spread. Julia probably confided in one person and human nature took its course throughout the building."

"Any idea how or why there was such secrecy about it?" Chase asked, recalling his conversation with Nolan Reed about the affair being absent from the files.

"How do you mean? Like I said, everyone knew."

Chase went on to explain that the affair was missing from the official record and did not exist in the FBI files despite the fact that Julia was Boyd's alibi for his father's murder.

"I realize it seems strange from the outside, but to me it doesn't," Barrett said. "When you hang around the Clevingers enough you learn *their* normal versus the rest of the world's normal. Essentially, they live in their own alternate reality."

"So, what do you think happened?"

"I think the Clevingers pulled some strings, maybe paid someone off."

"But why, when, like you said, everyone knows?" Chase asked.

"Well, I'm using the term 'everyone' loosely, Agent," Barrett said. "If *Dateline* would've caught wind of the affair, then everyone really would, essentially, know. The Clevingers are a proud family, proud people. Some of them less deserving than others. And like I said, they live in their own world. I'm sure they didn't want the rest of the real world to know that their blessed son is a cheat."

"Interesting," Chase commented. He was again disturbed at the notion of payoffs taking place inside the FBI. At this point, though, he had more important things to worry about. "Let's change subjects."

Barrett didn't reply. Instead he took a drink of his own Gatorade before crunching another chip.

"We executed a search warrant a couple of weeks ago for your condo," Chase continued. "You wanna guess what we found when we went in there?"

"Dirty dishes?" Barrett said with a chuckle. "Wow. A search warrant. You guys really *were* after me."

"Slow down a second," Chase said. "Do you really

think we found dirty dishes in your place?"

"Well, yeah," Greyson said. "It's not like I cleaned house before I left. What are you getting at?"

"The search warrant was to get a sample of your DNA."

"You should've just called me. Here, you can have some right now." Barrett pushed his Gatorade bottle across the table. "Just another way to prove to you I have nothing to hide."

"Your condo was spotless, Barrett," Chase said. "No dirty dishes, no dirty laundry, and not one bit of usable DNA."

Barrett twisted one corner of his mouth while he let the information marinate. "I guess it could've been…" Barrett suggested. "I don't know."

"We were looking for DNA because we found some at the murder scene that wasn't Otto Clevinger's," Chase said. "We wanted to see if yours was a match. Needless to say, we never could verify anything for sure. I mean, the techies said it was similar but not definitive."

"What does that mean, exactly?" Barrett asked.

"Not much," Chase said. "It could've been you. Might not have been you."

"Well, I wasn't joking," Barrett said. "You can have it now."

"Yeah, we'll get to that," Chase said. "But why would someone go inside your condo and scrub it from top to bottom?"

Barrett thought for a moment. "I suppose if they believed there was a chance I was guilty, maybe they thought they would be helping? I mean, I don't know. My mom, maybe?"

Chase nodded. "Your parents found out about the DNA at the scene prior to the search warrant. There was definitely an opportunity," Chase suggested.

"It's not illegal."

"No, not really."

The two men sat in silence. Barrett reached across the table and took hold of his Gatorade bottle again. Instead of drinking from it, he began to turn it in a circle on the table. Staring at the bottle, he spoke. "Are you going to let me out of here soon?" he asked in a soft tone. "I'm willing to do whatever I need to do. I know taking off was stupid. I realize it made me look guilty. But I'm not guilty. I didn't kill anyone."

Chase said nothing while Barrett Greyson continued his unofficial plea of innocence.

"I'll wear an ankle bracelet. Whatever you want. I'll be available to answer any questions or whatever you need. I'm more than happy to *help* you find the killer. I care about justice as much as you do. I'd like to know who did this. It obviously has had a massive effect on my life."

"Look," Chase began. "I have some good news and some not-so-good news for you."

"I'll take the good news first."

"I'm going to turn you loose," Chase said with a nod and a hint of sensitivity. He watched as Barrett sat up straight. "I realize how important it is for you to see your sick father. It would be for me, too."

"That is fantastic to hear," Barrett said. "Thank you."

Chase nodded. "Of course, I do still need to stay in touch with you. You were the last person to see Clevinger alive. You might have valuable information and not even know it. Technically, you will still be considered a 'person of interest' but not a suspect."

"Understood," Barrett agreed with a nod.

"And as strange as it might sound," Chase added. "I'll take you up on the Gatorade bottle offer. It'll go a long way with the bureau and Denver PD. Shows you're cooperating."

"As soon as I'm done drinking this, it's yours," Barrett said as he raised the bottle for another swig.

"So—" Chase said, but Barrett cut him off as he

finished swallowing.

"If you tell me the bad news is I have to spend more time with Randy and Nora, we're going to have a problem."

The men shared a quick laugh.

"No," Chase assured him. "I think you're safe from that happening."

"Good to hear."

"Here's the deal," Chase said. "I can't give you the money. Your money."

Barrett's shoulders slumped. "Why not?"

"Because it's been inventoried."

"What? Why?"

"Because that's how things are done when a car is stolen."

"But it's *my* money!" Barrett exclaimed.

"If I told you Randy said it was his money, would that surprise you?"

"Damn that guy," Barrett said, shaking his head.

"That's the problem," Chase said. "There's no way to determine who it really belongs to. A judge has to decide."

"But you know it's my money," Barrett said.

"You told me it's your money," Chase clarified. "And I happen to believe you. But this is the law. Look, if it's any consolation, this would've happened regardless of Randy saying it was his money. I can't just give it to you right now."

Barrett grimaced. "How long is it going to take?"

"Weeks," Chase admitted. "Months."

Barrett rolled his eyes and craned his neck. "Can I borrow a dime?"

***

Barrett's heart was racing. He hadn't been this nervous since watching two men die with gunshot wounds to the head a few months earlier. It wasn't that he was scared to speak to his mother, he was just afraid of what she might say regarding his father's condition.

Sheehan had been nice enough to let Barrett have a room to himself, one with a phone. The door was closed to give him privacy. He dialed his mother's mobile number and waited.

The phone rang once. Maybe she won't pick up when she doesn't recognize the number, Barrett thought.

The second ring began. If it goes to voicemail, what number would he tell her to call back? He opened the door and called out down the hall. "What's the number to this place in case I need to leave a message?"

"Hello?" a female voice said through the phone.

"N-never mind," Barrett said, calmer this time. "M-mom?" He closed the door behind him.

"Oh my God," Ella Greyson said. "Barrett, is that you?"

"It's me, Mom."

"Where are you? Are you coming home?" Mrs. Greyson asked.

"It's a long story but yes, I'm coming home," Barrett said. "I just need some help."

"Of course, whatever you need."

"Mom," Barrett said, this time slowing himself down.

"Yes?"

"Mom, how's Dad doing?" He cringed when he finished the sentence for fear of what she might say.

"Oh," Barrett's mother replied, "you know?"

"I saw it on TV," he told her. "On *Dateline*."

"I see," she said. "Well, he's um, he's hanging in there...I guess."

"How's that?" Barrett said, his heart beginning to race again. "What's wrong?"

"He's in the hospital, Barrett. He's been in a lot of pain. It's hard telling for sure what's going on."

"My God. I need to get there."

"Sure, sure. What can I do to help?"

Barrett told his mother a quick version of the story and how he ended up back in Gable. He explained how his money was tied up in police custody until further notice. "Can you buy me a plane ticket?" he asked her. "I really need to get back tomorrow — as soon as possible. It's going to be expensive, but you know I'll pay you back."

"Absolutely, Barrett," she said. "I'm at the hospital now. I'll see if they'll let me use a computer here to do it. They've been very nice to me — to us — since we've been here."

"How long has he been in there?"

"This is the third night. They haven't said a word to me about when he might get to go home. That scares me, Barrett. He hasn't been awake all day."

Barrett could sense his mother's anxiety through the phone. She needed him. She needed someone.

"Where's Milo?"

"He's back for Christmas break. He was here this afternoon," Mrs. Greyson told her son. "He's been working, too. Since it's Christmas Eve they needed him on the floor at the store until they close at five. He'll probably be up here in a while."

Barrett's younger brother, Milo, had worked at The Buckle since he had turned sixteen. Although Milo now went to school in Fort Collins, he was still able to pick up hours at the Aurora store over holiday and summer breaks. Barrett was old enough to remember when the store was called The Brass Buckle and teased his brother about it often, referring to his employer as "The Brass Knuckle," "Brass Tacks," and "Brass Balls." But Milo loved fashion, and working in the store was a perfect fit for him.

"I'll be home soon to help, Mom," Barrett told her. "Things are sorted out. It looks like I have the authorities off my back for now. I want to focus on our family. I miss you guys."

"Oh, Barrett," he could hear his mother begin to sob, "I'm so happy you're coming home. This is the best Christmas present I could've asked for. Your father will be so excited."

"One more thing, Mom," Barrett said, trying to keep his emotions under control. "I need a hotel room here. Why don't you call me back when you get the plane booked? Hang on a second. Let me get the number."

Barrett opened the door and once again asked for the number to the station. After relaying it to his mother, the two said goodbye.

"Remember, I need to fly out of Omaha. Check Southwest."

"I love you, honey," Ella Greyson told her oldest son.

"I love you too, Mom," Barrett said. "We're gonna be okay."

After hanging up the phone, Barrett paused for a moment to regain his composure. That was more difficult than he had expected. He was going home a free man. His father was, quite possibly, on his deathbed. How could something so good still feel so bad?

He took a deep breath and opened the door. Taking a sharp right turn, he walked back to the front of the building. When he reached Chief Perkins's desk his eyes immediately fixated on Claire, who had returned to the station. She was seated near the front door.

"Howdy stranger," she greeted him with a smile. "Long time, no see."

***

"What are you doing back here?" Barrett asked her. "I told you I'd call you before I left."

Claire stood up. "Well, I'm glad to see you, too," she said sarcastically. "Forgive me for, I don't know, not trusting you?" Claire ended the sentence with an awkward question mark.

Barrett understood what she was getting at. "I was actually just going to call you," he told her as he pulled her phone number out of his pocket.

"Now you don't have to," Claire said. She smiled again and slugged Barrett playfully on the arm. "I talked to my mom and...well...it's Christmas and...she agreed it would be a nice gesture. We'd like to have you come over tonight. I mean, assuming you don't have any plans or, umm, you aren't going to be confined to a cell or anything like that."

Barrett's eyebrows darted to his forehead and then retreated to their normal resting place. "That's very kind of you," Barrett said, "But I couldn't impose like that."

"You wouldn't be imposing. We asked you."

"Don't you think things would be a little weird?" he asked.

"How so?"

"To begin with, your mother doesn't even know me."

"She'll probably hardly say three words," Claire said. "I told her everything. That's why she's good with it."

"I'm flying back to Denver tomorrow, probably early in the morning," Barrett told her.

"That's okay. I'll take you to the airport. I'm off work. Stubby's is closed on Christmas. You can even stay the night, sleep on the couch."

Barrett hadn't felt this welcome since the last time he arrived in Gable. The feeling of being wanted instead of hunted was a massive relief.

"I don't even know what to say," Barrett said.

"Just say yes, because I'm not taking no for an answer," Claire said.

***

Before Barrett knew it, he was being ushered through the door of the house Claire shared with her mother. He had nothing to bring with him besides the clothes on his back. After reluctantly accepting the invitation, he was informed by Agent Sheehan that not only was his backpack of cash off-limits, but his duffel bags were, too. Inside were his clothes, toothbrush, and other essentials.

Before he left the police station with Claire, Barrett had remembered to call his mother about one more important thing. Amidst his excitement that he was going home, the recent runaway had forgotten that his driver's license and other identification were sitting on a dresser in his Lakewood condominium. No airline was going to let him board a plane without proof of who he was. Barrett considered trying to rent a car but figured the hassle would end up being just as impossible for similar reasons. Plus, the winter weather was unpredictable and, given the timing, he wouldn't be able to rent a car until the day after Christmas anyway. Following an extended discussion, Mrs. Greyson booked her oldest son a flight that wouldn't leave Omaha until the twenty-eighth. On the twenty-sixth she would overnight Barrett's driver's license and one of his credit cards to Claire's address in Gable. The flight would take off on the twenty-eighth at seven forty-five in the morning. With the one-hour time difference, he would be at the hospital by mid-morning. There was some consideration given to booking a flight for the twenty-seventh, but the possibility of the overnight carrier service screwing up the delivery of his license was too much of a risk. The Greyson family was all too familiar with the "We're sorry your package didn't make it, but we were backed up because of the holidays" excuse. Several decades in the logistics industry had that kind of effect.

The idea of a hotel was still possible, but Claire insisted he stay with her for the night. Things were finally in motion for his return, albeit far more slowly than Barrett had hoped for. The extra three days could be crucial given his father's condition. Even Sheehan showed signs of regret for not being able to do more to help. He did call the TSA to make sure there were no official red flags out for the name "Barrett Greyson." When it was discovered there were not, Barrett was relieved. But he was also embarrassed. All of the precautions he had taken during his time on the run — had they all been for nothing? The authorities had been looking for him, but not nearly as intently as he had assumed. If it wasn't for the *Dateline* segment, Randy and Nora never would've ambushed him. If Barrett hadn't fled Colorado the way he did, there never would've been a *Dateline* episode in the first place. He couldn't help but feel this entire thing had been a vicious circle of stupidity brought on by his own paranoia.

For years Barrett had prided himself on being smarter than the average young man. He always listened to his father's advice, and he learned from his own mistakes. The fact that he'd had the brains and wherewithal to disappear the way he did proved he was ready for the unexpected. Now that it was all said and done, Barrett felt more like a fool than a sharp guy. But getting back to his family was all that mattered now, even if it seemed like he'd been trying to get there for ages.

Despite his father's poor health, Barrett was beginning to sense he'd been given a second chance at certain things. Claire had proven to be the person he believed she was during his previous stay in Gable. Opening her home to him on Christmas after all he had put her through was a strong statement of virtue and heart. People with qualities like these were not easy to find, at least not in Barrett's experience. It was a "me first" world and a rarity that someone did something nice for him without wanting something in return.

Following a brief introduction to Claire's mother and a reunion with his cat, Wilson, Barrett was invited to take a seat on the couch. Wilson pounced on his former roommate's lap the instant Barrett sat down. Trish Mathison left the room to tend to dinner.

"Looks like he hasn't missed a beat," Barrett said as he stroked the cat's head.

"I'm going to go see if Mom wants help," Claire told her guest. "We usually make homemade pizza for Christmas Eve. And chocolate chip cookies, too. I know it's non-traditional, but it's what we do around here these days. You want anything while the food gets made? A drink?"

"Yeah, that sounds great," Barrett answered.

"Beer, wine, or margarita?"

"Margarita on the rocks would be perfect."

"You're in for a treat," Claire said. "This is a special recipe. It's got three different fruit juices in it and plenty of Cuervo Gold. This margarita will melt your eyeballs!"

"Just what the doctor ordered." Barrett grinned. Claire smiled back at him. It was the smile Barrett hadn't seen since the night of Chum's party. The one where her eyes sparkled, lighting up the rest of her face.

"One more thing," Claire said. "Come with me." She led him around the corner from the kitchen and down a short, narrow hallway. She opened up a closet and pulled out a white robe, handing it to Barrett.

"Are we gonna box?" he joked.

"No. You're gonna get out of those clothes so I can wash them," she said.

"Claire, you don't have to—"

"I want to," Claire said, cutting him off. She pressed the robe up against Barrett's chest and pushed him inside the bathroom. "Whites and colors," she commanded. "Don't be shy!"

Barrett shook his head and chuckled as Claire closed the bathroom door between them.

***

Jackson was on his way home and running only thirty

minutes late when his phone rang. He was surprised to see it was Chief Perkins calling instead of Caroline.

"Yes, Chief," Jackson greeted his boss.

"Merry Christmas, Jack."

"Merry Christmas, Chief."

"Thanks," Perkins said. There was a short pause before Jackson broke the silence.

"You still there? Did I lose you?"

"Yeah, yeah. I'm still here," Perkins said.

"Was that all you wanted, to say 'Merry Christmas'?" Jackson asked.

"Naw, there's something else. Did you realize Sheehan was going to a hotel tonight for Christmas Eve?"

"Uh, no. I didn't know that," Jackson replied. "I spoke to him briefly about the stolen mini-van arrests and Greyson, but I haven't seen him since late this morning."

"I just think that's sad," Perkins continued. "The guy's sister is missing, he's away from his family on Christmas, and he's going to a hotel."

"Yeah," Jackson agreed. "That's too bad." He had a feeling he knew where Perkins was going with this conversation.

"I'd take him in at my place for dinner tonight," the Chief said, "but I've got a full house already. I don't think it would work. He'd probably be pretty uncomfortable."

"Yeah," Jackson said, realizing his instincts were correct. "You want me to see if I can talk Caroline into having him over for the evening." He said this more as a statement than a question.

"Would you?" the chief asked. Jackson could almost see Perkins's dark beady eyes beaming through the phone.

"Yes, Chief. I will." Jackson rolled his eyes and pulled into his driveway.

"Thanks, Jack," Perkins said. "We don't want to look

like a rude, bassackwards PD to the FBI. I won't forget this. I owe you one."

"You already owe me at least five, but…" Jackson kidded.

"Tomorrow's Christmas. Maybe Santa will square us up."

"Doubt it."

The men hung up.

"This is *not* ideal," Jackson mumbled to himself.

***

"Would you like some more spaghetti, Agent Sheehan?" Caroline Jackson asked. Her family was seated at the table with their holiday dinner guest. The Jackson children were on her left and Chase was on her right. Sergeant Jackson sat at the opposite end of the table.

"Please, you can call me Chase. It's not necessary for you to be that formal. I mean, I appreciate the respect. And yes, please."

"I'm sorry I didn't have time to make anything fancier," Mrs. Jackson said, handing the bowl to him. "I've got a turkey to cook tomorrow. You're welcome to join us again at noon."

"I guess we'll just have to see what happens," Chase said. He filled his plate with another pile of spaghetti and spread some sauce and meatballs over it. This wasn't how he'd planned to spend the evening. If he couldn't be with his family on Christmas Eve, he'd rather be sulking in a hotel room alone, trying to figure out what happened to Delia. When Jackson called him, he had no excuse to not come over for dinner. He didn't want to be the stuck-up FBI agent who snubbed a family's values and hospitality. As uncomfortable as he was in an unfamiliar house with people he didn't know, he couldn't deny the spirit of Christmas giving that had been extended to him.

Sergeant Jackson took a roll and began to butter it. In the process, he accidentally dropped his knife. The sudden clang of the utensil on the table startled the children.

"Daddy!" little Kaitlyn screeched. "You scaaaarrrred me!"

"Me, too!" Tyler chimed in, but his laughter indicated he was more amused than anything.

"Do it again, Daddy!" Kaitlyn said.

"No honey, I'm not doing it again," Jackson said.

"Katie, are you done eating?" Caroline asked her daughter.

"Yep!"

"Why don't you go wait for us in the living room?"

"Do we get to open a present?" Kaitlyn asked, her smile revealing a missing front tooth.

"Just one," Caroline said. "But you wait for us."

"I'm coming, too!" Tyler exclaimed. "Come on, Kaitlyn. Let's go figure out which ones we want to open!"

The children bolted from the table and raced to the living room, squealing with glee.

"Do you have kids, Chase?" Caroline asked.

"I do. I have a daughter. She's eight, a second grader." Chase stabbed a meatball with his fork before completing his thought. "Being here with you and your children, it's nice. Feels a little like home and kind of takes my mind off of other things."

"Anything you can talk about?" Caroline's gaze went from Chase to her husband and back to Chase. "I mean, I know you can't always discuss your work. John explained a little bit about that to me."

Jackson spoke up. "That's up to you, Agent."

Chase wiped his mouth with his napkin and took a sip of his Heineken before joining in. "Well, there's one thing going on here we can't really talk about yet," he said. "But what I can tell you is I'm actually here on vacation. My sister works for the DEA. Her last known whereabouts were somewhere between here in Adler and Gable."

"What?" Caroline Jackson exclaimed. "Your sister is missing?"

"I'm afraid so." Chase nodded. "Not a trace of her for a few days now."

"Oh my God! That's awful! What do you think — I mean — what could've happened? I mean, is there any possible reasonable explanation?"

It was clear to Chase that Caroline Jackson was not used to dealing with this type of drama. She was trying her best to say the right things, completely unaware that there were no right things to say in a situation like this.

"It's hard to say," he said. "Delia and I are pretty close. We're twins, actually. She has never been out of touch like this. We're always texting or calling to let each other know what's going on."

"Hmmm," Caroline uttered with a pout, seemingly trying to solve the case. She looked across the table at her husband. "You're awfully quiet, mister."

The police sergeant shrugged. "I already knew all of this. It's horrible. And frustrating and perplexing."

Mrs. Jackson turned her attention back to the FBI agent. "Is it true what they say about twins? Do they have a connection that other siblings don't?"

"Believe it or not I don't get asked that very often. Here's the thing…I can't tell you what it's like for everyone else. All I know is Delia and I have an extremely strong bond. And I haven't been myself since she went missing."

Chase pulled his phone out and opened up the same picture of him and Delia that he had shown Maddison and Claire earlier that day.

"She's pretty," Caroline commented as she held the phone. "Is she married?"

"Divorced. No children," Chase said. He took his phone back and pushed away from the table. "The meal was fantastic, thank you so much. I'm going to use your restroom to clean up, if that's okay."

"Of course," husband and wife said in unison.

As Chase got up from his chair, he reached for his left shoulder and groaned. "Man," he said. "I got something going on here. I don't know if I slept on it wrong or what the deal is." He continued to massage the shoulder as he made his way to the bathroom.

"There's some Bengay in the medicine cabinet if you think it'll help," Jackson called out to him.

Chase closed the door to the bathroom and looked at himself in the mirror. His eyes were bloodshot. He looked ten years older which, coincidentally, was exactly how he felt. "Where are you, Delia?" Chase said under his breath, still staring at himself.

He opened the medicine cabinet door and found the heat rub Jackson had mentioned. He undid three buttons on his shirt and smeared some of the cream onto his throbbing shoulder. Under normal circumstances, Chase would be self-conscious about the aroma that was now emanating from his body, but he planned to find a hotel shortly and would soon have some time to himself. Chase splashed some cold water on his face and washed his hands before opening the bathroom door. Jackson was standing in the hallway.

"Just got a call from Adler PD," the policeman said abruptly. "They found a woman in a ditch just north of town about an hour ago. She's unconscious, but alive. She's pretty beat up. They think it might be your sister."

It didn't take long for the gravity of Jackson's news to smack Chase in the face. He ran to the kitchen and grabbed his jacket. "You coming with me?" Chase asked him.

Jackson looked at his wife and then at his children.

"Crap. It's Christmas," Chase said. "That wasn't very

thoughtful. Stay here with your family, Sergeant."

"Go ahead and go, John," Caroline spoke up. "The kids will just open a small present with me and go to bed. I've got this."

Jackson moved over to his wife and gave her a kiss on the cheek. "Thank you, sweetheart," he said, quietly. "I won't be late. I just want to help him out in any way I can."

"Of course," his wife told him with a smile. "That's the good Samaritan in you. You just can't help yourself."

XXVII

When Jackson and Sheehan arrived at St. Mary's Regional Hospital in downtown Adler they were met by two uniformed police officers. Jackson walked up to them immediately and shook the older one's hand. "Thanks for calling me, Mark," Jackson said. He turned and motioned to Chase. "This is Agent Chase Sheehan of the FBI. Chase, this is my counterpart at the Adler PD, Sergeant Mark Hines."

Chase nodded at the police sergeant and shook his hand. Hines was in his mid-forties and a couple of inches taller than Jackson. His stomach hung slightly over his belt, making him the obvious heavyweight of the bunch. He introduced the other man, a young officer, as Murray McGee. McGee was a tall, lanky, baby-faced guy in his early to mid-twenties. It looked to Jackson like the kid was still waiting for his first shave.

"So, what do you have, Sergeant?" Chase asked.

"Come on," Hines replied. "Let's walk while we talk." The four men walked down the hall in the direction of the elevators as Sergeant Hines told them what he knew. "We got a call about ninety minutes ago from a family driving into Adler from Merchant for Christmas," he began. "One of the kids in the backseat said he saw something in the ditch. I guess the dad didn't want to turn around and have a second look at first. Probably thought the kid was B.S.-ing him. But eventually they did and lo and behold they discovered a badly beaten woman. Alive, by the way."

As the men took their turns entering the elevator Chase spoke up. "Brunette?" he asked. "Dark hair?"

"Yes," Hines confirmed. "We had caught wind of your sister — Agent DeMarco's —disappearance from Chief Perkins in Gable. When I first laid eyes on her in the hospital bed it took me a few minutes to even be able to guess an approximate age. I have to warn you, Agent. She's in pretty bad shape. I mean, someone beat her up pretty good. But they say she's going to be okay."

Chase took a deep breath and nodded as the elevator crept to the fourth floor.

"But after I spent some time in her room I began to realize this could be Agent DeMarco," Hines continued. "I mean, I haven't been able to ask her. She's been unconscious for a while now. She was out in the cold and, like I said, the injuries have probably taken a lot out of her."

"Was there anything on the scene that might clue us in to what happened, I mean, other than the obvious?" Jackson asked. This was a big moment of truth. If this woman was DeMarco, it meant Pablo had followed through with Jackson's suggestion. That was a good sign for the future. It meant Jackson might have some control of the situation after all. But the discovery of DeMarco also meant he would have to rely on her to stick to her word and cover for Jackson on the disappearance — and soon to be recovered body — of Chum.

"Officer McGee was the first on the scene," Hines said. "Go ahead and tell them what you know, McGee."

The door opened and the group stepped off the elevator. McGee spoke as Hines led them down the hall to ICU.

"When I got there the husband — Robert Cobb is his name was the only one outside the family vehicle. He hadn't moved her or anything for fear he could do more damage. Good thing, too. She's got a separated shoulder and a concussion."

Jackson shook his head and looked at Chase to try and

gauge how he was taking the news so far. He seemed to be in control. No doubt he had seen a lot of things in his line of work, just like Jackson had. But when it happens to someone you love, it can be an entirely different ball game.

"She was barely conscious when I arrived," McGee continued. "Cobb was talking to her. She wasn't saying much. Mostly groans. It was obvious she was in a lot of pain."

Hines stopped walking when he reached the closed door of room 409.

"But to go back to the original question," McGee said, "there wasn't anything there to get clues from. She didn't have an ID or phone on her. Just the clothes on her body and a coat."

Before anything else was said, the door to the room in front of them opened and a woman wearing street clothes came out. She had a stethoscope around her neck. Her hair was short and black.

"Dr. Langston," Hines said as she closed the door behind her. "This is Agent Chase Sheehan of the FBI. We think Jane Doe might be his sister. She's with the DEA."

After some quick introductions, Dr. Heather Langston took over the conversation. "Between her concussion, facial contusions, and separated shoulder, she's in a lot of pain. We moved her shoulder back into place about an hour ago and then put her under heavy sedation to help her sleep comfortably and let her build some strength back up. The good news is, she's going to be fine. I don't see any internal injuries other than the concussion. She took a pretty big blow to the head, so it's going to be a few days before you're really going to be able to talk to her. The concussion looks severe enough to be between a grade two and three. She's got a pretty big knot on her head. There could even be some memory loss, but we won't know for sure until she can stay awake and talk for a few minutes. We'll just have to wait and see."

"Can we see her?" Chase asked. "I'd like to confirm it's Delia."

"Yes, but just for a minute," Langston said. "I'll go in with you. Sergeant Jackson you can come, too, since it's going to be brief."

Jackson and Chase followed the doctor into the room while the Adler police officers remained in the hall. They stood behind her as she slowly opened the curtain around the hospital bed.

At first it was difficult to discern any facial features of the person under the oxygen mask in the bed. The hair was dark but the face was, too, covered in bruises that were highlighted with multiple cuts. Chase approached the bed first as Dr. Langston stepped aside.

"Delia, my God," he whispered, reaching out to touch her hand. Jackson moved next to Chase. Langston spoke quietly from behind them.

"She's your sister," she said. The answer was already obvious.

"Yes," Chase confirmed under his breath. Jackson turned to the doctor and nodded in agreement. As thankful as he was that DeMarco was alive, he wondered what had happened. Why had Pablo felt the need to put her in this condition?

Chase picked up his sister's hand and began stroking it. "You're going to be okay, sis," he said. "And I'm going to find who did this. I'm not leaving here until I do."

He bent down and kissed his sister's limp fingers as Jackson covered his eyes with the palms of his hands and pressed. He knew this move would make it appear he was agonized over the injured DEA agent in front of him. And he was. But not nearly as much as he was disturbed by what Sheehan had just said.

***

When she had eaten her share of pizza and chocolate chip cookies, Trish Mathison retired to her bedroom and left her daughter alone with their holiday guest. Claire sat on one end of the couch with her elbow on the armrest, holding her third margarita. Barrett sat on the other side with his own margarita. He was still dressed in the white bathrobe she had given him earlier. Claire wore a pair of flannel pajama bottoms and a button-down light blue shirt.

"Did you steal this robe from a hotel?" Barrett asked with a giant grin. He ran his hand over the soft material.

"I can honestly say I have never stayed in a hotel that had bathrobes," Claire said. "I don't know where that thing came from. It's been in the closet for a while now."

"Well," Barrett said, "I can honestly say I have never worn one in a situation like this. I think the alcohol is helping me not feel as self-conscious."

"Your clothes should be dry soon," Claire said.

Barrett nodded and took a drink of his margarita.

"So, what do you have to be self-conscious about?" Claire asked. "The fact that you're naked under that thing or that you don't think white is your color."

She giggled before finishing her drink in one swallow. After setting her empty glass on the end table, she slid to the middle of the couch.

"I don't even know how to answer that question," Barrett said.

"I was just thinking," Claire said. "Why couldn't I just drive you to Colorado?"

Caught off guard by the sudden subject change, Barrett gave her an inquisitive look. "To start with, I guess the winter weather is a good reason not to," he said. "Flying is a lot more reliable. And faster. That's a huge plus."

"I've never been to Colorado," Claire said, pointedly ignoring his objection. "I'd love to see the mountains. I've seen pictures and it looks so beautiful."

"It's a long trip," Barrett continued. "Over five hundred miles. You'd have to drive back by yourself."

"I think I could manage," she said.

"Let me put it to you this way, Claire. You're not driving me to Denver."

Claire frowned.

"I'm sorry, but I'm sick of driving across the country," Barrett explained. "It's nothing personal. I need to get back there and I want to do it the fastest way possible. If I could have Scotty beam me out there, I would."

After crossing her arms, Claire tossed herself backwards against the sofa. "Can't get out of here fast enough again, can you?" she grumbled. Wilson, who had been sprawled out atop the sofa, decided he had seen and heard enough. He leaped to the floor and disappeared down the dark hallway.

Barrett shifted closer to Claire, putting his hand on her knee. "You do understand this has nothing to do with you, right?"

"I thought I was never going to see you again," Claire said. "I wasn't even sure I wanted to see you again. Then when it happened, all of my old feelings for Henry came back. I can't stop thinking about how perfect things were for that week when we were hanging out. We were like little babies, completely ignorant of the truths around us." She paused before continuing. "Well, *I* was oblivious, anyway. But I understand why you took off that night, and I understand why you need to get back to Colorado so fast, but…" Her voice trailed off as she sat up and repositioned herself. Barrett's hand moved to the middle of her flannel-covered thigh.

"But what, Claire?" She shook her head and stared across the living room.

Barrett reached for her face with his other hand and turned her head so he could speak directly to her. "What do you want from me?" he whispered. As he looked deep into her eyes he swore he saw flecks of every shade of green and brown imaginable.

Barrett knew exactly what he was doing, what he was saying. He didn't care anymore. He had nothing to lose. It was different this time. He was completely free now. There was no need to hide. In fact, being vulnerable and wide open would feel good for a change.

In answer to his question, Claire tilted her head towards his. His hand still on her cheek, Barrett gently guided her face to him until their lips met and melted into one another. That's what the sensation felt like to Barrett, anyway. He was amazed at how good Claire's mouth tasted despite the food and alcohol. This immediately made him worry about how bad his own breath might be. But Claire showed no signs of slowing down as she slipped her tongue between Barrett's lips and teeth. She let out a slight groan as they continued to kiss passionately.

It was all coming back to Barrett now. The feelings he had the first time they had kissed that night in the farmhouse and he had put an end to it before things went further. Or all the way. Back then he didn't want Claire to get tied to him. Tonight was different. He had feelings for her, and there was a burning desire inside of him to prove his feelings to her before leaving her behind again.

While the two continued to kiss, Barrett stroked Claire's cheek, hair, ear, and neck. Hands began exploring other areas of anatomy as their animal instincts assumed control. They had been taken over by an urge that was larger than life. There would be no stopping their sudden outbreak of lust.

Claire began to stand up as Barrett's hand wandered to the buttons on her shirt. At first he thought she might be shutting things down, but her lips remained fastened to his and Barrett quickly realized she wanted to move to another room. He rose with her as they continued to kiss. She pulled him by the collar of the robe as they moved in the direction of the hallway. At one point, finding it difficult to simultaneously make out and maneuver through an unfamiliar house, Barrett turned too early and whacked his elbow into a doorjamb.

"Ouch!" Barrett cried out as he rubbed his elbow.

"Shhhhh!" Claire said, placing her finger in front of her lips and giggling at the same time.

"Funny bone," Barrett whispered to her. "That hurt."

"I know," she said softly, still snickering.

"It's not funny," Barrett quipped. But he was only joking with her, and she could sense it.

"No. No, it's not," Claire whispered. She moved close to him again. "It's serious business. You poor baby." She rubbed his elbow through the robe. "Come on," she said. "Let's go have a closer look at it." Claire took him by the hand and led him to her bedroom.

***

Christmas came and went in Gable and the surrounding areas just like it did every year. The Jacksons enjoyed the day at home in Adler opening presents, listening to holiday music, and eating a homemade meal. The children played so hard with the new toys Santa had brought them that they fell asleep together in the recliner watching *A Christmas Story*. Caroline Jackson remained silent about the sudden exile to Minnesota. She figured things must be better if John had let them come home. Sometimes it was best to not poke the bear. Her husband had always done right by their family; there was no reason to question him now.

Sergeant Jackson hid his stress and apprehension deep inside the pit of his gut. He did not want to ruin Christmas for his family by being a grumpy old scrooge. DeMarco's return was supposed to have been a good thing, as long as she kept her word. She and Sheehan would leave town, and life could return to normal in Gable. But instead, the FBI agent planned to track down the person or people who had beaten his sister into unconsciousness. Pablo had defeated the purpose of Jackson's request for DeMarco's release.

Maddison Chumansky went to her parents' house in Maydale, the town she had grown up in about an hour east. Still considered small by most standards, Maydale was larger than Gable. Large enough, in fact, to have its own private university. Maddison spent her Christmas Day wondering and worrying about her ex-husband's fate. When her parents inquired about Tom, she responded with vague and elusive statements about him being busy at work and trying to make it to his parents' home. It wasn't like he was supposed to be with her for the holidays: they were divorced. Maddison kept her sanity by being thankful that through all that had happened, she still had her own health and that of her unborn baby. Even if Tom was gone forever, there would still be a piece of him left on Earth. It wasn't ideal, but she tried to focus on the positive.

Randy Fowley and his mother, Nora Ferguson, spent their Christmas in jail eating a holiday meal of turkey and mashed potatoes from the Boston Market in Adler. Chief Perkins didn't want to hear how he had mistreated the pair during a holiday and thought it best to go out of his way. The mother-son duo would be transferred to Des Moines on the twenty-sixth and given their fair shake at a trial in the near future. It wasn't Randy's first rodeo. He didn't want to go back to prison, but the reality was beginning to sink in. All he could do was his best to create doubt and confusion. Nora, on the other hand, didn't seem to be giving in so easily. She would be charged with a lesser crime and, because of her age, she hoped to find leniency within the legal system.

Chase spent the rest of his Christmas at the hospital watching over his sister. Officer Murray McGee was nice enough to make a visit on Christmas day. A single man, McGee explained that he had finished the day's festivities at his parents' place and decided to stop by. The two men spent an hour discussing various subjects including the possibilities of who might have kidnapped and assaulted Delia. The men agreed it was probably related to the narcotics case she was working on, but it was difficult to say who had done it. Even more confusing was why they had let her go the way they had.

After a sizzling Christmas Eve in Claire's bedroom, Barrett woke up Christmas morning feeling like a thirteen-year-old boy. Not surprising, Claire was giddy most of the day, too. Her mother, on the other hand, did not seem enthused by any of it. It was obvious Trish Mathison knew what had happened in her house the night before, but she never mentioned it. Instead, she and her daughter fixed a hearty breakfast of pancakes and eggs. In conversation over several cups of coffee while Claire's mother was in the shower, Barrett learned what had been happening in Gable since he'd left. Claire told him about Maddison's plan to retrieve the hidden drug money and split it up and how something had gone wrong, and now Chum and Eddie were missing. The first thought that came to mind when Barrett heard this was how much of a snake Chum had been for almost getting everyone killed over money and drugs he had the entire time. That Chum had now disappeared and could possibly be dead was an appropriate case of karma as far as Barrett was concerned. But Claire's sensitivity towards Maddison's well-being was admirable, and Barrett listened intently to everything she said.

The Mathison women felt awkward opening gifts in front of their guest, but Barrett insisted they not let his presence affect their Christmas any more than it already had. Mother and daughter opened three packages each while Barrett looked on. Claire's favorite gift from her mother was a gold chain and crucifix. Trish told her daughter she hoped it would inspire her to go to church more often. At first Barrett thought he sensed tension between the two regarding the subject. But the women laughed it off almost immediately as Claire reminded her mom that she didn't attend church often herself. The rest of the day was spent hanging around the house talking and munching on goodies. The weather had cleared up and the sun shone brightly for most of the afternoon. All things considered, Barrett was appreciative of the hospitality and the opportunity to spend the holiday with the Mathisons. To his delight, Claire was proving to be the young woman he had thought she was. Wise and mature beyond her years in many ways, she was not afraid to let herself go and be a simple, fun-loving person. Everything about her was attractive to Barrett. This had been true when he'd first met her, but he had kept himself in check at the time because he didn't feel comfortable getting too close. Especially not when he was using an alias and hiding everything about who he really was. The slate had been wiped clean now, though. He would have to put things on hold for a while, but he truly did plan to continue some type of relationship with Claire. In what fashion, he did not know yet. Barrett always believed these things had a way of working themselves out.

The day after Christmas was a busy one for both the Adler and Gable police forces. Around seven thirty in the morning, Officer Hodge arrived at the Chumansky property with two Adler officers to finish digging around the fingers and hand they had found two days before. Sergeant Jackson made his way to the scene about fifteen minutes later to observe and supervise the task. When Eddie Clark had vanished again, Jackson felt he had two options. One was to move Chum's body during the holiday shutdown. But that idea didn't fit into his family holiday plans. Besides, the thought of going back into the woods in the dead of winter and doing more digging and then hauling a one-hundred-forty-pound body out of it and disposing of it somewhere else was not appealing. Instead, Jackson had gone in another direction.

The sun continued to shine throughout the region that morning as the temperature soared to forty degrees. This helped Hodge and his team dig the body up more quickly than anticipated. At eight forty-five an ambulance and the county coroner were called. It was clear to everyone that the deceased was Tom Chumansky. Jackson examined the body as if he were witnessing it for the first time, pointing out to the team how there was little if any decomposition, suggesting the subject had not been buried very long. He also observed and commented on the obvious gunshot wound to the chest, presumably the kill shot. After scribbling a few notes, Jackson stated that it was now in the coroner's hands to make everything official.

By ten thirty in the morning, the Chumansky property had been cleared out and the body moved to Adler for an autopsy. Maddison Chumansky returned home from Maydale around eleven fifteen and promptly returned a voicemail from Sergeant Jackson. Not wanting to deliver bad news over the phone, Chief Perkins and Jackson made the short drive back to the house to tell her in person about her ex-husband's death.

The pregnant divorcée did not take the news well. Perhaps it was the illusion that Chum would've made a good father for their baby that caused Maddison to break down the way she did. Or maybe she was simply upset because her devious plan to gain control of the hefty sum of money had failed miserably and wound up getting her baby's father killed. Maybe she felt like it was her fault. Whatever was causing the outburst of emotions, Jackson had more urgent things on his mind. He felt bad for Maddison, but not nearly as bad as he would have had she not tried to play him like a fiddle. Strangely, he could thank Pablo for pointing him in the right direction that night.

***

On the evening of the twenty-sixth, Chase was in the St. Mary's cafeteria eating a cheeseburger and tater tots when Dr. Langston approached him.

"Can I sit down?" she asked as she pulled out a chair.

"Of course," Chase said. Another physician had been on call Christmas Day, so this was the first time he had seen his sister's doctor since Delia had been brought in.

"I have some good news," Langston said. "Your sister is awake."

"What?" Chase exclaimed. "That's great!" He stood up and began to gather his food.

"Wait a minute," Dr. Langston said. "Take your time.

There's no hurry. You don't want to go up there and inundate her with questions right now. We need to go easy on her."

Chase sat back down and took a deep breath.

"The best thing you can do for her right now is to go up there and let her see your face," Langston continued. "But let her control the conversation. I mean, if she feels like talking. You do not want to put pressure on her to remember anything. Only go where she wants to go right now."

Chase nodded.

"I know you want to find out what happened, but I'm sure you agree that Delia getting back to normal — her health — is even more important." Dr. Langston reached across the table and touched Chase's hand. "Come on, I'll go up with you."

On their way to the elevator, Chase made polite conversation. "What made you become a doctor?" he asked her.

"Same thing that made you become an FBI agent," Langston replied.

"You like shooting bad guys?"

"No," she said. "Passion." She pushed the up button for the elevator.

"I guess you could call it that for me," Chase said. "But I think of it more as annoyance. I can't stand seeing people get away with crimes."

The elevator door opened and they walked in.

"So, you're passionate about it then?" Langston smiled.

"Yeah, okay." Chase chuckled.

"When I was a child I loved going to the doctor," she confessed and then paused, letting it sink in.

"That's pretty weird."

"I know," Langston said. "Children hate going to the doctor, primarily because their earliest memories of the doctor's office is getting shots." The elevator door opened. Dr. Langston got off first and turned to face him as she kept talking. "My mom would take me for a checkup or whatever and I would go crazy wanting to play with all the instruments. It was a given that my doctor always had to let me listen to his heart, take his blood pressure, and check his throat."

"It stuck with you then," Chase said as they walked down the hall to Delia's room.

"If my pediatrician hadn't been so nice about it I don't know if it would have," Langston explained. "But I think he recognized an opportunity to help encourage my growth, even at such a young age."

"My story's not nearly as heartwarming as yours," Chase said as they arrived outside Delia's door. "I just enjoyed playing cops and robbers, I guess." He stared at the closed door and concluded his reminiscing. "I'd always try to make Delia be the robber. It was an argument we had every time."

"Come on," Dr. Langston said softly. She moved forward and pushed the door open. As she entered the room, she stepped to the side and allowed Chase to head directly to the bed. Delia's eyes were closed, but as her brother approached she opened them slowly.

"Dee," Chase said under his breath. "Delia," he said a little louder. Chase touched her arm and watched a faint smile spread over her face.

"It…hurts…when I…do anything," Delia managed to utter.

"I know," Chase said.

"When I…breathe," she said. Dr. Langston stepped between them and began regulating the flow of some IV bags dangling next to Delia's bed.

"I'm going to help you out with that," the doctor promised. "We're trying to make you as comfortable as possible, Agent DeMarco."

Delia closed her eyes as Langston finished her

adjustments.

"I'll leave you two alone," she said. "Only a few minutes tonight," she added, looking at Chase and grabbing his arm. "Remember our conversation…"

He nodded and watched Dr. Langston leave the room, closing the door behind her. When Chase looked back to Delia it was obvious she already felt better. Her eyes were wide open and she turned her head from left to right.

"Wow," she mumbled. "Like magic." Her voice was weak and her speech garbled.

Chase's pursed lips turned into a lopsided grin. "Take it easy, sis. You've got a nasty concussion. You don't need to be tossing your noggin around."

"Heeeeeeeey," Delia exclaimed. She reached out with her right hand to her brother. "What are yoooooouuuu doing heeeeeere?"

Crap. Those pain meds are working *too* well, Chase thought. He grabbed his sister's hand and squeezed it before replying. "I came here to find you."

Delia swung Chase's hand back and forth. "Shilly goosh," she slurred. "I wasn't losht."

Chase gained control of their moving hands and pulled a chair over with his other hand so he could sit down next to her. He leaned in closer and whispered. "Delia, you were missing. Do you remember what happened?"

She squeezed her bruised eyelids closed and reopened them. "Surrrrrrre," she said. "I was...working."

"I know that, Delia. But what happened to you? How did you end up here in the hospital?"

"Here for...druuuuuuuuuuugs," Delia replied with a giggle. Chase wasn't sure if she was referring to the ones in her system or her job as a DEA agent. He decided to continue digging.

"You were trying to track down some missing money and cocaine. Did you find it?"

His sister shut her eyes again. This time she kept them closed while speaking. "Chumansky," Delia said. Her voice was quiet again, like it had been when Chase first entered the room.

"Yes, yes. Exactly. Did you get anywhere with him? Did he lead you to it?"

"Dead," Delia groaned. Her face was creased in pain, and she turned her head away from Chase.

"What?" Chase bellowed. He sprung up from his chair and leaned over the bed. "Delia, wh-what did you mean by that?"

As he said this, the door opened and Dr. Langston appeared in the room. Chase continued the interrogation of his sister. "Did you see something? What are you saying, Delia?"

"Agent Sheehan!" Dr. Langston cried. "You need to stop *right now!*" She walked to the bed again as Delia kept her eyes closed and moaned. "She's not ready for this. I told you!"

"I know, but she was saying something that's critical to..." Chase didn't finish his sentence. He watched as his sister drifted back into wonderland. "I didn't realize..."

"Go ahead and sleep it off, Agent DeMarco," Langston said. "I've just increased your drip. I can tell you're feeling better already."

A smile crept over Delia's face. Her eyes started to open, and then closed again. "Shee you at the shtation, Jackshon," she uttered in another hodgepodge of garbled words.

Startled again by what his sister had just said, Chase looked at Dr. Langston. "Did you hear that?"

"Barely," Langston said as she grabbed his arm to lead him out of the room.

"Did she say 'See you at the station, Jackson?'" Chase held his ground.

"Maybe," the doctor said. "You can ask her in a couple of days. Let's go. She needs to rest and it's clear you're not able to control yourself."

Langston escorted the FBI agent out of the room, but not before Chase glanced over his shoulder one last time at Delia.

XXVIII

The day after Christmas did not turn out quite the way Barrett and Claire had planned. Since Claire was off work, the two headed to Adler to eat lunch and see a matinee movie. Arriving in town at ten in the morning, it was too early for food or a movie. Instead, Claire drove to the nearest S-Mart Superstore and bought Barrett some new clothes to wear on his trip back to Colorado. As they were eating lunch and trying to decide what movie to see, Claire's mobile phone rang. It was Maddison informing Claire that Chum had been found and that he was, indeed, dead. Barrett watched as Claire's expression went from happy to distraught, and then to sympathetic. He observed her as she listened to Maddison weep on the phone. For a moment, Barrett thought Claire was about to cry, too. She ended the call by telling her friend that she would be at her house in less than an hour. Then she spent the next twenty minutes apologizing to Barrett.

"I'll make it up to you," she told him.

"You don't have to. You've already done enough for me."

Barrett had no interest in going to Maddison's house to sympathize with her while she grieved. His entire relationship with everyone in this little town was already far too muddled. He had apparently worked things out with the one person who mattered to him. He didn't need to complicate things by pretending to forgive Chum for almost getting everyone killed. Claire didn't even ask Barrett to come with her. He assumed this was because she was intelligent enough to know better.

Trish Mathison also had the day off from her job at one of the jewelry stores in the Adler shopping mall. She said nothing to Barrett as he dozed off on the couch while she sat in the recliner and watched soap operas.

Around three thirty Claire returned home. The opening of the door woke Barrett from his lengthy snooze. Trish offered to fix them a late afternoon snack, but they each politely declined. When her mother went to the kitchen to make herself something to eat, Claire gave Barrett some brief details about Chum's death and how Maddison was handling it.

"They found him buried in the area with all those trees behind the house." She sniffled a little. "He had a...a bullet hole in his chest. I guess they're doing an autopsy now but I don't know why. Sounds like they know how he died."

Barrett shook his head and walked over to Claire, giving her hug. "You wanna get a drink?"

Around five thirty the twosome headed back to Adler. Barrett insisted that he was tracking how much money Claire was spending on him and promised to pay her back, one way or another. They began their evening at an Adler sports bar called Hashmarks. Barrett drank a couple of light beers while Claire enjoyed some tequila sunrises. It seemed no subject was off-limits. When the topic of ex-lovers came up, Claire fired off first.

"My first real boyfriend was also my last," she said.

"How did that happen?"

"We began dating when we were sixteen. When we graduated from high school he went to college at the University of Iowa. It ended shortly after that."

"Too much of a distance?" Barrett asked.

"That and he became too interested in all the new college girls." Claire snorted. "I never actually caught him doing anything, but I might as well have."

"And you haven't dated anyone seriously since then?

That's like four or five years ago, right?" Barrett was astonished by this.

"Yep."

"Why?"

"Crap, Barrett. Look where I live." Claire said.

"I guess I can see your point," Barrett said. "But you must not get out much either. You have places here in Adler you can go and—"

"I just pretty much stay holed up in Gable."

Barrett took a drink of his beer and Claire grabbed a menu before continuing her thought.

"When we first met, you said something to me about how maybe I hadn't found the right reason to leave Gable yet."

"Yeah, I seem to remember that," Barrett said.

"Well, I think you were right. I mean, I'm still relatively young by today's standards, trying to figure out what I want to be when I grow up."

Nodding, Barrett flagged their server down and asked for another beer; Claire ordered the chicken nachos for an appetizer.

"These drinks are giving me the munchies," she said.

"Did you ever consider going to college?" Barrett asked.

"For starters, I couldn't afford it. But the real reason was because I didn't know what I wanted to do. I still don't."

"Fair enough."

The two paused for a minute. The bar and grill was busy. Barrett figured it always was the day after Christmas. People were sick of being closed up with their families over the holiday and were ready to get out for a few hours.

"What about you?" Claire asked.

"Oh, I went to college. I had to in order to become a CPA."

"I meant girlfriends." Claire snickered.

"Oh," Barrett said, also chuckling. His fresh beer arrived and he took a sip off the head. This was not a topic he enjoyed discussing, but he knew he owed Claire some more honesty.

"Since I'm a little older than you I've probably got a few more stories to tell," he began. "I'll keep it short for now."

"Wait," Claire said, holding her hand out like a traffic cop. "Did you leave a girlfriend behind in Colorado?"

"Nope," Barrett answered without hesitation.

"Thank God!" she exclaimed. "It honestly didn't occur to me until now. I guess that's what happens when you're 'inactive' for such a long time."

Barrett laughed again, mostly because of the way Claire used air quotes when she said the word "inactive." If she hadn't been with a guy for several years before the other night, Barrett sure hadn't detected it. Although it might explain her unbridled passion, he thought.

"Sorry I cut you off," Claire said. "Go ahead. I wanna hear."

A sudden roar exploded from one corner of the bar. A college bowl game was on the big screen television, and Barrett could see from where he was sitting that someone had just scored.

"It's really not very interesting," Barrett said, resuming eye contact with Claire. "I didn't date anyone seriously in high school. In college I met a girl and we dated for a while. She was a freshman when I was a sophomore. It lasted about a year and a half before we broke up."

"Why?"

"I found someone else I wanted to date." Barrett cringed inside when he finished the sentence.

Claire shrugged. "Okay. I mean, you broke up with her first?"

"Yeah, actually I did."

"There's nothing wrong with that. I mean, I don't

think there is. Maybe I'm missing something."

"Well, that's what I thought, too," Barrett said. "But of course she didn't quite see it that way."

"I suppose," Claire said. Their nachos arrived and they dug in, taking a couple of bites each before they continued their discussion. "So," Claire said, washing down some food with a drink of water, "what happened with the new girlfriend?"

"I married her," Barrett replied.

Claire immediately covered her mouth so she wouldn't spit out the water she was drinking. Instead, she swallowed the wrong way, bringing on a fit of coughing. "You did not!" she said once she finally recovered. Her eyes were as big as saucers.

"Yeah, I did," Barrett admitted. "It didn't happen overnight. We dated for about a year."

This was a part of his life Barrett had pushed so far aside that he had almost forgotten about it. He watched as Claire leaned forward with her elbows on the table, placing her fists under her chin.

"I didn't realize it then, but our relationship was fueled by alcohol," Barrett explained. "You know, you're in college and you kind of get caught up in things. We went out a lot, and there was always drinking."

Claire nodded.

"One night we wound up in Vegas and..."

"Oh my God," Claire said.

"Yeah. To this day I still hate Elvis."

"Were you actually married by—"

"By an Elvis impersonator? Yes. Yes we were."

"Holy crap!" Claire couldn't contain her laughter any longer. "I'm sorry," she said. "I'm not laughing at you. I'm laughing at the picture you just put in my head."

"I know," Barrett said. "I totally get that."

When she regained her composure, Barrett concluded

the story.

"So, I was twenty-one, she was twenty, and we were in school. Needless to say, it didn't last a year."

"That's too bad."

"Not really," Barrett said. "It was a mistake to begin with. I did a lot of growing up beginning the day after the wedding."

"You don't see her anymore?"

"Nope."

"At least you didn't get her pregnant."

"No kidding." Barrett reached across the table and closed Claire's hand in his. "I've dated off and on over the years since then," he said, "but I haven't gotten serious like that since. I might be a little gun-shy, I don't know. I've mostly focused on my work instead, I guess."

"Kind of like me in some ways," Claire said. She settled her free hand on top of his and lightly massaged Barrett's knuckles with her fingertips. "I really like you, Barrett. I feel a spark when I'm with you. It gets stronger every time we're alone."

"I know, Claire. I feel it, too." Barrett said. "Being with you these few days has helped me forget why I'm even going back to Colorado. In some ways I feel guilty about temporarily forgetting. But I also can't stop smiling when I'm with you."

"Did you know you're quite the romantic?" Claire asked him.

"No clue."

She smiled and flagged down the server. "We better get out of here if we're gonna make it to the movie on time," she said.

"Whatever you say."

"Besides," Claire added, "it'll be easier to make out in a dark theatre than in here."

She winked at him and Barrett pumped his fist as if he had just thrown a game-winning touchdown pass. They cracked up as their waitress dropped off the check.

***

"You wanna tell me why you felt the need to beat the living shit out of Agent DeMarco before you dumped her in a ditch?" Jackson belted out as soon as he knew it was Pablo on the other end of the phone. He could hear a soft snicker before the Hispanic man responded.

"Come on," he said. "I had to make her think I showed her mercy. I couldn't just let her walk out the door."

"Yes. Yes you could have. And you should have," Jackson snarled. "You almost killed her. And guess what else? Because you had to show her who was boss, her brother the FBI agent is staying around here until he finds out who did it!"

"Then I'll take care of him," Pablo stated coldly.

"No you won't. No more bloodshed, remember? Just chill out."

"I'm not the one who's worked up, señor."

It annoyed Jackson when Pablo was right. He took a deep breath before speaking again.

"I'll keep an eye on him, help him. Lead him on a wild goose chase. He won't get close and if he does, we'll deal with it...together." I can't believe I just said that, Jackson thought.

"You better make sure he doesn't find me," Pablo warned. "Your own freedom depends on it."

Jackson knew Pablo meant he would rat out the police sergeant in an instant. "Yeah," Jackson replied, "I got you."

"I called you for a reason, señor, and it was not to argue," Pablo said, changing the subject. "I actually must compliment you."

"Oh yeah?"

"Sí. Señor Timmons has done very good during his

first couple of days as our distributor."

Jackson smiled. Not because he was happy Timmons was doing well. But because of the way Pablo pronounced Bart's last name: "Tea-moans."

"Great to hear," Jackson said. "I knew he wouldn't give you any trouble."

"If you know anyone else that could—"

"Let's not let this get too weird, okay?" Jackson interjected.

"Sí."

The men hung up and Jackson's mind immediately began racing through his priorities. First and foremost, he would need DeMarco's help to make anything work. There was no telling what she was going to say once her recovery hit a certain point. He heard that she had woken up briefly the night before, but apparently she wasn't able to say much before going back to sleep. Chum's body was being examined by the coroner. There would be no surprises and although the murder would be investigated, Jackson was the last person they would suspect. The cartel would be at the top of the list for both Chum's death and DeMarco's abduction. That would've been a good thing if Jackson didn't now have to worry about protecting Pablo.

As he pulled out of the police station parking lot, a white taxi drove by on the highway. He couldn't be sure, but he thought he spotted Bart Timmons in the backseat. Jackson followed the cab to Main Street in Gable. The vehicle turned right and headed east, heading towards Bart's home as it went over the railroad tracks and merged onto a county highway. Jackson knew the Timmons farm was a mile east of town. Three minutes later, the taxi stopped just short of the long gravel driveway that led to the blue two-story farmhouse. Parked a hundred feet behind it, Jackson watched as Bart struggled to remove his large frame from the backseat of the cab. He pulled out a wad of bills and paid the driver. As the taxi U-turned its way back towards Gable, Bart jogged over to the squad car and. Jackson rolled down his window.

"Hi, Officer," Timmons greeted him.

"I'm a Sergeant, Bart."

The farm boy frowned. "Oh. Sorry."

"What's the deal with the taxi?"

As soon as Jackson asked the question out loud, the answer hit him.

"I don't have a license anymore, sir," Bart said then corrected himself. "Um, Sergeant."

"I forgot," Jackson said. "It got taken away when you got charged with another DWI. You've been conducting your business in Adler via taxis? That's got to be expensive."

"Yeah, it is. I'm barely breaking even right now. I mean, not that I applied for this job or anything. This is like delivering pizzas but having to pay for a cab to deliver them. It's kind of counteractive."

"Counterproductive," Jackson said.

"Yeah, that's what I mean."

"And you might not have asked for this job, but no one made you get behind the wheel of your truck last week when you were sloshed, either. This is your ticket out. A second chance."

"I know," Bart said. He kicked the gravel with one of his big shoes. "What sucks is I wasn't even that drunk."

"You blew a point two three!" Jackson exclaimed.

"I don't even know what that means!" Bart snapped back, throwing his fists down in frustration. "All I know is I felt way more drunk the first two times I got caught."

Jackson shook his head but let a half-smile form on his lips. "Did I say 'second chance'? I meant this is your fourth chance," the police sergeant said.

"Right."

"Look, Bart. Don't pay for a taxi," Jackson said, realizing he had another thing to add to his to-do list. "Drive your truck. I'll take care of your entire charge and license suspension on my end within the next couple of days. In the meantime, drive slow and safe. Don't get pulled over for anything. You're just going to make this more difficult for me to take care of if you do."

"Got it. Yes, sir. I mean Sergeant."

Jackson put his car in drive and moved forward, following the taxi's tire tracks and making his own U-turn. As he reached Bart again, he slowed the vehicle to a crawl and spoke. "And if your new boss instructs you to kill anyone, you let me know."

"Kill some — what?" Bart shouted. But Jackson was already driving off in a cloud of dust.

***

Both Claire and Trish Mathison had to work on the twenty-seventh, leaving Barrett alone in their house for a good portion of the day. Barrett was intrigued by how trustworthy they were. Of course, there wasn't much damage he could do. Burn the house down? Steal back his cat? Instead he waited patiently for the delivery of his driver's license and credit card.

At nine-thirty, shortly after Trish left, Barrett heard the delivery truck park in the street. Thirty seconds later, the doorbell rang and his special package was in his hands. He walked to the kitchen and set it on the table. Wilson followed, probably hoping there was something in it for him. Barrett looked around for a pair of scissors but was only able to find a steak knife. His mother was a thorough packer and had used plenty of tape on the mailing envelope. He assumed it was because she was worried someone might open it and steal his stuff, but he also knew from experience she simply liked to wrap things. Ella Greyson worked overtime and went overboard at Christmas and birthdays when it came to wrapping gifts. All packages were neatly wrapped and tied with festive ribbons. It always made Barrett feel bad to open any of his presents because he knew how much time and energy she had put into wrapping them. He often found himself trying to open the gifts with care, in an attempt to not destroy her artwork. But his mom would always laugh and tell him to tear into it because that's what he was supposed to do.

Today's present was one he wasn't interested in preserving. Barrett took the knife and dug his way through the tape and the opening of the mailer. It took a couple of minutes, but he was eventually able to reach his fingers inside the hole he had made and rip it open. The contents fell on the table. Barrett could tell his license and Visa card were there, but there was also a piece of paper that landed on top of them. He turned it over and read it.

Barrett,

Your father was awake on Christmas day. I told him that you were coming home. He is very excited to see you. We don't expect he will be released before you get to town. He even had me go home and get something for you. See you soon, honey.

Love,

Mom

Barrett folded the note and set it aside. He looked at the credit card and was thankful to see it had not expired yet. Next, he slid the driver's license in front of him with two fingers, as if he were moving a piece on a checkerboard. He stared at his face in the picture. The shot had been taken two years ago and strangely, Barrett remembered the day very well:

Boyd Clevinger was becoming more active in the family business, and Barrett had started to realize there was nothing anyone could do about it. Accepting it was one thing, but working *around* him in order to keep the business successful was no easy task. Barrett and a number of others at the Clevinger Group had agreed they would do everything in their power to keep any and all important business as far away from Boyd as possible. The guy never completed anything he started, which would also cause Barrett to have to cover for Boyd.

This particular day, Barrett was taking an extended lunch break for his father's birthday. Frank Greyson picked his oldest son up and together they stopped at the nearby DMV to renew Barrett's license before heading to their favorite lunch spot, a restaurant called Renegade. Mr. Greyson even got silly while Barrett was having his photo snapped, making faces at him "like your mother and I did when you were a baby."

Thankfully the line wasn't long at the DMV, so they arrived at Renegade before the lunch rush hit. Shortly after being seated, Barrett's cell phone rang. It was Rob from one of the Clevinger Group's larger clients, Coleman Systems, and he was not happy. After a few minutes of taking a verbal beating through the phone and having no idea what Rob was talking about, Barrett excused himself from the table and went outside to continue the phone call.

Twenty minutes later he returned to the table and apologized to his father for the interruption. Barrett went on to explain how Boyd had gotten a wild hair one day to do some work, so he began a project for Coleman Systems but didn't finish it. This wouldn't be a terrible thing if he hadn't also mailed the incomplete work to the government. When the error was discovered Barrett received the call because he was the go-to person for the Clevinger Group's key clients. The last thing he was going to do was throw the owner's son under the bus. So he took the blame himself and promised he would get things worked out.

Despite two more phone calls — one from Rob and one from the boss himself, Otto — the Greyson men were eventually able to enjoy a meal and some casual conversation together. Barrett could tell his father was displeased with the situation that was going on at the Clevinger Group and how it was affecting his son. Over the years they would occasionally discuss things like this. But these talks would always lead to one conclusion: learn to deal with it or get out.

Barrett had gotten out, all right. He just hadn't done it the way most people would.

For the rest of the day Barrett hung around the Mathison house, watched some TV, gave Wilson his share of affection, and took a nap. He had found himself unusually tired the last few days. Maybe it was the stress he was feeling — and pushing aside — regarding his father's condition. Barrett was doing his best to concentrate on Claire and enjoy the time he had with her. He did plan to keep her in his life. He just didn't know how yet.

At two o'clock, Barrett was yanked out of a deep sleep when the home phone rang. At first he thought it was an alarm clock until he realized it was the middle of the day and he hadn't set one. It took him four more rings to find the phone. He wasn't sure if he should answer it but figured it might be important since it hadn't rung once during his stay. He picked up the receiver slowly.

"Hello?" he said.

"Hey, what are you doing?" an energetic Claire asked him. "I wasn't sure you'd answer."

"I didn't know people still had landlines," Barrett joked.

"Iowa didn't get microwaves until 1998."

"Well, the good news is you'll be one of the last to die from all the radiation, right?"

Claire laughed. "You're still a funny guy, bud. And you make a good point, too."

"Hey, I was just thinking," Barrett said, "instead of leaving at a ridiculously early time tomorrow morning so I can catch my flight, why don't we leave after you get off work today? We can stay in a hotel. This time on my dime. I got my credit card and license today."

"I think that sounds like a great idea," Claire replied.

Barrett could hear the smile in her voice. It made him smile just thinking about her smile. "Then let's make it happen."

"Hey, Barrett," Claire said.

"Yes ma'am?"

"I'm not looking forward to saying goodbye."

"I know," Barrett said. "That's kind of why I want to make the last twelve hours or so a little more special."

"That's nice of you."

"And also don't forget, this is in no way 'goodbye,'" Barrett reminded her. "It's temporary. I like to think of goodbyes as forever."

"I guess that explains why you left in the middle of the night without saying it to me a few months ago," Claire quipped. "You must've known you'd be back."

Barrett could tell she was joking again. "Hey, that wasn't me," he said. "That was Henry Fields."

"I can't argue that," Claire agreed. The two said goodbye and Barrett flopped back down on the couch.

***

Jackson and Chase stepped off the elevator at St. Mary's on the fourth floor and turned up the hallway. They immediately saw Dr. Langston standing near the reception area. Chase picked up his pace and rushed over to her. "Wow! What a difference twenty-four hours makes," he exclaimed.

"These things are unpredictable," Langston said. "You still need to be cautious as you speak to her. But she's willing and able to put forth an effort."

"That's great!" Chase said.

Yeah, wonderful, Jackson thought. He was present for a variety of reasons this evening. Ultimately, he wanted DeMarco to recover. She didn't deserve what Pablo did to her. At the same time, she wasn't supposed to be there when

Jackson took care of Chum and his hidden treasure. They had made a deal with each other after she witnessed it. All Jackson could do now was hope she honored it. If she did, he felt good about his future. Other than the part about being the ringmaster between the Mexican cartel and a farm boy distributor.

"Hey, Dee!" Chase greeted Delia as the three of them walked through the door. "You look great!" He leaned in and gave his sister a kiss on the forehead.

"I'll have to take your word for it," Delia said. "They won't let me have a mirror to see. Which tells me how bad it actually is." She shot a glance at Dr. Langston, who shrugged in response.

"Your speech is great, too," Chase added. "Last night was a bit of a mess."

"I wouldn't even know you had been here if she hadn't told me," Delia admitted, motioning at Langston with her right arm. "Totally blasted from my mind. We could've been at an R.E.M. concert last night and it would've been a waste of money for me."

"No big deal. You want to talk a little about how you ended up here?" Chase asked as he motioned behind him. "You remember Sergeant Jackson?"

Jackson winked at Delia as he took a step closer to the bed. He kept a straight face and stared into her eyes until she responded. He wasn't trying to be intimidating, but he needed to jog her memory. At least he hoped that was what he needed to do.

"Uh, yes," Delia said. "Hello again."

She showed little if any emotion with the greeting, but Jackson also noted she hadn't shown much emotion at all since they had entered the room.

"I'm going to be just outside the room," Langston informed them. "Give you some extra breathing room. If you need anything..." Langston was speaking to Delia but trailed off as she poked Chase in the back. "You behave yourself, mister."

Chase smiled and saluted her before she turned and walked out the door. "What happened, Delia?" he asked delicately, pulling up a chair and sitting next to her.

Jackson was positioned slightly behind Chase, giving him the opportunity to make eye contact with Delia, when possible. He did his best to flash her a pleading look, even though he wasn't sure how to accomplish this. Staying as serious and attentive as he could while she spoke was the best he could think to do.

"I came to town and it didn't take long to track Chumansky. I think it was my first night," Delia began. "Or maybe it was my second. I can't really remember."

"That's okay," Chase said. "Where did you track him?"

"I-I…" Delia's wheels were spinning. She closed her eyes for a long blink and when she opened them, she was looking directly at Jackson. "I was running surveillance from his old house, the one his ex lives in."

"You just happened to be there at the right time?" Chase confirmed.

Delia gave her brother a disoriented look. "Wait a minute," she said. "That's not right. I'm sorry, Chase. This is harder than I thought it would be."

"That's okay," Chase told her. "Take your time, sis. There's no hurry."

"How about a drink of that water, there?" Delia asked. Chase grabbed the Styrofoam cup and handed it to her. After downing it like a shot of tequila, she handed the cup back. "Let's try this again."

Delia sneaked another extended glance at Jackson. Chase remained unaware. She seemed to be timing them when her brother was looking away.

She's telling me something, Jackson decided. He placed his hands behind his back so he could cross his fingers without anyone noticing.

"I followed him," Delia continued. "It was from his work. I followed him all the way to his ex-wife's house. He had no idea. I parked up the road and walked to the house. Then I made my way into the wooded area. Just at the edge so I could stay undetected."

"Good," Chase said, encouraging his sister. "This is great. Very helpful."

"Eventually he came outside. I could tell he was up to something. He walked into the woods. I was able to follow him at an angle because of the light on his cell phone. He was using it to find the spot he was going to."

Chase nodded. Jackson remained still.

"When he stopped, I thought I had lost him. But then I realized he had started digging through the snow and mud. The noise he was making helped cover up the sounds I was making as I kept trying to get closer to him."

Delia sniffled and asked her brother for a Kleenex. When Chase reached for the box she shot another look at the uniformed police sergeant.

Please, please, please, Jackson said to himself.

After blowing her nose Delia picked up her story. "I got close enough to see everything that was going on. Once I was able to visually confirm that he had the coke in his possession, I stepped into his line of sight and drew on him."

"Then what happened, Dee?" Chase asked. "Do you remember? Take your time."

Jackson took a deep breath. He could tell Delia noticed it. He brought his hands back around and crossed them in front of his body.

"Yes," she said quietly. "Someone else was there." Delia looked at Chase and then to Jackson.

No, no, no! Jackson screamed to himself. He hadn't exhaled in fifteen seconds. He felt like he was having an out-of-body experience. As if this moment were a dream, like it wasn't really happening. Except it was. And life as he knew it was about to end.

"Okay," Chase said. "Who was it?"

Delia closed her eyes again. This time when she opened them they were focused between Chase and Jackson, at the wall or the door. Or nothing.

"It was a Hispanic male," she said. "He had a gun."

Jackson silently blew out the air he had sucked in a half minute ago.

Thank you, Jesus. No. Thank you, *Delia*, he thought. Jackson nodded ever so slightly. He figured if Delia saw it, she would know what it meant. If Chase happened to notice it, he would assume Jackson was merely indicating he was not surprised by who else was involved.

"What happened then?" Chase asked her. "Did he shoot Chumansky?"

Delia shrugged and shook her head. "I don't know," she said. "Someone else got me from behind. I blacked out immediately."

Jackson watched Chase's shoulders sink.

"I might know more," Delia added. "But I think I need to rest and let my memory come back to me, slowly. I'm kind of feeling sick to my stomach right now."

Chase stood up. "Okay," he said. He put the chair back in its place. "Get some rest, girl." He bent down and gave his sister another kiss on the forehead.

Jackson nodded at Delia again. "Thank you, Agent DeMarco," he told her. "Thank you very much for telling us what you did."

XXIX

The two-hour drive to Omaha in Claire's car was a journey filled with music, singing, and plenty of conversation. When they finally arrived at a hotel near Eppley Airfield, Barrett figured the car stereo had been turned up and down no less than a hundred times during the trip. He didn't have a problem with most of the music Claire enjoyed, but he hoped to never hear "Poker Face" by Lady Gaga again.

Before they left Gable, Agent Sheehan had made a brief house call to Claire's. He wanted to verify a few more details with Barrett before he left town. They agreed to meet again in the next few weeks and put their heads together in an attempt to solve the Clevinger murder mystery. Barrett doubted he'd have much to contribute — a detective he was not. But he also had nothing to hide and knew that providing as much information as possible would continue to weigh in favor of his innocence. Speaking with the FBI with mutual respect was a far cry from running in the opposite direction.

After a sit-down meal at a steak house, Barrett and Claire headed back to their hotel room. It was nine o'clock in the evening and although they were well aware they needed to be awake early the next morning, they both had other activities on their minds.

Barrett hooked the Do Not Disturb sign on the door and closed it, making sure to turn all of the locks. As he turned around and tried to decide how to make his move, he was pushed against the closed door by an already half-naked Claire. Because she had shoved him as he was turning around, he landed awkwardly against the door handle.

"Oww!" Barrett howled. "Damnit."

Claire pressed herself against him and kissed his lips hard. Barrett used one arm to stroke her hair and face while using the other to massage the pulsating pain in his side. After fifteen seconds he drew his head back but kept her close to him.

"Do I always have to get the tar beaten out of me during foreplay?"

"Nope," Claire said. "But you have to be ready at all times. I got needs, man."

Barrett grinned, leaned back in, and continued kissing her. Sometimes there was nothing else to say. Why ruin the moment?

The next morning the alarm clock blared with an unwelcome reminder that his flight was leaving for Denver in less than three hours.

"Nooooooooo," Claire groaned.

"I know. I feel the same way," Barrett told her. He meant it, but he was also happy to be heading home.

Claire sat up in bed with the sheet pulled up over her chest. "These last few days feel like a dream," she declared.

"Again, I know what you mean."

"This didn't seem possible a week ago," Claire continued.

"Ya think?"

"I don't know what I'm going to do without you near me," she whimpered.

Barrett crawled up beside her and turned her face to his. "You're going to be fine, Claire."

"You don't understand how much strength you give me," she told him.

He leaned forward and kissed her. "It's going to be okay."

"I believe in you, Barrett," Claire said. "I can tell how special you are. I know you didn't kill anyone. You're not capable of it. I think that's why I was so confused after you left and the accusations started pouring in."

Barrett smiled and leaned back against the headboard with her. "Hey," he said, suddenly, "I didn't tell you, I saw you on TV."

"Oh God!" Claire exclaimed. "The camera added ten pounds didn't it?"

"No," Barrett said. "I enjoyed seeing you again. You said nice things about me. Your smile brought back some good memories."

"I did smile, didn't I?"

"Yeah, when you were talking about me."

"What does that tell you?" Claire asked.

"It tells me you have a thing for me," Barrett answered. "Or maybe you have a thing for Keith Morrison."

"Wow!" Claire laughed out loud. "First of all, you already knew I had a thing for you — and you still took off, by the way — and second, that's gross!"

Barrett laughed. "I've always liked him. Although I don't think I like him as much now since he slandered my name in front of America for two hours."

"I guess he was nice," Claire admitted. "But he's a couple of years older than I am."

They snickered together this time.

"I'd like to hear him read *'Twas the Night Before Christmas*," Barrett said, glancing at the clock. "Crap! We've been sitting here for fifteen minutes. We need to get moving!"

He bolted from the bed, went into the bathroom, and turned on the shower. Claire didn't move.

"I'll use the shower first," Barrett hollered.

"Okay."

Her voice was barely audible through the sound of

running water and the wall that separated them. Barrett was certain she had a pout on her face.

Despite her obvious unhappiness, Claire showered and dressed at a brisk pace once Barrett was finished. They were only fifteen minutes from the airport, so the drive was a quick one. And a quiet one, too.

"You pissed or something?" Barrett asked. She had said nothing during the first five minutes of the drive.

Silence.

"You can't be mad," Barrett said. "There's nothing to be mad about."

More silence.

"Why aren't you talking to me?"

"You want me to drop you off here on the side or what?" Claire asked without taking her eyes off the road.

Frustrated, but not wanting to end their time together on a sour note, Barrett answered in an even tone, despite Claire's sudden attitude. "Park it in the lot, please. I'll mail you some cash to cover it."

"I can pay for it," Claire said. "I've got a job."

Barrett wasn't sure if that was a dig at him or if she was just trying to make herself not look needy. After all, Barrett *didn't* have a job.

They walked across the parking lot together. The only thing Barrett had with him was a plastic grocery bag that contained his one change of clothes and a few other essentials Claire had hooked him up with. Under his coat he was wearing a button-down white shirt and khaki slacks she had bought him the day they went to Adler. Barrett was beginning to sense he might be flying the friendly skies with an uncomfortable feeling in his stomach about Claire. That feeling subsided in an instant when Claire surprised him by grabbing his hand as they walked through the terminal. She didn't let go until Barrett got in line to check in and get his boarding pass. Claire stood back while he was doing this. When he was finished he walked back up to her and without warning threw his arms around her and held her close.

"I'm gonna miss you, Claire," Barrett said. "I can't thank you enough for all that you've done for me."

He could feel her reciprocate the embrace, but she said nothing in return. Barrett could tell she was squeezing harder as the hug continued, and he was not at all shocked to see tears falling like raindrops on her cheeks when he pulled back.

"You'll call me?" Claire asked, sobbing.

"I have the number right here." He pulled a piece of paper from his pocket and unfolded it.

"As soon as you land, okay?"

Experience had taught Barrett that crying was not attractive on any human being. But somehow Claire was pulling off a ridiculous stunt: she actually looked sexier while crying.

"Of course," he said.

"I just realized something," she said as she reached inside her purse for a tissue.

"What's that?"

"I haven't had a cigarette since you came back," Claire said.

"That's great," Barrett said.

"Yeah."

She reached up and pulled him down, kissing him this time with more passion than he could remember during their sexual encounters. It was so full of raw emotion Barrett became self-conscious, wondering if they had an audience beginning to surround them. When Claire finally released him, Barrett took a quick look around to confirm there was no crowd gawking at them.

"I need to go," he said.

"I know," Claire agreed. "Go."

Barrett couldn't think of anything to say. He leaned in and kissed her one last time. "For now," he said as he began walking backwards. "But not forever." Barrett blew her a kiss and waited for her to do the same before turning his back. He knew she was beginning to cry again, but he refused to look back because he knew the effect it would have on him.

***

Claire turned the ignition and began to back her car out of the parking place. She took a deep breath and exhaled before reaching behind her to look out the rear window. After paying the fee to exit, she made her way through the winding roads and eventually found herself back on the interstate. She didn't need to be at work until two, but she was ready to get home. The faster the better.

Twenty minutes passed before Claire looked in the mirror and realized she had been crying. She wiped her face, eyes, and nose with the back of her hand and turned the radio on, hoping to find something to occupy her mind. After flipping through the channels and finding nothing worth listening to, she turned it off and began singing to herself.

A few minutes into her personal concert she stretched to the passenger seat and grabbed her purse, pulling out her cigarettes.

***

For once, Jackson woke up feeling refreshed. He even took a shorter shower than usual and spent a few extra minutes with the family at breakfast. The children were already up, which was nothing unusual. Neither was the type to sleep in. Tyler was playing with his handheld game unit and Kaitlyn was watching *Dora the Explorer* on the TV. Caroline had even poured her husband a cup of coffee as he walked into the kitchen. This was not something she normally did.

Today feels different, Jackson thought. He hoped it

was because of what had taken place last night. There was a period during the meeting in the hospital room when he wasn't sure what was going to happen, but by the time he left it was clear that Agent DeMarco was sticking to her word and protecting Jackson.

After a quick bowl of cereal and some kisses, the police sergeant headed out the front door for his twenty-minute drive to work. The idea of living in Gable had never crossed his mind. Even if the idea had been on the table, when he and Caroline had kids it would've been thrown out the window. They had nothing against the Gable school district, but they had both grown up in Adler and graduated from high school there. They felt far more comfortable raising Tyler and Kaitlyn in a community they were familiar with.

At the top of Jackson's agenda today was to fix things for Bart Timmons. He had some ideas on how to do it, and would take things in whatever direction he could. Once he finished this, Jackson hoped he could put a little distance between himself and that entire situation. Sheehan hanging around the area to get justice for his sister was not good. Maybe once DeMarco was released he'd change his mind. Or maybe Jackson would need to have a private conversation with the DEA agent to convince her to persuade her brother to leave town. Granted, she had already done plenty for Jackson. But if push came to shove, he wouldn't be too proud to ask for more.

When he pulled into the station he saw Sheehan's rental car was already there. Jackson wondered if the guy was getting any sleep at all. What on Earth could be so important that he needed to be here this early in the morning?

As he opened the door and stepped into the lobby his question was answered. Chief Perkins was seated at his desk, his arms crossed. Sheehan was planted on the edge of Perkins's desk, one foot on the floor. He was facing someone who was sitting in the chair across from the desk. When Jackson walked in, they all looked up at him. The person in the chair turned around: it was Fast Eddie Clark.

Sheehan immediately pushed himself off the desk and strolled to Jackson, putting his hand out in front of him, as if to stop him from going any further. "Come here," Sheehan said. "Let's talk."

Jackson didn't say a word. He knew what was going on. He needed to get his story together, fast. Chase led him past Perkins, making sure to stand between Jackson and Eddie.

"Morning, Jack," Perkins greeted him.

"Good morning, Chief," Jackson said. "I think…?"

The two men entered the interrogation room and Sheehan closed the door.

"What's going on?" Jackson asked.

"Eddie Clark out there says he watched you shoot Tom Chumansky in the chest and then bury him."

"That's bullshit!"

"Okay, okay," Chase said. "Calm down."

"There's a guy out there accusing me of murder and you want me to calm down?"

"You know what I mean. Just chill out for a minute. Sit down."

The two men sat down at the table.

"He was running away from me the other day, Chase," Jackson said. "He might be the one who did it. He could've killed Chum and then scored the loot for himself."

"He says he was hiding and then running from you because he was afraid you were going to kill him. Said you might know he saw it happen."

"Oh for God's sake. Why in the hell would *I* kill Chum?"

"The money?" Chase suggested. "Maybe?"

"Are you insinuating—"

"No, I'm not. You asked a question."

"This is freaking ludicrous," Jackson said.

Chase rubbed his chin and continued. "Delia said she saw a Hispanic man with a gun before she blacked out."

Jackson was quick to react to the inconsistency. "Yeah, but it was dark. Who knows? It could've been Eddie. Besides, she's got a major concussion. I mean, come on. There's no way to know for sure."

"Maybe," Chase said.

"I mean it could've been Eddie that she saw or it's also possible Eddie was working with the cartel," Jackson suggested. "Maybe the guy she saw *was* Hispanic, but the guy who knocked her out was Eddie." That came together very well, Jackson thought.

"Hmmm," Chase said. "That's a good point. I hadn't thought of that."

"Can I talk to him?" Jackson asked.

"Who? Clark? God, no!" Chase replied.

"Why not?" Jackson already knew the answer.

"Conflict of interest, Sergeant. You know it."

"Will you do me a favor?" Jackson asked.

"What's that?"

"Ask him if we can search his home."

"I already searched it," Chase reminded him.

"Yeah, but how thoroughly? You were looking for signs of where he was. Now you're looking for signs that he committed a murder."

"Hmmm," Chase said again.

"If he hesitates to let us do it without a warrant, that could be a sign he's hiding something."

"It might also just mean he's not going to let us do it without a warrant," Chase said.

"Yeah, but still…"

"Okay, stay here."

Sheehan left the room. Jackson was pleased with the way this was panning out so far. He had hoped Eddie Clark would disappear forever, but now it was time to work things in a different direction — a direction Jackson had already planned for. Five minutes passed before Agent Sheehan returned. He closed the door again before speaking.

"Well, he's going to let us search his place."

"Did he hesitate?"

Chase shrugged. "Nothing unusual. He had to think about it for a minute."

"Great. Let's go!" Jackson got up from the table.

"Whoa, Sarge. You're not going anywhere. I'll take Hodge with me." Chase was still shaking his head when he finished his sentence.

"Oh yeah," Jackson said. "I forgot. Sorry. This is a little...weird."

"That's an understatement," Chase said and walked out.

***

Barrett wasted no time getting to the hospital. When his plane landed at Denver International Airport, he hurried through the terminal to the exit. The air was cold and dry, reminding him of how different the winter weather can feel out west compared to Iowa — or Maine. Within minutes he was in the backseat of a taxi and on his way.

The flight had been a bumpy one, off and on. When things were calm, Barrett had been able to drift into a light sleep. The time he had spent with Claire had been nothing short of fabulous. It had been a long, long time since he'd had that kind of experience with a woman. But he needed to focus on his family now. His father's health, his mother's needs. This was one of those times in life where everything else had to be put on hold. The irony of thinking this way after deserting his life in Denver only a few months earlier was not lost on

Barrett.

After the cab dropped him off on the street corner, Barrett jogged up the sidewalk and into the hospital. The lobby's clock told him it was ten forty. Not having luggage had significantly cut down the time it had taken to get out of the airport. With no phone to contact his mother, he went to the front desk and asked for guidance. A young clerk who was filing some folders told him that all the cancer patients were treated and housed on the third floor. Barrett hustled to the elevator and, once inside, pushed the button labeled with the number three. He positioned his arms behind his back and took a deep breath as the door closed and the car began its rise. Ten seconds later the elevator stopped and the door opened, signaling him to step forward.

As soon as he set foot in the hallway, Barrett could smell it. He didn't know what it was for sure, but he knew it wasn't good. Was it chemotherapy? Or was it...death? He had never smelled anything like it, which was probably why it made him so uncomfortable.

Barrett approached the nurses station in the middle of the floor. A short redhead was seated in front of a computer. She was wearing reading glasses and typing something but stopped when Barrett cleared his throat.

"How can I help you?" she asked, looking over the top of her glasses at him. Barrett guessed she was in her early fifties.

"I'm looking for my father. He's a patient here. Frank Greyson."

"Oh yes," the woman said. She stood up and pointed down the hall. "He's right down there in room 346. You must be the other son."

"Yes. Yes, I am." Barrett said. He could now read her name tag: Regina M. "Thank you very much, Regina."

He began to walk in the direction she had pointed, but Regina had more to say.

"You're welcome. They've been talking about you."

Barrett stopped and turned back to her. "They?"

"Your family."

Barrett stood, silent.

"I'm sorry," Regina said. "I didn't mean to make it sound bad. I just meant they've been talking about how you were on your way home and how great it was going to be to have you here. Your mother, especially."

"Oh," Barrett said.

"Mr. Greyson, I should tell you before you go in there...and this is off the record and just my personal feelings," Regina began. "I know it's none of my business, but I'm glad you're here for your family right now. Your mom is a nice lady, but I think she's in desperate need of...you. Coming back was a very good decision."

Caught off guard by her candor, another "Thank you" was all Barrett could muster up in response.

"My pleasure," Regina said with a smile. "If you need anything I'll be here until three."

As he moved down the hall to his father's room, Barrett wondered if Regina had just implied that she knew who he was, where he'd been the past several months, and why. It was probably a good idea to begin accepting this kind of possibility now. It was a part of his life that would be haunting him for a while. He couldn't just forget it had happened like he did with his marriage. People weren't going to let him.

When Barrett came up to room 346, the door was opened a crack. He listened from outside for a few seconds but could only hear the sound of machines. And there was still that damned smell. It was strong in the hallway, but as he pushed the door to his father's room open the odor overwhelmed him to the point of shuddering. He quickly regained his composure, however, and softly knocked on the door as he walked in.

"Anybody home?" he asked, immediately realizing he should've been more prepared for what he was seeing.

Barrett's focus was solely on the hospital bed. The man in it was wearing a nasal cannula that was supplying him oxygen. He was lying on his back with his eyes closed, dressed in a light blue hospital gown with a snowflake design. Barrett knew the man was his father, but it looked nothing like him. He continued to stare at the figure in the bed as his mother stood up from her chair to greet him.

"You're here!" she said in an excited whisper as she ran into him, throwing her arms around his neck. "Your father is resting. He had a rough night last night."

Barrett took his eyes off the bed and turned to his mother, giving her a kiss on the cheek. But this greeting wasn't good enough for Ella Greyson. She grabbed her firstborn's face and pulled him down to kiss him full on the lips — first once, then twice, and finally a third time before letting go.

"Rough night?" he asked.

"A lot of pain," his mother said with a grimace. She reached in again and hugged Barrett, this time putting her arms around his waist. When she did this he became aware of another person in the room. Sitting in a rocking chair in the corner and holding a book was his brother, Milo.

"Yo, little brother," Barrett said with a wave.

"Hey," Milo said with minimal enthusiasm. Barrett glanced at his mother who shrugged.

"This has been hard on all of us, honey. In different ways, of course," she clarified.

Barrett nodded.

"Come in here. Join us. Let's catch up," she continued. "My gosh, you must have a lot to tell us."

He followed his mother deeper into the room and walked around the bed to the sofa against the window sill. After removing his coat, he sat down next to her. Barrett looked at Milo, who had put his nose back in his book, *The Fault in Our Stars*. His brother was dressed in designer jeans and a peach button-down shirt.

"Actually Mom, I don't really feel like dumping everything out right now," Barrett said. "I just want to help in any way I can and focus on us...us and Dad, right now."

Ella Greyson put her hand on her son's knee and rubbed it like she was trying to start a fire.

"That's perfectly fine, dear. In fact, I think we'll leave you alone with your father for a while. Milo and I can go get some snacks. We've been here since eight and could use some refreshments and stretching."

Milo looked up from his book and closed it. "The food here sucks," he said, glancing at Barrett while rubbing his clean-shaven head.

"That's why we're going to leave the hospital to get something." Mrs. Greyson almost smiled. "In fact, we might as well just grab lunch for the three of us. By the time we get back—"

"That would be great," Barrett said. "Just surprise me. You know what I like."

Milo and Mrs. Greyson put on their coats and headed to the door. Before leaving, his mother gave Barrett one more hug and a kiss on the cheek. "I'm so glad you're here," she told him.

"Me too, Mom."

She walked out the door and closed it behind her.

Alone now, Barrett sat on the couch and picked up where he had left off, staring at his sick father. The situation was as bad as he had imagined. But imagining it and witnessing it were two different things. His father must have been forty pounds lighter, and he didn't have that much to spare in the first place. His skin was pale, his arms and hands bruised from needles and God knows what else. The only movement Barrett could see was the slow rise and fall of his chest.

This isn't fair, Barrett thought. Dad never did anything to deserve this. He's a good guy. He always tried to do right by everyone.

But Barrett knew that life wasn't fair. Bad things happened to good people every day and there was nothing anyone could do about it. He put his hands on his forehead and leaned back on the couch. The agony he was feeling deep inside was beginning to seep its way up and out of his body. He could feel himself ready to explode in a fit of rage and tears.

Not here, he thought.

Barrett took his hands from his face and shook his head back and forth like a wet dog. Standing up, he pulled the rocking chair next to the bed and reached through the safety rails to hold his father's hand. "Dad," he said softly. "I'm here."

The sick man did not react. Barrett fixated on the hand he was tenderly holding.

"I have so much to tell you, Dad," he said. "There's so much I want to talk to you about. I was so stupid to take off the way I did. I just...panicked. Stupid, I know. I thought they were going to pin Otto's murder on me. I really did. I didn't do it, though. I would never do something like that. I know you know that."

Frank Greyson took a deep breath. It startled Barrett, making him think something was wrong. He waited several seconds before his father finally exhaled and went back to his regular sleep breathing.

"I can't imagine what you're going through right now, Dad. I would take your place in a heartbeat if I could. You know that...right?"

Barrett felt the tears beginning to pour from his eyes. He held back the best he could, wiping his face with his free hand. Instead of saying more, he rested his forehead on the safety bar. Several minutes of silence passed. A few more tears drained from Barrett and fell to the edge of his father's bed. When he finally looked up again, Barrett was surprised to see his dad's eyes were open and gazing at the ceiling.

"Dad?"

The elder Greyson slowly turned his head. "Hey, son." He spoke groggily and smiled an uneasy smile. "It's great to see you."

Barrett squeezed his father's hand and felt him trying to reciprocate the affection. "I've missed you so much, Dad."

"Me...too." Frank Greyson winced as he attempted to shift his body.

"What are you doing?" Barrett asked, releasing his father's hand.

"Move...moving. I get...stiff and sore."

"Oh."

"And...that has nothing" — his father took a deep breath in the middle of the sentence — "nothing to do with the cancer."

"Can I do something?" Barrett offered. He didn't know what else to say or do.

"Yeah. Go...I have something...for you." Mr. Greyson did his best to motion to the other side of the bed. Barrett got up from the rocking chair and walked over to the nightstand on his father's left.

"There's just a cup of water, a pad of paper and pen, and a key chain with a key on it," Barrett said.

"The key," his father instructed. "Bring it."

Barrett did as he was told. When he returned to the other side of the bed he reached out the key to his father.

"It's for you," Frank said.

Barrett examined the key. The key chain had a number written on the tag. "Three, seven, three," Barrett read.

"Safe...deposit box," his father said. "There's stuff...you need."

"Dad," Barrett objected, "I don't want to talk this way right—"

Despite being deathly ill, weak, drowsy, and in tremendous pain, Frank Greyson was still able to cut his son off before he finished his sentence. "No. Listen."

Barrett went quiet.

"American Bank. Downtown Denver. Broadway."

The torment Barrett's father was going through was obvious with every word he managed to speak.

"Okay, Dad. Thank you." Barrett put the key chain in his front pants pocket.

Frank Greyson tried to reach for his son's hand but was unable to raise his arm far enough. Barrett saw this and helped his father by sitting back down in the chair next to the bed and reaching through the bars again.

"Barrett..." Mr. Greyson began. He closed his eyes and Barrett spied a lump in his father's throat. He couldn't tell if it was due to emotion or the weight loss. "Barrett, I love you."

Hearing those words in his father's sickly voice sent Barrett into another powerfully emotional moment. He wasn't as good at controlling it this time. Sputtering as his eyes welled up and tears streamed down his cheeks, he leaned down and kissed his father's bruised hand. "I love you, too, Dad."

A tear made its way down Frank Greyson's cheek as well. He closed his eyes again and reopened them a few seconds later. Barrett wondered if the pain was at its worst this time of day.

"And...I'm sorry," Mr. Greyson said.

"Sorry?" Barrett wiped his face dry with his arm.

"I'm sorry for...anything I've done to hurt you...in any way."

"Dad, what are you talking about?" Barrett said. "You've never done anything to hurt me. You've always been there for me. That's why I came back. I want to be here for you."

His father closed his eyes again and this time when he opened them they were as big as silver dollars. "Will you get...the nurse?" Mr. Greyson asked his son. Barrett could tell his father was in distress. Without saying a word he dashed out the door and looked for the nurse, any nurse. When he found one they rushed back to the room. Mr. Greyson's eyes were still wide open and he was flinching every few seconds. The nurse immediately announced she was going to increase the morphine drip to help with the pain. Within half a minute Frank Greyson was completely relaxed. Another sixty seconds passed before he drifted off into a deep sleep.

When the nurse left the room, Barrett returned to the couch, this time lying down on it. His intention was to take a nap, but there was too much information spinning through his mind to relax enough. Instead, he rested peacefully and listened to his father's heart monitor while waiting for his mother and brother to return with lunch.

***

Jackson had hoped the time he spent waiting around the station for Sheehan and Hodge to return would be a good opportunity to fix things for Bart Timmons and his DWI charge. But the task proved to be impossible with Chief Perkins watching him like a dog eyeing a bone.

"You're not buying his bullshit, are you?" Jackson finally asked him. "*You* don't think I killed Chum...do you?"

The chief shook his head. "I never said that. I'm just doing what the fed told me to do."

"And what was that?"

"Make sure you don't try anything," Perkins said.

"Like what?" Jackson asked.

"How the hell am I supposed to know?"

"Come on, Chief," Jackson pleaded. "The guy's nickname is 'Fast Eddie' — because he's a slick salesman. Get it?"

Perkins shrugged.

"I can't believe this. Of all the people to fall for something so ridiculous. You're the last person I would've—"

"I never said I believed him, Jack."

"Then stop looking at me like that."

"Like what?"

"Like you're afraid I'm going to club you over the head with my baton any minute now."

Perkins shook his head and put his face back in his paperwork. Not another word was said until Sheehan and Hodge returned. When they entered the station, Hodge was carrying several evidence bags. Jackson immediately rose from his desk. "Well?"

Sheehan wasted no time filling them in. "We didn't find any coke or gobs of cash," he said.

Jackson frowned.

"We did find some pot," Sheehan continued. He reached out to Hodge, who handed him a bag. "And this."

Chief Perkins stepped forward and took the bag from Sheehan. ".357 Magnum," he said.

"And it's only got five in the chamber," Hodge added. "Looks like it's been fired."

"Ha! See?" Jackson exclaimed, slapping Perkins on the shoulder. "I told you it was all crap!"

"We're gonna need to run ballistics on it and compare it to the bullet that was pulled out of Chumansky during the autopsy," Sheehan cautioned. "Fingerprints, too. The usual stuff."

"What did Eddie have to say?" Perkins asked.

"He doesn't know," Sheehan said. "We kept things under wraps. As far as he knows, we found nothing of interest. Until we know for sure there's a match, we can't arrest him. But we also don't want him running because he knows something's up."

Perkins stroked his chin before asking another question. "Where'd you find it?"

"Inside a vent," Hodge said. "It was hidden but not

that well-hidden."

"All right," Sheehan said, taking charge. "Let's get the gun to ballistics in Adler and do what we need to do. The sooner we figure this out, the sooner we can move on to other things."

Jackson nodded. "Anything I can do?"

"You can make the call to ballistics and the coroner in Adler, let them know what's going on," Sheehan suggested. "And then you can go catch a speeder or two. I can't believe how fast people drive out there on that highway of yours. And I'm from Atlanta, where everyone drives like an Andretti!"

"So, I'm a free man again?" Jackson confirmed.

"Of course," Sheehan said, holding his hand out. "Thank you for your patience, Sergeant. I hope you weren't too terribly offended. I had to be cautious."

"Don't mention it," Jackson said as he shook the agent's hand. "I understand completely. We're all on the same team here." He shot Perkins a look as he walked past him to his desk to make the phone calls.

***

Twenty minutes later Jackson left the station presumably to do just what Sheehan had told him to do: write some tickets. Still suspicious, Chief Perkins pulled Chase into the interrogation room and closed the door.

"Something doesn't add up, Agent," Perkins said.

"Ya think?"

"So you know?"

Chase smiled. "I appreciate the fact that you've been in law enforcement far longer than I have, Chief. But I've been trained to investigate highly complex cases. And this one is *not* highly complex."

"What do you think is really going on then?" the police chief asked.

"I don't know for sure yet," Chase said, "but you're right when you say something doesn't add up. Why would Clark come to us and tell us Jackson killed Chumansky, let us search his house without a warrant, all the while knowing he had left the murder weapon on the property?"

"Assuming that gun really was used to kill Chum," Perkins added.

"Right. And something tells me it was."

"Really?"

"Yeah, but I'm guessing we'll find no evidence that the gun was ever in Clark's hand," Chase said.

"No prints, you mean," Perkins said.

Chase nodded.

"But who and why?" Perkins rubbed his chin as he had earlier.

"I have to say, I think your sergeant is at the top of the list," Chase said.

"Damn him," Perkins groaned. "That's what I was afraid you were going to say. Why would he do such a thing?"

"It's too early to tell, Chief. That's why I let him go. He thinks we're off his trail. He's not going anywhere."

"Sonofa…" Perkins groaned. "I can't believe this."

"You've gotta act like nothing's wrong when you see him. Can you do that?" Chase said.

"Yes."

"Hodge doesn't know yet, either, by the way," Chase warned.

"What do we do now?" the chief asked.

"Can you go through your evidence records and check on any and all .357 Magnums that have been inventoried?"

"Sure."

"Just get a list printed out or whatever and then double check it against what you're supposed to have here physically."

"I see where you're going here," Perkins said as he opened the door. "And it's scaring the bejesus out of me."

"I know," Chase said. "Thanks, Chief."

Perkins waddled to his desk as Chase closed the door of the interrogation room again. He pulled out his phone and dialed his boss.

"Nolan Reed."

"Nolan, it's Chase. I'm going to fill you in on everything, but first I need to ask you to check on something."

"Holy crap!" Reed cried. "You're still there? Did you go home for Christmas at least?"

Chase remained silent.

"Good God, Chase." Reed said.

"Can you ping another mobile phone for me?" Chase asked, changing the subject. "I need to know where this person was around the same dates and times I gave you a few days ago, when Delia disappeared."

"Okay," Nolan agreed. "What's the number?"

Chase pulled a piece of paper from his pocket and recited Sergeant John Jackson's cell phone number to his boss.

XXX

The rest of the day at the hospital was uneventful for the Greyson family. Frank Greyson continued to sleep, and it seemed to Barrett that his father might be drifting away. Early on during his sleep he would groan, snort, twitch, or simply make an uneasy face filled with pain. But by four o'clock that afternoon he was no longer showing any signs of restlessness. When the doctor on call stopped by at four thirty during his final rounds of the day, Barrett tried to pick his brain by following him out the door when he was finished.

"Dr. Augustine," Barrett called from behind him. The doctor stopped and turned around. He was wearing casual street clothes with a stethoscope around his neck and a name badge clipped to his shirt pocket. At first glance Barrett thought he resembled Gerald McRaney.

"Yes," Augustine replied, glancing down at his clipboard.

"I'm sorry to bother you, but I was just wondering if you could tell me a little more about what's going on with my father," Barrett said.

The doctor thumbed through his clipboard before looking up to respond. "Well, I can't say for sure," Augustine said. "It does seem that his vital organs are beginning to slow down."

"That's not good, right?"

"It's not." Augustine said this with no emotion, the implication being that it was so obvious there was nothing more to say.

"Is he dying?" Barrett had to ask the question, but when he heard it come out of his mouth he thought it sounded stupid.

Augustine's eyebrows darted to his forehead. "Probably."

"How long does he have?" Why did every question sound so ridiculous? Barrett thought.

"Could be days," the doctor said as he glanced at his clipboard again. "Or it could be hours."

Barrett bit his bottom lip. "But his organs slowing down—"

"Would indicate sooner rather than later, yes," Dr. Augustine said, finishing Barrett's sentence. "I just can't tell you any more than that. I've seen patients hang on in this condition for a very long time. And I've also seen the opposite. It's highly unpredictable."

Barrett nodded and looked down at the tiled floor. "I understand."

"Anything else?" Augustine was ready to move on.

"No," Barrett replied. "Thank you, doctor."

The prospects weren't good, but Barrett wasn't sure what to do with the information as he walked back into the room. Another hour passed as his brother continued to read his book and listen to music on his phone while their mother watched television and occasionally walked to Frank Greyson's side and either stroked his forehead or held his hand. Barrett remained on one corner of the couch, thinking. Every fifteen minutes or so he would take a walk up and down the hallway. Regina had been replaced at the front desk by a younger, black woman, who would flash a smile at Barrett each time he passed by. He would reciprocate the smile and raise a hand, but he wasn't in the mood for conversation with strangers. Of all the things that had happened to Barrett over the last few months, his father's devastating illness and inevitable fate were what seemed the most unbelievable.

Frank Greyson had always seemed like such an indestructible human being. Unflappably strong, even in the face of difficult times. The ups and downs of his job were a perfect example, but even as a child he had faced plenty of adversity. Barrett's grandfather had left his wife, two daughters, and his son when Frank was only six, and young Frank Greyson fast became the man of the family. College was out of the question, financially, but he finished high school and began working full time almost immediately as a driver for a regional freight carrier. Working his way through the ranks over the next twenty years, Mr. Greyson became a well-respected employee and was recognized on several occasions for his outstanding efforts for his company and the industry. When he lost his job fifteen years ago, he did not miss a beat. Using the contacts and knowledge from his years of experience, he opened his own small third party logistics company. As the internet began to take over the world, it also helped Frank Greyson's business succeed in a manner not even he could've predicted.

"Sometimes bad things have to happen to people before good things do," his father had once told Barrett.

As five thirty rolled around, Ella Greyson talked her sons into going out to dinner together. She instructed them to take their time and bring her back a steak salad. Barrett was surprised that Milo was as open to this as he was. He had barely spoken three sentences since his big brother had arrived, and it was unclear whether he was simply in a funk due to his father's condition or if there was something else bothering him.

The young men spent an hour at Jeffrey's, a middle-of-the-road restaurant a couple of miles from the hospital. During their meal, the brothers, who had little in common, did their best to reminisce about the good times regarding one of the few things they did share: their father. Being ten when Milo was born, Barrett remembered many of the details surrounding his brother's birth. His favorite story to tell Milo was how he had wanted to name his baby brother "Elway" after the Denver Broncos quarterback, John Elway. His parents shot the idea down, though even Milo agreed the name "Elway Greyson" had a nice ring to it. This story would often lead to another, one that was built around the notion that Milo had been named after a waiter their parents had been served by on their first date at Casa Bonita in the late seventies. Casa Bonita was a unique restaurant when it first opened. It served a buffet-style Mexican meal and also featured a mariachi band, fire jugglers, and a waterfall with cliff divers. Apparently the story was only partially true. The couple did have an interesting waiter assisting them at Casa Bonita, but his name was not Milo. At least not to the Greysons' knowledge. That first date had been so long ago, neither Frank nor Ella remembered the server's name. All they recalled was how he had curiously disappeared for a long period, only to return with wet hair. They later found out he had taken a dive into the waterfall on a dare by his coworkers. Somehow Barrett had twisted the story over the years to make the mysterious waiter his brother's namesake.

"So, that book you're reading," Barrett mentioned when they returned to the hospital. They had just exited the elevator and were staring at the television attached to the wall in a corner of the waiting room.

"Yeah," Milo replied, still staring at the TV.

"Isn't that about a kid dying of cancer or something like that?"

"Yeah," Milo said. "It's a coincidence."

"How's that?" Barrett asked.

"It's required reading for a lit class I'm in."

"Oh."

"I guess it's inspired by Shakespeare, but it's kind of...meh," Milo said.

"I've heard that everything written is inspired by Shakespeare in some way," Barrett said.

"Yeah, I've heard that, too."

The brothers stood still and watched the forecast on the Weather Channel in silence. New Year's was only a couple of days away and the outlook was unseasonably mild for the celebration, with temperatures in the Denver area expected to reach the fifties.

Milo moved to one of the sofas in the waiting room and sat down. He leaned back and placed his palms over his face.

Sitting down next to him, Barrett put a hand on his brother's knee. "You okay?"

Milo took his hands from his face. There were tears in his eyes. "No." The three-word exchange immediately caused Milo to break into an uncontrollable sea of sobs. Although he was caught off guard by the sudden outburst of emotion, Barrett pulled his brother's smooth bald head to his shoulder for comfort.

"I just can't help but feel like I've not been a good enough son for him," Milo whimpered in his brother's chest.

"That's not even close to true," Barrett said. "Dad loves you. He loves to come up and watch your wrestling matches. He's very proud of you."

"I don't know," Milo continued. "Sometimes I blow him off when he tells me things."

"I've done that before, too. Dad knows what it's like to have a twenty-one-year-old son, Milo. You're his second and, in case you forgot, he used to be a twenty-one year old, too."

"Yeah?" Milo pulled his head away from Barrett and looked at him.

"Yeah. Absolutely."

Milo began to wipe his eyes and face and reached to the end table for a tissue. "I'm sorry," he said. "I'm sorry for losing it like this. I didn't mean to."

"Hey, it's all right," Barrett said. "We're family. I understand. This is hard for all of us. We're all dealing with it in our own way."

"So, you came back because of this?" Milo asked, clarifying the brief story Barrett had told him at dinner regarding his last few months.

Barrett nodded.

"Funny how that works," Milo said.

"What do you mean?"

"I mean, if Dad hadn't gotten sick and if you hadn't

seen it on the tube, you'd be in Canada right now and still thinking you were a wanted man."

Barrett considered his brother's epiphany. He hadn't taken the time to analyze the chain of events that had brought him here. At least, he hadn't looked at it in the same manner Milo had.

Before either of them had the opportunity to explore the point further, the door to the waiting room exploded open and the young black woman Barrett had silently greeted earlier during his walks appeared.

"I'm sorry," she said, out of breath. "You're...Greyson...right?"

Barrett and Milo stood up in unison as if they were soldiers coming to attention.

"Yes," Barrett replied.

The woman motioned with her hand. "Come quick!"

Rushing through the door, Barrett knew this had to be it — the worst was happening right now. As the three sprinted down the hall to room 346, a run that took seconds seemed to take ten minutes to Barrett. Peculiarly, he felt as if everything were moving in super-slow motion. Maybe the stress of this life-changing moment was overwhelming his brain. Much the same as everyone remembered where they were when they first heard of the events of 9-11, Barrett was now soaking up his surroundings and the details of this deeply personal tragedy.

As he ran past the desk, he could see patients and visitors peering from rooms on the other side of the hallway. Barrett knew they were wondering what the commotion was about.

Nothing to see here — go back to your own problems, Barrett thought.

After making a sharp move to avoid a man with a ponytail pushing a cart, Barrett followed Milo and the girl into his father's room. At first he thought everything had gone back to normal speed, until he saw the distraught look on his mother's face.

"What happened?" Milo cried out.

Ella Greyson spoke through her tears. "He took a massive breath. A big inhale. And...and that was it. He's...gone, boys. Your father passed away."

"Oh my God, Dad!" Milo bellowed as he bent down to his father, who was still lying in the same position he had been in when they left for dinner. Ella and her youngest threw their arms around the motionless body and cried hysterically for Frank Greyson to return to them.

Barrett could feel the tears streaming down his face but again, the world around him was moving in a strangely slow and distant manner for him. He glanced at the young woman who had just ushered them to the room. He could now see her name tag clearly: Shawna S. She was assisting a sandy-haired woman doctor who was leaning over his father, checking his pulse.

"Time of death, seven ten PM," the doctor announced quietly. Shawna wrote the information down on her clipboard.

Moving to his brother and mother, Barrett knelt down behind them and gently hugged them to join the mourning. He was crying too, but he almost felt like he had left his body and no longer had control over it.

His father was gone, just like that. Barrett had been talking to him earlier today and now he would never speak with him again. It all felt like a dream —a nightmare — and this was probably why Barrett's brain was having a difficult time processing it. The slow motion, out-of-body feeling was his mechanism for dealing with the stress. He wanted to believe this wasn't real. But it was, and he knew it. He also knew he needed to get a grip, even if it was just for a short while.

Pulling away from his family, Barrett retreated to the edge of the couch. Milo and Ella Greyson continued to sob but had pulled themselves together enough that they were now able to keep their heads up and wipe some tears from their faces.

"Take as much time as you need," the doctor who had pronounced Frank Greyson's passing said. "We'll be right outside here if you need anything."

Barrett gave them a quick nod and the women left the room. After a few more minutes, Milo joined his brother on the couch. Their mother had moved the chair next to the bed and was holding her husband's hand while stroking his cheek with the other. She was whispering to his lifeless body, but Barrett could not make out what she was saying. He figured it was probably best that way.

When Ella Greyson finally stood up, her sons did the same. She turned to them and Barrett could see she had regained most of her composure. Her eyes were still red, but now they were dry. She dabbed her nose with a tissue. "I suppose," she began, "we need to find out what to do next."

"Yeah," Milo said.

"Can I get a few minutes with Dad?" Barrett asked his mother.

"Of course, honey." Mrs. Greyson looked at Milo. "Maybe your brother will come with me to speak with the nurse and doctor."

"Sure, Mom," Milo said. She grabbed her purse and they left Barrett alone with his dad.

The room was eerily silent. It seemed strange to Barrett that his father was in the room but not making a sound. At any moment he expected his father to twitch or open his eyes and say, "Boo." But the only noise Barrett could hear was his own footsteps as he took a seat in the chair next to the bed. He gazed at his father for what he knew would be the last time in this natural state.

"I don't know what to say, Dad," Barrett began. "I don't know what I'm going to do without you. I missed you so much for the few months I was gone, how am I going to get through a lifetime?" A tear left the corner of Barrett's eye and traveled to his chin. He wiped it away and continued. "I know you will always be with me in some form. I promise I will make you proud. I will not let you down. I will live my life by following in your footsteps and take what you've taught me and apply it to everything I do. I want to be just like you, Dad. It's all I've ever wanted. You showed me how to do it right. I'm your oldest son and I will uphold our family name with respect."

Three more tears uncontrollably streamed down Barrett's face. The words had flowed from him as if he had prepared a speech, even though he had not. Instead, each sentence was straight from the heart. Barrett meant every bit of it and knew his father had heard him, wherever he was at right now.

He bent down and kissed his father's cheek for the last time.

"I love you, Dad."

***

It didn't take long for the results of the ballistics report to climb their way up the chain. Chase had made a couple of phone calls to speed up the process. Being a federal agent had its perks, and pushing tests through the local facilities was one he used often. Instead of having the information sent to the Gable PD, Chase specifically requested he be notified by phone when it was ready.

The next morning while Chase was eating breakfast at his hotel, the call came. He spooned up the last of his lukewarm biscuits and gravy and grabbed a banana on his way out the door.

The findings of the test did not surprise Chase. The bullet pulled out of Chumansky during the autopsy without a doubt had been fired from the .357 Magnum recovered from Eddie Clark's house. No fingerprints were found on the gun. It had, in fact, been wiped completely clean. The entire scenario smelled like a setup to Chase, but he couldn't be certain. Either Eddie was really dumb — not out of the realm of possibility as far as Chase was concerned — and had wiped the gun clean but hadn't had the sense to get rid of it, or he was being set up to take the fall. The prime suspect to do such a thing was Sergeant Jackson, but that was only because of Clark's allegation. There was no evidence to even suggest it, not yet anyway. At this juncture, Chase had no choice but to move in the direction the gun was pointing.

Before leaving the station in Adler, Chase arranged to have Sergeant Hines assist with making the arrest. Then he called Officer Hodge and instructed him to swing by the Adler PD and join Hines to arrest Eddie Clark. Chase gave Hodge the details but asked him not to explain any of it to Clark, that Chase would personally do this at the station within the hour.

He also asked Hodge to not mention the arrest over the radio. Chase thought Hodge seemed intelligent enough to know something was up, but he was also wise enough to not object or question the federal agent.

When Chase arrived at the Gable Police Station, Chief Perkins was the only one in. Jackson had taken the day off, so Chase quickly filled Perkins in.

"I thought we agreed this case was heading in another direction," Perkins said.

"It is," Chase said, "but we've gotta do it this way. Which reminds me, how are things coming with your inventory?"

"A pain in the ass," Perkins said. "It's not that there have been a lot of firearms used around here. It's just that our system isn't as organized as I thought it was."

Chase poured himself a cup of water and took a quick drink. He tossed the cup in the wastebasket and peered through the blinds of the window near Perkins's desk. "Looks like they're here," he announced.

"I'll have the physical inventory done by the end of the day," Perkins added as the front door opened.

"You wanna tell me what the hell's going on here?" Eddie Clark barked at Chase as he was led into the lobby by Hines and Hodge. His hands were cuffed behind him.

Chase waved at them to follow. He led them down the hall to the interrogation room. Hodge cuffed Eddie to the table and closed the door, leaving Chase alone with him.

"I'm waiting, man," Fast Eddie said. "This is a crock of crap!"

"You ever seen this before?" Chase lifted the bagged .357 Magnum from the counter next to him. He pushed it across the table at Eddie. With his free hand, Clark examined the gun through the plastic.

"I don't know," he said. "I've seen a lot of guns. It's one of my things. You know, a hobby."

"So you don't know if you've ever seen this gun, or if this one is yours?"

"I mean, I've seen a .357 before," Eddie explained. "But I don't own one. I have no idea if I've *seen* this one before."

He's genuinely perplexed, Chase decided.

"Wait a minute," Eddie continued, patting the gun with his hand. "Is this—"

"This was the gun used to kill Tom Chumansky," Chase said. "We found it in your house yesterday."

"What?" Eddie cried. "Where?"

"In an air vent."

"Man, I didn't kill Chum!" Eddie exclaimed. "He was my friend. Someone must've planted that gun in my place." He pursed his lips and frantically shook his head back and forth. "I know just who it was, too."

"I know," Chase said, rolling his eyes. "It was Sergeant Jackson, right?" He was mocking Clark. But not because he didn't believe him. He simply wanted to see what the accused would say.

"It was!"

The two men stared at one another. When Eddie finally caught his breath he spoke again, this time more calmly. "Listen to me," he pleaded. "I watched him shoot Chum. It was point-blank in the chest."

"You could know that and still be the one who did it,"

Chase said.

"Let me finish," Eddie said. "I didn't tell you this before. I wasn't the only one who saw it happen."

"What? What are you talking about?"

"That lady DEA agent was there, too," Eddie explained.

"You're lying." Chase was beginning to wonder if he was wrong about Jackson. Maybe Fast Eddie Clark *was* trying to pull a fast one.

"No, listen," Eddie continued. "I was supposed to meet Chum out there. We were gonna dig up the money and coke. I got lost trying to find the spot in the woods, showed up late. By the time I got there, Chum was being held at gunpoint by Jackson and the DEA agent."

Chase shook his head in disbelief. "Are you telling me that Jackson and Agent DeMarco were both involved in Chumansky's shooting?"

Eddie curled his lip and pulled his head back as if he'd been served spoiled milk. "What? No! The opposite."

"Will you finish your story before I decide to shoot *you*?" Chase snapped, holding up his thumb and index finger. "I'm this close."

Eddie nodded. "I don't know who got there first or if they got there together, but Sergeant Jackson was going psycho and the DEA agent was trying to calm him down. And then he shot Chum and the agent was just as surprised by it as I was. And then Sergeant Jackson turned his gun on the agent."

"What? Really?"

"Yes!"

"And then what happened?"

"He took her guns and her phone from her. And then…" Eddie took some extra time before finishing the sentence, "he buried Chum."

"And then…?" Chase knew there had to be more.

"He led the agent away with him," Eddie said. "I mean, he had his gun pointed at her. And no, I didn't follow them. I'm not stupid. Whatever was going on with Sergeant Jackson, I was pretty sure he'd have killed me too if I'd've shown up on time. No, I was freaked out. I got the hell out of there."

Chase's mind was catching up with all of the new knowledge that had just finished pouring in. Things were beginning to make sense. A lot of sense. Too much sense.

"Stay here," Chase said, getting up from the table. "I need to leave for a little bit."

"Where am I gonna go?" Eddie asked. He tried to hold up his cuffed and chained hand from the table, but the FBI agent had already left the room.

***

The drive to Adler seemed much longer than it had previously. Chase had already made the trip several times since coming to Iowa, but this was the most important one. He drove as fast as he could without endangering anyone else on the road.

The information that Eddie Clark had just spilled to Chase was huge. More than likely it explained why, when Delia was fading in and out of consciousness, she mentioned Jackson by name. If everything Clark had said was true, Delia had a lot of explaining to do. Why would she lie about what had happened to her? Chase tried to give his sister the benefit of the doubt, thinking it would make sense for her to lie when Jackson was present. Chase hadn't had the opportunity to speak to Delia alone since she began feeling better, so maybe that was why he hadn't heard the truth from her lips yet. He felt good about his theory and prayed to God he was right.

When he was about half a mile from the hospital, Chase's phone rang. He checked the caller ID and realized it was, coincidentally, St. Mary's Hospital calling him. "Hold your horses," Chase said out loud to no one. He figured there was no point in answering the call. Whoever it was would probably see Chase within the next five minutes.

He parked the car in the visitor's lot and raced across the street. After taking the elevator to the fourth floor, he ran down the hallway to room 409. Throwing the door open, Chase burst into the room.

"Delia, you need to tell me what really…"

He stopped himself when he realized the person in the bed was not his sister. Instead, a man in his forties was lying on his back, unconscious. Chase could hear a ventilator keeping the man alive.

He spun around on one foot and retraced his steps out of the room. When he reached the hallway again he heard his name.

"Agent Sheehan!"

Chase looked to his right and saw Dr. Langston rushing to meet up with him.

"I just tried to call you a few minutes ago," she said when she got within earshot.

"Where's my sister?"

"That's what I was calling you about," Langston said. "She's in four eighteen now, but there's something else..."

Chase began to follow the numbers down the even-numbered side of the hall.

"Agent Sheehan…" Langston called out to him. Chase pretended he didn't hear her, and the doctor moved swiftly behind him, continuing to speak. "We moved her out of ICU the day after you were last here," she explained frantically while tailing him, "but just an hour ago she had a relapse."

Dr. Langston completed her sentence just as Chase opened the door to room 418 and witnessed Delia once again lying unconscious in a hospital bed.

"Blood has built up in her brain, a swelling," Langston said, this time with more bedside manner. "It's called epidural hematoma."

"You said she was okay," Chase said without turning to look at her.

"All indications pointed in that direction. But she took a massive blow to the head," Langston said. "That kind of trauma to the brain can be very unpredictable."

Still standing in the doorway, Chase closed his eyes to ask his next question. "What's next?"

"Surgery," Dr. Langston said. "Like, within the hour. That's why I called."

Chase's chin dropped to his chest. He let out the slightest of groans. It was so soft that the doctor almost didn't hear it while standing directly behind him.

"I'm sorry, Agent Sheehan."

***

The day after Frank Greyson's passing was a busy one. Barrett and Milo joined their mother at the funeral home around ten to make arrangements. There were also phone calls to make, flowers to purchase, life insurance paperwork and a litany of other things. And they also had to answer the door to allow family friends to drop off food: there were meat and cheese trays, a six-foot sub sandwich, cookies, pie, cupcakes, lasagna — even restaurant gift cards.

Milo left for work around two fifteen, but not before he ate a heaping plateful of lasagna and two cupcakes. Barrett and his mother contemplated the ritual of bringing food to families who have experienced a death. They came to the conclusion that people felt so helpless that the only thing they could think to do was bring food to the house. It gave them a reason to stop by and offer their condolences in person. It was a nice gesture, and Barrett felt no ill will towards any of the nice people who had dropped by with their offerings. Of course, all of them would also utter some form of "If there's anything I can do," before they left. It always sounded like an empty offer but customary, just like the food.

Barrett knew most of the people who came over to visit. If any of them were curious about his return to Colorado, none of them gave so much as a hint. He assumed they knew about his departure four months earlier. How could they not? He and his parents had all appeared on a network television show. But he was glad he didn't have to explain himself to any of them. In fact, the only person he really wanted to explain himself to had just died.

After a big sandwich and slice of peach pie, Barrett decided to head over to his condo and make an attempt at settling back in. He had slept at his parents' house the night before, but his long-term intention was to return to his previous residence. He owned it, after all. And his parents had been nice enough to keep up with the payments during his absence, though his mother had mentioned this morning that they would've eventually sold it had Barrett not returned.

Since he no longer had an automobile, Ella Greyson automatically gave her son the keys to her SUV. He kissed her goodbye, telling her he'd be back in a couple of hours. She seemed to be handling herself well so far, considering the circumstances. Barrett knew the next hurdle would be getting through the visitation and funeral. Because of the upcoming holiday those rituals would take place three days later, on the second of January. It was not something he was looking forward to, but Barrett knew it was all for show. He had already said goodbye to his father and pledged his future to him. The funeral was more for everyone else. The rest of Barrett's life without his dad had already begun.

As he drove out of the Morning Glory subdivision, he remembered the key his father had given him during their final talk. Amidst the chaos of Frank Greyson's passing, Barrett had completely forgotten it in his pants pocket. His mother had washed yesterday's clothes earlier that morning so he could wear them again today. Still driving, Barrett positioned himself so he was able to slide his hand into his pocket. Feeling the key, he breathed a sigh of relief and pulled it out. The tag was a bit worn from the water, laundry soap, and dryer, but he could still read the number without difficulty.

After glancing down at the digital clock on the dashboard, Barrett decided making a pit stop at American Bank wouldn't hurt. He had the time, and the bank would still be open since it was only a quarter to four. With the holiday and funeral coming up, it could be several more days before he would have another opportunity. Barrett was curious as to what his father had given him, and this was a wonderful chance for him to have some more private time with his father in his thoughts.

American Bank was an old building in downtown Denver not far from Coors Field. Barrett hated driving in this area. Of course there would be no baseball game to cause traffic jams today. But the one-way streets, traffic lights, and odd turns were enough to cause even the most skilled drivers to pull their hair out if they weren't familiar with it. The truth was, Barrett was familiar with it and still hated it. The Clevinger Group was located nearby, and for years he had fought the maze of downtown Denver during his drive to and from work.

At least when he was driving to work every morning Barrett knew he would have a place to park when he got there, thanks to the parking garage. But today, going to the bank, he assumed parking would be an added stress. Luck was on his side, however, as he quickly located a spot and pulled the big black SUV into it. After using his credit card to pay the parking meter, he walked a block and a half to the front steps of American Bank. He looked at the massively wide stairway that led to the front of the large stone building. If it weren't for the red, white, and blue sign above the doors that read "American Bank," Barrett knew most people would assume the landmark was a government office. Maybe a courthouse or police station, a place where important decisions were made.

Not knowing for sure what to do or who to see, Barrett walked through the front door and looked over the layout. Directly in front of him were a number of teller windows where people were standing in line to make their final withdrawal or deposit for the year. To his right were some restrooms and to his left he saw what looked like an office area for executives as well as an open space with desks for other bank personnel.

Barrett figured approaching one of those people

would make more sense than standing in line and asking a teller who probably wouldn't be able to help him anyway. As he rounded the corner, a man sitting at the first desk immediately made eye contact with him.

"Hello there," the man said popping up from his chair like a finished piece of toast. "Can I help you with something?" Barrett figured the man was in his late fifties or early sixties. His hair was white and he was tall and lanky.

"Yes, I need to get into a safe deposit box rented by Frank Greyson," Barrett replied, pulling out the key. He read the number from the tag: "Three, seven, three."

"Well, you've come to the right place," the man said. "I'm Bill Gallagher, by the way."

"Barrett Greyson," Barrett responded with a handshake.

Gallagher pulled a manila folder from his file cabinet and skimmed through some paperwork before continuing. "Looks like you're the only other person authorized. We'll just need you to fill out some paperwork and then I'll take you to it." After inviting Barrett to sit down, he handed him a form to fill out and then asked for his driver's license so he could make a photocopy. When all of the formalities were out of the way, Bill Gallagher stood up again.

"Follow me," he said. Barrett took the key from the desk and walked behind Gallagher, past the other desks in the room. It wasn't that Barrett was *trying* to walk behind him. Gallagher's long legs were simply carrying him that much faster. They strolled thirty yards or so before the tall banker turned right and opened a door. After walking another ninety feet, Gallagher stopped and pulled a key chain from his pocket. As he searched for the key he needed, it gave Barrett a chance to catch up.

"I know it's one of these three," Gallagher said without looking up. He tried the first key. "Nope, not that one. I bet it's this one." He put another key into the lock. "Aha!" The door opened. "Here we go."

Gallagher entered the room and turned around, signaling Barrett to join him. Along the two walls on either side of him were row upon row of individually numbered doors.

"What was that number again?" he asked.

Barrett glanced at the key to be sure. "Three seventy-three."

Gallagher assessed his position in the room. "Okay. Should be down here." He put his finger out in front of him and followed the numbers. Barrett took his time and soaked up the strangely ominous atmosphere of the room full of safe deposit boxes. For a moment he thought the compartments resembled miniature morgue drawers. Shaking the disturbing notion from his mind, he made his way to Gallagher's side.

"Here it is," the banker said, tapping the numbers on the box. "Go ahead and give your key a try."

Gallagher took two steps back and Barrett stuck the key in. It turned without a problem and the door pulled open.

"I guess you're good," Gallagher said.

"Does this come out?" Barrett was clueless. He had never been inside a bank vault or seen a safe deposit box.

"Yes. And if you want I can escort you to a private room to do whatever you need to do with the contents," Gallagher explained.

"I guess that would be okay," Barrett said. "I don't really know what I've got here but..."

"It's not a bad idea," Gallagher said. "Not that we ever have any problems, but I'm always skittish about leaving people in here alone. I mean, I'm not worried you're going to steal anything. But if something did turn up missing or whatever, we go back through the records and whoever—"

"Makes complete sense. I understand." Barrett put his hand up politely to stop him from continuing.

"You can go ahead and pull that out then and follow me," Gallagher told him. The two walked back through the door of the vault and turned left, heading further down the hall. The next door on the left was also locked. After Gallagher unlocked it, he held it open for Barrett.

"Here you go," he said. "I'll be right across the hall when you're finished."

Barrett thanked him, and Gallagher closed the door as he left. Placing the box on a table, he moved a chair out of the way and stood over it as he removed the top.

The contents of the box immediately perplexed him. The first thing Barrett identified was his father's mobile phone. He might not have recognized it were it not for his ongoing attempt to persuade his dad to get rid of his Android and make a move to the "dark side" with an iPhone. When Barrett picked it up he could feel something attached to the back. It was a sticky note. In Frank Greyson's handwriting it read: "Play Videos."

As he waited for the phone to power on, Barrett reached for another item in the box. He was already assuming the phone contained a "goodbye video" from his father.

Something to make me cry again, Barrett thought.

But the next keepsake he was now looking at was so peculiar it yanked his mind away from shedding more tears, instantly. Inside a one-gallon Ziploc bag was what looked like a plastic grocery store shopping bag. In large, handwritten block letters on the outside of the bag was the phrase: "DO NOT OPEN."

Barrett's forehead wrinkled with confusion. The phone made a sound signaling it was now ready for activity. Fingering through the icons, he found the one for the camera, pictures, and video. Taking a deep breath and exhaling in preparation, Barrett touched the first video in the menu.

The first five seconds of the video were completely black, but the audio gave a clear indication that someone was holding and maneuvering the device. When Frank Greyson's face came into view, it was obvious he was holding the phone in front himself, filming "selfie-style."

"My name is Frank Thomas Greyson," his father said on the video. "I'm shooting this video with the expectation that it will be used as needed when I'm gone."

The video moved so quickly that Barrett didn't have a chance to ponder what was being said, although none of it was making sense to him.

"Tonight I have committed a heinous act," Frank Greyson continued. "I'm not proud of myself. But I am owning up to it, at least in theory, by way of this video confession."

"Confession?" Barrett repeated out loud. Without warning, the angle of the video changed and suddenly the screen showed a horrific scene. Lying on the floor behind Frank Greyson was the lifeless body of Otto Clevinger.

Barrett could feel his heart pounding with more intensity than it ever had before. The beats had tripled in a matter of seconds. Feeling light-headed, he reached for the chair he had abandoned a few minutes earlier. As he sat down, the angle of the video changed again. This time Barrett could tell his father was behind the phone in order to shoot a close-up of Otto. As the video moved closer, it became clear that the dead man's eyes were still open. Barrett looked away, but as he did Frank Greyson spoke again.

"This is what was used," he said as his hand appeared from behind the phone holding a plastic shopping bag. Barrett immediately recognized it as the one in the Ziploc bag in front of him. His father shook it in his bare hand, making the annoying crackling that all shopping bags made these days. The video went black again, but only for a split second. When the picture returned, so did Mr. Greyson's face.

"My name is Frank Greyson...and I murdered Otto Clevinger."

Book 4

Smoke and Mirrors & White Lies

XXXI

Chase picked up the latest issue of *Sports Illustrated* for the third time in ninety minutes and began thumbing through it yet again. Delia had been in surgery for two hours. The longer it took, the more nervous he got. Dr. Langston was unable to tell Chase how long the procedure would last. She had it explained it was impossible to know how much pressure there was to relieve until they opened up his twin sister.

Things had gone from bad to better to really good and suddenly to complete shit in a matter of days. Chase tossed the magazine onto the coffee table in front of him. He pressed his palms to his face.

Good Lord, I have a splitting headache, he said to himself and then immediately felt guilty for complaining about pain in *his* head. Chase's thoughts were quickly interrupted by the sound of boots coming his direction at an uneven pace. He glanced up as Chief Perkins made his way to where the FBI agent was sitting. Chase began to stand.

"You don't need to get up, Agent," Perkins said with the wave of an arm. Chase did anyway, and the two men engaged in a handshake. The chief placed his left hand on top and held it there to express his concern. "I'm so sorry, son," he said. "I can't imagine what you must be going through right now."

"I appreciate that," Chase said. Perkins let go of his hand and the two men sat down in adjacent chairs.

"If you wanna talk…" Chief Perkins said.

Chase wasn't sure if Perkins meant it or not, but it didn't matter. Instead of talking about Delia's condition, he wanted to change the subject and keep his mind on other things. "Anything new on the Chumansky murder?" he asked.

"As a matter of fact, yes," Perkins replied. "That's the other reason I'm here. I have good news. Or, I guess it's actually bad news."

"I figured you'd find something eventually," Chase said.

The chief shook his head and snorted before continuing. "Technically, just the opposite. I found something that was *missing*."

"That's what I meant."

"I gotta hand it to you," Perkins said. "You knew what you were talking about. It shouldn't have taken me as long as it did. It's not like there have been that many guns entered in evidence at our station. On the other hand, there's been a lot of crap put in there. And I'm a bit embarrassed at how crummy our filing system has been over the last couple of years; but I finally discovered the record of a .357 Magnum that is not in inventory."

"No empty bag, nothing?" Chase asked.

"Zilch," Perkins confirmed.

"Makes sense. If you're a cop and you're going to steal it, you take any evidence that it ever existed in the first place." Chase let his words echo through the waiting room as he pondered them for a few extra seconds. "But now that I think about it, why wouldn't he delete it out of the computer system?"

Perkins smiled. "That's an easy answer," he explained. "He couldn't. We're a laid-back, small town department, but every once in a while I do things that make sense. See, I'm the only one with the password to the inventory system."

"Ahh," Chase said in delight. "So if something was

missing from inventory *and* the system…"

"It would have to be *me* who did it," Perkins said. "Of course, I never expected something would ever actually happen. Guess it shows what I know."

Chase leaned forward. "Chief, it's imperative that you don't say a word about what you've discovered to Jackson."

"Of course not."

"And it's also extremely important to not let him know about Delia's condition," Chase said. "I'm waiting to hear back from my office about one other thing regarding your sergeant. Depending on what information comes back to me, I may need him to think Delia has leveled with me and finally told me 'the truth' about what happened to Chumansky."

Chief Perkins raised his eyebrows in surprise. "You think your sister was involved?"

"I'm fairly certain she knows more than she's told me," Chase said, "but that's all I can say for sure."

"Wow," Perkins said with a sigh.

"I was coming here to chew her ass about it…" Chase added contritely.

Chief Perkins responded with a sympathetic pat on the FBI agent's knee. "You'll still get a chance to ask her about it," he said.

Chase nodded.

"You need anything?" Perkins asked as he rose from the chair. "I'm gonna head out."

"I'm good, thanks," Chase said.

"You'll keep me posted?" Perkins said.

"Yes, sir. Of course."

The police chief turned and began to hobble back up the hallway but stopped short and spun around to face Chase again. "Hey, one more thing," Perkins said as Chase looked up. "How about you don't refer to him as 'my sergeant' anymore, okay?"

***

The entire notion was absurd, unfathomable. He continued to glance at his father's phone as if it might grant his wish and disappear, making the last thirty minutes nothing more than a nightmare. But every time he looked down at the passenger seat next to him, the phone was still there. It was all real. Too real. And so insane.

Just down the street from his condo, Barrett pulled into a strip mall with a liquor store. His friends always made fun of the establishment because it was next door to a dentist office. The adjacent neon signs were the same color and type style and read "Liquor Dentist" when seen from a distance. He had no idea why he was here but after opening the door Barrett marched straight for the hard stuff.

His heart hadn't stopped racing since he first saw Otto Clevinger's cold, lifeless stare on the cell phone video. He skimmed through the bottles on the shelf: whiskey, rum, gin, vodka. When he came to the Everclear he paused. Grain alcohol. Why not? After paying for the bottle, he hopped back in his mother's SUV and drove on home.

When he entered his condo he made a mad dash for the kitchen. Although it had been four months since he had been inside, Barrett took no time to look around. He did notice that it smelled oddly clean, but this was not surprising after hearing Agent Sheehan's observations a few days ago.

Dad probably cleaned the place up to wipe away any DNA, Barrett thought. And it was a good thing he had, too.

He went to the cupboard and grabbed a glass. After placing it on the kitchen table, he sat down in front of it and the bottle of booze. He pulled the phone from his pocket and set it down on the table, too. Scrolling to the videos, he pressed play again. Initially, Barrett thought he would be able to force himself to sit through what he had already watched. But after a few seconds, he realized this was not going to happen. He pressed fast-forward until he reached the section of the video where he had stopped watching and left the bank.

"My name is Frank Greyson…and I murdered Otto Clevinger."

Barrett's entire body shuddered in disbelief, just as it had earlier when he was alone inside the private room at the bank.

"When I learned my body was being destroyed by cancer, a number of things went through my mind, including all of the experiences I would miss out on. I would never see my sons get married. Never hold my grandchildren in my arms. There were even surface-level things like never getting the opportunity to retire and enjoy life without having to go to work every day. But there was also a deviously selfish idea that I would soon be gone and could not be punished for any crimes I might commit between that moment and my death."

"Good Lord, Dad," Barrett murmured out loud.

"Having never been a deeply religious man, I'm not concerned about being judged for this heinous act in the afterlife. I have witnessed my hardworking son, Barrett, become as loyal to Otto Clevinger as he was to me. Maybe more so. But I did not end Mr. Clevinger's life out of jealously. I ended it to right a wrong that disgusted me because of the nepotism. Otto Clevinger has shown great favoritism to his son and completely disregarded my son's loyalty to him and his business. In return, I am showing favoritism towards my son with this deed."

"What?" Barrett said.

"I probably have murdered the wrong person. It might have made more sense to dispose of that clueless son of his. But my rage is not as much with Boyd Clevinger as it is — or was, anyway — with his father, Otto. It is he who allowed this situation to progress to what it is today. Barrett now works in the shadow of an inferior Clevinger, aggressively dealing with Boyd's flaws in both character and work ethic. If Otto Clevinger had not blindly allowed his son to take over his company without having any idea as to what the hell he was doing, this would not have happened."

Who is this guy? Barrett wondered.

"But as it stands, I had nothing to lose by doing what I did only a few minutes ago."

This knowledge that his father had felt compelled to share with him was causing Barrett nothing but torment. What was he supposed to do with this information? Live with it? Give it to the FBI to clear his own name and anyone else's? Had Frank Greyson even considered how this was going to affect the world after he had left it?

Barrett was beginning to feel like he never knew his father. If he was capable of something like this, what else had he done that his family wasn't aware of? And rooted deep within, Barrett also wondered who he might really be as Frank Greyson's son. Was he capable of these kinds of things as well? He didn't think he was, but could he be certain? Could he share this information with anyone? His mother? His brother? If he did, how would it affect his life? Their lives? The burden of the information and of what to do with it was overwhelming.

Instead of opening the bottle of Everclear, Barrett grabbed the only beer from a nearby craft brewery left in his refrigerator. Under normal circumstances he would've poured it in a glass and sipped it for an hour. But this wasn't normal circumstances. He cracked it open and took a long swig directly from the can.

"Wow, that's good," Barrett said out loud. And to think he might never have had the opportunity to drink it again if he had made his way to Canada. And if he had gone to Canada he also knew none of this would be happening to him right now.

The afternoon had not turned out quite the way Barrett had planned. But at least he had made it back to his condo. He turned the television on but, as he had assumed, the satellite service had been disconnected. There was also no running water. There was, however, still power. He flipped the stereo on in the living room and began scanning the radio channels. Nothing grabbed his interest. A couple more sips of beer before flipping to satellite radio. No service.

When Barrett disappeared he had left behind a lot of favorite personal items. His iPod was one of them. He went to his bedroom and shuffled through his things before he found it almost exactly where he remembered leaving it months ago. He brought it out to the living room and placed it in its dock on the stereo. Then he sat back down in the recliner and began to scroll through his 15,000 songs. Barrett was almost done with his beer when he finally settled on Pink Floyd's *Dark Side of the Moon.* He fell asleep before the song "On the Run" had ended.

***

"They're treating me like a criminal around here," Randy spouted off.

Derrick Janssen glared at the client he'd been appointed to represent. "You *are* a criminal, Mr. Fowley," he reminded Randy.

"Not *this* kind!" Randy cried, yanking his handcuffed wrists from the table between the men.

"You're a registered sex offender, you stole a car in front of twenty-seven people in a restaurant, and you threatened a small child and fired a gun multiple times in front of those people. Are you kidding me? Oh yeah, and you also stole a minivan." Janssen was proud of himself. He hadn't even needed to refer to the file while reciting the offenses.

"Are you here to defend me or crucify me?" Randy asked with a snarl.

"If you want me to defend you, I'm going to need your help. You can start by being honest," Janssen said.

"For the record, I didn't steal the car at the restaurant," Randy explained. "I traded it in. But it sounds like you've already got everything figured out."

"You need to be honest with yourself," the attorney continued. "You're a repeat offender. An ex-con. You went haywire at that truck stop in front of all those people. No judge is going to let you off with a slap on the wrist."

"Then don't let it get to a judge," Randy said.

"Yeah, great idea. How?" Janssen asked. "Stealing the minivan is a Class D felony. You could be looking at five years, and that's just for *one* of the stolen vehicles and not taking into account your random public firing of a gun. And yes, you stole the car, too. You weren't at a dealership." Derrick Janssen shook his head in amazement. He hated defending these guys; they were all morons. Trying to get criminals off the hook was not what he had in mind when he went to law school. "Do you have anything else to say?" he asked Randy. "Anything at all? Something that could help me save you, maybe?"

Randy lifted his chin higher this time as he spoke. "Yeah," he said. "That guy who was with me. Greyson."

"Yes, Barrett Greyson," Derrick said, this time checking a document inside a brown folder.

"Yeah. He made me do it."

"What? No he didn't." What the hell is this guy thinking? Derrick wondered.

"Yeah," Randy repeated. "He did."

Janssen tilted his head as if it would help him understand what the big, goofy blonde guy was saying.

"Get it?" Randy added, slowly. He stared at his attorney.

"Sure," Derrick replied with a slow nod. He didn't but assumed it was better to not let on.

"You seem young," Randy said. "Are you sure you're a lawyer? Or did one of the security guards send their kid in here to play make-believe?"

Derrick finished the note he was writing and then closed the folder. "I assure you, I've passed the bar."

"How old are you?" Randy asked him.

"Twenty-nine."

"Jesus Christ!" Randy exclaimed. "Did you just pass it last week?"

"Are we done here?" Derrick asked. "I've got nothing else." He got up from his chair and turned towards the door. Knocking on it, he signaled the guards outside that he was ready to leave.

"Hey," Randy called out from the table. Derrick turned around. "I need to get out of here. I'm begging you."

The door opened and the guards entered.

Counsel made eye contact with his client one last time and nodded before heading through the doorway. When he made it to the front lobby, he opened up the folder and read the note he had written: *Reminds me of Dad.* Janssen didn't even know what this meant or why he had written it down, other than the fact that it was true. Making fun of Derrick's youthful appearance, saying things that should make sense but didn't. The only difference was his father had never spent time in prison.

Maybe it was time to twist and turn the facts to the point of uncertainty and create reasonable doubt. Most people would call it "lying." But lawyers didn't think of it that way. It was their job to do this kind of thing. It was something they were good at. Derrick was no exception — he knew he was already a pretty damn good lawyer. And despite how much it repulsed him to help a guilty man beat his charges, the desire to succeed in what seemed like an impossible situation was much stronger. It wasn't even a desire for Derrick. It was a need. That's what Derrick told himself, anyway. It was easier than opening his eyes to the similarities between the criminals he represented and himself.

He was going to get Randy Fowley what *he* wanted. What *he* needed. They both had the same goal of getting him off the hook. It was just for different reasons. And, of course, he reminded Derrick of his old man. The dad who never seemed to be pleased with him.

***

Claire scooped up the tip Cameron Dahl had left her on the bar for his late afternoon ritual of beers and an appetizer: two Bud Lights and a plate of fried pickles. She wiped up the wet spots with a dish towel: one from his water glass and one from his bottles of beer. She turned around and looked at herself in the mirror. She looked like hell. Her hair was coming out of her ponytail and the rings under her eyes gave the impression she hadn't slept all night — and she hadn't. Thoughts of Barrett continued to haunt her that afternoon at work. She wasn't sure how to proceed in this so-called relationship. Was it a relationship? She wasn't even sure. Barrett did call her from his mother's mobile phone a couple of hours ago. He hadn't said much except that his father had had a difficult night. When Claire told him that she missed him he told her he missed her, too. There wasn't much more before he ended the conversation by saying he'd "be in touch soon," whatever that meant.

Claire simply couldn't help but think there was something else she was supposed to be doing. Something didn't feel right. The man she had a strong romantic interest in was losing his father, and here she was six hundred miles away working the same dead-end job she'd had since before she was old enough to work, legally. The urge to call Dr. Hammond was fluttering at the edges of her consciousness. She could use more advice from that down-to-earth shrink of hers. The cost was getting ridiculous, though. Claire knew better than to try and turn Hammond into her own personal paid friend. At least she was smart enough to realize the inclination was there and was inappropriate. What could Dr. Hammond do, anyway? She'd probably tell Claire to figure it out herself. Maybe that was the answer. Instead of paying Dr. Hammond for her clarity, perhaps it was best for Claire to have her own therapy session inside her head.

"What can I get for you today, Phil?" Claire asked.

"I'll just have a Bud and a cheeseburger," he told her. Phil Belmar worked at the nearby dairy plant and came in two or three times a week.

Claire knew what Dr. Hammond would tell her right about now: She needed to stop playing the victim. Okay great, Claire thought. What else would she say?

After writing down Phil's order and hanging it up for the kitchen to cook, Claire popped open a bottle of Budweiser and set it down in front of him.

"You ever get a crazy thought in your head and almost do it?" Phil asked Claire before taking a swig of his beer.

"Huh?" She was caught off guard.

"Let me give you an example," Phil said. "Today I was so pissed off at my boss. I won't bore you as to why; let's just say he's a passive-aggressive jerk. But anyway, I was so angry I almost got in my car and left during morning break. Had the car in gear and everything."

Claire held her position. "Really? What made you not do it?"

"Sensibility, I guess. I need the job. If I took off — quit — I would be without income, indefinitely."

"But you'd be free of the crap," Claire reminded him.

"Yeah," Phil agreed. He stared at himself in the mirror over her right shoulder. "I could probably get by for quite a while. I'm not married, don't have any kids."

"Sounds like you're trying to talk yourself into it."

"Well, the more I think about it, the more I'm not so sure if taking off was the sensible thought and not doing it was the 'crazy' one," Phil said.

"Hmmm," Claire said. She could feel her own wheels turning inside her head.

"Who knows," Phil said. He paused again before shutting down the subject. "Maybe someday."

Claire looked at the entrance to Stubby's, half

expecting Henry Fields — well, Barrett Greyson — to come bouncing through it the same way he had that Sunday afternoon last September. If she had a chance to do it over again, would she have done anything differently? Probably not. She had pulled out all the stops, taken all of the steps she thought were necessary. The late evening with the wine and sleeping on his couch. Attending Chum's party with him. Despite the tragedies that occurred that night, Claire wouldn't change a thing. She had gotten too much good out of the risks she had taken during the week Henry/Barrett was in town.

***

"Do you have any idea how long you're going to keep my client here without charging him with a crime?" Lucy Brock asked. Her short haircut made her look like she was a colonel in the Army instead of a lawyer. She was hovering above the chief, who was seated at his desk.

"Look," Perkins said to Eddie Clark's attorney. "I'm only doing what the Federal Bureau of Investigation is telling me to do."

"You are aware that they still need to abide by the law, right?" Brock barked. "Just because they're the FBI doesn't mean they get to hold someone and not charge him."

"Yes, counselor. I'm well aware of a citizen's rights. I also know that we can detain him for seventy-two hours."

"What's the holdup?" she asked.

"The holiday."

"It wasn't a holiday when you arrested him," Brock said.

"Again," the chief began, "I'm only doing what I'm told to do. I can't release him. Federal orders."

"Well then, you need to get me on the phone with someone who can." Lucy Brock marched to the interrogation room and slammed the door behind her.

Chief Perkins picked up the phone in front of him and

dialed a number. "Hi, Agent," he said. "How's Delia?"

"She just got out of surgery a little while ago," Chase reported from the other end of the line. "The doctor told me she's still in critical condition. It's impossible at this point to say whether or not the surgery did any good."

"I'm sorry to hear that," Perkins said. "I'm praying for her, son."

"I appreciate it, Chief. What else is going on?"

"We've got to do something with Clark. His attorney is going apeshit."

"I was afraid of that," Chase admitted.

"What's the plan?"

"I'm still waiting to hear back from my office on a couple of other things and when I do, if my suspicions are correct, we'll be able to let him go," Chase explained. "And then we'll have another arrest to make."

"Oh boy," the chief said unenthusiastically.

"Stall him a little bit longer, please," the FBI agent requested.

"It's a 'her,' and you don't know this woman," Perkins said. "She's a pit bull disguised as a poodle. She's liable to bite my fingers off."

"Then we'd have another lawsuit on our hands," Chase joked, trying to lighten up the mood.

Perkins sighed. "All right. But let me know as soon as you know something. I don't want her here any longer than necessary."

After hanging up, the chief made his way down the hall and timidly tapped on the interrogation room door as if he were not in his own police station and not the police chief.

"Yes," Lucy Brock called from inside. Perkins opened the door.

"I'm working on trying to get you out of here," Perkins said, trying to diffuse the situation. "I understand the frustration, and I'm on your side."

"Just a minute ago you weren't," Brock reminded him.

"Wrong. I said I was only doing what I was told. Believe me, I probably want you to leave more than *you* want to leave. Just sit tight. I have a call in and it's being checked on."

"I've heard that one before," she said, frowning.

"Chief Perkins," Eddie spoke up. "You know I didn't do this, don't you? I can tell."

"You need to be quiet," Brock said.

"I don't have to do shit."

"I strongly advise you to shut up then," she snapped back.

"I'm not saying anything wrong," Eddie said. "Chief, admit it. Not only do you know I didn't kill Chum but you know who did. It was Jackson. You know it, don't you?"

"I'm gonna tape your mouth shut," Brock grumbled. Eddie continued to stare at Perkins, who broke his silence.

"I don't know a damn thing about anything," Perkins said roughly and closed the door.

***

"Happy frickin' New Year, everybody!" Boyd Clevinger hollered at the top of his lungs. He lowered his glass and stepped down from the sofa he'd been standing on. It was only eight o'clock on New Year's Eve, but Boyd was already hammered.

"Thanks, Boyd-oh!" a voice called from the crowd in front of him. "But save it for midnight, bro!"

"Ah, screw you!" Boyd belted from his seat on the sofa he had just dismounted. He poured himself another glass of Crown before rising and weaving amidst his guests. His wife, Fredrika, had chosen to drive to Durango to spend New Year's with her parents. Things hadn't been the same since

Boyd's father had died. Or since she had found out about his running around on her.

Getting married was something Boyd *had* to do. It was required — expected. He was an only child in a prominent family. The next step was to have children. The only problem was the idea of it scared the hell out of him. It was easier to have safe sex with other women than it was having unprotected sex with Freddy and risk her getting pregnant. Instead he used every excuse in the book to not be intimate with his wife. On the occasions that they did end up doing it, Boyd would often pull out a last-minute birth control method, so to speak. At first Freddy questioned this odd behavior for a married Catholic man, but Boyd would merely mumble, "I forgot what I was doing" or some other lame excuse. Eventually, Fredrika Clevinger learned to simply be happy that her husband still had an interest in her.

Boyd was only a little surprised she had taken off for the holiday the way she did. Knowing what he'd been doing the night his father was murdered, he'd assumed she wouldn't let him out of her sight for the rest of his life. And it had been that way for a while. But Boyd figured she had grown tired of trying to micromanage his life, and at some point the phone calls, texts, and efforts to police his every move had decreased.

Tonight was supposed to be a celebration — the Baby New Year was arriving. And yet Boyd felt more alone than ever before. His father was gone, and there was a strange feeling of emptiness inside him. It wasn't depression. Well, he *was* depressed. But there was something flowing through Boyd Clevinger that made him feel at fault for his father's murder. He hadn't killed him. He had no idea who had. Treating his father horribly all those years had never been something he'd thought about while in the moment. He had no inkling that, when his father was gone, he would no longer have anyone else to blame for his own shortcomings. No one other than himself.

"Boyd! Want a bump?" A male voice called out to the

party's host.

"On my way, Trav!"

The offer to snort some cocaine violently jerked him away from deep thoughts about life, death, and unhappiness. Boyd approached the table where his friend Travis Harrington stood inhaling deeply and wiping excess white powder from his nose.

"Have at it, bro!" he said.

"Don't mind if I do," Boyd replied. "Since I bought it."

The young men laughed in unison as Boyd snorted a short line of his own.

"Woooow-weeee!" he howled and then shook his head rapidly like a wet dog. "Gooooooood morning, 2015!"

"What!" someone yelled from behind them. "Did we miss the countdown?"

"Was the microphone turned on?" Travis countered while whipping around to see who had asked the stupid question. "Don't worry, you'll know when it's time!" He shook his head as he turned back to Boyd. "What an idiot," he muttered under his breath.

"Who was that?" Boyd asked.

"No clue," Travis admitted before they both let out another hearty guffaw.

"I'm gonna go mingle," Boyd told him.

"Dude, you're the CEO of a company. You don't 'mingle,'" Travis told him.

"I don't? Well then, what do I do?"

"I don't know. But just don't use that word. It sounds like something you'd find in a teenage boy's gym shorts."

"Not appealing," Boyd said.

"You see? Exactly. Don't mingle."

As Boyd shuffled through his party, he continued to ponder the notion that he had indirectly killed his own father.

Maybe he was too wasted right now to think sensibly. If he said it out loud — actually heard the words — he would probably come to his senses and realize it wasn't his fault. Was it possible that someone had hated his father enough to murder him? Well yeah, it was. It had happened, after all. But who? Otto Clevinger had made enemies over the years. But so had Boyd. Sitting inside the top three was Barrett Greyson. Had he killed Boyd's father?

He probably should've killed me, Boyd thought. Why would he kill Dad?

The day of the funeral had been difficult for Boyd, but it was easily forgotten when the riches of his late father began to appear in his bank account. There was no one else. Boyd never knew his mother — she had been killed in a tragic car accident when he was just a baby. He had no siblings. It all flowed right to him. Along with the responsibility of the Clevinger Group.

Boyd knew there were probably people who thought he had killed his father. Yes, his father annoyed him. And yes, there were times when he had said some horrible things that were overheard by others. But he was not a murderer. He was not the type of person that would take a human life.

I don't think I am, anyway, Boyd said to himself.

The coke was making his mind race, and there was only one way he could think of to reverse the trend once the clock struck midnight and the partygoers began to file out.

Boyd scanned the room for Travis. He wasn't difficult to find thanks to the orange flannel shirt he was wearing. When he reached his friend, Boyd placed a hand on Travis's shoulder and leaned into his ear. "A little later, you wanna shoot me up?"

XXXII

"You knew I was going to find something goofy when you asked me to check into this, didn't you?" Nolan asked the moment he picked up the phone.

"You must have something big," Chase replied quietly from the waiting room. "Talk to me."

"Well, Sergeant Jackson was with Delia the evening she disappeared. Or at least they were in the same vicinity."

"Same as Chumansky and Clark, too, right?" Chase surmised.

Nolan shuffled some papers around on his desk before he found the document that verified the hypothesis. "Yep, you got it. Holy hell. What happened out there?"

"I don't know for sure, but it's enough info to justify digging deeper," Chase said.

"You gonna bring Jackson in?"

"Tomorrow morning."

"Okay. Let me know what else you need. Keep in touch with me about Delia, too. We're praying for her."

"Thanks, Nolan."

"Happy New Year," Chase said bitterly after he hung up. He'd skipped genuine New Year's wishes for Nolan and cut the conversation short on purpose; he didn't want to get into a long conversation about his sister.

This trip to Iowa has been the most insane, off-the-grid investigation imaginable, he thought. He didn't regret it though. He'd *had* to do it. His sister was missing. And now he was finally going to get some answers.

Sergeant Jackson knew more than he was telling. Was he not the person everyone thought he was? How much did the Gable PD really know about this guy? Why did Delia presumably lie about what had happened? Was she scared of Jackson? The entire ordeal was mind-boggling and Chase hoped to God he really was on the right track. Regardless, Jackson had some explaining to do.

He pulled the contact list up on his phone and dialed Chief Perkins.

"Perkins."

"Chief, I have the news you wanted to hear but didn't want to hear," Chase said.

"Uh-oh."

"You got that right. Sergeant Jackson was in the same area as Delia, Chum, and Eddie Clark the night people started disappearing."

Chief Perkins remained silent.

"Chief? You still there?"

"Yeah."

"I'm sorry," Chase said.

"Me, too."

"Maybe there's a logical explanation," Chase suggested.

"I doubt it."

"Me, too. But you never know." Chase swallowed hard and changed the subject back to the investigation at hand. "So, what can you tell me about Jackson? I'm going to do a thorough database search on my own but thought I'd ask you first."

"Well, I'm not sure," Perkins said. "What do you want to know? What are you looking for?"

"Really just anything out of the ordinary. About his

past or…it's hard to say. Anything unusual about him."

"I don't know. I've always liked him," the chief admitted. "Always found him pretty normal. You know, a wife and kids. You met them all."

"I know it seems strange to think like this, but what do you know about his past?" Chase realized Perkins was having a difficult time fathoming there could be a darker side to his sergeant that he was unaware of.

"I'm gonna have to think about this, Agent. I mean, he was in Saudi for Desert Storm. And I know he worked some security jobs before he came here. He grew up in Adler," Perkins said. "I realize that's not unusual or very helpful. I'm just not thinking straight right now."

"That's okay, Chief," Chase said. "I'll do some snooping of my own, and I'll let you know what I find. We can talk tomorrow morning, early. What time does Jackson usually show up?"

"About eight."

"Let's meet at seven. Good for you?"

"Normal time for me, yep," Chief Perkins agreed. "I'll sleep on this."

"One more thing — about Clark," Chase said.

"Oh yeah," Perkins said. "I almost forgot. That wouldn't be good. I'd end up in the pit bull's doghouse!"

"You can let Eddie Clark go now. But it's under two conditions. He needs to go straight home and cannot go out in public until eight tomorrow morning. And he needs to understand he is still a person of interest in the case."

"Got it. Do I need to write anything up?"

"You mean to have him sign off on? Naw. With an attorney there right now it's pointless. You'll be there all night trying to get the wording to her liking. Just…I don't know…make Clark spit and shake on it or something like that. Sounds like something he'd understand, right?"

"We're gonna arrest Jack tomorrow, aren't we?"

Perkins asked the FBI agent.

"You don't have to be a part of it, Chief. I can handle it. I don't want you to feel like you—"

"I got this one, Agent," Chief Perkins interjected. "I kind of feel like I should, ya know?"

"Yeah," Chase said. "I understand. Completely."

***

No one likes funerals, this much Barrett knew. But the discomfort multiplied when the funeral was for a family member. Funerals weren't designed for the family to say goodbye. They were a way for everyone else to say goodbye. Open caskets, eulogies, and the reception afterwards — it was all designed to help people through the difficulty of losing a loved one.

Barrett would rather not have to go through another viewing. It was too creepy, too haunting. After the visitation the night before at the funeral home, he had seen enough of his father's motionless body. But it wasn't like he had a choice. He needed to be there for his mother and for Milo, too. Both of Frank Greyson's parents had preceded him in death, but he did have a brother, Dale, who had flown in from New Hampshire for the funeral. He was three years younger than Frank and hadn't been very close to him for many years. Unaware that Frank was even sick, it was quite a shock to Dale Greyson when he learned of his brother's death.

A number of Frank Greyson's coworkers had shown up for the visitation. Barrett knew only one of them well, Curt Ryerson. Curt had worked with or for Barrett's father for many years. He started as a forklift driver, then was a local delivery driver, and eventually became a terminal manager. When his father was let go from his job many years ago, Curt was devastated and eventually teamed up with him again when Frank Greyson started his own business.

"Your father is going to be missed so much," Curt

said as he shook Barrett's hand firmly and pulled him in for an embrace.

"Yeah," Barrett said. "Thanks."

"He was such a special person to me," Curt continued. "He was always there for me, lending a hand when I needed it. I don't think he had a cruel bone in his body."

Not knowing what to say, Barrett simply nodded. It wasn't in agreement, necessarily. But what Curt didn't know wouldn't hurt him. It's not like Barrett could try to explain to him why he was wrong.

"He thought very highly of you, too, Barrett. You know that, don't you? He never stopped talking about you."

"Milo, too, I'm sure," Barrett said.

"Well, yeah but…" Ryerson paused for a beat before finishing his thought by lowering his voice, "he *really* loved you."

Barrett nodded. "Thanks, Curt."

"You're a good man. Keep doing what you're doing, Barrett. Follow your father's lead and you'll be just fine." Curt began to walk away with a pat on Barrett's arm but leaned in to whisper one more thought. "And I don't know why you took off or what happened with your boss. I mean, it's not my business. But I'm sure you left town for a good reason and I'm also sure your dad knows it, too."

Barrett managed a meager smile. "Thanks again. Yeah, it's…umm…all good. Thanks." When Curt had moved on, Barrett shot a quick glance in the direction of his father's casket.

The main feature of the service was Pastor Spaulding's eulogy. Barrett had declined to be an additional speaker, citing his distress over the loss of his father and his desire to avoid breaking down in front of all those people. The truth was he was having a difficult time processing what he had learned only a couple of days earlier and felt he was in no condition to say much of anything good about his father.

As the pastor spoke, Barrett listened halfheartedly as he tried to figure out whether or not his own life had been a lie to this point. Who was he? Where had he really come from?

"When you lose a parent, the child in you dies," Pastor Spaulding said through the microphone at the podium. "We still have the memories, but the innocence is gone. No longer is our beloved father the indestructible superhero we once thought he was."

There was sniffling in the seats behind Barrett, Milo, and their mother.

"We are here today to show our love and support for Frank Greyson's very precious family. Not only have we experienced our own personal feelings of loss over Frank's passing, but our hearts have been drawn to them and will continue to be with them.

"It is our human nature to want to understand everything now, but faith requires that we lean and rely heavily on God even when things seem unclear."

"My name is Frank Greyson…and I murdered Otto Clevinger."

"Throughout his life, Frank Greyson combined a carpe diem attitude with faithfulness to his family and an untarnished professionalism at work. Everything Frank Greyson did, he did with integrity. He was also loyal, sometimes to a fault."

"I probably have murdered the wrong person."

"Whatever pickle someone was in, no matter how busy Frank was, he would drop everything to help. He would give anyone the shirt off his back. Yet while his principles were rigid, he was no stiff. He could find humor in absolutely every situation."

"I had nothing to lose."

When the service ended, almost everyone who had attended followed the hearse to the cemetery for the brief burial ceremony. Despite the trauma Barrett had been experiencing by himself the last few days, he was still capable of putting on the sad face for his mother and brother and anyone else who expressed their condolences or grabbed him for a hug. Underneath it all, Barrett Greyson was being torn apart in a different way and for a different reason.

***

"Did you know about Jackson's issues in the war?" Chase tried to take a sip of the piping hot coffee Perkins had poured him.

"Issues? What issues?" The chief leaned back in his chair and waited for an explanation.

"It wasn't too big of a deal," the FBI agent explained. "But I guess he had some problems distinguishing between fantasy and reality."

"What? Come on!" Perkins said, flashing a look of disbelief across his desk at Chase. "You're saying he's cuckoo?"

"No, that's not what I mean," Chase said. "I don't really know what it means, but we might need to find out more. His records mentioned some psychotherapy when he returned to the states and was discharged, but that's not necessarily anything unusual."

"See? I mean, the guy was probably just having a hard time with the war. That had to be awful," Perkins said. "I was lucky. I was just barely too young for Vietnam. I never had to deal with any of the trials and tribulations of fighting overseas and watching people die and stuff."

"Sure, I hear you, Chief," Chase agreed. "It could be nothing. Like I said, I was just looking for unusual stuff."

"Well, I stayed up late last night and couldn't come up with anything fresh or new or exciting to tell you about. Jack has always done me and our little department right. I keep going back and forth on this. One minute I want to punch him in the face because it seems so obvious. The missing gun from evidence was the real kicker for me. But knowing him the way I do, I just have a hard time imagining he's involved."

Chase shrugged and held his hands open.

"I know," Perkins added. "It looks like he is. And I'm honestly looking forward to finding out what he has to say about it all."

"I'm pretty sure I'll know it if he tries to lie," Chase said. "I've gone over things in my head rigorously and can't think of any other logical explanations."

"It would be nice if you were wrong and there actually were some logical explanations."

"I understand why you feel that way," Chase said sympathetically. "But that would also mean we're not even close to solving any of this — pardon the elementary term — 'mystery.'"

"We still have Eddie Clark," Perkins reminded him.

"I just don't think he's guilty of anything other than being in the middle of Chumansky's mess."

"The cartel, though."

"Well, yeah. What about them?"

"They could've killed Chum," Perkins suggested.

"Oh, I still think they're involved," Chase agreed. "I find it hard to believe they're not behind all of this."

From outside the window next to Chief Perkins' desk came the sound of a car pulling into the parking lot, crunching the snow that covered portions of the asphalt.

"Well, this is a rarity," Perkins murmured. "I hope you were done talking. Jack's here early."

"Okay. Just follow my lead, Chief. No cuffs just yet."

Chief Nathan Perkins took a deep breath in preparation for what would surely be the most uncomfortable confrontation he'd ever had.

"Morning fellas. What's new?" Jackson asked as he entered the station.

"You're not usually here until eight," Perkins commented.

Jackson shrugged. "It's a new year. New beginnings. I thought it would be good to get started early."

Perkins looked down and shook his head.

"We need to have a talk, Sergeant," Chase said calmly.

Jackson looked surprised but recovered nicely, like a shortstop bobbling a ground ball but keeping it in front of him.

"Sounds serious. Is everything okay? Am I in trouble....again?" He offered a half smile combined with hesitant nervous laughter.

"Let's go into the other room," Chase suggested.

"The interrogation room?"

Chase said nothing. Instead he stood up and walked to the interrogation room and held his hand out, motioning for Jackson to follow and enter.

Just then the front door opened again and Officer Ryan Hodge walked in. "Morning all. Happy New Year!"

Hodge had barely finished his greeting before his boss gave him his first instructions of the year. "Perfect timing, son," Perkins said while heading down the hallway with the familiar hitch in his step. "I need you to watch the front."

"Sure, what's going on?"

But Chief Perkins had already entered the interrogation room and closed the door.

***

"What do you know about .357 Magnums in evidence?" Chase asked Jackson as soon as the door closed behind them. The three men were still standing. Jackson's face immediately went pale but miraculously regained its color almost as quickly.

"I'm not quite sure what you're asking," Jackson said.

"I think you are, Sergeant," Chase countered.

Jackson glanced at Perkins, who kept a straight face behind Agent Sheehan. "What's going on here, Chief?"

Nathan Perkins remained silent.

"I don't understand what you're trying to say," Jackson pleaded, looking back at Chase.

"Oh for God's sake, cut the bullshit, Jack!" Perkins bellowed with a menacing point of the finger. "We know what happened! We know what you did!"

"The gun that was used to murder Tom Chumansky — the one found in Eddie Clark's apartment — came from the evidence inventory here at the station." Chase crossed his arms on his chest as he finished the sentence.

Jackson did his best to act surprised. "What? How is that possible?"

"There's only one way, Jack," Perkins interjected.

Three beats passed before a response from Jackson was uttered. "Wait a minute. You think I…how could you think I'd do such a—"

"Christ, Jack! No one else could have done it!" Perkins said.

Jackson shook his head before responding again, this time in a quieter tone. "Well, *you* could have…"

A look of shock swept over Perkins. He darted forward as quickly as his bad knees would let him, hands and arms out, ready to grab his sergeant.

"You son of a—!"

Chase arm-barred the big man before he made contact with Jackson. "Hang on, Chief. Let's calm it down. We have more to tell."

Red-faced, Perkins took a step back at Chase's request while still glaring at Jackson.

"Sit down, Sergeant," Sheehan said.

"I'm good," Jackson replied.

"It wasn't a suggestion," Chase said, this time more firmly. "Sit down."

Jackson hesitated and then obeyed while the other two men remained standing.

"The night Chumansky went missing and presumably the night Delia disappeared, we know where everyone was at that time because we ran GPS reports on their mobile phones," Chase reported. Jackson nodded. He was already aware of this. "Including yours," Sheehan added.

Jackson's shoulders sank, but only briefly, before recovering. "I…" was all he could manage to say. It seemed he was running out of explanations and misdirection plays. Perkins remained in the background, biting his lower lip, hands on his hips.

"Jackson," Agent Sheehan said. "We know." The veteran police sergeant attempted to look perplexed. "Delia told us," Chase told him. Jackson's shoulders lowered again, and this time they stayed there.

"I…uh…" he began.

Chase continued, but with more precision. "We know you guys were together that night. She told us what happened to her. The only thing she didn't tell us was why."

Jackson thought for a moment before answering. "I should have a lawyer here, shouldn't I?"

"Are you asking for one?"

Now with glassy eyes, Jackson replied. "Not yet."

"We just need to know what happened. I need to figure out the truth in this mess," Chase said calmly. "Help me?"

Jackson looked again at his boss, whose position hadn't changed. Locking his eyes on a space on the wall between the two men, he shook his head and began to speak. "They called me and threatened my family."

"Who? The cartel?"

"Yeah, something like that. I mean, they don't really

call themselves that, but—"

"Hang on a second, back up. You need to start from the beginning," Chase said as he sat down at the table across from Jackson.

"All right, sorry. This is…awkward," Jackson said.

A grunt of sarcasm came from Chief Perkins.

"Go ahead," Chase said. "When did they call you?"

"I guess it was that Friday, whatever the date was. They didn't give me much notice, which makes sense. They didn't want me to figure out a way around things."

"What did they say? Who was it?" Chase asked.

"All I know is the guy's name is Pablo. I don't have a last name or anyone else's first name." Chase scribbled in his notepad as Jackson went on with his story. "They threatened to slaughter my wife and kids if I didn't do what they told me to do."

"What did they tell you to do?"

"I mean, they *knew* my family. They knew my house. They knew what my little girl wore to preschool that day," Jackson explained.

"Answer the agent's question, Sergeant," Perkins commanded. His tone had leveled off a bit, and he was doing all he could to sympathize with the situation Jackson had been in.

"They told me to get Chum to give me the money he had stolen from them," Jackson said.

"Okay," Chase said as he wrote another note.

"And they told me to get rid of Chum," Jackson said, resentment clear in his voice.

Chase stopped writing and looked up. He didn't say anything, he simply nodded.

"You don't seem surprised," Jackson said. "How'd you figure it all out?"

"You're not done with your explanation, yet," Chase

reminded him. "Go ahead. Keep it moving. What happened after you took the call from this Pablo guy?"

"Well, for starters, I debated what my options were. I didn't know what else to do other than follow through. I mean, I didn't want to commit murder but…my God they really scared the shit out of me, at least at that moment."

"You didn't think to come to me?" Perkins said.

"I didn't think — I mean — I was afraid for my family," Jackson explained. "I didn't want to take a wrong step and end up getting them killed."

"So, I'd make a wrong step, that's what you're saying?" Perkins moved towards him.

"Chief Perkins, please. I don't want to force you to leave the room," Chase said calmly but firmly. With a slight hint of embarrassment, Nathan Perkins stepped back and mouthed the word "sorry" in the agent's direction.

"It's not like that, Chief," Jackson said. "You didn't hear the vivid detail that this guy used to describe what he would do to Caroline…the kids…I was scared of that happening. The only way I felt I could insure their safety was to do what they told me to do."

"So you stole a gun from inventory to do the deed," Chase said.

"Yeah, I guess that's the best way to say it," Jackson admitted. "I didn't know it would get traced the way it did. Figured the chances were slim. It was my only play to get a gun for something like that on such short notice."

"You could've considered another way," Chase suggested.

"Believe me, I considered it. But I figured that was the easiest, quickest way. If I did it any other way, it would take time, precision, and effort. I didn't want time to think about it. I was afraid I'd chicken out and cost my family their lives."

"So how'd you end up getting to the money? Did Chum just take you there?" Chase was still trying to tie Delia into this entire thing, but he couldn't let Jackson know she hadn't actually told him anything.

"That was the weird part. This Pablo guy told me to keep an eye on Chum Saturday evening, that he would lead me to it. And he did."

"Wow. These guys are the real deal. They must have listening devices in all the right spots." Chase recalled planting the bug in the Greyson home and that all he had learned from it was how much stress the couple was under.

"That's exactly what your sister and I assumed," Jackson said.

"Okay. I'm glad you brought her up. Explain to me how you two got connected in this whole thing," Chase said. "In *your* words," he added, in an effort to convince Jackson he'd already heard Delia's version.

"Well, I tailed Chum from Mecca Warehouse to his old place — Maddison's house, now. He didn't spot me following him. From the east end of the property, the back side, I was able to watch him move into the wooded area. I followed him from there. Little did I know Agent DeMarco was doing the same from a different angle."

Chase looked up from scribbling in his notebook and nodded, as if he already knew this.

"She actually made her presence known to Chum before I did," Jackson continued. "Shortly thereafter, I came out from my secluded spot. Surprised both of them, I suppose."

"Delia must've been mighty surprised when you shot Chumansky, too," Chase suggested.

Jackson paused. He stole another glance at Chief Perkins then darted his eyes back to Sheehan, all without moving his head.

"What?" Chase said, but Jackson remained silent.

"Jack," Perkins quipped, "what the hell are you doing?"

"I think it's time for a lawyer," Sergeant Jackson finally said.

"What the hell?" Perkins growled.

"It's okay, Chief," Chase said. "I'm not surprised." He stood up from the table and led Perkins through the door and into the hallway.

***

"That son of a bitch," Perkins hissed under his breath.

"Come on," Chase said, trying to soothe the angry man. "He's not stupid. We know what happened. He knows we know what happened. And he knows how the law works. It's okay for now."

"I just can't believe this."

"Chief, I know. But it happened," Chase said. Putting his hand on the big man's shoulder, he asked, "Are you ready to do this?"

"Nope. But I have to do it," Perkins said solemnly. He pulled his handcuffs from his belt and reopened the interrogation room door. Chase watched and listened through the open door.

"You have the right to remain silent…"

XXXIII

It was a long drive, a seemingly endless night. Claire hadn't taken much time to think about what she was doing. She knew if she had, she would've never followed through. After punching out at Stubby's, she drove home and packed a suitcase. Following a quick explanation to her mom (who was less than enthusiastic) Claire climbed inside her car and hit the highway. She made it to Interstate 80 by seven thirty in the evening, but that was only the beginning of the road trip. While planning the journey in her head, Claire had told herself that once she got west of Omaha it would be smooth sailing. In a sense, she was correct. The weather was certainly cooperating, with temperatures staying around the freezing mark and no precipitation to speak of. But the ten-hour drive was exhausting. Every ninety minutes or so Claire would stop at a gas station to use the restroom and get a cup of coffee or something to eat. She needed to shake it up every so often just to stay awake. It probably didn't help that she was also desperately trying not to smoke. She made it as far as Kearney before finally giving in to her craving and lighting up.

Claire Mathison had never driven a car longer than four hours at a time, and never by herself. This was a new experience for her, and she wasn't sure she liked it. But it was all for a good cause, she kept telling herself. No, she wasn't driving for Jerry's Kids or UNICEF or anything like that. It was for love — the love of her life. She couldn't stand being away from Barrett, and she was positive that driving all night to get to him was exactly what she was supposed to be doing right now.

Every pit stop she made, Claire was careful to lock her car doors, hold her purse close to her body, and keep the can of pepper spray her mom had given her tight in her hand. Trish Mathison might not have been thrilled with her daughter's sudden decision to drive six hundred miles to be with a man, but she was more concerned with her only daughter's safety.

There were plenty of interesting-looking characters at every break Claire took, but thankfully no one bothered her. It was easy to fear the worst after hearing Barrett tell the story of what happened to him at the bus station in Chicago. These things could happen to anyone, and there was a better chance it could happen when you let your guard down. Claire did her best to stay on high alert in case anyone had the guts to try and harm her. Not that she would beat them down or anything like that, but she was confident she could hit an assailant square in the eyes with a couple of quick sprays and maybe even a punch to the stomach or groin.

All of the stops put her in the Denver metro area at around four thirty in the morning. Claire didn't think it would be a good idea to knock on Barrett's door before dawn, though it wouldn't be the first time she had done something like that to him. Instead, she spent two hours at a Danny's Restaurant in the suburb of Englewood eating breakfast, drinking even more coffee, and occasionally dozing off while stretching out in her booth. Her server was a nice older lady named Helen who didn't bother Claire too much. At one point Helen asked her if she felt okay.

"Oh, I'm fine," Claire said. "Just really tired. Long drive from Iowa. All night long."

"Oh my," Helen said as she filled Claire's coffee mug for the seventh time. "You're a long way from home, aren't you?" She wiped up a wet spot before smiling and asking, "Is it a guy?"

Claire smiled back. "How did you know?"

"I guess you could call it experience," Helen said,

flipping her dishcloth in the air and catching it. "I'm old."

At six thirty-five, Claire decided it was time to shuffle on and make her way to Barrett's condo. If not for the grace of the Internet on her mobile phone, Claire might've been unable to surprise Barrett by showing up on his doorstep. But when she conducted a thorough Google search she was blessed with what she was fairly certain was the address of his condominium. Had this not worked, she would've been forced to call his mother to find out where he was. Of course, there was always a chance that he was not living in the condo right now and Claire might still have to do that. For now, she was assuming he would be there when she arrived.

What she really wanted was sleep. A lot of sleep. In fact, she considered finding a cheap hotel and crawling into bed for ten or twelve hours. It was a tempting idea. But she convinced herself it was more important to see Barrett and maybe then catch up on some sleep. Claire missed him so much — she simply wanted to see his face again, sooner rather than later. She feared she would pay for the hotel room and then not be able to sleep because of her anxiety about surprising the man she was crazy about.

When Claire reached Barrett's condominium, it was almost exactly as she had pictured it: a modest dwelling, but certainly not cheap or rundown. From the outside, the place seemed to be the perfect size for a single person. Claire checked the time on her phone; it was five minutes after seven in the morning.

There are worse things I could do, she thought before ringing the doorbell.

As she waited, she wondered if she should ring it again if no one came to the door. Claire strained to listen for sounds inside. At one point she thought she heard some movement, but she wasn't sure. While she contemplated this, the door suddenly sprang open.

The look on Barrett's face was, quite simply, one of surprise. Certainly more so than the time she woke him up at the farmhouse in Gable late one evening last September. He clearly was not expecting to see Claire.

"What the hell?" he greeted her.

"Surprise," Claire said. It was a halfhearted exclamation that ended with more inquiry than excitement.

"Wh-wh…" It almost sounded like he was about to repeat himself.

"I know, I know. You weren't expecting me. I'm sorry."

Barrett stepped aside and motioned for her to come in. "Well, no I wasn't. Umm, how did you get here?"

"I drove."

"All night?"

"All night long," Claire said. "Took me longer than it should've. I have a small bladder. And actually, I just got done having an early breakfast at the Danny's up the street."

"Wow," Barrett said, still processing her arrival. "Here, have a seat. You want some coffee?" The living room and kitchen were in an open area separated by a breakfast bar. Barrett walked into the kitchen and began to prep the coffee pot.

"Oh, no," she said. "I've had plenty already."

Once the coffee started brewing, Barrett returned to the living room and sat down next to Claire on the couch.

"So is there a problem?" he asked her. "Why are you here?"

Claire couldn't be sure, but she thought she detected a tone in his voice. One she hadn't heard before. Aggravation? Frustration? Or maybe she was just exhausted and needed some sleep.

"No. Well, kind of. I just really needed to see you," she explained.

Barrett nodded slowly. "I see."

"I get it," Claire said. "You're not excited. I'm sorry. I

just missed you. A heckuva lot."

Recovering a little, Barrett spoke up. "No, no. I – I – I just have a lot going on. A lot on my mind."

"I can understand that," Claire said.

"The funeral was yesterday and…"

Claire could tell he was struggling with expressing his thoughts. "Look," Claire said. "I really am sorry to be-bop in on you like this. Would it be okay if I caught up on some sleep and maybe we could talk more later today when we're both more together?"

"Sure," Barrett agreed.

Claire went out to her car and brought her suitcase in. When she returned, Barrett showed her to the guest bedroom. Without changing her clothes, Claire slid under the covers and dropped off but only after wondering if she had just made a huge mistake.

***

"Good morning, Julia."

"Good morning, Boyd."

"How was your New Year's?" Boyd asked her.

Everyone knew he didn't really care, and so it had become standard to give a routine answer. "Just fine," Julia answered her boss. "And how was yours?" She knew the only reason he had asked about her holiday was because he wanted her to ask him about his.

"Tremendous!" Boyd responded. He stood next to her desk in the front office and picked up a couple of papers from a pile, pretending to look at them. She knew she needed to ask him for more details.

"So what did you do?" Julia asked.

"Oh nothing much," Boyd said as he stretched his arms above his head. "Just hung out at home with Freddy. We had a nice time just having some drinks and watching some of those bad year-end TV shows and eating Chinese food."

"Sounds like it was tremendous," Julia said with a hint of sarcasm.

Before the pretend conversation went any further, Antonio Barnes came down the hallway.

"Hey, Boyd. I didn't know you were here yet," he said.

"How was your New Year's, Tony?" Boyd asked him.

"No complaints," Barnes replied. "How was yours?"

Julia put her face back in her paperwork while Boyd repeated the story he had just told her. It was the same thing, all the time. Boyd would walk around the office for half the morning and ask how everyone's holiday went because if he didn't do this, he'd never get the chance to tell anyone what he did. Because no one cared. The Clevinger Group had never been a chummy bunch. With Otto and Barrett both gone, it had gotten worse. It started and ended with Boyd — because for the most part no one liked him much. Or at least they didn't respect him.

Since Barrett had left the city under a cloud of suspicion, and by most accounts had deserted or resigned from his job, Tony Barnes had done his best to take over as many of Barrett's duties as he could. He was doing an okay job, but he was no Barrett. Unfortunately, that was all the Clevinger Group had these days.

"Hey, I was reading the paper the other day and I saw that Barrett's father passed away," Tony said, changing the subject so he didn't have to hear any more about Boyd's holiday.

Julia interjected before Boyd had a chance to say anything. "Yeah, I knew he was sick after watching the Dateline special."

"I knew that too," Tony said. "I just didn't realize he was in such bad shape already."

"It's a nasty disease," Julia said and then turned around towards her work again.

"Well, that's not all I learned," Tony continued. "Meg Schrader went to the wake. She worked for Mr. Greyson for a while until she had her first kid."

"I remember her," Julia said. "She used to work part time here until...well, until she had her second baby."

"Was she the one with the big black mole in the middle of her forehead?" Boyd said.

"No, that was Lucretia," Tony said. "Meg had the big—"

Julia whipped around and glared at Tony before he finished his sentence.

"Eyes."

Julia shook her head.

"Oh sure," Boyd said. "So anyway, back to your story." Even the clueless Boyd Clevinger sometimes knew when it was time to move on.

"Well, I ran into her the other night at The Warlock and guess what? Barrett's back in town. He was at the viewing and I assume the funeral, too."

"What?" Julia and Boyd exclaimed simultaneously.

"Hand to God," Tony said.

"Did she talk to him?" Julia asked.

"Apparently, but only briefly. It sounded pretty formal."

"I guess he caught wind of his father's death or something," Julia suggested. "Makes sense he would come home for that."

Boyd said nothing for a minute or so. Abruptly, he made a beeline for the hallway, headed into his office, and closed the door.

"Hmmm," Tony murmured. "Still a sore subject."

"I probably didn't use the best choice of words there," Julia said.

"Do you think — you don't think?" Tony stammered.

“No, I don’t think Barrett did it,” Julia said. “And I think Boyd struggles more with losing a father he treated poorly than worrying about who really murdered his dad.”

“And yet he still complains about his dad to me,” Tony added. “That’s weird.”

“It is,” Julia agreed. “It’s a sad state of affairs, that family.”

"And their company," Tony said. "I mean, I'm worried. I'm doing the best I can but I don't know that it's enough."

"We all know you are," Julia told him. "That's all anyone can expect from you. No one planned for us to lose our two most knowledgeable employees within a few days of each other."

***

Bart Timmons was actually starting to like his new job despite it being illegal. Pablo had been treating him okay so far. Bart had done everything asked of him and Pablo in return had paid him and given him no grief. He could drive his truck again without worrying about going to prison. Things were going pretty well.

It was Thursday evening, and Bart was on his way back to Gable after making some deliveries and collections. Working nights at this job worked out nicely for Bart because he had so much other work to do during the day. Farmwork. He could handle the farmwork and did a decent job with it. It wasn’t necessarily something he wanted to do for the rest of his life, though. But ever since he was a kid it seemed that was what was expected of him. He was born into a farming family in a farming community. He was a farmer’s son, and so naturally the expectation was that he would be a farmer. No one ever asked him what he wanted to do or be when he grew up. The truth was, Bart liked doing something different for a change. Maybe this was something he could do long term. He was making more money per hour delivering coke than he would ever make as a farmer.

Of course, Sergeant Jackson's involvement in this business was perplexing. Why did he ever get into it? Maybe he liked the money, too. All Bart knew was he was thankful for the help on the drinking and driving charge and also for the new business opportunity. As he approached the midway point of his travel back to Gable, Bart pondered whether he should ask Sergeant Jackson about a long-term opportunity in this business. Or maybe it would be a better idea for him to speak with Pablo about something like that.

As his mind wandered, he didn't immediately notice the flashing red and blue lights behind him. When Bart finally did see them, he pulled over and prayed that it was Sergeant Jackson. After a rap on his truck window, he rolled down the glass and saw a lanky police officer he didn't recognize.

"Good evening," the policeman said.

Bart wasn't sure if the officer was a highway patrolman or a local cop from Gable or maybe Adler. He thought he knew the Gable policemen pretty well, but this one could be new. "Uh, evening, sir. I mean, Officer." Bart did his best to be as polite as possible. It was in his nature.

"Were you aware you've got a taillight out?" Officer Murray McGee asked him.

"No. I didn't know that," Bart said. Actually, he was pretty sure he did know this. He just didn't know how or why he knew. It could've been something he noticed during a drunken stupor, the memory planted deep in his brain while sleeping things off.

"Well, it's illegal to drive around like this and know about it," McGee explained. "Under normal circumstances I'd have to write you a fix-it ticket. But I'll give you a verbal warning. I just need to see your license and registration, please."

In a matter of seconds, Bart went from relieved to panicked. He didn't have his license. The officer who'd pulled him over a couple of weeks ago had taken it from him because of his multiple DWIs. Before saying a word, Bart reached into the glove compartment of his truck and pulled out his registration. Next, he reached into his pocket to pull out his wallet, but stopped short on purpose.

"Officer, you're not going to believe this, but I didn't bring my wallet," Bart lied. "I guess I left the house too quick. I hope that's okay."

McGee sighed. "Well, technically I'm supposed to write you a ticket for that, too. But heck, it's a new year. I'm in a good mood. I'd rather give you a mulligan." He took the registration from the big guy in the driver's seat. "Wait here. I'll be right back."

Well, that wasn't so bad, Bart thought as he rolled up his window. He wondered if Sergeant Jackson had fixed the problem yet. As it stood, it didn't seem to matter. This police officer was being awfully nice. Maybe the tide had turned for Bart. The only thing that hadn't changed for him was his craving for alcohol. In fact, a whiskey and Coke would sure hit the spot when he got home.

After waiting a few minutes, Bart began to wonder what was taking so long. He glanced in his rearview mirror to see if the officer was making his way back yet. He could see the outline of the man sitting in the driver's seat of his squad car. Bart knew enough to stay in his truck. One time, he had tried to exit after being pulled over and the cop pulled his gun on him. You're not supposed to get out of your vehicle when you've been pulled over. That much he knew.

Five minutes passed. Then ten more. Even for his past DWIs Bart hadn't waited this long to get handcuffed. Five more minutes passed. Finally, he decided he would get out of his truck slowly with his hands in the air. The least he could do was let the policeman know he wasn't trying to be aggressive or cause any harm. At this point, he was legitimately concerned. What the hell was taking so long?

"Sir? Officer? Is everything okay?" Bart stepped out of his car and put his arms in the air. "My hands are above my head. I'm coming back there. Please don't shoot me. I just want to make sure you're okay."

Bart continued to trudge slowly towards the police car. Its lights were still flashing red and blue on top. As he approached the driver's door, it became even more difficult to see inside the vehicle. The big guy was shocked to have made it this far without so much as a word from the officer. Coming up next to the cruiser, hands over his head, Bart squatted down and tried to find an angle to see inside through the closed window. As he did, a car drove by on the highway, its headlights providing just enough light for him to get a glimpse inside.

And after he did, Bart Timmons ran back to his truck faster than he had ever run in his entire life. He turned the key, pumped the accelerator, and shifted into drive so fast his entire body jerked backwards as the truck accelerated forward. He didn't even remember to close the door until he had driven fifty yards up the shoulder.

Bart didn't know what had just happened, but if he went home and hid under the covers, maybe it would all go away.

***

"Sheehan."

"Hi, Agent Sheehan. This is Barrett Greyson."

"Hey, thanks for calling me," Chase said.

"Well, you asked me to stay in touch and I have nothing to hide," Barrett explained. "I also wanted to give you my new number."

After scribbling it down in his notebook, Chase continued the conversation. "Anything new?"

"I'm sorry to say, no," Barrett answered. "How's my money?"

"Same as before. Locked away in an evidence room somewhere in central Iowa," Chase said before changing the subject. "Have you seen your buddy Boyd?"

"Not hardly. I don't work there anymore," Barrett reminded him. "Also, *not* my buddy."

"Ah, good points. I guess I hadn't thought about how you probably don't have a job at the Clevinger Group anymore. Any leads on what you're going to do for income yet?"

"Not a clue. I haven't been home long enough to figure that out. We just buried my dad yesterday."

"I'm sorry. That's never fun."

"No. No it's not. But..."

Chase waited, but Greyson said nothing more.

"But what?"

"Oh, I was just wondering the other day. I had a hypothetical question I wanted to ask you," Barrett said.

"Sure. Hit me."

"Well, let's just say that — again, this is all hypothetical so don't get all jumpy on me — but imagine that the person who killed Otto Clevinger was immune from justice."

"Huh?"

"I mean, what if the person who committed the murder couldn't be prosecuted?" Barrett asked again.

"I don't even see how that's possible," Chase said. He was beginning to think Barrett needed to get some sleep, find a job, and put his father's death behind him.

"Oh, I know. But I was just wondering. I mean, well, I don't really know what I mean either, I guess."

"Is there something you're not telling me, Barrett?" Chase asked.

"Nope."

"If you know something, you really need to tell me."

"I'm aware of that," Barrett said. "I know nothing. I was just trying to figure things out myself. Apparently I'm not very good at it."

"I told you to just stay out of it."

"But you also said you wanted my help," Barrett reminded him.

Chase thought about this. "That's true. But whatever you were just trying to say to me, it didn't make much sense. Are you sure you're okay?"

"I'm fine," Barrett said. "Maybe a little tired."

"Get some rest then," Chase told him. "Call me in a couple of days."

"Wait a second. Let me try this again," Barrett said.

"Really?"

"Hear me out, it'll take ten seconds."

"Okay, go."

"What if I did know who killed Otto but that person couldn't be prosecuted. They had complete immunity. Hypothetical, of course."

"I still don't get it," Chase said, frustrated.

"Pretend," Barrett said.

"Okay, I'm pretending."

"So?"

"So, what?" Chase asked.

"Would it matter if I knew who did it even if that person couldn't be put on trial or thrown in prison?"

"You know something, don't you?" Chase said.

"I told you, this is just a situation I came up with in my head."

"Let me put it to you this way, Barrett. If you know something, you better tell me. If you don't know something, then you're wasting my time with these questions. I have more important things to do than take the trolley to the land of make-believe with you. Call me the day after tomorrow," the FBI agent said and hung up abruptly.

***

Officer Murray McGee had not been seen or heard from since the previous night when he'd checked in for his shift at the Adler PD. Peculiar things had happened that night, too. Around ten o'clock, a couple phoned the department and reported their concern that a patrol car was on the shoulder of Highway 57 with its emergency lights on. When dispatch asked what was so unusual about this, they explained that it had been there for no less than three hours. The young man and woman lived in Gable and had driven to Adler for dinner when they noticed the patrol car on the side of the road. On their way back home, the car was still there, which seemed strange to them. It wasn't until later on in the evening that dispatch realized Officer McGee had not responded to any of their calls.

Sergeant Mark Hines had a bad feeling as he headed north towards Gable in his own radio car early the next morning. The conservative community of Adler had been shaken recently by the revelations of drug running and murder. When it came to small towns, Hines knew that even local problems with crime could send shockwaves in a fifty-mile radius. There simply weren't many good reasons why Murray McGee might be pulled over on the side of the road for hours and not responding to dispatch. He could've been in an accident, but it didn't sound like that was the case according to the couple who had driven by twice. It's possible his car had broken down or lost power, but a mobile phone or emergency flares would help in either situation. At this point, the only thing anyone had seen was a police car with flashing lights on top. Something wasn't right.

A few miles down the highway, Sergeant Hines finally spotted the patrol car on the east shoulder, red and blue lights flashing, a silent testament to what had happened just hours earlier.

"Damnit," Hines cursed under his breath. He stopped his car twenty feet behind the other squad car and reached for the radio.

"Adler PD, I've found the vehicle in question. About seven miles north of the station on 57, east shoulder. I'm moving in."

He exited his car and armed himself. He slowly moved forward, holding his gun out in front of him.

"Office McGee," Hines called out, "are you okay?"

No response. The sergeant moved another ten feet.

"McGee? It's Sergeant Hines."

Still nothing.

"What hap—"

Hines stopped himself. He thought he saw someone in the driver's seat, but he couldn't be sure.

"Are you okay?" He moved faster, gun still drawn. As he came up on the driver's side window he pulled his flashlight out with his free hand. It was still early enough in the morning that additional illumination would be handy. He shined the light inside the police car.

Mark Hines had seen many things in his law enforcement career, many dead bodies. Bloody ones, body parts missing. But nothing would ever compare to what he was witnessing now: a twenty-five-year-old police officer he knew well, staring at the roof of his car, lifeless.

The police sergeant dropped his flashlight on the frozen ground and fell to one knee, holding back tears and praying for Murray McGee's soul.

XXXIV

"You do understand that you need to show up for your court date, right?" Derrick Janssen knew the answer to his own question, but it made him feel better to clarify, especially since his client didn't seem to care much about procedure.

"Man, I understand how this works. I've been to prison before," Randy scoffed.

"I know. That's what worries me."

"I don't know how you did it, but you did good, kid," Randy said. He patted his lawyer on the shoulder as they walked through the parking lot.

"There's always a way to make things happen," Janssen said. "It just depends on how much it's worth to you." He opened the passenger door of his car and reached down to maneuver the seat back.

"What made you do it for me?"

Janssen stood back up and looked at the ex-con. "It's not like you care, Randy. So why bother wasting oxygen trying to explain it. Just stay out of trouble and make sure you're back here for your next appearance." He motioned for Randy to get in the car and then hustled to the other side, throwing himself behind the wheel.

"How's Mom?" Randy asked.

"Again, do you really care?"

"Of course, I do. She's my mom."

"She's fine," Janssen said.

"Good," Randy said.

"I told you you didn't care."

"What's that supposed to mean?" Randy snapped.

"Nothing," Janssen replied. He didn't feel like getting his butt kicked by the client he had just bailed out of jail.

"Just take me to the bus station, wherever that is," Randy said.

"No problem."

"There's one more thing," Randy added.

Janssen took one hand off the wheel and grabbed his wallet from his coat and handed Randy a wad of bills. "That get you going?"

Randy took the money from the attorney and added it up quickly in his head. "Yeah, I think so. How'd you know?"

"How'd I know how much or how'd I know you'd ask for it?"

"Both, I guess," Randy said.

"I thought like a criminal," Janssen explained.

"Now that right there," Randy said, "that sounded condescending."

"No offense, Randy. It kind of was."

***

"What? You're kidding me," Chief Perkins said into the phone at his desk. "What the hell happened?"

Chase walked over and sat down across from him, curious as to what was going on. Hodge was on patrol, and Sergeant Jackson sat uncomfortably in a jail cell waiting for his attorney to arrive.

Perkins listened intently. "Do you want help?" he asked then waited to hear the answer. "You just let us know what we can do to help. I'm, umm, down a man right now, but Agent Sheehan is still here. We'll do whatever." He paused again. "Okay, just let us know, Mark."

The chief hung up the phone and turned his attention

to Chase.

"What's that all about?" the agent asked.

"You remember that kid cop from Adler, McGee?"

"Sure. Murray. He came up to the hospital and hung out with me on Christmas."

"He's — he's — dead," Perkins managed to spit out.

"What? What happened?" Although he didn't know McGee well, he had enjoyed the kid's company and found him to be a smart cop with a bright future.

"He was found in the driver's seat of his patrol vehicle on the east shoulder of the highway, about seven or eight miles from here," Perkins explained.

"Wh-what was the cause of death?" Chase asked.

The big man took a deep breath before replying. "He was strangled with some type of wire or…or a string or something like that."

"Holy shit."

"You can say that again," Perkins said, massaging his face. "I don't understand what the hell is going on around here. It used to be such a nice area. The trouble was limited. I mean, Adler has its issues, it's bigger. But nothing like this or what's happened recently has ever taken place near here. And then this thing…with Jack…" Perkins shook his head and looked down at the floor between him and his desk.

"Can't help but wonder if it's all connected, can you?" Chase commented.

"That was Sergeant Mark Hines from Adler on the phone," Perkins said. "He found McGee. He sounded pretty shaken, but he's going to interview the couple who drove by the squad car twice in three hours, see if they noticed anything at all that might tell him what happened."

"I'd like to help," Chase offered.

"He said he had it under control for now."

"Of course he said that," Chase said. "No one ever

wants to involve the FBI until it's too late. Give me his number."

Perkins obliged and Chase made arrangements to meet Hines at the couple's house in thirty minutes.

***

"I realize I probably shouldn't have come here," Claire said. She and Barrett were sitting in his living room and having their first talk since she had fallen asleep ten hours earlier.

"Why do you keep saying that?"

"Because there's something wrong here," she said.

"I don't understand," Barrett said. He did, but he wasn't about to tell her how right she was. Not yet, anyway.

"My biggest fear when I took you to the airport in Omaha was that things would never be the same again. The instant you opened the door this morning I could tell something was wrong."

"There's nothing wrong," he lied.

"Barrett, come on," Claire said. "*Everything* is wrong."

"I mean, I lost my dad almost as soon as I got back here," Barrett said. "I don't have a job and everyone here looks at me cross-eyed because they're wondering if I'm a killer. But other than that, nothing is wrong."

Claire nodded. "Is there anything else?"

"Like…?"

"How do you feel about me?" she asked. "I mean, now. After I showed up here like this."

Barrett shrugged. "No different, I guess."

"You guess?"

"I've just got a lot on my mind already," he explained. "I wasn't expecting you. It was a surprise. Sometimes surprises can be stressful even when it's a 'good' surprise."

"So you still have the same feelings for me that you told me about a few days ago?" Claire clarified.

"Of course."

"Then kiss me," she commanded.

"What?"

"Get over here and kiss me. I'll be able to tell if you're lying."

Barrett moved next to her on the couch. Although nervous that Claire might actually have superpowers and could read his mind if he kissed her, he smiled and cupped her face with both hands. Pulling her head to his, he delicately kissed her lips. He held the kiss for several seconds before gently pulling away.

"Did I pass?" he asked her.

"B-plus," she said.

"Hmmm. I can do better."

"I know. But given the circumstances, it's a passing grade. You're all right."

Barrett pretended to wipe sweat from his forehead and the two shared a laugh.

Claire took his hand and squeezed it.

"Are you sure there's not something you want to talk about? I'm a good listener."

Barrett was beginning to wonder if this was a sign. The girl sure was intuitive. On a whim, he decided it wouldn't hurt to get some things off his chest and see where it led.

"Okay," he said. "I could probably use a little therapy session."

"Lie down here," Claire said. "Put your head in my lap. Talk to me."

Barrett did as he was instructed.

"So, what's on your mind?"

"Well, you've lost a parent," he said. "You kind of understand, I expect."

"But it's a different situation for everyone," Claire reminded him.

Barrett began by relating the events leading up to Frank Greyson's passing in his hospital bed. He told her about his conversation with his father, how he had bizarrely apologized and also given him a key to a safe deposit box. Before she had the chance to ask questions, Barrett fast-forwarded, telling her about the visitation and funeral and how some of the guests who had come to pay their respects seemed surprised to see him.

"You're not really shocked by that, are you?" Claire's hand, which had been stroking his hair, paused as he spoke.

"I guess I hadn't thought about it until it started happening."

"You don't have to explain anything to them," Claire said. "It's none of their business."

"That's true," he agreed.

"So have you checked out the safe deposit box yet?"

She doesn't miss a beat, Barrett thought. Should he, or shouldn't he? "Yeah," he responded slowly.

"What was in it?" Claire asked. "Some pictures or some sort of keepsake?"

Barrett hesitated. "Not…not exactly." Then he thought about it again. "Well, kinda."

"I'm sorry. Is this too much? I understand. I don't want to pressure you," Claire said.

Pulling himself up upright again, Barrett looked her in the eye but said nothing.

"What?"

He continued staring, looking as far beyond her hazel eyes as he could. He wanted to be sure. But he knew he never could be, completely.

"What?" Claire repeated, this time with a nervous laugh. "Stop it."

"I need to show you something," Barrett said. He patted her knee. "I'll be right back."

Sixty seconds later he returned with his father's cell phone.

***

"We appreciate you meeting with us, Mr. and Mrs. Gunderson," Sergeant Mark Hines said as they sat down in the young couple's small living room. Chase and Hines planted themselves on the couch as the Gundersons sat on a love seat together.

"You can call us by our first names," Mr. Gunderson said as he pushed his wire-rimmed glasses up the bridge of his nose. "Daryl and Kelly."

"Fine," Hines said. "Tell us about the first time you drove by the police car."

"We were on our way to Adler for a steak dinner at Theodore's restaurant," Daryl Gunderson explained. "I guess it was a few miles before we got to Adler that we drove by the car and saw it."

"It had a pickup truck pulled over," his wife said.

"No, it didn't," Mr. Gunderson said, giving her a perplexed look.

"Yes, it *did*," Kelly Gunderson insisted, setting her shoulder-length blonde hair swaying.

"Wait a minute," Hines interjected. "It makes sense that the squad car would have someone pulled over. But this is the first you've mentioned it."

"You didn't tell them?" the lady of the house asked her husband.

"I didn't *see* it," he pleaded. "Are you sure there was a truck there?" His wife folded her arms and gave him a look. "Okay. I guess I didn't see the truck. I don't know why. It was getting dark and the police car's lights were flashing on top. Kind of blinded me, I guess."

"Do you remember what the truck looked like, Mrs. Gunderson?" Chase asked. He had pulled his notebook out and was taking notes.

"Well, like Daryl said, there wasn't a lot of light out there other than the blue and red flashers," she explained. "I think it was an older model, but I can't be sure."

"Any idea how old?" Hines asked.

"I'm sorry. I don't know anything about cars or trucks."

"Color?"

Kelly Gunderson squeezed her lips together and shook her head in disappointment. "I guess it wasn't a dark color. I can tell you that much," she said.

"So, like white or silver…" Hines offered.

"Sure. Or maybe cream or yellow?" she suggested. "I'm sorry. I know it was there, I just don't recall any details."

"I'm sure they understand, baby," Daryl Gunderson told his wife while taking her hand. "We drove by at sixty miles an hour."

"Totally understandable," Hines agreed. "We're just here to see what you can remember."

"So, on your way back," Chase said, "what did you see?"

"Same thing," Daryl said.

"Except there was no truck," Kelly added.

"There wasn't? Oh heck, I don't know," Daryl explained to the officials. "I can't remember what I saw and when I saw it. If she says there was no truck, there was no truck. I mean, I was driving both times. Keeping my eyes on the road, you know."

"That makes sense, Mr. Gunderson," Chase said. "When you drove by on your way to Adler there was nothing unusual about a police car on the side of the road, lights flashing. You didn't catch any additional details, like the truck. When you came through there on the way home, you did see the cruiser by itself and that's what stuck in your brain when you called the authorities. How long had it been since you drove by the first time?"

"Nearly three hours," Daryl said.

"How do you know it was in the same spot both times you drove by it?" Chase asked.

"Ahh," Kelly interjected. "We asked each other the same question as we drove by it the second time. But almost immediately we both remembered where we had been in relation to the IDP signs on both sides of the road. That's how we knew it hadn't moved, or if it had it certainly hadn't moved very far."

Chase gave a confused look to the three locals in the room. "IDP?"

"Iowa Dairy Processing," Hines explained. "I can confirm what they're saying. It's right between the two billboards. There's one on each side of the highway."

"And visible in the dark?" Chase said.

"They're well-lit," Hines continued. "It's a big deal around here. They employ about two thousand folks in the area."

Chase nodded and made another note in his pad.

"So you didn't see any people either time you drove by?" Hines asked the couple.

"No," Daryl answered. "I mean, did we?" He looked at his wife for confirmation.

"I didn't. It was just too dark both times to see much of anything," Kelly said. "I mean, I assume there were people in the vehicles, but I never saw anyone. I'm sorry."

"You have anything else, Agent Sheehan?" Hines asked.

"I'm good."

Daryl Gunderson ushered the two men to the front door, while Kelly went to the laundry room to move around some clothes. As Sergeant Hines made his way out of the house and to his car, Chase turned back to Gunderson. "I do have one more question," he said.

"Sure," Daryl said.

"How long have you been married?"

"Three months," the newlywed admitted. "Is it that obvious?"

Chase shrugged. "Well, when you've been married for nearly ten years like I have, it's not that difficult to spot. Been there, done that."

Daryl Gunderson nodded. "I see."

Chase patted him on the shoulder before heading down the front steps. "And don't worry. It gets harder." He chuckled to himself as he trotted to Hines's patrol car. "Well, that was worthless," he said, leaning in the driver's side window.

The policeman turned to show he was on the phone. "Hang on a second," he said and then held the phone away from his face. "You know a Bart Timmons?"

"No. Is he from here?" Chase asked.

"Yeah," Hines said and then returned to the call. He asked the person on the other end to text him some information and then hung up. "We've got a lead," he explained.

"Really?"

"My guys found a vehicle registration on the floor of McGee's squad car."

"Let me guess: Bart Timmons," Chase said.

"You wanna guess what kind of vehicle, too?"

"I don't think I have to," Chase said.

"I'm gonna kill this guy," Hines said.

Chase tried to dial things back. "I know you're upset, Sergeant, but we need to take this one step at a time."

"I know," Hines conceded. "This has just all been so frustrating. And…devastating." A bell rang once from his phone. Mark Hines took a quick look and turned back to Chase. "Wanna go give this Timmons guy a visit?"

"I'll be right behind you," Chase said, and hopped inside his rental car.

***

The trip from the Gundersons' was a quick one. Chase followed Hines to some farmland east of Gable. The FBI agent knew they had arrived when he read the name on the mailbox. They pulled their vehicles up the long driveway to an older house sitting next to a large barn. With snow on the ground in the middle of winter, Chase didn't expect to see a lot of farming going on. However, a familiar farm aroma still lingered. In the distance he could hear the mooing of some cows. He could also smell them.

"We don't know anything about this guy?" Chase asked as they walked to the front door.

"I ran some checks on our way over here," Hines explained. "Apparently, this is the family farm where Bart Timmons grew up. And he's had a bunch of DWIs."

"That could have something to do with what happened to McGee," Chase said.

"Really?" Hines seemed surprised. "Driving drunk is a reason to kill a cop?"

Chase smiled a sympathetic grin. "I know it sounds crazy. But when you're an FBI agent, you look at every possibility no matter how ridiculous. I read a quote once from an author," Chase continued. "Can't remember who it was, but he said something like, the only difference between real life and fiction is that fiction needs to make sense. I thought that was a perfect saying to keep in mind during investigations. This is real life. Things often don't make sense. They're not always logical."

"Hmm," Hines said. "I'll have to remember that." He raised his hand to knock on the door but stopped short. "One more thing before I forget," he said. "Bart Timmons just had his third arrest for driving while intoxicated a couple weeks ago. Happened here in Gable."

"Wow," Chase said.

"Something still doesn't add up though," Hines said and rapped on the screen door. The men waited thirty seconds until the door finally opened. A woman in her late forties, but dressed like she was in her seventies, answered the door. She was wearing a one-piece, flower-covered dress, and her hair was pinned up in a bun.

"Oh my," she said as she unlatched the door. "What has he done now?"

"Sorry to impose ma'am," Hines greeted her. "Is Bart home today?"

"Well, of course he is. He's a farmer, ain't he? He's out there somewhere feeding something. Let me give him a call for you," she said.

"Can we come—" Hines was going to ask if he and Agent Sheehan could come inside the house and wait, but the woman stepped forward onto the porch and let out a bellow.

"Barrrrrrt! Company!"

The woman listened in silence. Hines opened his mouth to speak again but was unable to get a word in before the woman let out another screech.

"Barrrrrrrt! There," she said with a smile, "that oughta do it. Come on in, gentlemen. May as well make yourselves at home. The only time the authorities show up here is when Bart's done something wrong. I usually know what it is, too."

The two lawmen followed the woman into the large two-story house. The floors were wood, and the furniture was old. The scent of mothballs assaulted them immediately.

"Can I get you anything to drink?" she asked. Both men declined and remained standing in the hallway between the living room and the kitchen. "Well, make yourselves at home then," she suggested. "He should be here any minute. I could hear him off in the distance."

Chase and Hines looked at each other, puzzled. They were both trained professionals and neither had heard a thing. But, as promised, the back door opened shortly after and a large man walked through the kitchen, into the hallway.

"Bart Timmons?" Hines asked him.

"Yes sir," Timmons replied.

"We'd like to ask you a few questions, if you wouldn't mind."

"Sure," the big guy responded. "What about?"

"Is there a place we can talk privately? Maybe have a seat?"

"All right," Timmons replied. "Follow me, sirs." He led them down another hallway in front of the kitchen to an empty room. Timmons pulled three folding chairs out of the closet with one hand and opened them up. He sat down on one of them and motioned to the two men to join him.

After he and Sheehan introduced themselves, Hines cut to the chase.

"Bart, do you have any idea how your vehicle registration could've ended up in a police officer's car when, by law, you shouldn't even be driving?"

Chase already assumed Bart Timmons was not a very bright man. While profiling was technically not a fair assessment, it was certainly something that investigators did on a regular basis without thinking. Chase could immediately tell that Timmons was caught off guard by Hines' question. The look on his face went from concerned to panicked. However Timmons' vehicle registration had ended up in McGee's patrol car, the farm boy had sincerely forgotten about it until this moment.

"I don't know," Timmons responded with a halfhearted shrug.

"Bart," Chase said, "the police officer is dead. Did you know this?"

"I-I don't know," Bart repeated.

"You got another DWI charge a couple of weeks ago. What were you doing out?" Hines said, now clearly aggravated. "You were driving…illegally."

Tagging onto Hines, Chase repeated his words from moments ago. "The police officer is dead, Bart. Did you do it?"

"God, no!" Timmons exclaimed. "I wouldn't kill anybody."

"Why were you driving, Bart?" Hines asked him again.

Bart's eyes darted around the empty room. Chase could tell the guy was searching for an answer.

"Have you guys talked to Sergeant Jackson yet?"

***

"How would you feel about me getting a job here?" Claire asked Barrett. She had used her own money and purchased some food from the grocery store to fix a meal for them.

"Sure. Whatever," Barrett responded as he took a bite of the broccoli chicken casserole she had made.

"That doesn't sound very enthusiastic," she said.

"I'm sorry," Barrett said. "I just…I have a lot on my mind."

"I know you do," Claire said. "I understand. I really do. I'm just trying…trying to fit in, I guess."

"Sure," Barrett said.

"Sure what?" Claire said. "Sure you wouldn't mind if I got a job or sure you understand that I'm just trying to fit in?"

Barrett raised his eyebrows. "Both?"

Claire immediately noted the inflection of a question. "I'd…umm, live here," she said under her breath. "Right?"

Another bite of broccoli, cheese, and grilled chicken entered his mouth before he spoke. "Sure."

"Barrett, my God! I get it. I know you're dealing with a lot of fucked up shit right now. And no, I can't relate to any of it. But for God's sake throw me a bone, will you?"

Barrett jerked his head backwards and showed Claire that she now had his attention. "I'm with you, Claire," he said. "I'm sorry. I don't mean to neglect you. I want you to know that nothing has changed for me. I still feel as strongly for you as I did before I flew here from Omaha. You have my word."

"Are you sure, Barrett?" Claire asked. "I don't have to be here. I can go back. All you have to do is tell me."

"I want you here, Claire," Barrett said calmly. He smiled at her. "Really."

She watched him closely for a few seconds, searching for any hint of sarcasm or lack of interest. Finally, she turned her attention back to her plate.

"So, have you thought at all about what you want to do, for a job I mean," Claire asked him.

"I'm trying to wrap my brain around everything that has happened," Barrett said. "And to answer your question, no, I haven't. But I'm going to make a few phone calls today and see what I can drum up. My credit card should be able to keep me going for another week or two, but after that…"

"That's why I'm getting a job," Claire said. "I don't have a lot of experience doing much of anything but waiting tables or tending bar, but if I can end up at the right restaurant I can make some good money in tips."

"Promise me something?" Barrett asked her.

"Anything," Claire said.

"Oh, don't say that," Barrett replied. "Promise me you won't turn down any tip, no matter how big it is."

"You're right," Claire agreed, "I can't promise that."

"You ever gonna tell me the story as to why you have such a hard time with tips over a certain amount?"

"Yeah," Claire said.

"How about now?"

"I don't know…" Claire said quietly.

"You know what?" Barrett said suddenly. "That's fine. I don't like to pressure anyone with things that might be sensitive. You'll tell me when you're ready."

Barrett got up from the table and took his dirty plate to the sink. As he rattled some dishes around, he could sense Claire was considering her options. When he was finished, he kept his back to her and paused briefly. It was as if he knew she needed him to be looking the other way before she began to share her dark secret.

"My Uncle Stubby molested me…more than once…for…money."

XXXV

Chase plowed through the interrogation room door of the Gable Police station. Jackson stood up from his chair, though still cuffed to the table. Chase didn't stop at the door. He moved like a linebacker towards the police sergeant and slammed his palms into the man's thick chest, pushing him backwards and causing him to slip.

Jackson fell to the hard floor but only as far as his handcuffed arm would allow. He shuffled to regain his balance and stand back up. "What the hell?" he shouted at Chase.

"You better start telling me what the hell's going on!" Chase howled back.

"I have been," Jackson said. "Sorta," he added.

"Well, you haven't been telling me enough," Chase said. "Sit down." Jackson did as he was told. "So, you're running cocaine for him too?"

Jackson raised his eyebrows. "No."

"No? Why did Bart Timmons just tell me that then?"

"Who's that?" Jackson asked.

"Would you knock off the bullshit?" Chase said. "He also told me that you were supposed to fix his DWI problem."

"What?"

"Yeah, that's right. So he could be the middleman for

you," Chase said.

"Well," Jackson said, "I'm sure if you check the record, you'll see I did nothing of the sort."

"Yeah, already did that," Chase said. "Let me give you a little more information so you can understand how serious this is getting. Officer Murray McGee is dead."

Jackson hesitated before responding. "How did that happen?"

"He pulled over Bart Timmons the other night."

"Bart Timmons killed him?"

"No, I don't think so," Chase said.

"Well then who did?"

"That's the million-dollar question, Sergeant Jackson," Chase quipped. "Who's doing all the killing around here? Ironically, the person with the most answers is a cop who's not saying anything."

Jackson considered this as Chase continued his rant.

"Okay, Chumansky's death. I'm not saying that should've happened, but him being gone is one thing. But then my sister ends up on her deathbed, and now we have a local cop strangled in his own cruiser. What the hell is going on around here? I know you know, Jackson. And you're gonna help me make this right."

Chase turned around and slammed the door.

***

"I didn't get Sergeant Jackson in trouble did I? I didn't mean to," Timmons moaned from inside the room across the hall. He was seated at a table similar to the one in the interrogation room. Chief Perkins and Chase stood over the big guy.

"So you're telling us that Jackson came to you and asked you — no — told you you were going to sell cocaine for this Hispanic guy named Pablo," Chase clarified. "And in return Jackson was going to make your most recent drunk driving charge disappear. Is that right?"

"Yeah," Timmons said sorrowfully, head bowed. "That's what happened. But I didn't kill anybody. In fact, Sergeant Jackson told me if they — I mean Pablo or whoever — told me to kill somebody, that I was supposed to tell him."

"So what happened the other night? You got pulled over, right?" Chase asked.

"Yeah, for a taillight that was out," Bart explained. "He asked for my license, but all I had was my registration. I told him I had forgotten my license."

"But that wasn't true, was it? It got taken away a few weeks ago, right?" Perkins said.

"Yes, sir."

"So what did you do?" Chase asked.

"I waited."

"Okay."

"For a long time."

"How did you end up leaving?"

"Well, I got out of my truck and went back to check on him," Bart said.

"And?"

"And I did that. Went to his car to see if he was okay."

"What did you discover?"

"That he wasn't okay," Bart said. "I saw his eyes...they were glued open. He was looking up. Like he was watching an airplane. But he...he looked scared. He wasn't...moving."

It was evident that Timmons was telling the truth, reliving the horror of seeing such a savage death up close like that. But Chase still had to ask the tough questions.

"Are you sure you didn't kill him because you knew he was going to run your name through the database and find out the truth and arrest you?"

"What? No. I didn't even—" But Bart was unable to finish his thought as Chase kept pressing the right buttons to see what would happen.

"You know what kind of trouble you're in, right? This is serious business, Bart. Driving without a license, trafficking drugs, murdering a police officer..."

Bart closed his eyes and shook his head. "I know everyone around here thinks I'm a big dummy and a drunk. And...well, I guess I am. But...I'm no killer. I didn't shoot that police officer. I don't even own a gun."

Chase motioned for Perkins to step into the hall with him.

"He's telling the truth," Perkins said, beating Chase to the punch.

"Yeah. McGee was strangled from behind," Chase said.

"What now?"

"The only thing that makes sense is the cartel," the FBI agent suggested. "We need to get Jackson to help us set these guys up in a sting."

"Or Bart," Perkins said.

"Definitely. Both of them."

They stepped back into the room with Bart. This time,

instead of hovering over him, Chase sat down across the table from him, while Perkins remained standing.

"We know you didn't kill Officer McGee, Bart."

"You do? Oh gosh, that's great. Thank you so much, mister." After saying this, Bart's wheels began to visibly spin. "Sorry. I meant to say 'Agent.'"

"No problem, Bart," Chase told him. "You need to know that I'm on your side. And Chief Perkins' side. You two are on the same side, right?"

"Yes. I think so," Bart stole a glance at the chief. "Yes."

"Good. Because I'm gonna need your help."

From behind the table, near where Chief Perkins was standing, a custom ringtone began to play — John Mellencamp's song "Small Town."

"That's my phone," Bart announced. Chase looked at him. "Well, that's one of my phones," he added. "It's the 'special' one." Perkins reached for the device and handed it to Chase.

"Perfect timing," Chase said, handing the phone to Bart.

***

Maddison Chumansky was sound asleep on the couch in the middle of the afternoon when the doorbell roused her with the Mecca Warehouse jingle. Despite the fact that she now owned the two stores, she planned to get the doorbell changed, soon. She wasn't surprised that Tom hadn't changed his will to reflect the divorce. Whether he ever planned to or not, Maddison wasn't sure. Thankfully, the stores ran by themselves for the most part. Being very pregnant was her priority right now.

She waddled her way to the door as quickly as possible, but apparently not fast enough as the jingle began again.

"God, I hate that song," Maddison grumbled out loud. When she opened the door, she was surprised at who she saw.

"Hi. Is Chum here?"

At first Maddison felt a numbing sense of déjà vu. After fighting off a dizzy spell that also hit her, she took a moment to reflect on the question the big bearded blonde man had just asked her. And then she burst into tears. It wasn't because she was upset about Tom's death. She *was* upset. But more than anything, Maddison was pretty sure this was a case of pregnancy hormones and emotional instability. She immediately covered her face and moved back to the sitting area where she had just come from, leaving the door open.

"Was it something I said?" Randy asked her as he let himself into the house. He closed the door behind him and followed her.

Maddison continued to sniffle and weep as she sat on the couch again. She reached over to the coffee table and pulled a tissue from the box. "I'm sorry," she said.

"Lady, I just asked if Chum was home."

The sound of Tom's nickname sent Maddison into another wailing tirade.

"Look lady, I realize you're upset already, so I want to apologize for making you more upset with this," Randy said as he pointed a revolver at her. "Where's Chum?"

Maddison looked up through her tears and saw the gun pointed in her direction. She was surprised but not nearly as surprised as she would've been a few months ago.

"Don't you get it?" Maddison sobbed. "My husband's dead."

"Right," Randy said. "So how about the money?"

"My God," Maddison said. "You really don't know what's going on around here, do you? Tom is dead. The Mexicans killed him and took their money back. I can't help you with anything."

"What?" Randy said.

"I'm serious," Maddison said. "Why do you think I'm crying? Also, I'm onto the fact that you're not on the up-and-up. You're too old to have gone to high school with Tom."

"I'm going to believe you because I really don't want to hurt you," Randy said. "It does make sense. But what about that Barrett guy? Where is he at?"

"I don't know," Maddison said. "Last I heard, he was here hanging out with Claire. She was with him when they told me Tom's body had been found. That's all I know, though. Whether he's still here in town or not I couldn't tell you. And, no offense, but I don't really care where he's at. I've got enough on my mind. Maybe you noticed when you came in?" Maddison stood up and showed him her pregnant belly.

"Who's this Claire? Where do I find her?"

"She's a friend of mine," Maddison explained. "She was the other person who was here that day you came and gave me your bullshit story. And if you think I'm going to tell you where to find her, you're out of your mind."

"Lady, don't get tough with me." Randy took a step closer to where she was still standing, her baby bump pushing out her maternity blouse.

"Tell you what I'll do," Maddison said. "She works at the only restaurant in town, on Main Street. It's called Stubby's.

Go there and see if you can track her down that way. At least it'll be in a public place and you can't be a menace to society that way."

"You really don't know me very well," Randy said with a snigger. He turned and walked out the front door, leaving it open.

***

"I've got this thing set up," Chase told Jackson. "I need you to help out. Help Bart."

Jackson refused to give in. "I'm not doing shit."

Chase wanted to pounce on Jackson again but knew it would not be professional nor would it get him what he needed.

"I'm still waiting on my lawyer," the sergeant added.

"We don't have time to wait around for you to play tiddledywinks with your attorney," Chase said. "You need to start being honest with yourself about what you've done and how you can help fix things."

Jackson shook his head viciously. "Do you have any idea what will happen to my wife — my children — if…look, I beg you *not* to try and set these guys up. We'll *all* end up dead."

Chase stepped forward. "Have you thought at all about the people you've involved in this thing?"

"Me?"

"Yeah, you," Chase said. "Chumansky, his wife, his unborn child, Bart Timmons, your family, my sister…do I need to continue? What about Murray McGee?"

"That's where you're wrong, Chase. My family hasn't been affected by this. At least not to a point where our lives have changed. I'm trying to prevent that from happening. You force me back into it like this and they're all dead. You've got a little girl. Put yourself in my position. What would *you* do?"

Chase's phone vibrated in the front pocket of his pants. He pulled it out, looked at the screen, and saw that the call was from the hospital in Adler. "I'll be right back," Chase told Jackson as he answered the phone and wandered into the hallway. "Sheehan."

"Agent Sheehan, this is Heather Langston — Dr. Langston. I need you to come to the hospital right away."

"What?"

"I need you to come to the hospital," Langston repeated. "It's about your sister."

This time Chase could sense a hint of concern, or was it empathy, in her voice. "What's going on?" he demanded.

"There's been a change in Delia's condition…Chase," the doctor said.

"Just tell me what happened. I'm a big boy. I can handle it. I don't want to think about it while I'm on my way there. What's going on?"

"Agent Sheehan…Chase…Delia is…she…she's gone. She passed away 15 minutes ago."

"What?" Chase couldn't believe his ears.

"I'm so sorry," Dr. Langston said. "I promise you I did everything I could. There was just too much pressure in her skull."

"No," Chase said. "You're full of shit."

"I'm sorry," Langston said. "But it's true, Chase."

***

Chase had never driven a car so fast in his life. Despite

the high speed, the drive still seemed to take an hour instead of eleven minutes.

"I'm so, so sorry," Dr. Langston said the moment she saw Chase.

"What happened? How...I thought..." A distraught Chase was lost for words.

Langston shook her head. "It's like I said before the surgery; head injuries are frighteningly unpredictable. The surgery relieved some pressure temporarily, but it returned. And when it did, it didn't give her a fighting chance. She ended up with multiple aneurisms and massive bleeding in the brain. There was nothing we could do at that point."

Chase dropped his chin to his chest and rubbed the top of his head.

"I feel stupid apologizing all the time," Langston said. "Please let me know if there's anything I can do."

"Where is she?"

"You know where she would normally be right now," the doctor replied.

"Yeah, the morgue."

"I knew you were going to ask to see her. I wanted to put her someplace less...morbid...for you. Follow me."

Dr. Langston led Chase down the hall as he fought back tears. They turned the corner and walked to the end of another hallway, where an orderly was sitting in a chair.

"Thanks, Terry," she told the man. "Please wait down the hall. Give Agent Sheehan his privacy, and when he's done and has left, you can go ahead and finish up."

"Okay, will do," Terry said and moved himself and his chair down the hall a hundred feet.

"If you need anything," she said, trying to make eye contact with Chase, who was staring at the closed door, "just let Terry know. He'll either help you or find me."

Chase responded by taking a deep breath and exhaling. He pushed the door open and Langston slowly walked away behind him.

Inside the room he could see his twin sister lying on a gurney, motionless. As he approached her, he could see that her face was already turning pale. Her shaved head was still wrapped with bandages. Chase moved closer and stared at Delia's face. Though he was still trying to refrain from crying, a tear dropped from his eye and landed on the blue sheet that covered Delia's body.

"Oh, Dee," he groaned, his voice echoing throughout the otherwise empty room. "This wasn't supposed to happen. I...I don't know...I don't know what I'm going to do without you."

He placed the back of his hand to her cheek. It was cold, but it brought a sense of comfort to Chase for a few brief moments.

"Delia..."

His sister was dead. This moment was surreal to him. All of the teasing and playful disagreements were over for good. Delia would never have the chance to meet the right man or have kids. And Chase was going to have to tell their parents about this. How could this be happening?

"Delia, I'm going to make this right. I promise you," Chase told her lifeless shell. "I'm going to take care of the people who did this to you. Every last one of them. I won't be able to rest until I do. And I doubt you will be able to either."

He leaned down and kissed her on the portion of her

forehead that was visible beneath the bandage.

"I love you, Dee," he sobbed.

XXXVI

While sitting in a tedious meeting with a recruiter, Barrett had received a voicemail from his mother on his new mobile phone. A recruiter's office was not where he had expected to be spending his time today, but he'd made the mistake of answering a generic ad online for a "numbers nerd" with an accounting degree. It had been a long time since Barrett was interviewed by a headhunter, but today's meeting had brought it all back. He really did try hard to respect this occupation, but every experience he'd had was fruitless and boring. Almost none of these guys seemed to care one bit about him and were only concerned with finding the one applicant their client ended up hiring — before another recruiter did it first. What a farce.

The voicemail from his mother informed him that his former coworker Julia McGregor had been trying to reach him. Not knowing for sure if Barrett actually wanted to speak with Julia, Ella Greyson took the information down and relayed it to him.

Julia had always been a good work friend during his years at the Clevinger Group. He had no reason to think she was trying to reach him for any kind of vindictive reason. As he drove away from the recruiter's building, he dialed Julia's number on the Bluetooth system of his mother's SUV.

"Hello?"

"Julia, it's Barrett Greyson. How are you?"

"Hi, Barrett. It's so great to hear from you. I wasn't sure if the message would reach you."

"My mom's pretty good about that kind of thing. Don't get me wrong, sometimes she gives me messages that I never return, but..."

"I'm so sorry about your dad, Barrett."

"Thanks."

"Is that what brought you back?"

"To make a long story short, yeah."

"I hope I don't need to tell you that I never once believed you had anything to do with Otto's death."

"I appreciate that."

"So, you're apparently, uh, not in trouble. A free man, I mean." Julia was trying her best to be sensitive.

"Yes, I am. Like I said, it's a long story. So, what's been going on there? I mean, at the office."

"Use your imagination. With Otto *and* you gone, you-know-who is in charge. That's kind of why I called."

"Hmm, okay." Barrett wasn't sure what she was getting at.

"He just doesn't know what he's doing, and...I'm not saying you'd ever come back, but..."

"Come back? Boyd probably thinks I killed his dad. I don't see how he'd even consider bringing me back."

"I'm not so sure he thinks you did it," Julia explained. "I'm starting to think he believes *he* did it."

"Huh?" Barrett wondered how preposterous that

would sound if he didn't already know it wasn't true.

"Well, not literally," Julia explained. "At least, I don't think so. But I think the regrets he has about the way he treated Otto are beginning to take a toll on him. Catch up with him. He kinda blames himself."

"You been sleeping with him again?" Barrett had to ask. The way Julia was acting was peculiar. Like she had been pillow talking with Boyd or something.

"No!" she said immediately. "I might be stupid, but I don't make the same mistake twice...usually. Call it intuition, I guess."

"I have to be honest, Julia. I really don't care. I mean, I tolerated Boyd because I had no choice at the time. But I do now. This is a new beginning for me. I think coming back to the Clevinger Group would be a step in the wrong direction."

"Would you consider just talking to him?" Julia asked.

"Really? About what?"

"He doesn't have anyone. He's parentless now and an only child."

"He's got friends, a wife, employees. Why don't you talk to him?"

"For starters, he doesn't listen to women. And it also might be seriously awkward, given the history I have with him."

"I just don't know what I have to offer him right now," Barrett said.

"Just think about it, will ya? For your old pal Julia."

"Fine, I will."

"Thanks, Barrett."

"Save your gratitude for when I actually do

something," Barrett cracked as they hung up.

***

"I'll tell you one thing, Jack. Be thankful you don't need a public defender because you have me. This is a mess!"

Rick Masterson had been friends with John Jackson since junior high school. The two had played basketball together in high school and never lost touch.

"You don't know the half of it," Jackson said.

"How much are you going to tell me?" Masterson asked. "You know I can't help you if you don't tell me the truth."

"I realize that in theory," Jackson said. "But I've got a lot riding on this. We're talking about my family's lives here."

"I understand that, but there are other lives that have already been changed forever because of your actions," the attorney said. "Chumansky is dead. Murray McGee is dead. And Delia DeMarco, too."

"What? She's not dead."

"Yes, Jack, she is," Masterson said empathetically. "I was just walking in the door here at the station when the FBI agent got the news. DeMarco is his sister as I understand it."

Jackson's jaw dropped. "She died?"

His attorney didn't feel it required another response.

This was all becoming too much to handle. All Jackson ever wanted to do was live a peaceful life. Enforce the law, get married, have some children. Now, look at what had happened. Despite the fact he hadn't asked for any of this trouble, he couldn't help but feel responsible for every bit of it. He'd probably made the wrong choice the first time Pablo had called him. No. There was no "probably" about it. He had messed up.

"You still with me?" Masterson waved a hand in front of his friend and client's face.

"Yeah," Jackson said quietly.

"So, where do you want to begin?"

"Here's the thing," Jackson said. "You need to strike a deal right now."

"What? Really?" Masterson asked. "You sure?"

"Yeah," Jackson said. "But I want immunity. Total immunity. For everything."

"And what are you gonna give them in return?"

"Everything," Jackson replied.

***

Claire entered the Danny's restaurant where she had eaten breakfast only a few early mornings ago. She was pleased to see Helen at the cash register, where she had just finished ringing up a customer.

"Hi," Claire said. "Remember me?"

A warm smile spilled over Helen's wrinkled face. "I do. How are you? On your way back to Iowa?"

Claire smiled back. "Ye have little faith. I'm here for the complete opposite reason —I'm staying."

"Well, good for you. What can I do, then?" Helen asked as she stuck a receipt under the credit card machine.

"I need a job to help get my feet on the ground," Claire said. "Are there any openings here?"

Helen scanned the restaurant to make sure no one was

in earshot. She leaned down before responding. "Honey, you're not going to make much money here. People who frequent Danny's are crappy tippers. Some of them pay for their meals in coins and wind up leaving you pennies."

"I don't really mind," Claire explained. "I just need to get the ball rolling. I might not stay long, but…"

"I understand," Helen said. "I only work here because I can draw Social Security at the same time. I don't make enough to worry about it. I mean, as long as I die soon enough and don't run out of the government funds."

"Oh my," Claire said. "Don't say that."

Helen cracked a weary smile. "You'll understand some day."

"I have tons of experience waiting tables," Claire continued. "I've worked in a bar and grill for years."

"You'll probably start out at about five and a quarter an hour, plus your tips," Helen said.

"That's fine," Claire said. "It's actually a quarter more than what I was making in my hometown."

"Well, okay," Helen said. "This would all be great if I was the manager — and I probably should be — but I'm not. Let me see if Ross is available. What's your name again, honey?"

"Claire. Claire Mathison."

"Be right back," Helen said.

Claire took a seat on the bench at the front of the restaurant. Assuming she was offered a job, she knew it wouldn't be long-term. But she needed a quick fix to show Barrett she was in it for the long haul. She wanted to be with him, spend more time with him, get to know him better. Even if she only brought in a couple of hundred dollars a week, it would show a commitment to being here with him.

"Claire?" A shorter than average man walked up to her. His hair was dark, as was his complexion. He was clean-shaven, but Claire could tell by the shadow that his beard grew in thick. His cheeks were rosy and his smile warm. He held his hand out as Claire stood up.

"Yes, that's me," she said.

"I'm Ross Richfield," the man said. His voice was gentle and had a hint of femininity to it. "I'm the general manager here. Helen tells me you're looking for a job and you have experience."

"Yes, that's true."

"Come on back to the office. Let's talk." Richfield led her through the restaurant to a small room adjacent to the kitchen. As Claire walked behind him, she was amused to note that she was slightly taller than he was.

The manager motioned for Claire to have a seat on a folding chair, while he sat next to her at his desk. There were papers scattered haphazardly around a computer monitor. Claire assumed there were a keyboard and mouse somewhere under it all.

"I apologize for the mess," Richfield said. "I have three shift managers and we share this office. I'm a neat freak, believe it or not. Clearly the others are not."

"I didn't even notice," Claire said.

"So, tell me about your work experience and what brings you here looking for a job," he said.

Claire gave Ross Richfield a brief overview of how she had worked in her family's restaurant since she was nine and understood how to give every customer a good experience no matter what kind of baggage they might have carried in with them.

"What brought you all the way out here?" Richfield asked. "Especially at this time of year."

"My boyfriend lives out here," Claire said. This was the first time she had used the term. It had just kind of rolled off her tongue. She was glad Barrett wasn't here to witness it.

"That sounds like quite a story," Richfield commented. "Not that I'm asking. You don't have to tell me anything personal. In fact, you didn't have to mention your boyfriend or anything like that. Just making myself clear. Danny's is very particular about these things. The big, stuffy, talking heads are scared to death of getting sued."

Claire snickered.

"Holy crap," Richfield said. "Did I say that out loud?"

They both laughed.

"Claire, I think I'd like to offer you a job," he said. "I can start you off at five and a half per hour because of your experience. But, sweet baby Jesus, don't tell anybody. They'll all go cray-cray if they find out."

"Thank you very much, Mr. Richfield," Claire said. "I accept."

"You keep all of your own tips, too, of course," Richfield added. "Also, you can just call me Ross. Or R-Squared, Double-R, or my personal favorite, R2."

"Like *Star Wars*," Claire said.

"Oh, yes," Ross said, waving his hand. "Lately, one of the cooks has been calling me D2, which can be confusing when you're used to all of your nicknames containing the letter R."

Claire nodded. "So, when would you like me to start?"

Ross shuffled through the papers on the desk. "Let's see, where is that damned schedule," he murmured to himself. "Ah, here it is." He held the piece of paper at arm's length in front of his face. "Honestly, I have reading glasses around here somewhere. But it could take me forever to find them in this chaos."

"I never would've guessed you were old enough to need them," Claire said.

Ross flashed a toothy white smile, tilted his head, and waved his hand again. "It's the tanning bed. It keeps me young."

They shared another laugh before Richfield continued. "How about the day after tomorrow? Umm, I should mention we usually start people off on the graveyard shift to get them used to things. Are you okay with that for just a few nights? It's eight at night to five in the morning."

Claire shrugged. "Sure."

Just then, a tall black man wearing a stained white hat stuck his head inside the doorway. Claire could tell by the way he was dressed that he worked in the kitchen.

"Hey, boss," he said. "Joe's here a little early. I'm gonna bug out now if that's okay with you. The old lady texted me and said our eight-year-old is sick. I'm gonna stop by the drugstore on the way home."

"Go for it, Austin. Get out of here," Ross told him.

The man gave Claire a nod before smiling at his manager. "Thanks," he said. He took off his hat and began to exit. "See you tomorrow, R5 minus three," the man added.

Ross did a double take before responding. "What's that supposed to mean?" But Austin was already out of sight.

A cackle could be heard in the distance.

"See what I mean about the nicknames?" Ross said. "We try to have fun around here. Work hard, play hard, I guess."

"I like that mantra," Claire said.

Ross grabbed a pen and wrote down some notes. After a few words, he stopped and brought the pen to his lips in thought. "R5," he said, shaking his head. "What the hell is R5?"

Claire decided it would make her funny new boss feel old if she told him that R5 was a famous pop rock band.

***

Gathering the information he wanted upon his return to Gable, Iowa, was easier than Randy had expected. Especially after talking to Chum's wife. He went to Stubby's and immediately asked about the girl named Claire who worked there. Randy learned all sorts of things that he didn't care about in the process of finding out where Claire was. He discovered that Claire's aunt was the widow of the owner of the restaurant and a rather chatty woman. She told Randy that Claire had taken a trip to Colorado to see her "friend." Apparently this vacation that her niece had taken was without much notice and having an effect on the restaurant. Her aunt now needed to work extra hours to fill in during her niece's scheduled shifts and was clearly not happy about it. With all the excessive talking, Randy thought it was strange she never asked who he was and why he was trying to find Claire.

Driving a car he'd stolen in Iowa upon his release from jail, Randy was already running out of the cash Janssen had given him. At this point he had only one priority: find

Barrett Greyson and turn him in. Or better yet, find Barrett Greyson and get the money he was owed. If there was one thing that enraged Randy, it was getting screwed over. A deal is a deal. Greyson needed to pay up like he had promised, and *then* Randy could turn him in.

Now that Randy was in Denver, he would be able to operate more efficiently and spend less money. He might need to sleep a night or two in the car and skip the luxury of a hotel, but that was okay. All he needed was to find his man and get what was rightfully his. Randy knew he never should've spent the money the way he had the first two nights, staying in nice hotels that ran him well over one hundred dollars per night. But after those days in jail recently, he really needed to relieve some stress. It made him feel better sleeping in a comfortable bed and using the Jacuzzi in the pool area. So what if people looked at him funny because he was wearing his tighty-whities in the water? They were all he had. Besides, wasn't wearing his underwear in the pool better than skinny-dipping? The people at the Hampton Inn acted like they had never seen a partially naked former wrestler before.

Randy's next move was to find a public library where he could use a computer and the Internet for free. He would conduct an exhaustive Google search and find out where Barrett Greyson or somebody from his family lived. Things might not wind up as easy to uncover as they were in Gable. Randy was sure people wouldn't give up information as nonchalantly this time. But if he wasn't able to find Greyson directly, there were plenty of news articles online about him with quotes from other people the guy knew: coworkers, friends, etc. Someone was bound to have information that would lead him to Barrett Greyson. Randy would simply cross each bridge as needed.

Whatever it takes, he thought and then touched the gun tucked away in his jeans.

***

"Honey, I'm home," Claire joked as she bounced through the front door of Barrett's condo, her ponytail swinging behind her. "And I bring good tidings."

Barrett strolled out of the bedroom, having recently returned from the day's exhausting job search. "I like tidings," he said as he reached out and gave her hug and a peck on the lips.

"I got a job," Claire blurted.

"Wow," Barrett said. "That was fast."

Claire took his hand and led him to the sofa. "Waitress jobs are easier to get. I'm less skilled than you are."

"I don't know about that," Barrett replied.

"Well, let's not compare our talents right now," Claire said. "The job isn't exactly glamorous. I'm not going to be making a lot of money. It's at the Danny's up the road."

"You're working at a Danny's? But you have all of your teeth." Barrett laughed.

"Ha ha," Claire said. "My boss seems really nice. I think he might be gay."

"Well, I…" Barrett wasn't sure how to respond to that one.

"I'd rather be working at a higher end restaurant and making more in tips," Claire continued. "But this is just something to get me started. I'll keep my eyes and ears open. I know I could really do well at a steak house or something like that."

"I'm sure you could," Barrett agreed.

"So, how did your search go?"

"Not so good," he said. "I really don't want to talk about it."

"Okay."

"But I did have an interesting voicemail earlier," Barrett said. Over the next few minutes, he told Claire about returning Julia's phone call and his former coworker's thoughts on the Clevinger Group's new CEO and the business's future.

"She thinks you should talk to Boyd?" Claire confirmed.

"Yeah."

"That seems like it would be weird now, wouldn't it?" Claire commented.

"I mean, it would be weirder if I had murdered his father," Barrett said. "But it's even more awkward for me knowing what I know about who did do it."

"I know." Claire tossed her arm over the back of the couch and rested her head on Barrett's shoulder. She massaged his chest with her free hand. "I know," she said again.

Barrett responded to her sincere attempt to soothe him. "I'm extremely thankful you came here, Claire," he told her. "I don't know what condition I'd be in right now if I hadn't been able to confide in you."

She leaned up and kissed a spot on his cheek, close to his ear. "That's the sweetest thing you've said since I got here," she whispered.

"I'm sorry it's taking me so long to warm up," Barrett said, this time more quietly. "There's just still so much going on in my head."

"I have something else to tell you," Claire said. "Actually, a couple of things."

"Okay."

"Today, while I was interviewing with my new boss, he asked me how I ended up out here from Iowa," she said. "Without thinking, I told him 'my boyfriend' lives here. It just kind of came out that way."

Barrett snorted. "The easy joke right now would be for me to say something like 'He does? What part of town does he live in?' But I'm bigger than that."

"You just said it."

"Technically, that's not true," he clarified with another laugh.

"Are you making fun of me?" Claire asked with a slap on the stomach. The impact made Barrett grunt.

"No," he said after catching his breath. "Not at all."

"Good, because you're making me not want to tell you the other thing."

"I'm sorry," Barrett said. "Seriously. Please continue."

Claire placed her head back on his shoulder. "I don't know how you feel about that —me referring to you absentmindedly as my 'boyfriend' — but I can tell you it flowed naturally for me. It just felt…right. I feel so strongly about you, Barrett. I've risked embarrassment to come here. I've opened myself up to you. I've never done anything like this before. And you shared a deep, dark secret with me and believe enough in me to know I will remain by your side." She paused and began playing with the fabric of his shirt. "I'm falling in love with you, Barrett Greyson. You are very special to me."

Barrett sat up, forcing Claire to do the same. He wasn't caught off guard one bit by her proclamation. He shared many of her emotions, he just had so many other things rattling around in his brain. "Claire," he said, "you're very special to me, too." He reached out and touched her cheek with his fingers before gently sliding them down to her chin. "I feel the same way. I'm falling in love with you, too." He leaned forward, drew her face to his, and softly kissed her lips.

"Are you sure?" she said.

"Yes," he said. "Most definitely." Barrett leaned in and kissed her again, this time more passionately. After thirty seconds he pulled away. "I'm so glad I met you, Claire. We had to go through a lot of crap to get here, but I can't say I would change a thing about it. If anything was different, we probably wouldn't be here together right now."

Claire smiled and leaned in to give him another quick kiss on the lips. "So, when do I get to meet your mother?"

***

Chase exploded through the door of the Gable Police station. He passed Masterson and Chief Perkins standing near the watercooler in the lobby. Before giving either of them a chance to greet him, Chase beelined for the interrogation room where he had left Jackson earlier.

"Hey, my client wants to extend an offer," Jackson's lawyer tried to tell him.

Chase pretended not to hear, slamming the door behind him and locking it.

When Jackson saw Chase, he immediately began to speak. "Chase," he said, "I'm so sorry—" but that was as far as he got.

Chase reached out with one hand and grabbed Jackson's thick neck as tight as he could. Voices could be heard in the hallway, one of them Masterson's as he pounded his fist on the door.

"Sheehan!" the muffled voice said. "You better behave yourself in there!"

Chase squeezed his fingers tight around Jackson's throat. The policeman's eyes bugged wide open. It felt to Chase as though he might pull Jackson's windpipe right through his neck. He wasn't really thinking right now. Still handcuffed to the interrogation table, Jackson used his free hand to try to relieve pressure from his assailant's grip.

"You got my sister killed, didn't you?" Chase growled.

Jackson tried to deny the charges but was unable to form any words as he continued to claw at the FBI agent.

When the reality of what he was doing finally hit, Chase immediately released his grip. Jackson caught his breath, coughed, and massaged his now red throat. Not knowing for sure what to say next, he picked up where he had left off.

"Chase," Jackson said, "I am so sorry about Delia. I promise you this isn't my fault. I want to help."

"I want to hear everything," Sheehan said. "You owe it to Delia."

Jackson nodded. "I do."

Once both men had regained their composure, Chase turned around and opened the door. Rick Masterson practically fell into the room. "What the hell was going on in here?" he asked.

"Police talk," Sheehan said.

"Oh yeah? You okay, Jack?" Masterson asked his high

school chum.

"I'm fine," Jackson replied.

"Let's get this going," Chase said. "We don't have a lot of time."

Jackson's attorney spoke first. "My client wants complete immunity, and in return he will cooperate in any and all ways."

"Total immunity, huh?" Chase said. He raised an eyebrow at Jackson.

"What were you expecting?" Jackson asked.

"I don't know. Why don't you spill your beans first? Then after I hear all of the crooked crap you did, I'll tell you what I think is reasonable."

"He's not talking until the paperwork is done," Masterson said.

"Fine," Chase said. "Get it drawn up. Fast. I need to get it signed off on, and the clock is ticking. We've already got something brewing with your buddy Pablo." Chase looked at Jackson again. "By the way, before you bother writing up the paperwork, it's probably a good idea to let your client know that this is going to include his involvement with a sting operation."

"Are you okay with that?" Masterson asked his client.

"I have a family," Jackson said with a shrug. "I don't see that I have much choice. So go with it."

"Atta boy, Jack," Chase said, patting him on the shoulder.

Jackson looked up at Chase. "Seriously, I am very, very sorry about Delia."

"You're gonna have your chance to prove just how

sorry you are," Chase said.

XXXVII

Chief Perkins had joined Chase, Jackson, Rick Masterson, and Bart Timmons in the main interrogation room. The paperwork had been signed and sealed and was now out of the way. In the process, Masterson had worked a similar deal for Timmons at Jackson's request. It was easy for Chase to agree to helping Timmons out. The guy hadn't killed anyone. Wiping a single DWI from a person's record was one thing, but this was Timmons' third offense. Because of this, the FBI insisted that Bart check himself in to Adler's alcohol and drug rehab center once his assistance was no longer needed.

Now that the sting discussion was under way, Jackson's handcuffs had been removed. Every few minutes he would rub his wrists. Chase wasn't sure if this was because they hurt or because he was nervous.

He oughta be nervous, Chase thought before he began speaking.

"We did some research on Pablo and have reached the conclusion that he is more than likely Pablo Garza. Garza was next in line to Franco Salazar in this geographical division of the Mexican drug cartel. Salazar was the main man who was arrested up the road at the Corner Store a few months ago."

"I know who he is. I wrote the local report," Jackson informed him.

"So, Garza called Bart's phone a few hours ago to check in," Chase continued.

"He does that every day or so," Bart commented.

"But I figure he also wanted to feel out his middleman to see if there were any issues, especially after the job he did on Murray McGee."

"How do we know he isn't already aware of what's going on here?" Jackson asked. "He always seems to be a couple of steps ahead of everything."

"Pablo told me he wanted to meet with me tonight," Bart piped up. "And he seemed…kind of surprised when I said I would."

"I think meeting with Bart is his way of testing the waters," Chase said.

"Why on Earth would he show up if there's a chance he could be ambushed?" Jackson wondered out loud.

"He might not. But if Bart can convince whoever does show up that everything is okay—"

"I don't think you know who you're dealing with here, Chase," Jackson said.

"You got a better idea?"

"No, I'm just sayin'."

Chief Perkins chimed in. "You know, my Granny Lucy was five feet of concrete and would stare you down and stand her ground. She lived till she was ninety-three. I'll never forget the last two things she said to me from her hospital bed when I was just a kid. My God, she looked frail that day. She said to me, 'Nathan, never tell someone they're going the wrong direction unless you can show them why they should be going another direction.'" Perkins glared at Jackson. "She also told me not to grow too fond of the bottle," he continued, this time shooting a glance at Timmons.

"You're still pissed at me, aren't you?" Jackson shot back.

"Forevermore, John Jackson."

"Wow," was all Jackson could manage in response.

"All right you two," Chase interjected. "As we discussed, you're going to be a part of this as well, Jackson. You'll join Bart for his meeting."

"I figured that. But what are you going to be doing?"

"Waiting in the wings."

"You think they won't know?"

"I know what I'm doing, pal." Chase turned to Masterson. "You better tell your client to shut his trap and follow my instructions to the letter. If he has something of importance to offer, great. Otherwise, shut him the hell up!" He directed his attention back to Jackson with the last sentence. Jackson rose from his seat, but his friend and attorney Rick Masterson stuck his hand out, letting his client know it would be a good idea to sit back down.

"We're on your side, Agent," Masterson said while looking at Jackson. A silence swept over the room before the attorney turned his attention to Sheehan. "I trust this will all be done on the up-and-up."

Chase shrugged. "What are you implying?"

"Just want to make sure you plan to bring these guys in. You know, arrest them. Let justice take its course," Masterson explained.

The FBI agent scanned the room before responding. "Isn't that why we're all in this business?"

"Just making sure," Masterson said, glancing at Jackson and then Perkins.

"Can I speak to you for a second, alone?" Perkins asked Chase.

"I guess, sure. We need to hurry, though. Time's wasting."

Perkins walked Chase out to his desk, leaving the other men inside the interrogation room.

"Chase, son. You've been through a hell of a lot since you got here. With your sister's passing…well, no one would blame you if you weren't up to this," Perkins said. He cringed when he finished.

Chase recognized Perkins' good intentions and chose to treat the suggestion with the respect it deserved instead of misdirecting his pain and anguish. "Chief, I get it. And I appreciate it. But I got this. This is my job. I need to take care of things. It's what I do."

"But you're going to cuff 'em, right? No funny business?"

"What have I done to make you think I would ever do otherwise?" Chase asked.

Perkins shrugged and began to wobble back to the interrogation room. "Nothing, son. I was just asking." Chase pondered this while he followed behind the chief. "Everything's fine, Rick," Perkins announced once he and Chase joined the others. "Let's concentrate on laying out this plan so we can get these men out for the sting."

Chase surveyed the room as all eyes redirected to him.

"I realize there are a lot of frustrations and feelings flying around this room right now, many of them coming from me. But it's time we set aside our differences and get back to what we all signed up for years ago, present company excluded." Chase nodded at Bart. "Let's put our heads together and go bring in thc *real* bad guys."

He wasn't sure he believed the baloney he had just spewed, but Chase knew it would sound good on the record down the road, just in case.

***

It felt to Barrett like he had been gone from the Clevinger Group for years instead of months when he walked through the door of the business. Otto's sudden death and Boyd being thrown to the fire had caused more change than Barrett could've imagined. A redesigned logo adorned both the building and the stencil on the door. Instead of an easy to read "CG," the company letters were now represented with a fancy, interconnected font. Because it was so difficult to make out, Barrett thought for a moment the Clevinger Group had moved. But as he entered the lobby he saw some familiar decorations and accessories — and Julia McGregor. When she saw him, her face immediately lit up. Barrett gave a brief wave as Julia scrambled to greet him.

"My God, you came," she said in a low voice.

"I'm not sure why."

"I am," Julia said. "It's 'cause you care." She gave Barrett a half-hug greeting before leading him into the front office.

"It's just really awkward," Barrett said. "Otto's murder is still unsolved and…"

"It will be okay," Julia said.

"How do you know?"

"Because I know you, and you're not going to let it turn into anything," she explained.

"I don't think I'm the one you have to worry about," Barrett countered. "Have you forgotten all the yelling he's done right here in this office? At me, at Otto, at others?"

"And did anyone get hurt?" Julia asked. "Nope."

"I didn't come here to get yelled at."

"Why did you come?"

"I already told you: I don't know," Barrett reminded her.

"You'll be fine. Stay here a minute."

Julia walked down the hall near Otto's old office. Barrett assumed Boyd had claimed the spacious area as his own shortly after his father's death. He could hear Julia's voice coming from it but couldn't make out the words. Thirty seconds later, his former coworker returned.

"You can go on back."

"Does he know it's me?" Barrett asked her. Julia remained silent. "He doesn't, does he?"

"Barrett, I promise you I prepped him. He's going to be calm."

"But he doesn't know it's me, does he?"

Julia shook her head.

"I'm glad you trust *me*," Barrett told her as he made his way down the hall.

The door to Otto's office was open when he arrived. He stood in the entryway and observed the changes Boyd had made to the room. There were no more old paintings on the walls; the pictures of family that included Otto's late wife, Sandy, had also been removed. Boyd was seated at the desk, his blonde head looking down at some paperwork.

Barrett cleared his throat and rapped on the doorjamb with his knuckles. Boyd took his time looking up from the papers, as if he was annoyed by the interruption. When he made eye contact with Barrett, his reaction was more relaxed than expected.

"Well, holy shit."

"Tell me about it."

"Why are you here?" Boyd asked, standing up and straightening out his shirt and tie.

"Can I come in?"

"I guess. Why are you here?" Boyd wasn't letting up.

Barrett moved slowly to the chair in front of the large desk. He decided to use silence as a tactic. Boyd Clevinger played right into this and continued speaking.

"Julia said there was someone here to see me and that I needed to be prepared for some emotions, that I needed to keep myself under control. I must admit, I knew you were back in town, but I didn't think you'd have the balls…"

"Well, surprise," Barrett said. "Here I am: me and my balls."

"Seriously, Barrett. What the hell are you doing here?" Boyd folded his arms and scowled.

"Seeing how you're doing, I guess."

"I'm fine, thanks for stopping by," Clevinger said.

Barrett ignored him. "I didn't kill your father, Boyd," Barrett said. He said it with care, making sure it didn't sound like a desperate plea.

"Why'd you run?"

"I got scared after being questioned by the Denver

Police," Barrett explained.

"So you ran away?"

"Not my best decision," Barrett said.

"They've cleared you?"

"Yes. Because I didn't do it."

"How do they know?"

"No evidence that I did anything."

"They had DNA, but…"

"I think that was a hopeful piece of evidence that ended up being a dead end," Barrett said. "Besides, even if it was my DNA wouldn't it make sense? I drove him home that night. We were in a car together." He hadn't thought of this until now, but it sure sounded logical when he said it out loud.

"I'm pretty busy right now," Boyd said. "I really don't have time…" His arms were still crossed, but his tone had changed ever so slightly. He seemed less agitated.

"I can tell," Barrett said, trying not to sound sarcastic. "I just wanted to stop by and offer you my condolences since I didn't get a chance to before."

"Why don't you come by my place tonight?" Boyd said unexpectedly.

"Huh?"

"Yeah, come on over. Fred's out of town. Have a drink. We can kick back a little more and talk," Boyd suggested.

"I don't know, I've got a lot—"

As a spoiled only child, Boyd Clevinger had never gotten used to taking no for an answer. He cut off Barrett's excuse. "Don't be a wuss, Greyson. Don't run away again," he said. "Eight work for you?"

Barrett shook his head. He hadn't missed this guy one bit. "All right," he agreed.

"Great," Clevinger said. "I'll see you then. Now, if you'll excuse me…" He sat back down at his desk and began looking at the papers in front of him again.

"Sure," Barrett said. He turned and left the CEO's office. There were no goodbyes. No handshake. No thank you. Once again, Barrett wasn't sure how he had gotten to this point, or why he was even doing any of it. For as uncomfortable as this meeting had been, tonight's was going to be far worse. If there was a goal, Barrett was unaware of what it was. And that factor made tonight's get-together even more unpredictable and frightening. Deep down, Barrett was sure Boyd Clevinger had invited him over for a reason. He just didn't know what it was.

***

Jackson was becoming all too familiar with the abandoned warehouse outside of town. The land had once been owned by a local farmer. He had put the building up on the property and leased it as warehouse space to area businesses in Merchant, Gable, and Adler. When the farmer had died a few years ago, no one had given it a second thought when the building became and remained vacant. The farmer's widow was still around but had become a recluse. Now that Jackson was aware of how the building was being used, he couldn't help but wonder if the widow had sold out to the cartel for a nice sum. Technically, the building was still in the widow's name. But that didn't mean anything.

"Are you scared, Sergeant Jackson?" Bart asked him as they pulled into the warehouse parking lot in Jackson's personal vehicle.

"No," Jackson said. Of course, he was lying. He had been a nervous wreck ever since he was commissioned to kill Chum and return the loot. Telling Timmons this, though, would only make the rendezvous more stressful.

"That's good," Bart said. The two strolled to the door of the warehouse before another word was said. "Me neither."

Jackson looked at the large young man. Bart dropped his eyes to the snow- and gravel-covered ground.

"Bart, look at me," Jackson murmured. Timmons did as he was told. "You need to be as cool as a cucumber in there. This is not the time to look or act scared. You start being a Nervous Nellie and they're gonna smell a rat. Be cool. Got it?"

Bart nodded. "Yes, sir. Sergeant."

"Don't speak unless spoken to. And you're probably going to be spoken to, so be ready," Jackson said. "Again, be cool. Fold your arms or something. Look tough."

"Okay."

Jackson pushed the door open, and the men entered the warehouse together once again. This time every light in the building was turned on, lighting the large room up like a concert venue.

They don't want anything to slip by them, Jackson thought. The bad guys were on high alert.

As soon as the heavy door closed behind them, the door at the opposite end of the building opened. One Hispanic man entered. Another, shorter, man came from behind an old piece of machinery not far from where the first one had come in. Jackson was pretty sure they were the same men who were present the two times he had met Pablo here. Neither man was Pablo, however. They were both holding Uzi semiautomatics.

"Hands up," the shorter one, who had been hiding inside, commanded.

"What's this?" Jackson called out.

"Hands up," the man repeated. Jackson and Bart obeyed as Pablo's men approached them.

After frisking both and finding them free of weapons, the other man spoke. He had a small tattoo of a trident on his face, between his eye and his cheek. "Take off your clothes," he told them.

"What?" Bart cried. Jackson shot him a look.

"Where's Pablo?" Jackson asked them.

"We're not going to ask again," the short man said, clearly annoyed.

Giving a nod to Bart, Jackson took off his winter coat and unbuttoned his shirt collar. It was obvious that Bart was less comfortable removing his clothing than the fairly well-chiseled police sergeant. Timmons disrobed slowly, letting out occasional whimpers and whines that Jackson hoped were mistaken for groans due to the physical activity. So far Bart was having a difficult time keeping it together the way he had been instructed. It wasn't like he hadn't been warned at the station that this would probably happen. Apparently the big farm boy thought the experienced lawmen were exaggerating. For the finale of his awkward striptease, Bart removed his CAT cap and took off his oversized black T-shirt, exposing so many fat rolls that it almost looked like he wasn't wearing any underwear.

Both men were down to their shorts and socks, shivering.

"Your watch," one of the henchmen told Jackson. The policeman shook his head and unfastened the band. He tossed the timepiece on the pile of clothes in front of him. Bart slapped his cap back on his head.

"Your hat, too," the man said.

Hesitating, he tossed the cap on top of his own pile. The shorter man picked up the piles and walked backwards with them to the door through which his companion had entered.

"Where's Pablo?" Jackson asked again, this time more firmly.

"He's coming," the man with the tattoo said. "Why are you here?"

"Because this is my deal. I set this entire thing up to begin with. He's my guy." Jackson pointed a thumb at Bart. "I need in on what's going on."

"Hmmm," the man said with a nod.

"What does that mean?"

The man said nothing.

"I'm standing here naked; we're supposed to be seeing Pablo. What the hell is going on?" Sell it, Jackson thought.

The shorter man returned with their clothes, dropping them in the middle of the group. "Clean," he said.

"Even the hat?" the other man clarified.

"Sí."

The man with the face tattoo looked back to Jackson and Bart. "Correction, señor. You are not naked. Take them off, both of you." He pointed with his machine gun at their skivvies.

"Are you kidding me?" Jackson exclaimed.

"Aw, no," Bart moaned.

The man with the tattoo stepped forward. "Do it

now."

Bart looked at Jackson, who could give no other reaction than a shrug. He reached down to his waist and pulled down his black boxer briefs. Bart pulled his white briefs down as well and kicked them off in front of him. If there was a bright side to this situation, it was that neither of the men in front of them seemed to care what they were looking at. They were only concerned with being watched or heard. This time the man who had taken their clothes earlier put on a pair of winter gloves before picking up their underwear. He rushed outside again, this time running and not looking behind him. Within ninety seconds he had returned.

"Nada," he reported. He dropped the underwear with the rest of the clothes.

"Go ahead," the man with the tattoo said. "Put your clothes back on." The other man removed his winter gloves and after giving them a disgusted look, threw them in a corner near some boxes.

"Seriously," Jackson said as he pulled his shirt up over his arms. "Get Pablo in here now. I'm pissed. I don't understand what the hell is going on here, but—"

"Get your clothes on first," the tattooed man said, cutting him off.

Jackson shook his head and continued to dress. When both he and Bart were finished, the police sergeant turned back to the men. "Come on," Jackson said. "Obviously, we're clean. We want to see Pablo."

The man who had examined their clothes turned to the back of the building and whistled loudly. The door opened and a figure appeared in the entryway, mostly hidden in the darkness of night.

***

Chase had been lying flat on his stomach for more than two hours on the roof of the abandoned building. The hand and foot warmers he had brought with him had cooled off over an hour ago, and at this point he was colder than he could ever remember being in his life. No training could've prepared him for something like this. During the meeting of the minds at the police station, Chase had determined that the only way to insure he could remain in place undetected was to be situated long before the bad guys arrived. Jackson had already informed him that hiding inside would probably be a death trap for all of them. It would have been impossible to stay on foot outside the building without being seen and still be close enough to arrive when the time was right. As Chase expected, the men from the cartel showed up thirty minutes early and two of them swept the area and the building, inside and out. Because Chase had watched them arrive in their black van and conduct their search, he was confident there were no additional vehicles or men hiding in the area. What he didn't know was how many men were still inside the van.

The audio transmission from inside the building was not crystal clear, but it was good enough to hear what was transpiring. Chase and his team knew the building would be searched for cameras and audio devices, and they were fairly certain Jackson and Bart would be searched extensively. But the good guys had that part covered, too. Literally.

Knowing where everyone was was a good thing. Not knowing how many guys were in the van was concerning, but Chase did have policemen nearby in unmarked vehicles, armed to the max. The problem would be getting them to the scene quickly in the event they were needed. The closest backup was

Hodge, and he was roughly three miles away. None of them had moved into position until Chase had given them the okay — once the black van was parked and the two men had entered the building to meet Jackson and Timmons.

In his earpiece, the agent heard Jackson demand to see Pablo. Soon after, someone whistled. Chase could hear a door open. He waited.

"Pablo, vienen aquí," Chase heard one of the men say. "Todo ésta claro."

Chase translated the words to English under his breath: "Come here, Pablo. It's all clear." He's there, Chase thought. He flipped the switch on his radio. "The pheasant is present," was all he said. Office Ryan Hodge knew this code phrase meant that Pablo's arrival had been confirmed and that Chase was going inside shortly. It also signaled Hodge to move his other teams into place strategically and proceed with caution.

After receiving confirmation from Hodge, the FBI agent flipped the radio frequency back to the audio emanating from the large room below him. Chase stood up and jogged as light-footed as possible to the place where he had climbed the building earlier. Moving his body was warming him up, and it felt good.

He reached the rafters and swung like a carefree monkey to an old, rusted fire escape. Releasing his grip, he flew through the air to safety, landing perfectly and, thankfully, quietly. If he had missed, there's no telling what condition he would've ended up in. Apparently the year he had spent with Delia as the only boy in her gymnastics class had paid off.

The twins were eight, and a dare had turned into an agreement: Chase joined her for gymnastics, and when he was ten and began playing football, she would try out for the team. Gymnastics bored him to tears, but he followed through as promised. He hated standing around all the time waiting his turn to use the beams and bars. Even at the age of eight, Chase felt it was about the least masculine sport he could ever be a part of. But Delia had dared him — he *had* to do it. And he was really looking forward to seeing Delia get smacked around the football field in a couple of years. Unfortunately, another ten-year-old girl beat Delia to the gridiron and was badly injured in the process. As a result, by the time the twins were ten, the area athletic association had developed a football program for girls, appropriately called "Powder Puff." Delia had no interest in playing touch football with a bunch of other girls, so she was never able to hold up her end of the bargain.

Chase hadn't thought of that stupid gymnastics class for more than twenty years. It had been so meaningless and worthless in his life until now.

As he moved down the metal staircase, the audio in his earpiece faded in and out. The reception was always iffy with this equipment, more so when either the receiver or unit was moving. When he reached the ground, Chase kept close to the building and ended up outside the closed front door. He knew he should wait for the backup that was on its way. The audio from inside was still choppy and bounced between English and Spanish.

"What…Pablo…to…qué…cómo…"

What the hell is going on in there? Chase whispered out loud to himself. He pressed his ear against the door. It was cold, thick steel. No conversations were going to make their way outside to him. He waited another thirty seconds.

There were times as an FBI agent that making the "right decision" was a complete crapshoot. This was one of those times. Sometimes people looked at agents like they were superheroes. Like little kids looked at firemen. It was assumed that these types of professionals never made mistakes. But the sad truth was they were just like everyone else, not perfect. As in any profession, there were times when you had no choice but to go with your gut. In the FBI, sometimes you were right; sometimes you ended up dead. This was not an ideal situation for Chase.

"Help me, Delia," he begged softly. "I need you now. Give me some guidance." Chase closed his eyes and listened. He wasn't sure what he was expecting to hear until he heard it.

At first there was static, but what he could make out was Jackson's voice, and he was yelling.

"That's — Pablo — re —!"

The garbled mess made no sense to Chase. This was one of those moments where he was going to have to rely on instinct. Jackson sounded desperate. Something wasn't right. He grabbed the doorknob and swung the door open just as the gunfire inside began.

XXXVIII

The first thing Chase saw when he opened the door, besides machine gun fire, was four men running in different directions. The two closest to him were Jackson and Timmons. Timmons had somehow managed to tromp his way behind some wooden crates to his left. He looked like a dancing circus bear as he moved in graceless fashion while trying to protect himself from the deadly lead flying through the warehouse. Jackson was moving in the other direction and had made it behind a yellow forklift. Chase made these observations in less than a couple of seconds as he dove into the room and began firing both of his handguns at the two Hispanic men wielding Uzis. He rolled from the open area inside the door to a position behind a pile of wooden crates not far from where Bart had taken cover. The third man seemed confused and had yet to brandish or fire a weapon. Instead, he was also trying to take cover but seemed unsure which direction to go. Was this Pablo? Chase had seen pictures, but it was impossible to tell from this distance during the chaos.

Just as Chase was contemplating the identity of the third man, a handgun slid across the slippery warehouse floor towards the unknown individual. Although he wasn't far from the back door, the man chose to grab the gun, cock it, and immediately begin firing in Chase's direction behind the crates. He didn't realize the only reason Chase hadn't shot him thus far was because he wasn't posing a threat. Now that the FBI agent was certain he had eyes on a bad guy, he took quick aim and laid the man down with one bullet to the midsection. In some ways, Chase hoped he hadn't just killed Pablo. It was too easy, and lacked a retribution speech for Delia.

"Bart!" Chase shouted into the continuous echo of rapid fire. There was no answer. At least not one that he could hear. And it was impossible to know if this was because Timmons didn't hear him or if he was simply too frightened to raise his head and make a noise. Of course another possibility was that he had been hit and was bleeding out, or dead.

Chase hollered in the other direction, across the warehouse where he'd last seen Jackson. "Jackson! What the hell is going on?"

Again, no response. Were they both down?

Continuing to fend off the danger by returning fire, Chase was able to nick another one of the men in the shoulder when he mistakenly rose to reposition himself. Although Chase knew the man was still alive, it helped to know the guy wouldn't be raising a gun again in the next few minutes.

"Jackson! Timmons!" Chase called out. Fewer shots being fired gave him hope that communicating would be easier.

"I'm here!" Jackson's voice echoed through the warehouse. "Not much I can do unless you can get these guys to come out and box me!"

"They're down to one!" Chase yelled as he fired. He saw Jackson's head pop up from behind the forklift. "I've got an extra piece!" Chase took his second gun, reloaded it, and slid it across the floor in the same fashion he had witnessed earlier. But he underestimated how hard he needed to push it, and the gun ended up fifteen feet away from Jackson in an open area of the floor.

"You did that on purpose, didn't you?" Jackson yelled.

"I'll cover you!" Chase answered, ignoring the question. He waited for Jackson to make a move for the gun. Nothing happened. "I'm waiting!"

Finally, Chase spotted movement as Jackson appeared at the back end of the forklift. The two men made eye contact. It was obvious that Jackson was nervous about putting himself in harm's way. Agent Sheehan gave Jackson an aggressive nod and waited.

I don't have time to soothe your bruised ego, Chase thought.

A few more seconds passed before Jackson, keeping as low as possible, scooted out into the open. Chase turned and fired in the direction of the lone gunman. Jackson snatched the gun and, instead of returning in the same manner, elected to dive back with a half somersault, half roll. As he did this, the sound of different gunfire came from where Chase had wounded one of the men earlier. With his healthy arm and shoulder, the man had risen and was shooting in Jackson's direction with a handgun.

It all happened so fast, there was little time for Chase to think. The instant he heard the firing of an additional gun, he turned and located the target, aimed, and fired. The man disappeared behind some corrugated boxes with a bullet in the center of his forehead.

"Sonofa…" Chase looked back to Jackson's location and figured he had made his way behind the forklift again: He was nowhere in sight.

"Jackson!"

A brief pause before a response. "I'm here." This time

the police sergeant's voice was not as strong.

"You hit?" Chase asked.

"Maybe."

"What does that mean?"

"It means I'm trying to pretend I haven't been shot!" Jackson's voice was more intense this time.

"Where?"

"Around the hip bone. I'm okay. Just hurts a lot."

"You gonna be able to help me take this pain in the ass out?"

"Now that I have a gun, I definitely want to kill *somebody*," Jackson joked.

"Can you get in position to cover me?"

"Yeah, I think. Give me a minute."

The possibility that the Hispanic gunman knew English and could hear every word he and Jackson were saying crossed Chase's mind. But they were more than a hundred feet away from the guy and he was firing a machine gun. They really had no choice but to conspire directly in front of him and hope there was too much commotion for him to comprehend it.

"I'm good. Ready," Jackson said.

"You have a full clip in there, but that's it," Chase informed him. "Use it wisely."

The FBI agent took a couple of deep breaths while he loaded his own firearm with a new clip. "Now!" he barked as loud as he could. Chase leaped over the crates in front of him and fired into the area where the Uzi was continuing its assault. He could hear Jackson doing the same with his gun. As Chase continued to hurdle containers and boxes while moving towards the last gunman, he tripped on a loose chain and bumped into a pile of wooden crates, causing it to tip over and crash to the floor. When the disturbance finally settled and Chase regained his balance, the entire warehouse had gone silent.

"Jackson!"

"I think I got him!" the policeman responded.

"You think?"

"Take a look. I'll cover you. I've still got ammo."

Chase did not respond but instead began to shuffle his way to where the man had last been seen.

"See anything?"

"No."

Keeping his gun drawn, Chase worked his way around a mess of machinery. On the floor was the third gunman. He had been shot in the chest and had already bled out. His machine gun was lying next to him.

"Nice work. You got him," Chase informed Jackson as he picked up the Uzi.

"Yay for me," Jackson grunted.

"What the hell was going on in here when you were yelling, before I came in?" Chase asked as he made his way back to the forklift and Jackson.

"I was trying to tell you that the guy wasn't Pablo. You didn't hear me?"

"The audio was loaded with static. I couldn't make it out," Chase explained as he approached. "How are you feeling?"

Jackson was lying on his back and staring up at the FBI agent. "I've been better, but I think I'm going to live."

Chase raised his gun and aimed it at Jackson.

"What are you doing, Chase? Come on." Jackson put his hands up in surrender.

"My sister is dead," Chase said. "How responsible do you feel for that?"

"Well, I…" Jackson was befuddled. "Chase, I…she wasn't supposed to get hurt. I told you the story. You know I didn't mean for anything to happen to her. Please don't blame me. I know you're hurt."

As quickly as he had pulled his gun on Jackson, Chase now holstered it and took the conversation in a different direction. "So that guy wasn't Pablo?"

Even more perplexed now, Jackson put his hands back down to his side and answered. "Yeah, yeah. Seems he was a decoy," Jackson explained. "When I realized it wasn't Pablo, I tried to warn you through Bart's wire."

Hearing Bart's name rang a bell in Chase's head. "Where is he? Bart!" He spun around to look for the missing farmer, but when he did he was met with a bullet from a semiautomatic pistol. It hit Chase square in the chest and catapulted him backwards to the hard floor.

Hearing the shot, Jackson called out. "Chase! What happened?" He could see nothing from his position, but it didn't take long for him to discover what had happened. From around the corner Pablo appeared, gun still drawn.

Jackson began to reach for his gun.

"No, no, señor," Pablo said as he cocked his gun.

Jackson put his hands up, just as he had for Chase only a minute earlier. "You're a sonofabitch, you know that?"

"My, you are cocky for being in such a position,"

Pablo countered.

"Nothing to lose," Jackson said with a shrug. "Just get it over with will you, hotshot?"

"I'm disappointed you betrayed me the way you did," Pablo continued. "You tried to set me up. Did you think I wouldn't know?"

"You didn't leave me much of a choice when you killed a police officer the other day," Jackson said.

"Well, that wasn't me," Pablo explained. Jackson gave him a look of doubt. "I mean, it was my guy," Pablo clarified, "but I didn't make the call. He did. And it was the right one. That police officer was about to discover Señor Timmons' prior arrest."

"That's all you guys do, isn't it?" Jackson said. "Kill people who get in the way of your business."

"I'm not sure there's a more efficient method," Pablo said. Before he could say anything else he was showered with a barrage of bullets from behind. He fell face forward to the ground in front of Jackson. Pablo was dead.

Another figure, this one much larger, appeared from around the back of the forklift to greet the surprised look on Jackson's face. Bart Timmons stood over Pablo's corpse, still holding one of the Uzi semiautomatics.

***

As far as Claire was concerned, things couldn't be going much better. Sure, there was the matter of her boyfriend's dead father being a murderer. She knew Barrett would be dealing with that secret for a long time, assuming he wanted to keep it a secret. Claire wouldn't blame him no matter how he decided to handle it in the long run. She just wanted to give him the support he needed and deserved. The same support he had given her the other night when she told him her own story about the disgusting things her Uncle Stubby had done to her when she was younger. Getting out of Gable was the best thing for Claire right now. It had enabled her to free herself from hiding the filth deep inside her.

She had called her mother earlier and told her the latest, about her new job and the plan to move here permanently. Trish Mathison didn't take the news well, but after a conversation about growing up and "growing out of Gable," she wished her only child the best and made her promise to come back and visit as often as possible. Claire agreed, saying she'd like to bring Wilson to Denver to live, too. In the meantime, her mother would care for the cat.

As she was about to leave for her first night on the job at Danny's, there was a knock at the door. Barrett was already gone for the evening, having chosen to accept Boyd Clevinger's invitation for a visit to his house, despite Claire's objections. It was Claire's opinion that nothing good could come from this meeting, that going to the office was daring enough. But going to his house would be a different story because it was Boyd's turf, his comfort zone. Barrett promised to keep his guard up and even concealed a knife in his pants pocket for the evening, just in case.

Claire looked through the peephole and was surprised to see a familiar face, but she wasn't about to let him through the door. It was the big blonde man who had come to Maddison's house a couple of weeks before when Claire was there.

Randy is his name, she reminded herself as she continued to observe him through the small hole. Being extra careful not to make a sound, Claire soon realized she was barely breathing.

He knocked on the door again and this time pressed the doorbell three times in a row. Thankfully, there was only one dim light on in the living room. There was no television on or music playing, no strong evidence that anyone was home.

Why is he here? Claire wondered. She ran through the story Barrett had told her about the crazy former wrestler and his wheelchair-bound mother and it dawned on her: It had to be about money. But how was he even here? Randy was supposed to be in jail. Obviously, he had gotten out somehow.

Just go away, she thought. Leave Barrett alone. Leave us alone.

She watched as Randy tried to peek through the peephole from the outside. Claire instinctively pulled her head back for a brief second before realizing he couldn't see her. Finally, as if he had someplace else to be, Randy turned away from the door and bounced down the steps. She didn't want to be seen looking out, so Claire moved to the sofa and listened by a window covered with thick drapes. She soon heard an engine turn over and a car drive away. Her cell phone was already in her hand. She pulled up Barrett's number and pushed the call button. After four rings, it went to voicemail.

"Barrett, you need to be careful. That Randy guy just came to the door of the condo. I didn't answer it. I think he left, thank God. I thought he was in jail, but…he knows where you live, Barrett. Honestly, after what you told me about him I'm surprised he didn't try to break in here. Maybe I should've called the police. I'm going to work right now. Be careful. Call me when you get this. I don't like this at all."

Claire hit the end button, gathered her things, and cautiously made it to her car with the can of pepper spray her mother had given her in one hand. Making the jump from a small town to a big city was a huge change for Claire. Not knowing what to expect, she wanted to be prepared at all costs. After all, enough violent and horrific things had happened right before her eyes recently, and she didn't want to be caught in the middle of any more.

Driving to her first night of work, she was thankful she had the pepper spray. She might've spent the entire night locked in the condo if she didn't.

***

The hospital in Adler was getting used to accident and gunshot victims. Today's arrivals were in better shape than many of the previous ones. Sergeant John Jackson of the Gable PD was in surgery to remove a bullet from his left hip. His family impatiently waited in the lobby with their attorney, Rick Masterson. Masterson told Caroline Jackson, who was unaware of her husband's arrest, that he was there to support them in their time of need and make sure there were no issues with health insurance. It sounded like a load of crap to Chief Perkins, but since he already knew the truth it didn't concern him. It was probably best that Jackson be the one to tell his wife what he'd done, anyway.

Officer Ryan Hodge had also arrived at the hospital to connect with his chief.

"Everything taken care of out there?" Perkins asked.

"Yes, sir. Bodies taken care of, clean-up crew, the whole nine yards," Hodge reported. "How's Jackson?"

"He'll be fine, lucky for him," Perkins said. He was still distraught over the betrayal of his finest officer, even knowing the circumstances. "Since you're the expert on the electronics, I'm going to have you take care of Timmons. Come on."

Perkins led Hodge down a hallway and into a private room guarded by an Adler police officer. Perkins waved the guard off as he entered the room. Inside was Bart Timmons, sitting on an examination table.

"Are you here to get this thing off of me?" Bart asked immediately.

"Yes, Bart. Officer Hodge is going to help you," Perkins said. "Take off your shirt, son."

Bart lifted his shirt over his head just as he had earlier at the warehouse.

"You're probably going to need to stand up to make it easier for both of us," Hodge suggested. Bart pulled himself from the table and stood with both feet on the floor. "Can you lift this up, please?" Hodge asked him, pointing at the largest roll of fat hanging from Bart's belly. Embarrassed and relieved, Bart grabbed his own blubber and lifted it up towards his chest, revealing a mess of wires, tape, and a microphone. When Hodge was finished with the front, he asked Bart to turn around. With the help of Chief Perkins, they lifted the roll of fatty tissue and skin on Bart's lower back and removed the small receiver box that the microphone had been plugged in to.

"Thank God," Bart said as he pulled his head through the neck hole of his giant shirt. "I was scared shitless they were going to find that thing."

"You did good, young man," Perkins told him with a pat on the shoulder. "Officer Hodge is going to need to get your official statement about what happened in there and how you ended up taking out Pablo Garza the way you did."

"I ain't never killed anybody before, sir. I mean,

officer," Bart said.

"You killed the right one," Hodge chimed in.

"And don't ever kill anyone again," Perkins added. "Have at it, Hodge. I'll be back."

As he hobbled down the hallway, he heard Hodge's voice reminding Timmons that Perkins is a "chief" and not an "officer." A smile crept to the corners of his mouth. He turned right and made his way down another hallway to another room being watched by one of Adler's finest. Nodding at the officer, Perkins pushed the door open and ambled into the room.

Lying on the examination table flat on his back was a shirtless Chase Sheehan. He lay motionless, with his eyes closed. Perkins gazed at the large black-and-blue mark in the middle of Sheehan's chest.

"That's a nice bruise you've got there, Agent," Perkins observed.

Without opening his eyes, Chase responded. "I've had worse, but they usually wind up on my face."

"You always wear a vest?" the chief asked him.

"I do in situations like that," Sheehan said.

"I can see why."

"What a disaster that was out there."

"I don't know," Perkins said. "The bad guys are dead, you're still alive, Bart's still alive, Jackson…he's…still alive."

Sheehan opened his eyes and carefully sat up on the table, wincing slightly. "You seemed to mention that last one with regret," Chase said. "Were you really hoping I'd take him out with some kind of revenge killing that looked like he got caught in the cross fire?"

Perkins shrugged. "I don't know."

"Come on, Chief. You're not like that."

Perkins shrugged again.

"Even as pissed as I am — Delia's death, McGee's — what Jackson did and why…I can't blame him for it. He did what he thought he needed to do to protect himself and especially his family, right or wrong. And I certainly believe — and this is just my opinion — that he never wanted to hurt you or the department."

"But he could've come to me," Perkins countered.

"That's between you and him," the FBI agent suggested. "Maybe he felt he couldn't for some reason."

The sound of Chase's mobile phone ringing interrupted the discussion.

"Sheehan."

"Chase, it's Nolan. You aren't going to believe this."

"You might be surprised," Chase shot back.

"Randy Fowley was bailed out a few days ago."

"I thought for sure he'd be held without bail," Chase said.

"I think there was probably some kind of payoff," Nolan Reed suggested.

"Damnit, why do you always suggest that as a reason for things?"

"Where there's smoke, there's fire. I'm just saying. Sorry."

"Who bailed him out?" Chase asked.

"His court-appointed kid lawyer, a guy named Derrick Janssen," Reed said.

"Weird. Does he realize Randy's not coming back for his court date?"

"Yeah, I think after sitting on it for a couple of days he realized what he had done, developed a conscience. And he came to the FBI instead of going to the judge. Kind of suggests—"

"I'll be damned, he paid off the judge?" Chase said, cutting off his boss.

"Appears that way," Nolan said. "But he's not admitting it. Janssen's biggest concern is us finding Randy and bringing him back to Iowa. He thinks he's on his way to Colorado to hunt down Barrett Greyson."

"Good Lord," Chase grumbled. "When is this madness gonna end?"

"So, hey," Nolan said. "It's been a while since we spoke. Before I forget to ask, what's the latest on Delia?"

***

As Randy was driving away from the condominium complex's parking lot, he noticed a car with Iowa license plates in the lot. This confirmed what he'd already heard from the blabbermouth aunt at the restaurant in Gable: Greyson's girly-friend was in town. Of course, it didn't mean she was at the condo right now. Even if she was, Randy didn't really care. It was Barrett he was looking for. There were other ways to find him. He had to be around somewhere.

He needed to concentrate, so Randy pulled the stolen car over and looked through the papers he had printed off at the library. Included were the addresses for both Barrett and his family members. Also in the pile were news articles about the dead boss and the family accounting business, the Clevinger Group. Randy skimmed through the clippings and wondered if he was going about it all wrong. He had already been to Greyson's parents' house and no one was home there, either. What about friends? Barrett Greyson had to have friends, right?

There had to be someone he could talk to who would lead him in the right direction. If all else failed, Randy would simply camp out at the condo until Greyson finally showed up. This is what any logical person would do. But Randy Fowley was far from logical or normal. He was impatient as hell and still hung up on the agreement he and Barrett had made in Chicago. Randy wanted his money, now.

The blonde giant smirked when he thought about his Doogie Howser-looking lawyer, Derrick Janssen. It was a massive stroke of luck to end up with such a gullible attorney. Randy didn't know for sure what additional strings the kid had pulled, if any. But it felt like a sign from beyond that he had been released on bail at all, as if he were supposed to pursue the big payday he had been promised.

Randy continued to scan the names in the articles in front of him: David Dixon, Julia McGregor, Carla Dreyer, Antonio Barnes, Boyd and Fredrika Clevinger. Was Greyson with any of them now? Chances were good he was with his girl, Claire, since her car was sitting outside at the condo and no one seemed to be home. But it was hard to say. Maybe she was inside and saw him through the peephole. Maybe she called the cops. All the more reason not to hang out there and wait for Greyson to return.

The clock in the car told Randy it was seven thirty-five in the evening. If his memory served him correctly, the library was open until nine. After striking out at the first couple of stops he had made, it was time to gather more addresses.

As he made a U-turn and headed back to the library, he wondered if his good fortune would continue and help him stumble on Barrett Greyson's whereabouts. Denver was a big city, but it was worth a try. Randy could feel the momentum pushing him. What was the worst that could happen?

XXXIX

Although Boyd had set their get-together for eight that evening, Barrett decided he would be fashionably late. It was eight twenty when he pulled into the wide driveway of the home in Highlands Ranch. Barrett still wasn't sure what the purpose of the meeting was. When Julia had asked him to speak with Boyd, Barrett assumed there was something on fire, as usual. Something he could help with. If that was the case, Boyd showed no signs of duress when Barrett had dropped by the office.

Oddly, Barrett had relished looking Boyd in the eye and telling him that he was not Otto's murderer. Sure, this was the truth. It just wasn't the whole truth. But for one brief moment, Barrett was able to pretend he knew nothing.

He was still struggling mightily with the knowledge that his father — a man Barrett had respected more than anyone — was apparently a raving lunatic. Chances of ever understanding what had really been going on inside Frank Greyson's head were slim to none, but he had certainly sounded disconnected from reality during his confession. It made Barrett's stomach turn every time he thought about that video on his father's cell phone. So much so that Barrett had returned the phone to the safe deposit box the day before, setting it alongside the murder weapon, the shopping bag that had held Otto Clevinger's last breaths.

The real question in Barrett's mind was whether or not he would or even could tell anyone else about the heinous act Frank Greyson had committed. What was his father's intent when he left Barrett the evidence? Most of the time when he thought about it, Barrett was convinced it had only been left for him in case he needed to prove his own innocence. At this point, it wasn't necessary for Barrett to throw his father under the bus and crucify his name and memory. For one thing, it would break his mother's heart. That was the last thing Barrett wanted to do now. Or ever. And certainly Barrett had suffered enough already the last few months, being accused of the murder himself and being ignorant enough to run around the country looking for an escape from something he hadn't done. If the world found out who the killer was, how would that affect his own future? His brother's? His mother's? Would it follow them around for the rest of their lives? Probably. It was a frightening and massive emotional load to be carrying around the information Barrett had right now. And on top of it all he was somehow going to Boyd Clevinger's house to talk or do whatever it was the guy had in mind.

Barrett trotted up the stairs between the identical twin wrought iron lions. They reminded him of Graceland, Elvis Presley's home in Memphis, except these were bronze colored instead of white. Loud music leaked through the massive double doors. Barrett pressed the doorbell and waited on the well-lit top step. The volume of the music lowered and one of the doors opened.

"You're late," Boyd greeted him. He was dressed in what could easily be mistaken for pajamas: a long sleeved, white T-shirt and plaid flannel pants.

"Sorry," Barrett said. Once again there was no

handshake, no other greeting. There was even a nanosecond when Barrett considered turning around and never coming back, at least not to Boyd Clevinger's house. But maybe with all the bad that had been going on lately, this meeting with Boyd would bring some good to everyone. Maybe even put an end to all the awkwardness once and for all.

Boyd stepped out of the way so Barrett could enter the oversized foyer. Looking past his host, Barrett could see rooms decorated with expensive paintings and other pieces of art. The furniture was modern and the overall colors were bright, though it was difficult for Barrett to tell for sure since every light inside the house was turned off, save one that could be seen down the hall.

"Beer?" Boyd asked. "You know what, never mind. I'll just get you one. Make yourself at home over there." He pointed to the area in the living room where the dim light was coming from. Barrett made his way to one of the armchairs and sat down. He noticed the big-screen television was also turned on, but muted. It was showing a movie he instantly recognized as *The Time Machine,* the original Hollywood version of the H.G. Wells book starring Rod Taylor.

Boyd returned with two beers and handed one to Barrett.

"It's a great movie," Boyd commented. "Much better than that piece of shit remake that was done a couple of years ago."

Barrett twisted the top off of his beer and took a drink. He stole a quick glance at Boyd's face. He looked different. Maybe it was the poor lighting.

"How have you been?" Boyd asked, catching his guest off guard.

"Well, I mean…" Barrett wasn't sure what to say. He needed to up his game, but without the usual sarcasm. Keep it friendly, but play it by ear. Let Boyd lead the way. "Can't complain," he replied. God this is stupid, Barrett thought.

"Heard about your dad," Boyd said with a sniffle. He wiped his nose with the back of his shirt sleeve. "I guess we finally have something in common."

"Umm, yeah," was all Barrett could manage to say. This was starting off almost as badly as he had expected.

"How did you feel when you lost your father, Barrett?" Boyd asked, taking another swig of his beer.

"What?"

"Did you cry?"

"Yeah, I did," Barrett said, frustrated and not enjoying the conversation. "Why?"

"Because I didn't," Boyd explained and then stood up. "Nope. I didn't cry one tear for the death of my old man. The sudden *murder* of my old man." He began pacing around the living room like a dog stressed out by a raging thunderstorm. "Why do you think that is, Barrett?"

Barrett watched Boyd continue to strut around the room. "I don't know," he said. "It's different for everyone, you know?"

"What's different? Being a son? Being a father?"

"No. I mean, everyone deals with the death of a loved one in a different way," Barrett explained.

"Loved one?" Boyd let out a cackle. "That's hilarious."

"Why?" Barrett was looking forward to seeing where he went with this.

"What is love, anyway?"

Oh for God's sake, Barrett thought.

"I'm not sure I loved the old man, Barrett," Boyd continued. "I couldn't cry about the loss. You know why?" He sauntered back to the couch across from Barrett and sat down. Leaning forward, he finished his thought: "Because I don't think I processed it as a 'loss.'"

Barrett tossed himself backwards in his chair. "Oh come on," he said.

"Why would I? Look at the gain I received from my 'loss.'"

"You had all of that, anyway. At least you would when the time was right." Such a self-righteous prick, Barrett thought.

Boyd suddenly stood up. He took the remote control and turned the music up louder. "I'll be right back," he said and walked down the hallway towards where he had grabbed the beers. A few seconds later, Barrett heard a door slam under the music.

What the hell was going on with this guy?

Barrett stood up and made his way around the living room. Because it was so dark, there wasn't much to see. The movement was more to keep the blood flowing through his body while he could. At the rate things were going tonight, there was no telling when he might need to make a mad dash for the door. If there was one thing he had learned while out on his own, it was to always be ready for the unexpected. Boyd was certainly unpredictable tonight. Barrett found this particularly amusing because during his days of working alongside Boyd, the spoiled son of the boss was the epitome of predictability. He could be read like a book — his emotional reactions, his lack of follow-through — it was always obvious to everyone at the Clevinger Group what Boyd was going to do or say next. Obvious to everyone but Boyd, that is.

A few minutes later, as the MGMT song "Time to Pretend" began to blare from the speakers, Boyd returned to the living room. He grabbed the remote immediately and turned the volume up even louder. "Don't you just love this song?" he shouted at Barrett over the music as he bounced in rhythm to the modern techno-poppy song. Barrett shrugged and sat back down in his chair. "I didn't get along with my father," Boyd said, his eyes closed and still bopping to the tune.

"Can you turn it down?" Barrett asked. "I can barely hear you."

Returning to the present, Boyd aimed the remote at the stereo and turned the music down again. "Music just takes me away, man. Ya know?"

"I get it," Barrett said. "You were saying something?"

"I don't remember."

"Something about not getting along with your father," Barrett reminded him. "I mean, I think that's what you said."

"Oh yeah. My father was an embarrassment to me."

"Come on," Barrett said.

"What? To me…he was," Boyd explained. He was suddenly more chipper than he had been previously. "No big deal. It's just the way it is. Or…was." He chuckled briefly.

"Are you okay, Boyd?"

"I'm fine, man. You want another beer? I'm not going to have one, but I can get you another if you want." Barrett's host began walking back down the hall.

"No, that's okay. I'm good. Still drinking this one."

"Okay, cool," Boyd said. He came back to the couch and grabbed the remote again, turning the stereo back up. "So, have you got a job yet?"

Barrett pointed to this ear to indicate he couldn't hear a word Boyd was saying.

"My bad. The music takes me to a different place," Boyd said after he'd turned the stereo down again.

"I think you mentioned that," Barrett said, toning down the snark as best he could. "So, what did you just say?"

"I forgot," Boyd said. "Oh yeah, you got a new job or what? You know, you deserted your job with me. I think legally you basically fired yourself."

Barrett shook his head. "I don't have anything lined up yet. Why do you ask?"

"I'm a caring soul, Barrett," Boyd quipped. "You sure you don't want another beer?"

"Nope. Why is it so dark in here?"

"Because it's nighttime," Boyd answered with another sniffle.

"Yeah, but people usually turn lights *on* in their house at night."

"There's a light on, right there." Boyd pointed at the lone lamp on the coffee table that sat between them.

"You hungry?" Barrett asked. You need to stop yourself right now, Barrett Greyson, he told himself.

"No, why?"

"Because it looks like you were eating powdered donuts earlier," Barrett said, pointing at a white, chalky substance near the base of the light on the table. Now you've done it, Barrett thought.

Boyd followed Barrett's finger to the white stuff.

"Yeah," Boyd said. "That's why I'm not hungry now. I already ate."

"I see," Barrett said, dialing things back. "How are things going for you at work?"

"Oh, good. Really good, actually. Better than ever. We…we're doing…good. Real good." By the time he was finished with his sell job, even Boyd himself didn't sound convinced.

"That's good," Barrett said with a nod.

"Man, I need to piss," Boyd announced as he began moving in the same direction he had gone ten minutes ago. "I'll be right back."

He's not even drinking anything, Barrett thought. He's gotta be doing something back there, probably cocaine. Many Clevinger Group employees had long suspected Boyd of drug use. Not that he had ever seemed to be wasted at work. But when he was younger and had yet to begin working for the family business, he had disappeared from public for a period of time. No one saw or heard from him for several months. Some stories had been told and passed around, but none of them revolved around what many had suspected: rehab. No one knew for sure. In fact, most people thought it possible that Boyd had checked in to rehab himself and Otto had no idea. His strange behavior tonight gave Barrett a pretty clear indication that Boyd Clevinger indeed had more problems than anyone else knew of, without a doubt.

When he returned from the bathroom, Boyd sat back down in front of Barrett and placed a revolver on the coffee table.

***

Oh come on, not again! was Barrett's immediate thought.

"What the hell is that for?" he asked, staring at the gun. This couldn't be happening again, right? More guns meant…more problems.

"I wanted to show it to you," Boyd explained. "I just got it today."

"Why?"

"I'm not sure."

"What do you mean you're not sure?"

"I mean I've always wanted a gun and so I got one."

"Today of all days?" Barrett clarified. "After you asked me over here?"

"You're paranoid," Boyd said. "You can't just walk into a store and buy a gun. There's a waiting period and crap."

"Not if you buy it on the street."

"I bought it legally. You wanna see the paperwork?"

"No. Can you put it away?"

"Why?"

"Because I've had a lot of dealings lately with guns and the stuff that comes with them," Barrett said.

"Really? Sounds like there's a story there."

"Not one I want to tell right now."

"Would you be interested in coming back to work for me?" Boyd said suddenly. The shock of the subject change made Barrett blink his eyes rapidly.

"Did you just…"

"Yes, Barrett. I asked you to come back to your job," Boyd said.

Barrett shook his head. "I don't know what to say."

"I'll give you more money and a better title. You can be the vice president."

"Where is this coming from?"

"My heart," Boyd said with sincerity then laughed out loud.

Even Barrett laughed. "Everyone knows you don't have one of those," he said.

"So, what do you say?"

"I don't think it's a good idea. We didn't get along well when your father was around. Have you thought about how it would be without him to keep the peace?"

"I'll be better, do a better job. I promise. I'll do whatever it takes."

"Empty promises, Boyd. I've heard this before."

"Come on, man."

"Never once did I consider coming back to work at the Clevinger Group."

"That's because you thought I thought you killed my old man."

"So, you don't think that anymore?" Barrett clarified.

"I'm not sure I ever did," Boyd said. He stood back up and wiped his nose again with the back of his sleeve before going into another one of his pacing rants. "Honestly, man. I don't know that I care who did do it at this point. I mean, I've been going apeshit for the last few months. I can't think straight. Most days I think to myself how it might have been my fault my father is dead and you know what? I don't give a shit. I know it sounds horrible, but it's just the frickin' truth. I don't know what's wrong with me. And again, I don't care. I just know what I feel."

"Come on, Boyd. It's not that bad," Barrett said. "Is it?"

Boyd Clevinger paced his way back to the coffee table. "You wanna know what, Barrett? You got me." He pointed at the white specks by the lamp. "I'm snorting coke. Done it three times since you've been here. Maybe it was two. I can't remember. And you know what else? I shoot heroin, too. Don't do a very good job of it by myself, but I can do it and have. And you know what else?" He picked up the gun. "You're right. I did buy this thing for a reason. Want to know what I got it for?"

Trying his best not to look frightened, Barrett answered. "I don't think I want to know."

Boyd took the gun and pointed it at his temple. "Boom!" he screamed.

"That's ridiculous," a startled Barrett said. "Why would you do something as crazy as that?"

"Because I *am* crazy! Can't you see that?"

"You are not," Barrett countered. "You just need to calm down and take life one step at a time."

"I lied earlier," Boyd said. He set the gun back down on the table and began pacing around the dark living room again. "The business is not good. I mean, it hasn't tanked or anything. But we've lost clients and aren't gaining any new ones. It's not a good thing, is it? That's bad, right Barrett?"

"I don't know," Barrett said. The longer Boyd's antics continued, the more difficult it was to find the right words. "It doesn't sound good, but it's impossible to know for sure without seeing the numbers and books and other stuff."

"Yes!" Boyd exclaimed. "That's why I need you to come back to work! Seriously. Whatever you need, whatever you want. Help me get this thing back on track. It's all I have, and I'm losing it."

He couldn't pay me enough to work for him, Barrett thought. But he didn't know how to tell Boyd no, especially not when he was in this condition.

"Can we just chill out for a while?" Barrett asked him. "Maybe I can help just by talking about it with you?"

"Chill out?" Boyd said. "I'm jacked higher than a jet airplane right now. I'd rather go jump off my roof." He paused before continuing. "Hey, you ever snorted coke before?"

Barrett rubbed his temples. "No."

"You want to?"

"No."

"Why not? I mean, just a little. It's not gonna kill you."

"Remember during sex ed when they said a girl means 'no' when she says 'no'?"

"Was that in sex ed?"

"I don't really remember."

"Well that's just plain stupid anyway," Boyd said. "You're not a girl and I'm not trying to bone you."

"I don't want any coke."

"Fine. I'll be right back," Boyd said.

"Hey, are you supposed to be doing that stuff this much?"

"I don't know," he called from the hall. "It didn't come with instructions."

This time Boyd decided to give Barrett a show. Instead of consuming it privately, he brought the small bag of powder out to the living room and set it on the coffee table.

"I was fine with you doing it back there," Barrett told him.

"It won't bite you," Boyd said. "Maybe watching will make you change your mind."

He poured a small amount of cocaine on the table. With a razor blade, he drew a line of the drug approximately two inches long. Next, he took a metal tube and set it near the line. Leaning forward, he moved his face near the table and stuck the other end of the tube inside a nostril. With a quick snort, the line vanished up through the tube and into his nasal passageway.

"Ahhhh," Boyd said. "That's good. You have to do it just right or it ends up in the back of your throat. Not too far. Here, I'll draw you a line."

"I said I don't want—" Barrett stopped short when he looked up at Boyd and spotted blood trickling from his nose. "Hey, your nose is bleeding. Is that normal?"

Boyd reached up, touched the spot on his face between his nose and upper lip, and looked at his finger. "Damnit," he said. "Not again."

"Does this happen often?"

Boyd didn't respond as he charged down the hallway. A few minutes later he returned with a wad of tissue shoved up his nose and a small suitcase in one hand. "I have an offer to make you, Barrett," he said. "And this is serious."

He set the suitcase on the table.

"What's in there?"

Before Boyd could answer, the doorbell rang.

***

"Who the hell could that be at this time of night?" Boyd wondered out loud. "It's like ten o'clock." He casually grabbed his new gun and placed it between the couch cushions where he was sitting.

It felt to Barrett like it was later than ten. So far his visit to Boyd Clevinger's had been a tennis match of volleys that included some ever-changing moods and unexpected moments. He reached inside his pocket to check the time on his mobile phone and realized he didn't have it with him. I must've left it in the car, he thought. He felt his other pocket and remembered the knife he had brought.

As Boyd made his way to the front door, the doorbell rang a second time. "Hold your horses!" he hollered.

Barrett remained seated in the living room, eyeballing the suitcase on the coffee table. He could hear the door open but could not see who had arrived. Not that he really cared. It's probably his drug dealer or something, Barrett said to himself.

"You're not going to believe this, but it's for you," Boyd called out as he made his way back down the hall.

The only person who knew Barrett was here was Claire. Or maybe it was Julia. That might be possible.

Boyd appeared from around the corner of the dark hallway. Before Barrett had the opportunity to respond, Randy came into view. Boyd stepped out of the big guy's way and extended an arm, as if to present Barrett to Randy.

"Here he is," Boyd said, oblivious to what was going on. "You want a beer, man?"

Randy was grinning from ear to ear. "Nope. I only came here for one thing," he said.

Boyd sat down on the couch. "Cool. How do you guys know each other?"

"Oh, Barrett and I go back a long way," Randy said. "Don't we…buddy?"

Up until this point Barrett had remained silent. His mind was racing. He was so sick of his mind racing. "Aren't you supposed to be in jail or something?" he finally said.

"Nope. Got bailed out."

"You been to jail, man?" Boyd interjected.

"A few times," Barrett answered for Randy. "How'd you find me? Or better yet, why?"

"It wasn't easy," Randy said. "No one was at your place when I went there earlier. Or at least no one came to the door. But maybe that cute little girlfriend of yours was in there, cowering in a corner."

Barrett's shoulders sunk. Even when you think you're unlisted, you're not. The Internet had changed all of that and so many other things in the world.

"That's right," Randy said, responding to Barrett's body language. "I know where you live. I know about your girl from Iowa."

"You brought a girl back here from Iowa?" a still clueless Boyd asked Barrett. "Cool. Hey man, you wanna sit down?" Like a pinball machine, the coked-up Clevinger changed his focus to Randy. The wad of tissue was still sticking out from his nose.

"Nope."

"How did you find me here?" Barrett asked.

Randy shifted his weight. "You know what's great about people?" he asked, making eye contact with both seated men. "They genuinely want to be helpful, and in doing so they often throw caution to the wind."

"What's he talking about?" Boyd said. "Is he talking about me?"

Barrett looked at Boyd. "No, he's not."

"Well, I could be," Randy corrected him. "He did let me in here."

"Boyd, who else knew I was coming here tonight? Did you tell anyone?" At this point it didn't matter, but Barrett was curious as to how Randy had found him. And with any luck the discussion would help Boyd snap into some semblance of sobriety.

"Well, I think Julia knew," Boyd said.

"Yeah, she did," Barrett agreed. "Because I told her about it on my way out."

"I almost forgot," Boyd said. "In the parking ramp, I was talking to Kevin Hollingsworth. I mentioned it to him, too. It was weird how it came up, but it did."

Barrett looked at Randy. "I barely know that guy."

"Apparently he wanted to help a couple of old friends find each other," Randy suggested with a shrug.

"Man, I don't understand what the hell is going on here," Boyd bellowed. He grabbed the bag of cocaine and pulled out another small cube.

"What you got there, guy?" Randy asked, already knowing the answer as he watched Boyd crush the white cube into powder.

"What do you think it is?" Boyd asked without looking

up. He worked with the razor to shape another line.

"Booger sugar," Randy quipped.

"Yep," Boyd said as he pulled out his snort tube. "Want some?"

"Nope," the former wrestler replied. "I want it all." Randy pulled a gun from his coat pocket and aimed it at Boyd, who finally looked up when he heard the weapon being cocked.

"What the hell, man?"

"You've got to have a lot of this shit around here," Randy suggested. "And I want it."

"Now just a goddamn minute!" Boyd retorted, pounding the coffee table with his fist and cracking the glass top. He began to stand.

"Sit down, bub," Randy demanded.

Boyd obeyed, but his intensity remained. "This is *my* house, asshole!"

Randy glared at him. "If you don't shut your yap right now, I'm going to shut it for you."

"Boyd," Barrett interjected. "Seriously. Do as he says."

"What's going on, man?"

Barrett didn't answer. Instead, he pretended to zip his lips and turned his attention to Randy. "So, take his coke and go, Randy."

"Yeah, it's not that simple," Randy said. "You owe me money."

"No, I don't."

"Yes, you do. We had a deal, remember?" Randy reminded him.

"I kind of thought that deal was null and void when

you went to jail for stealing a car and firing off a gun in a truck stop and all the other stuff you did."

"Well, I'm not in jail now, am I?" Randy said.

"I don't have the money right now, Randy."

"Where's the backpack then?"

"I don't have it," Barrett explained. "It's locked down in an evidence room somewhere. The judge needs to determine who it belongs to since it was found inside a stolen car."

Randy contemplated this. "You're lying."

"No I'm not," Barrett said. The room was silent except for Metallica's "Seek & Destroy" playing in the background. Boyd pulled the tissue from his nose and leaned down to the cracked coffee table. Using his other nostril, he snorted the line he had drawn out a few minutes earlier. Barrett flashed him a look of disappointment.

"What? I'm not going to waste it," Boyd explained.

"Your nose is going to melt before this night is over," Barrett quipped.

"Don't worry about me," Boyd countered, pointing with his thumb. "Worry about your whack job buddy over here."

"You're the moron who let him in."

"He said he was a friend of yours!" Boyd barked.

"All right, you two. Knock it off!" Randy howled. "Especially you, Ed Begley, Jr. Stop snorting my shit."

"Your sh—"

"Shut up!" Randy snapped, cutting Boyd off. After a deep breath, Randy refocused his energy. "What's in the suitcase?" He looked at Barrett when he asked the question and got a shrug in response.

Boyd raised his hand like a third grader who needed to go to the bathroom.

"Speak," Randy said.

"I know what's in the suitcase," Boyd said, his hand still up. "It's mine."

"Oh yeah?"

"Yeah," Boyd said. He finally put his hand down.

"So what's in it?" Randy asked.

"Your butt," Boyd said and then giggled like a little girl.

Randy had seen and heard enough from the cocky blonde guy in flannel pants. Without taking aim, he casually turned and fired his gun at Boyd. The shot rang out through the living room. Not knowing for sure where Boyd had been hit, if at all, Barrett's immediate response was to stop Randy from firing again.

"Randy, come on! What are you doing?" Barrett squawked. He looked first at Randy and then back to Boyd, who was holding his side.

"He shot me," Boyd cried. "Holy shitballs, he shot me."

"Because you wouldn't stop being an idiot," Randy explained. "What's in the suitcase?"

"Why don't we just open it and find out?" Barrett suggested. "And how about we call an ambulance for him?"

Boyd groaned. "Awwww, shiiiit. Am I dying?" He looked at Barrett with hollow eyes.

"I'm not worried about him right now," Randy said. Putting his gun back inside his coat, he moved to the coffee table and grabbed the suitcase. He pressed the gold buttons on top simultaneously and unlatched it. Because he'd turn the case towards him when he opened it, Randy was the only one who could see inside. Barrett watched a sinister grin appear on the big man's face.

"How much is in here?" he asked Boyd, turning in his direction.

"Half a mill. Was supposed to be for him," Boyd managed to utter, glancing in Barrett's direction.

Randy moved his gaze to Barrett and smiled again. "See? You do have money after all."

"Whatever," Barrett said. "Just go. I need to get him to a hospital."

Randy closed the suitcase and picked it up. "You know, I remember that day at the hotel room in Iowa when you told me how things weren't going to end well for either of us," he said. "Looks like you were wrong."

As Randy finished his sentence and made a half turn to leave, he locked eyes with Boyd, who was suddenly holding his gun on Randy as best as his wounded body would allow. Before there was a chance to react or object, Boyd began firing at Randy. The first bullet hit him in the right shoulder, causing the big man to drop the suitcase. The next one caught him on the right side of the chest, and the third one clipped his left shoulder. Still standing, Randy struggled to reach into his coat pocket to pull out his own weapon. Boyd continued to fire.

"That's not your money, asshole!" he wailed from the sofa. The next bullet hit Randy in the sternum and another buried itself in his stomach. Boyd's next two shots missed his target just as Randy raised his own firearm.

Although staggering around in a startled daze, Randy

was still standing and had the upper hand on Boyd as he began firing back, hitting the already wounded CEO in the abdomen twice. At nearly the same instant, Boyd managed to fire his gun one more time as well, and this time he hit pay dirt as Randy took the bullet in the throat.

As soon as the bullets had begun flying, Barrett had made himself as small as possible. First he dove from his chair to the floor and lay flat on his stomach. As the holy mess continued above him, he began to slither and wriggle away from the action and behind the chair he had been sitting in. This was no time to play hero again.

When Randy took the shot to the throat, he dropped his gun to the floor and grabbed at the wound with both hands. Realizing he could no longer breathe caused him to panic even more, and as he continued to bleed profusely, he lost his balance and fell, crashing down on the coffee table. Barrett had been watching the scene unfold from behind the chair. After Randy went down, Barrett bounced up from his haunches and darted to Boyd on the couch.

"Boyd," he said. "Where's your phone? I'll call 911."

He tried to raise his hand but couldn't. Instead, Boyd spoke. "Don't…wor-worry about it," he told Barrett between shallow breaths. "Hey. You kn-know what?"

"Where's your phone, Boyd?"

Boyd pretended not to hear Barrett's plea. Or maybe he couldn't hear him.

"I'm gla-glad I di-did all that coke-cocaine," he said. "Cuz I don-don't f-f-f-feel a thing."

Barrett grabbed Boyd's face and lightly slapped his cheek in an effort to revive his senses, if only for a moment. "Boyd," he said. "Let me help."

Boyd made eye contact with Barrett again. This time he was able to emit a crooked smile. "It's o-o-kay," he said. "I'm g-g-goo-good with this."

Barrett shook his head. He stood up and began looking around the dark room for a phone, or maybe even a brighter light. After a frantic search, he finally located a light switch in the hallway. His goal was to find a phone somewhere in the house. But the exploration never took place. When he returned to the living room, it was obvious that Randy Fowley and Boyd Clevinger were dead.

***

When Chase caught wind of Randy Fowley's newfound freedom, something struck him much harder than the bullet from Pablo Garza's gun had earlier. Things were finally seeming to cool down in the Gable-Adler area. But a voice inside Chase, one that sounded eerily similar to Delia's, told him he needed to get to Colorado immediately.

Instead of informing Nolan about Delia's death and derailing the conversation from the subject at hand, Chase neglected to give any details and simply told his boss "things were complicated." He then changed the subject to his need to get to Denver at all costs — fast.

Within twenty minutes, Chief Perkins had helped Chase charter a private airplane at a tiny airport just west of Gable. By nine thirty, the FBI agent was being flown to his destination. Initially, the plan was to land at Buckley Air Force Base. But during the flight, Chase was able to pinpoint Barrett Greyson's location by pinging his mobile phone and learned that he was currently in Highlands Ranch. Armed with this information, the pilot was granted permission to land at

Centennial Airport, which was much closer than the Air Force base.

Of course, Chase made several calls to Greyson from the ground and air, but there was no answer. According to Nolan, Randy had been free for the better part of a week. It was possible that he had already tracked down Greyson and done God knows what. What Chase did know was that Randy Fowley was considered a psychopath by most people who had dealt with him, according to the records. In general, a lack of understanding between right and wrong and having no concern or sensitivity towards people had placed Fowley in that category. But Chase had seen many men that were just like this and were actually worse than psychopaths. He wondered if Randy Fowley might be the same. These men and women knew the difference between right and wrong, but they just didn't give a damn. People like that were far worse because they were much less predictable than a stereotypical psychopath.

Chase had done all of his homework within the first twenty minutes of the flight and eventually took a few minutes to rest. His bruised chest was still sore and achy, but he'd be ready for whatever might be waiting for him in Colorado, if anything. His mind wandered to his poor sister being locked in a cold drawer at the morgue in Adler as she waited for her twin brother to take action and lay her to rest for eternity. Poor, sweet, innocent Delia. Why did this have to happen? Jackson had told Chase the story, and it all seemed believable. She was in the wrong place at the wrong time. Jackson had never planned to hurt her. He had locked her away for a period, but the two had joined forces when the policeman finally came to his senses the next day. It was a matter of circumstances that Delia was kidnapped by the cartel. Everything after that…well,

Jackson could've come clean sooner. It might've saved Delia's life. This was something Jackson would have to live with. More than a few times in the last couple of days Chase had wanted to kill Jackson. And the truth was he *had* given it serious consideration at the warehouse. But when the moment came, there she was again — Delia's voice in Chase's head. Chase knew he could never live with himself. The act would lump him in the same category as Jackson. And that just wasn't who Chase was. He wanted to be an "eye for an eye" kind of man, but when it came to taking a person's life, he was a by-the-book kind of FBI agent.

Not wanting to dwell on his sorrow over the loss of his sister, Chase's thoughts drifted to the peculiar conversation he'd had the last time he spoke to Barrett Greyson. What the hell was he talking about?

Imagine the person who killed Otto Clevinger was immune from justice.

Chase knew there had been some situations in history where government officials had immunity from acts and crimes, but that couldn't be what Greyson was referring to that day on the phone. If he hadn't been so busy with other things, Chase would've given this more thought earlier. But now that he had the time, he seriously believed Barrett Greyson knew something about Otto Clevinger's murderer.

What if the person who committed the murder couldn't be prosecuted?

In some regards, it sounded like Greyson was referring to double jeopardy, but that couldn't be it either. It wouldn't make sense in this situation.

What if I did know who killed Otto, but that person couldn't be prosecuted. They had complete immunity.

Chase laughed quietly to himself and shook his head as he sunk lower in his seat. He knew the only way a person couldn't be prosecuted for a crime he had committed would be if he was dead. He closed his eyes and drifted off for a brief power nap.

When he awoke fifteen minutes later, he bolted straight up in his seat.

XL

Once Barrett confirmed Randy and Boyd were dead, his brain seemed to begin shutting down. It wasn't like he was frozen with terror; he had been through too many violent and traumatic events recently to let this rattle him that way. No, it was more like he was numb to what had just taken place. He tried to make a decision about what to do next, but his mind refused to come to any conclusions. Instead, he found a dark corner of the living room near the fireplace, sat on the floor, and pulled his knees to his chest. Barrett Greyson had had enough of this crap.

Fifteen or twenty minutes passed. The only sound in the house was the stereo, which continued to play softly. Without warning, the doorbell rang. It startled Barrett enough to yank him out of his trance. The problem was he didn't know if he should answer the door or run out the back. Before he had a chance to make a decision, the front door gradually opened. Apparently Boyd had left it unlocked after letting Randy in. But who was letting himself in after ringing the bell, and what was he going to think when he witnessed the mess in the living room?

Barrett stayed in his dark corner, still iced with indecision. He heard footsteps on the wood floor moving in the direction of the living room. Barrett couldn't be sure, but the footfalls were heavy, most likely a man's. He hoped to God it wasn't Boyd's wife who had just entered. Why would she ring the doorbell?

A shadowy figure appeared in the hall near the living room. Indeed, the person appeared to be a man, though he had yet to enter the lit area near the coffee table. He also seemed to have a gun drawn.

Not again, Barrett thought. Seriously, not again.

The man crept into the light and checked for a pulse on each body. As he did, Barrett recognized him; it was Agent Chase Sheehan. Before he had a chance to consider his options, Sheehan spoke. "Barrett? Barrett Greyson?"

Responding seemed natural to Barrett. What else could he do at this point? "Yeah."

"Are you okay? Where the hell are you?" Sheehan asked.

"I'm fine. Back here. Hang on." Barrett picked himself off the floor and slowly walked to the center of the living room into the light. Agent Sheehan's weapon was still drawn. "I don't have a gun," Barrett told him.

"Surely you understand that, given the scene here, I'm not going to take your word for it," Sheehan replied. "Put your hands on top of your head." Barrett did as he was told. Sheehan turned him around and conducted a thorough search to insure Barrett was, indeed, unarmed. Once finished, Chase turned him back around. "What the hell happened?" he asked.

"They shot each other."

"And you just…watched?" Chase asked.

"Something like that. How…why are you here?"

"Because I heard that Fowley had gotten out and had made some comments about you being his priority," Sheehan explained. "I had such a strong vibe that you were in trouble that I got here in less than three hours. Of course, if you would've just answered your phone…"

"I must've left it in the car," Barrett said. "I kinda got used to not carrying one when I was wandering around the country trying not to be found."

"So seriously, what's the story here?" Chase asked again. Barrett could tell the FBI agent wasn't completely sold on his lack of involvement. "The last time I talked to you, you made it sound like you wouldn't be seeing Clevinger again anytime soon."

Barrett nodded and told Sheehan the entire story. How Julia had asked him to speak to Boyd, how he went to the office and Boyd invited him over, and how Boyd consumed copious amounts of cocaine that evening and had unknowingly let Randy into the house.

"So, I see the guns," Sheehan said as he combed through the destruction and bodies in the living room. "Good Lord, these two unloaded on each other. What's in the suitcase?"

"I didn't actually see it," Barrett said, "but I guess it's half a million bucks. That's what started the, um, gunfight."

"And you just sat there and watched?" Sheehan confirmed. He opened the suitcase and turned it towards Boyd to confirm that it was full of cash.

"What was I supposed to do?" Barrett said. "I didn't have a gun. I didn't have a phone. And I didn't exactly sit and watch. I hit the deck and crawled back there behind the chair. Then I watched."

"I'll be honest," Chase said. "I don't have any reason to disbelieve you."

"Just curious," Barrett interjected. "But why are we sitting around here discussing this? Why haven't you called this in or whatever it is you're supposed to do?"

"I want to ask you another question," Chase said. "When we spoke on the phone a few days ago, you said some strange things, asked some cryptic questions. I was too busy to evaluate it until recently. And then it finally struck me on the plane ride out here."

When he heard these words from the FBI agent, Barrett felt as if oxygen was no longer making it to his lungs. He did his best to not pass out, but he was certain his face was turning a ghostly white as all of the blood in his body rushed to the tips of his toes.

"At first it seemed like an outlandish correlation," Sheehan continued. "But the more I thought about the things you said, and the fact that you didn't seem to have these hypothetical thoughts until you came back here to Colorado…Barrett…did your father murder Otto Clevinger?"

Barrett knew this question was coming. After hearing it out loud, he closed his eyes and nodded his head ever so slightly. "Yes," Barrett said. The response was quiet. Barely audible over the soft music.

"You mind telling me how you know this?" Chase asked.

After regaining his composure, Barrett told the FBI agent another story — one about a safe deposit box, a video confession, and a shopping bag.

"I guess that would explain the close connection to you regarding the inconclusive DNA that was found at the scene," Chase surmised. "Your dad probably scrubbed your condo clean when word got out about the DNA."

"Yeah, I thought about that, too."

"Who else knows?" Chase asked.

"Claire. That's it," Barrett answered. "I didn't know what to do with the information. It's been a difficult truth to process. I don't even understand why he did it in the first place — killed Otto, I mean. And the only reason I can think that he'd even give me the evidence was in case I needed it to clear myself, prove my innocence. I just know when my mom finds out, it will probably kill her. That's why I've kept it to myself — with the exception of Claire — until now. I'm pissed as hell at Dad for doing this, putting me in this position, and it makes me wonder if I ever really knew my father. But I'm also not sure I'm emotionally ready to muddy his name with this just yet, either. It's all so…weird."

Chase paced around the messy, bloody living room, a lot like Boyd had a couple of hours earlier, only less frantically. He stroked his chin. He scratched his head. Barrett watched. He didn't know if he should speak or not. Finally, the agent stopped and faced Barrett again. "My sister died the other day," he said casually.

Caught off guard, Barrett replied with the first thing that came to mind. "I'm sorry to hear that."

"She was a DEA agent…my twin," Sheehan continued.

"Wow," Barrett said, looking at the floor.

"She got caught in the mess that was still going on in Gable. You know, Chumansky and the drugs, the cartel…"

Barrett nodded.

"She was actually murdered by some of those cartel guys," Chase said.

"Jeez," Barrett said. He realized there was a

connection — the obvious one — but he wasn't sure why it was relevant to the current discussion.

"I've learned a lot about myself these last few weeks," Chase said. "With my sister's death and being away from my family for a long period and dealing with people being in the wrong place at the wrong time. It's been enlightening. Even my sister was a victim of circumstance and difficult decisions that ultimately led to her death." Chase moved closer to Barrett, stepping over Randy's corpse. "I was pissed at her early on when I realized what had really happened to her. I thought she had made a bad decision that put her in the hospital. But soon after she died, it became apparent to me that she was simply doing her job. She was trying to help someone."

Barrett nodded. He understood and yet, he didn't. What did this have to do with the two dead guys in the room?

"If the world finds out that your father killed Otto Clevinger, it's going to do more than dirty your father's image and break your mother's heart," Chase said, jumping subjects. "It's going to destroy your name, too. The Greyson name. People are assholes. I think you probably know that by now."

"I hadn't thought of it quite like that," Barrett said. "I guess it's right, though."

"You can't tell the world the truth," Chase said. "And it's not necessary at this point. I think we have the missing link to Otto Clevinger's murder right here in front of us." He pointed to the carnage in the room. Randy's face was still planted in the coffee table; Boyd's eyes were still open but completely lifeless, staring into the darkness.

Barrett cocked his head. "What are you saying?"

"I'm saying we're going to let this scene play out the

way it looks," Chase explained. "It's all right here."

"Whoa," Barrett quipped. "Is it that easy?"

"No," Chase said. "You're probably going to have to tell a white lie or two to make it stick."

"You're serious?" Barrett confirmed.

"Very much so," Chase said. "Did you touch that suitcase?"

He thought for a moment. "No, I didn't."

"Perfect," Chase said. "Don't." He took a step back before continuing. "You need to understand something. I'm not a dirty FBI agent. That's not what's going on here. This is an off-the-chart situation that never, ever happens. It's not that I'm breaking the rules. Well, I am, but there's just no good way around this. Not for you, I mean. Unless we handle it like this."

Barrett shook his head and shrugged. "I don't know what to say."

Chase shrugged back in response but said nothing. In a surprise move, he stuck out his hand. Without hesitation, Barrett shook it firmly.

"Why are you helping me?" Barrett asked, still rather perplexed. Agent Sheehan already seemed to have his answer ready.

"Because I've learned this is the way the world works," he said. "It's not black and white like a lot of people want to think it is. It's extremely gray."

***

The next few days were busy ones for the Gable Police and Chief Nathan Perkins. The signed affidavits that were put together by Jackson's attorney, Rick Masterson, cleared both Jackson and Bart Timmons of all wrongdoing, including the DWI from around the holidays. As promised, Bart entered a rehab program in Adler. Jackson, on the other hand, was not let off the hook quite so easily. Extensive conversations took place between Perkins, the mayor of Gable, and a number of attorneys, including Masterson, about whether or not John Jackson could return to the force. After eight hours of discussion that did not include Jackson, it was decided that John Jackson would not be allowed to return to the Gable PD. Being released from the responsibility of the crimes he had committed was enough of a gift. Keeping his job would be too much. But Masterson did negotiate terms that included Jackson receiving his pension.

There was also the issue of WITSEC, and whether or not Jackson and his family would be interested in it. The thought of being put into the Witness Protection Program was not something that had even crossed Jackson's mind before. He was more interested in keeping his job. But when this didn't happen, hiding from the potential revenge of the cartel seemed like the safest move. There was no way of knowing for sure if the higher-ups in the Mexican drug ring would know what had happened to Pablo Garza and their other men. The media only reported that they'd been gunned down during a sting conducted by federal authorities.

After the "retirement" of Jackson, Perkins was in need of a new sergeant. Ryan Hodge was the logical choice and was promoted the next day. The two worked together to recruit a patrolman to fill Hodge's previous position, and a new era for the Gable Police Department began.

Eddie Clark was the luckiest of the bunch. Not only did he avoid any prosecution for his involvement in dealing drugs with Chumansky, he became the operator of both Mecca Warehouse stores. Maddison Chumansky continued to be the acting owner, but because she knew and cared nothing about the electronics business, she allowed Eddie to run them and paid him well to do it.

At first, the story that Chase spun about the mayhem at Boyd's place seemed too far-fetched. But to Barrett's surprise, it worked like a charm. The report that was filed was not as far from the truth as one might expect. Too many people knew that Barrett was at Boyd's that night, plus his phone GPS would be accessible and could also prove his whereabouts. The entire faux story that became the official report was built around Barrett's account of why the shootout happened in the first place. Chase's intent was to merely have Barrett plant the seed that, from what he could gather, Boyd owed Randy money for a job. The only other thing Barrett was to do was drop the words "dad," "dead," and "old man," and possibly "Otto." The story was constructed to imply that Boyd Clevinger paid Randy Fowley to murder his father. Since Barrett's fingerprints were not on either of the guns or the suitcase of money, the story was pretty credible.

Within a couple of weeks, it was evident that the ruse had served its purpose. Chase informed Barrett that both the Denver Police and FBI had put a lid on the Otto Clevinger case and closed it. Frank Greyson's dirty deed would die with Barrett, Claire, and Agent Sheehan.

***

Despite the closure that had come to Barrett's life in the month of January, he was still struggling with the knowledge that his father was a murderer. Knowing that he would never hear more as to how and why the decision to commit such an unspeakable act even crossed his father's mind would be a knife, forever in Barrett Greyson's heart. Not only was he not sure who his father really was or had been, it also left him questions about himself and how much of his father's dark moral character was buried somewhere deep inside of him. Claire suggested he see a psychiatrist, but it wasn't something Barrett was ready to do at this point. For now, he would have to learn to live with. Life would go on. His best move right now was to charge forward and grow from the experiences that he had been through.

At the end of January, Fredrika Clevinger called and asked Barrett to meet her at the Clevinger Group. Seated in the same office and chair that her father-in-law and husband had sat in before her, she asked Barrett to come back to work for the Clevinger Group.

"I'll make you president of the business," she said. "I know you know what you're doing. I know you'll make us both a lot of money. That's all I want. I have no interest in running a company. I just want to spend the money it makes."

Barrett chuckled at her honesty. "At least you're not bullshitting me," he said.

"I'm not my husband," Fredrika said. "Life's too short to play games or pretend you're something you're not."

"I respect that," Barrett said. "And I sincerely appreciate the offer, Mrs. Clevinger. I truly do."

"You can call me Freddy," she said.

Barrett nodded. "I just don't know that this is something I want to do."

The widow leaned forward on the desk in front of her. "I might've misunderstood my murder-for-hire, dim-witted, crazy, dead husband…but he seemed to imply this is *exactly* what you wanted when you were working here before."

"It was," Barrett agreed. "At one time. Back then. But so many things have changed these past few months. I mean, for me. And now that the opportunity is presenting itself, it doesn't feel right to me. Something's off."

"Really?"

"It's not you. It's me."

"Sounds like you're breaking up with me."

"It wasn't supposed to sound that way, sorry. But these experiences I've had have forced me to look at a lot of things differently. My life, my career, my future. And most importantly — who I am."

Fredrika Clevinger leaned back in the chair.

"I can't take the job, Freddy. I just can't. I'm sorry."

"I have to admit, I ignorantly thought this was all but a done deal." She exhaled deeply before continuing. "I suppose I should've had this conversation with you before I got my hopes up."

"You'll find the right person," Barrett said as he stood up and held out his hand. Fredrika rose from the chair and shook it. "Again," he said, "I'm truly sorry. I do believe this is the best for both of us and your business."

After taking a few minutes to say goodbye to Julia, Barrett walked out the door of the Clevinger Group for the last time. Not once did he ever consider whether Boyd's half a million dollars would've made a difference.

***

Breaking the news of Delia's death to the family was not an easy task for Chase. But shortly after he put a bow on the double homicide in Denver, reality hit the overworked FBI agent hard. He flew Southwest Airlines back to Atlanta and gave up on holding back the tears. The tension release felt good, but none of it was going to bring back his sister. He kept his face covered in his seat as best he could; he didn't want the other passengers to witness his sorrow and heartbreak.

He returned home to a wife and daughter who were ecstatic to finally have him back, safe. It was a bittersweet reunion, as the family of three also mourned the loss of a sister-in-law and aunt together for the first time.

Chase's parents, Gordon and Sandra Sheehan, lived in Raleigh, North Carolina, but agreed to lay Delia to rest outside of Atlanta, where she could be close to her brother and only niece. In fact, the loss of their only daughter helped them decide on their own final resting place — the same cemetery as Delia. The expectation was that Chase, his wife, and his daughter would outlive his parents. This way they could all be together in the end.

It was a somber thing picking out a casket and headstone — something Chase had never done before. Thankfully, Gwen Sheehan was there to stand by her husband with support and advice. Despite being home for the first time in many weeks, Chase had yet to get much rest. At least when he was busy working multiple intertwined cases at the same time, he was able to keep pace with adrenaline. But at this point there was no fuel left. Thankfully, Nolan Reed saw this coming.

"Take six weeks, Chase," Reed told him at Delia's visitation.

"I've only got three weeks coming to me," Chase reminded him.

"I insist," Nolan said. "You've earned it. Take some time and decide what you want to do."

"What does that mean?"

"It means if the field stuff has become too much for you, I've cleared the way for you to stay inside and still get heavily involved with cases," Nolan explained.

"Why would you think I'd want to get off the street?" Chase said.

Nolan gave him a look of disbelief. "I'm not even going to answer that question," he said, stealing a glance at Delia's lifeless body in the silver casket twenty feet behind Chase. "It's safer, and you wouldn't have to take a pay cut. Just think about it."

"Okay," Chase said. "You're a good boss." He reached out to shake Reed's hand.

"We're friends, Chase," Nolan said, and leaned in to hug him. Following the embrace, he stayed close and lowered his voice. "You also need to decide if you might just want to take advantage of WITSEC. I guess that's what John Jackson is doing. We really have no idea if the cartel will try to track you down."

"Screw them," Chase said viciously.

"You have a family," Nolan reminded him. "At least consider it during your time off and…watch your back, too."

Chase nodded. "Thanks again, Nolan."

When the darkness of the funeral had concluded and family and friends had cleared out of the church's gymnasium after munching on finger sandwiches and watered-down punch, Chase began his long vacation. He went home that afternoon and sat down in front of the television with his daughter. Although almost too old for it, Khloe jumped on her father's lap and watched a few minutes of an NFL playoff game.

"I'm glad you're home, Daddy," she said.

"Me too, baby," Chase said, giving her a squeeze and kissing the crown of her head.

They watched the game in silence for a few minutes, and then Khloe spoke tentatively. "Daddy?"

"Yeah, honey?"

"Was it a bad person that killed Aunt Delia?"

Surprised by the line of questioning, Chase answered cautiously, "Yes. Yes, it was, Khloe."

"There's lots of bad people in the world, right?"

"Yes, I guess that's true," Chase said. "But there are a lot more good people." He wasn't sure he believed this, but as a parent he knew it was the right thing to say.

"Your job is to stop all of the bad people from doing bad things to all the good people and put them in jail and make the world a better place, right?"

"Something like that, honey," Chase replied. "But I don't know about *all* of the bad people. That would be difficult to do."

"Oh," Khloe said. She leaned back and lay her head on her father's shoulder. Another minute passed before she spoke again. "So what's the point, then?" She hopped to the floor to face Chase after she said this.

"What do you mean?"

"I mean, if there's no chance to get *all* of the bad guys, what's the point of getting only some of them?"

"Well, I—" Chase began. "You see, honey, it's—" For the first time in a long time, the words weren't coming so easily for him. "It's complicated, sweetheart." Deep down, though, Chase knew his daughter had a good point. "You know, Khloe-girl, you're too smart for your own good sometimes," he joked with her. She jumped back on his lap again and gave him a hug.

"I love you, Daddy."

"I love you too, honey."

Father and daughter watched another play of the football game before anyone spoke again.

"And don't worry about getting all the bad guys," Khloe added. "I'm going to become an agent just like you when I grow up and I'll get the ones you don't get."

***

"I turned her down," Barrett told Claire at dinner. She had cooked an early meal for them at five thirty before her shift a little later that evening at Danny's. Tonight would be her last overnight shift. Ross was so impressed with Claire's can-do attitude, he already had big plans for her as a shift manager down the road. Next week she would begin working the mornings until two in the afternoon.

"How come?" Claire asked.

Barrett could tell she was beginning to get concerned that she had moved in with a lazy Millennial. "I just couldn't do it," Barrett explained. "Something didn't feel right about it."

"Okay," she said, taking a bite of casserole.

"I'm sure some of it is because I know more about what happened to Otto — and now Boyd — than anyone else," Barrett said. "I mean, besides you and Chase Sheehan. You know what I mean?"

"Yes, I can see that," Claire said and then paused before jumping back to the original point at hand. "What are you going to do, though? I don't make that much money."

"Claire, my love," Barrett said with a giant grin.

She smiled back at him, her eyes beaming the way they had the day he'd met her. Her face even had the same curiosity it did that day, except this time it was for a different reason.

"Yes, Barrett, my love," she said back to him, playfully batting her lashes.

"You'll learn that there's always an end to my means," Barrett declared.

Claire nodded slowly. "Kind of like when you recklessly leave behind your life to wander the countryside because you were questioned about a crime you didn't commit?"

"Touché," he said. "You got me there."

"Sorry," Claire said, laughing lightly, "it was too easy."

"Don't apologize," Barrett said. "But I really do have some good news. I spoke to Chase earlier today, before I met with Fredrika Clevinger. He told me that with Randy's death, my money is that much closer to making its way back to me. The family Randy stole the van from agreed they have no claim to it, so that leaves me and Nora."

"That's great, but how does the court know it wasn't the dead guy's money?" Claire asked, referring to Randy.

"Even if it were, it would go to Nora," Barrett explained. "But here's where the story gets cool. Randy's lawyer is also Nora's lawyer."

"Ah, the one who bailed Randy out, right?"

"Exactly. His name is Janssen," Barrett said. "Well, his

conscience is working him over, as Chase put it. Nora's arraignment is tomorrow and Janssen has her ready to plead guilty and also offer up the money to the court in return for a lighter sentence, asking them to release it to me immediately because it is not and never was hers or her late son's. Chase told me to call Janssen the day after tomorrow to have it transferred to my bank account. It's been counted and there's over ten grand left."

"That's awesome!" Claire burst out.

"It should buy us some time until we figure out what we want to do," Barrett added.

"What do you mean by that?"

"You know what I mean…until I find a job that meets our financial needs as a couple," Barrett said, making himself clear.

Later that evening, Claire went to work and Barrett hung out at home doing some heavy thinking. He listened to some music, he watched some television, and eventually he fell asleep on the couch. Around two AM, he pulled himself up and stumbled his way to the bedroom. After undressing, he flopped on the bed and slept soundly until seven. When he awoke, Claire was home and sitting in the living room, sipping coffee and watching the morning news.

"You're still up?" he asked while making his way to the coffee pot.

"I've been doing a lot of thinking," Claire said. "Not tired enough for bed yet."

"Thinking is dangerous," Barrett said as he scratched his already mussed-up head of hair. "I should know; I did lots of my own last night."

He moved to the couch and sat down next to her.

"What about?" Claire asked.

"Everything. Mostly how screwed up my dad must've been and I had no idea. I mean, who does that kind of thing?"

"I know. It seems weird, but" — Claire gave some careful thought to her next phrase — "I'm sure he loved you very much, regardless. I mean, love is pure. And based on what I saw in that video, your father thought he was doing a good deed for you."

"That's just so messed up," Barrett said. "He killed Otto. Jesus, if you're gonna kill someone, kill Boyd."

"Well, now he's dead, too," Claire reminded him calmly.

The nastiness of his last statement struck Barrett with embarrassment. "What I just said, that was wrong. I didn't mean it like that. I'm just frustrated and confused."

"I know," Claire said.

"And the irony is I just turned down the job that my father wanted me to have. The one that prompted him to commit murder."

The two reflected silently before Claire spoke.

"Do you think you might've turned it down to spite your dad?"

"You just read my mind," Barrett said. "I suppose it's possible, on some subconscious level. It does feel like the offer was tainted. It never would've happened if it weren't for the chain of events that Otto's murder set in motion."

"Of course, we never would've met, either," Claire said.

"The only good thing to come of it," Barrett said with a grin. "So, what were you thinking about?"

"Oh, just something you said last night at dinner about 'figuring out what we wanted to do.'"

"I'm not even sure what I meant by that," Barrett said.

"Yeah, but it made sense," Claire explained. "Do you want to live here?"

"I thought you did."

"I asked you first," she said. "But I will say, I want to be where things will work best for both of us."

"Well, so do I."

"Again, that doesn't really answer my question," Claire said. "Isn't it kind of awkward for you here?"

Barrett considered this for a moment. "Kinda, I guess."

"We don't have to live here, Barrett. I can get a job almost anywhere. I mean, not a great job but, you know..."

"I guess I hadn't really thought about any of this," Barrett said.

"Just consider it for a few days," Claire proposed. "We don't *have* to live here. I mean, I don't want to sound too ridiculous or delusional, but the world is our oyster. Let's take advantage of it and at least realize we have options."

With a nod, Barrett leaned over and kissed his girlfriend on the lips. "I will," he promised.

Later that evening, after Claire had pulled down eight hours of sleep, the couple enjoyed another homemade dinner. The weather was comfortable for January with temperatures during the day reaching the high fifties. Barrett cooked some hamburgers on the grill, and Claire threw together an "Iowa-style" potato salad. Accompanied by a bag of barbecue chips, the two ate and chatted for an hour.

When they were finished, they cleaned the kitchen together then moved to the living room. Claire had pulled a bottle of white wine from the refrigerator and was uncorking it when Barrett spoke up.

"I just had a thought," he said. "Go ahead and pour us each a glass. Then I want to do something with you. Together."

Barrett disappeared into the bedroom for a minute and returned with a small cardboard box. Claire had poured the wine as instructed and handed her man his glass.

"Thank you, my dear," he said. "Follow me."

He led her out onto the community patio, where he had grilled the burgers earlier. After setting his wine glass on a railing, he opened the box to reveal his father's mobile phone and the damning plastic shopping bag, still tucked away inside a clear Ziploc bag.

Although the coals were still warm, Barrett squirted lighter fluid on them before quickly striking and tossing a match inside, setting the entire grill off with wicked-looking orange flames. Claire moved closer to Barrett and pressed her head against his side in support, realizing what he was about to do.

Grabbing the shopping bag first, Barrett flipped the package onto the grill. The two watched it melt and smoke into nothingness. Next, he gripped the telltale mobile phone in front of them, allowing the small cardboard box to fall to the concrete below. Without hesitation, he pitched the device into the sea of flames.

The blaze engulfed and licked the phone into a pile of melted plastic as the couple continued to look on. It would soon be unrecognizable amidst the coals that had helped cause its demise. Although they remained silent, both Barrett and Claire desperately hoped the emotional damage that had been caused by Frank Greyson's repulsive act would burn into oblivion along with the last pieces of damning evidence that it ever happened in the first place.

Barrett reached over and snatched his wine glass.

"To starting over," he said, angling his glass towards

Claire in the form of a toast.

Claire reciprocated by clinking her glass to his. "To starting over."

They each took a drink and then leaned in for a quick kiss.

ABOUT THE AUTHOR

Brad Carl is a former radio personality who still earns part of his living as a voiceover artist. Growing up in the Midwest, Brad was influenced at an early age by the Hardy Boys mystery book series. When he was older he began to enjoy the work of authors like David Baldacci, James Patterson, and Clive Cussler.

Besides writing books and producing voice work, Brad is also a successful businessman in the textile and packaging industry. He currently resides in Kansas City, MO with his wife, Kristi, and daughter, Presley. The family also has a dog named Ali.

You can learn more about Brad including where to find his other books by visiting www.bradcarl.com. Be sure to sign up for the Mail List so you can get special deals on all new releases.

90551804R00375

Made in the USA
Lexington, KY
13 June 2018